I0735163

A Time for Memories and the Unthinkable

The Life of a Time Travel Spy

Paul D. Escudero

WORKBOOK PRESS LLC
187 E Warm Springs Rd,
Suite B285, Las Vegas, NV 89119, USA

Website: https://workbookpress.com/
Hotline: 1-888-818-4856
Email: admin@workbookpress.com

Ordering Information:
Quantity sales. Special discounts are available on quantity purchases by corporations, associations, and others.
For details, contact the publisher at the address above.

Library of Congress Control Number:

ISBN-13:   000-0-000000-00-0 (Paperback Version)
                000-0-000000-00-0 (Digital Version)

REV. DATE: 07/06/2022

A Time for Memories and the Unthinkable The Life of a Time Travel Spy

By

Paul D. Escudero

TABLE OF CONTENTS

Chapter One

Back in Time

Tinougl stepped into the time capsulee and sat down in the passenger seat. Kovloor reached over and helped snap his safety harness in place and hook up all his environmental sustainment hoses and connections. Tinougl's visor was still up, and his face exposed. Kovloor reached down to shake his hand. The two smiled at each other.

"Have a safe trip," Koovlar said and smiled feeling a degree of trepidation.

"I'll only be gone for one minute," Tinougl responded as someone from the present Dimension would see him gone for just one minute, but in the interdimensional portal time relationships shifted and either expanded or contracted in relative terms.

They would not know how long Tinougl lived in the other time domain until he returned with his story, provided he actually made it back.

Time travel was brief because the vast amount of energy required to sustain that time portal only allowed a minute at the most before the passenger would be sucked back into the present dimension.

At the destination, the amount of time a person existed could not be predicted as there were many unexplained actions that took place for no rhyme or reason.

Tinougl had spent the last 5 years training for this mission. He knew there were serious dangers ahead and of the dozen past time travellers, only half of them came back alive. The rest were killed in the line of duty in another time and place.

Where and when Tinougl would show up was very hard to predict, though efforts to fine tune the process to get them to an exact moment of time to do the actions desired was at best a 20% possibility. They would of course change history and the whole fabric of space time would evolve. The time skew that manifested may give the agent up to several weeks at the targeted locations, time, and date. But to those in the time transport area, Tinougl would be back in just a minute.

The goals were very moddest and the agent needed to leave a marker that cold be discovered in the future. If all went well, he would leave the marks behind in such a way they would not be able to be elimated but be observable in the future. If the time traveller did not make it back alive, nobody would know where to go look to see where he left his mark.

The time capsule launch was just about to begin. Tinougl lowered his visor that had a heads-up display in it. All the important information would be displayed.

Kovloor lowered the time capsulee cover and engaged the locking mechanism which made it airtight and prevented the magnetic and plasma field to get inside the time capsule which meant instant death for the occupant if it wasn't sealed. As the time machine ramped up sensors would relay telemetry down a steel pipe conduit that made up a faraday waveguide to the control room outside the vast concrete and steel dome structure.

Kovloor walked along the service entry platform towards the entrance of the chamber, exited the champer, shut the one-foot-thick steel door and pressed the control that would slide the service entry platform into the side of the building and away from the time machine. Hydraulic controlled panel then slid in place and now the time capsulee was left in the middle of the large spherical structure that had two large disks on the sides of the time capsulee.

Kovloor walked over to the control consoles area where a half dozen men were patiently awaiting the countdown. Kovloor calmly sat down in the chair in front of his supervisors control panel that stood up about a foot above the desktop. In front of him and all the other consoles now being monitored and operated by very well-trained scientists, would best be described as a movie theater screen where videos taken by cameras imbedded in the concrete sphere and inside the time machine capsulee showed all the areas of interest including the biological monitors.

"Stand by for countdown," Kovloor said.

"I'm ready, it's now or never," Tinougl replied through his communication link via the waveguide.

"One minute to launch," Kovloor stated.

Kovloor looked over at a scientist Miltonzy controlling the toroidal electromagnets in the two-time shifter disks on each side of the time capsulee.

In the vast simulations and the few time shots they performed, the expected actions were well known by everyone, and each person had a prompter on their control panel which gave them the ability to arm and activate their portion of the time machine when the interlocks were set, and a safe condition existed to transition to the next stage of the launch.

Out of protocol Miltonzy made the essential reports which conveyed the status of the launch. "Toroid fields are building. 4,000 amps are flowing temperature and field strength nominal."

Even though six feet of concrete and steel separated them from the time capsulee machinery, some of the toroidal resonances and modulations leaked through and the operators could hear the slight noise they expected which gave them faith everything was working as designed.

Up on the big screen in front of them they started to see the magic of the machine unfold. The surface of the discs seemed like they were spinning at ondulating rates. Because the video was time sampled it had the same effect as watching video of an airplane's propeller that sometimes appeared stationary due to the sampling rate. The discs were not actually spinning, the electromagnetic and electrostatic fields created by the toroids is what was spinning and growing in intensity. The illusion seemed to be like a sheet of steel glowing as it was being manufactured and ran through rollers to get the right thickness.

At 10 seconds before launch, Miltonzy announced, "All temperatures and field strengths are nominal."

The modulation they could hear seeping through the steel and concrete barrier had an eerie sound to it. Nobody in the control room wanted to be in the time machine.

Even though half of the Timestronauts, came back alive and functioned as normal and had no apparent medical conditions that resulted, half of them never came back and none of them left any marks or indications that could be found to suggest they arrived at the dimension targeted. Some theories suggested a skewness in space time could have sent them somewhere and by the nature of the journey, they might come back unexpectedly in 100 years or longer.

Tinougl's instrument panel on his time capsule gave him a green board meaning all equipment was operating as expected. However, since he was now inside the final 10 seconds of countdown, the big red PANIC button was suddenly extinguished and no longer available to him. If he tried to interrupt the time jump at this moment, he could be trapped in a phase lock and gone to unknown destinations without any hope of ever returning.

As he learned over and over during his training, it was too late to change his mind. Tinougl had until the RED PANIC butten illumination ended to abort the launch. He was now a time traveller to somewhere no matter what he did at this moment in time.

Tinougl had been subjected to vibration testing and Cosmic elliptical waves associated with the time machine. But it never got this intense because he was never launched in time. The strange sensation was the same as he felt in the past, just a lot stronger in intensity. As he watched the countdown timer on his control console when it reached the two second mark suddenly there was all kinds of strange colors around him. It was as if he was swimming in a sea of colors with no dimensions, no beginning, and no end.

The modulation of the waves slowly blended into a strange pitch unlike anything he heard in the past. It was as if all the modulation hit a resonance and a singularity happened. Suddenly there was no noise just quietness. Based on training, he knew the skin of the time machine would now be blisteringly hot.

Tinougl had no choice but to sit there hoping nobody in the past spotted his time machine so that when he stepped out of it there would not be a group of onlookers and his personal security at risk. One thing he would do as soon as instruments indicated cooldown was sufficient, he would step out of the time machine hoping he didn't find himself in a perilous scenario and remove his faraday suit as he had clothes on under that were designed for what was expected normal dress for the time and period they targeted. He also had a blaster with him to use if he had to to provide safety long enough to hop back in the time machine and hit the return button.

The time machine was always at the ready to immediately return. All he had to do was get inside, shut the cover, use internal controls to seal it and hit the BLUE return button and in a fraction of time reappear back where he started. In an emergency, he could forgo putting the faraday clothing on as it only provided nominal protection and in a bugout situation where life or death was at the essence, coming back with some injury was better than coming back dead.

There really wasn't a good way to measure the skin temperature of the time machine and based on a counter determine when it should be safe to exit. Hence the time scientists came up with a simplistic approach and simply measured the temperature upon return of a few time travels and the passenger would be given a simple "It's safe to leave the capsule," indicator based on time intervals they previously measured. They would then unlock themselves and exit the time machine and hoped that they were not in a perilous circumstance when they stepped out of the time machine.

The exotic materials used in construction of the time machine capsulee with neodimium, gadolinium, and thulium allowed it to shed heat very quickly. That was an important feature in allowing the occupant to obtain situational awareness as soon as possible.

In the span of a minute, the safe to exit indicator lit up and Tinougl released the securing mechanism allowing it to be opened, and he then got out. His targeted area was a location in the wilderness near a population center he was to visit, do his deed. Leave his mark and hustle back to the time machine and come back.

Tinougl stepped out of the time machine, verified by a few quick star references where he was at night and verified, that at least they got the location right, now the question was, did he arrive in the time slot anticipated?

Part of his possessions was a communicator of the type discontinued five hundred years prior. If he was close enough to a communication tower that no longer existed in modern times, his communicator would link up and in moments he could check the date to verify he reached his target in location and time wise.

Thanks to the fact they discovered a "hoarder" of junk, scientists were able to restore the communicator to fully operational and all the passwords were easily hacked so they could verify the settings it had and the accounts and services available to the former user that lived during their targeted period.

Tinougl was all set now as his mission now began. His adventure and his experiences would now transform him in ways he never imagined. As his journey began in a different time standard, that took weeks to complete, back in the world he left, he was back a minute later. The thoughts of existing in two different times coincidently defied the laws of physics and confronted the logic of philosophers. As expected, one minute later the temporal anomaly that gave that unique signature to the singularity that was photographically observed triggered the next set of actions immediately.

Once that anomaly appeared, the automatic shutdown began. Modal distortion of the light patterns on the spinning disks showed the expected harmonic oscillations as the spatial drivers spun down in a concise controlled manner. The pulsations were an indication Tinougl had a better than 50% probability of returning to the present time. Just like when Tinougl time traveled to his mission, sensors backed up the timer algorithms to let Tinougl. I know temperatures were now safe to leave the time travel capsule. A reverse of what happened before, a section of the wall moved out and upwards and a platform came out of a cavity hidden within that soon positioned around the time travel capsule.

The staff opened the top of the time travel capsule so that Tinougl could exit. He sat there. He didn't move nor did he say anything. His heads-up visor still covered his eyes, but due to the wireless interfaces that allowed the scientists to monitor his face and measure all his body functions, the only thing out of the ordinary was the tears coming from his eyes. There was definitely a scenario that occurred during his mission and those tears prompted significantly higher levels of interest. None of the other time travellers had ever come back in this fashion.

They all had undergone extensive psychological testing and preparation. Therefore, this behavior was not expected.

Tinougl's vital health indicators were normal. His blood pressure, pulse, body temperature, oxygen levels, and brain waves were nomally quite normal.

"Tinougl, you can get out of the time capsule," Kovloor stated.

Doctor Cocilglu the psychological mapper who cleared Tinougl for the mission and his chief neurological advisor stepped forward after observing all the telemetry and observing what transpired behind the heads-up face shield stepped forward and said:

"Tinougl, why don't you exit the time capsulee and go with me to my office so we can discuss some elements of you mission."

In Doctor Cocilglu's eyeglasses, he had a mini heads-up display and could see Tinougl's face and the strange behavior. He knew there had been an emotional spike. His Alpha, Beta, and Gama Brain waves recorded in his helmet had been sent via telemetry and Doctor Cocilglu knew those patterns often were exhibited by someone that had a serious emotional episode.

Tinougl still didn't respond, so Doctor Cocilglu's reached down and grabbed Tinougl's arm and tugged on it and recapitulated:

"Tinougl, please exit the time capsulee and go with me to my office so we can discuss your mission."

The physical touch seemed to snap Tinougl out of the trance and he stirred and started physical movement to exit the time capsulee. He didn't raise his visor which by itself gave an element of mystery, but it was designed to see through the heads-up data, and he climbed out and slowly followed Doctor Cocilglu who knew there was a very emotional aspect to how Tinougl acted. He followed Doctor Cocilglu through the control room where everyone was observing in a quite demure having seen the video knew now would not be a good time to approach Tinougl to welcome him back from his incredible time travel.

Chapter Two

Time Travel Debrief

They walked through a security boundary, then into a hallway and soon into an area with a private entrance that through the cypher lock was a hallway that led to several offices for the top staff and researchers on the project.

Tinougl had been to this office numerous times and Doctor Cocilglu had a wide range of instruments and devices he routinely used in his practice including brain wave monitors and neuronic precipitators.

Doctor Cocilglu shut the door behind them and asked, "Tinougl, please have a seat and I think you will feel more comfortable if you take off your mission helmet."

It was quite apparent that something big in Tinougl's life occurred on the mission. He also knew one thing they all knew is that even though Tinougl returned a minute later at the present time, that had no bearing on how long he existed in that other dimension in another time and place.

Tinougl may have existed weeks, days, months or even longer. Until all the reviews were done, and data extraction completed, they would have no time reference for how long Tinougl lived in that other dimension. They also would not know the scope of what it all entailed. His mission requirements were very modest. Their biggest hope was to get him there and back alive without damaging him. Now their worst fears were coming true, there was damage and even though there might not have been any apparent physical damage, obviousy there was some extraordinary psychological impact.

Tinougl eased out of his helmet, and he sat it on his lap and stared out into space. His tears had mostly crystalized leaving behind a slight trace of where the moist tears had been moments ago. His eyes were slightly puffy as expected from someone who was crying. The mystery was now deepening.

Some of the information was already coming to light that was astonishing the researchers. All helmet video recorded was in permenent nondestructive memory. What they now knew was that when Tinougl entered the time transport capsule he looked a lot older than he did now. While on the mission he had aged greatly indicating the passage of time and when he returned, he was young again. But the memories were not compromised it recorded all the events in the time travel capsulee, most specifically in all his helmet heads up video. This truly was an extraordingary event.

Tinougl could not see, nor did he care what was showing on Doctor Cocilglu semi-holographic 3D flatscreen display. A time lapsed photography showed the transformation in about a minute.

Doctor Cocilglu was unconventional. He didn't do everything by the book. Perhaps that's why he was more successful than most other psychoanalysts with his patients. It was moments like this he was prepared. The first thing he needed to do was pour himself and Tinougl a glass of Fonnegar Elixer alohol based drink spiked with psychiatric drugs.

Tinougl moved semi slumped over, obviousy in a semi-mental breakdown. Doctor Cocilglu knew not to assume anything. He was quite aware that during the mission the one minute gone resulted in Tinougl time travel into a singularity could have resulted in a long-life span in another dimension as time skews and shifts during such time travel events and there was much more to learn about it before they weaponized it.

Doctor Cocilglu pulled a couple clean glasses out of his middle drawer and the bottle of Fonnegar Elixer. He poured two glasses each about two thirds full. He then handed one of the glasses to Tinougl and said, "Here, take a drink of this, it will help you feel better in a couple moments."

Tinougl took the glass, took a sip, then in about 15 seconds drank the rest of the content, then sat the glass down on the small table in front of him without raising his face. Doctor Cocilglu took a couple drinks then waited. He knew the psychoactive drugs in the elixir would soon short circuit Tinougl's brain in a way that would unlock the mystery and slowly reveal the substantial event in Tinougl's life. What ever it was, he knew was heart breaking in some way.

Doctor Cocilglu was subtle and knew Tinougl would think he simply drank some popular alcohol and was feeling the buzz not realizing he was being drugged. These psychoactive drugs acted a lot like a truth serum without making the patient drowsy. Two for the price of one. Tinougl would feel the alcohol buzz and his mind would slowly be conditioned for Doctor Cocilglu's probing. Thanks to Tinougl's fast consumption the process would be hastened. Some patients who drank the substance slowly took upwards an hour or longer to reveal the results of their mission.

The discussion would be recorded an after a delay, other experts listening and observing the live video and audio feed would start analyzing everything Tinougl stated. Since the truth serum component of the drink would create a built-in vetting process, the researchers knew they would soon be receiving the unbridled truth no matter how ugly it might be. After they obtained all the information, they thought was pertinent to the mission Tinougl would receive treatments to help him forget his experiences during the time travel mission as to bury all the heart break and other potential negative side effects.

Doctor Cocilglu observed the time lapsed photography of the time travel facial recordings of Tinougl and knew he had left the present time, traveled through time, had experiences, then got back into the time machine as a much older man, then returned and reobtained his original physiology that had only one minute of time lapse. Hence, Doctor Cocilglu knew Tinougl had spent a lifetime away in another dimension and most likely had a lot of experiences dating from 450 to 500 years prior in an era when a lot of information was lost due to the massive wars and destruction that followed. Thus, Tinougl's statements would fill in a gap of what transpired in a period where little history was recorded, and it was feared wiped to hide possibly a very deadly period that touched most of their living beings one way or another.

One of the attributes of the Fonnegar elixir is it made people thirsty. Doctor Cocilglu knew this and refilled Tinougl's glass and as expected when he felt thirsty, Tinougl indulged in drinking more of the elixir. By the time Tinougl was halfway through drinking the second glass of Fonnegar, he exhibited drowsiness and made a statement, "I feel kind of sleepy."

"Tinougl, why don't you lay down on the couch and rest a bit, then you might feel like telling me about it later."

Doctor Cocilglu walked over to Tinougl and said, "Let me help you."

Tinougl complied very sheepishly as he was already now entering that mental condition sought by the researcher to unlock the past. Tinougl was helped to the couch and sat down and laid back and closed his eyes.

Tinougl had experienced the quintessential psychological transcendence during the time travel to the past and again when he returned to the present time. His mind was now accustomed to the strange holographic imagery his brain created in that voyage through time and space through the universe. And now thanks to the alcohol and the psychoactive drugs, he was once more in an unknown reality in similar mannerisms.

The way the truth serum worked that was part of the psychoactive cocktail, while Tinougl was in that altered mental state in a quiet room where outside noise was mostly extinguished, Doctor Cocilglu could interact with him and ask him questions which would trigger Tinougl to react in his dream state describing his experience. It was a refined hypnosis that truth gatherers excelled in unlocking valuable information the patient had no idea the interrogator easily obtained.

Doctor Cocilglu checked Tinougl's pulse with an instrument that indicated 45 beats per minute. His breathing was shallow, and he was nearly comatose. Tinougl's brain hemispheres were synchronized and his Delta and Xray brain waves were predominate. His Alpha, Beta, and Gama brain waves had achieved quiescence. It was time to probe.

Tinougl murmured something that Doctor Cocilglu could not make out, but he knew Tinougl's mind was now set up for probing and eventually Doctor Cocilglu would slowly get Tinougl to say more clearly what his words meant.

The common feature of drug induced hypnosis examination is the truth serums allowed discovering the passages through an almost cryptographic passage of Tinougl's memories. Humans are creatures where the messages that get processed that provide that mental holograph we know as human awareness, has a mapping system and passageways that are so complex, it would take many centuries of vast study for science to figure out the mapping system.

Unfortunately, each human is wired differently, so extending the findings from one human to another is almost impossible.

Therefore, the nagging process that Doctor Cocilglu now engaged was evidence current techniques for such investigations were considered primative at best. Doctor Cocilglu would pursevere and from his vast experience he would dig deep into Tinougl's memory at a pace no quicker than the ancient overland express of the horse and carriage. In his dream state Tinougl slowly divulged his journey in Time and Space that slowly filled in the blanks.

CHAPTER THREE

FIVE HUNDRED YEARS AGO

Tinougl's left the time travel machine after sealing and camouflaged it. He had a locater device imbedded in his cell phone designed to appear like the standard communications device at the time of his experienced. His mind had now traveled back to the past as if he had gone there. All his memories still existed. To the Holograph of his mind, he didn't know this was a dream world. This was a symmetrical recording in his mind where all the details and senses appeared real. At first Tinougl was confused. He had a sense he had done this once before.

About this time as he was taking all the luster of nature on the outskirts of a city in an undeveloped zone where builders would probably not arrive for another one hundred years. It was wild and it was remote, and the underbrush and poor visibility kept most hikers away from this particular spot. His glasses were a heads-up display and his hat had sophisticated sensors and a computer that had spatial processing ability to provide extra situational awareness. Any wild animal or human that got within fifty meters of him would be detected and he had ample training with devices he had with him that could quickly disable any threat.

These were none fatal but debilitating capabilities of his self defense equipment that would send bears running. His martial arts ability and physical fitness were second to none. He was a very lethal spy. The main difference is he was a time travel spy to discover who did what and when. And even though he was from the future, the results of being captured were just as deadly as being captured behind enemy lines.

There were great theorists who tried to come up with the answer to a nagging question: If a person is transported to the past and killed and can't make it back, how that works out for his timeline. Was that the reason why some of them never made it back?

Each time travel spy was given a special cyanide release system so that if they were captured and were going to be tortured, they could end it and not suffer. Their captors would never know who they were since they came from the future. That is unless they violated their oath and damaged the fabric of time by changing the future. A strange process was put in place to deal with that which other's surmised would entail sending a hit team back in time to silence the person and kill him as he was exiting his time machine.

Time travel espionage and sabotage was a very strange system. The prime orders were to get what they could without damaging the fabric of time. Therefore, the sabotage aspect of it was used very sparingly and a deep analysis was done to determine if there were time fabric consequences that would be adverse for the future.

The only possible sabotage that would be permitted without any concern would be to prevent others from developing time machines. They all knew what happened when more than one country developed nuclear weapons. The time machine was viewed as potentially a million times more destructive than any nuclear weapon.

As expected, as Tinougl passed through the heavy brush and triple canopy forest, he had numerous detections of wildlife. In a few instances his self defense system created that cacophony of noise that put fear in the dangerous animals. Most dangerous animals including the savage Trestodragons feared other animals so the sounds that mimicked such creatures and the scent synthesizer to help convince them, usually drove them away.

Slowly Tinougl made it to the outskirts of a city where buildings were sparse at first but quickly multiplied in numbers as he walked. Thanks to research of the era, the time travel group were able to dress Tinougl in clothing of the era even though styles apparently changed often. Tinougl was happy that he quickly discovered he was dressed relatively appearing as pedestrians he passed.

Tinougl had studied the city as it existed fivel hundred years ago, and scientists pulled out volumes of data that society had managed to preserve in spite of the major war that occurred a number of years past the targeted time travel date. His mission was to go discover information and get back with the results with the imperative he had to be leave that time by a certain date.

Tinougl walked down that familiar street he practiced many times in a large open building wearing three dimensional goggles to provide a fantastic holographic reality as if he were transported back in time. The imagery of his training was time stamped almost identical to his arrival date, so nothing was out of the ordinary.

As part of the mission planning, Tinougl walked to the Cuìlù Resort Hotel near a surface transportation center that operated high speed intercity Zingcraft transportation that are supersonic people carriers shooting through tubes pneumatic powered. Air pushing and air sucking at supersonic speeds propelled these devices currently in the tube.

The Cuìlù Resort Hotel looked magnificent as it was in it's finer days when Tinougl arrived. Scanning the area around him, Tinougl had determined nobody was following him and he arrived when the major commuter peak had just ended, and as expected pedestrian traffic had died down. As he walked down the opposite side of the street, he observed the Cuìlù Resort Hotel noting the exactness of it's image that matched his training completely. Tinougl was now going through his mental checklist as he checked off mission milestones and determined step by step what he needed to do next.

Since there were often people coming and going and suddenly

needing a hotel room, nothing would seem suspect of a person walking in and requesting a room.

The credit system used in five hundred years prior was not much different that present day. It was all based on crypto currency, and every day the intelligence directorate received harvested credits sucked out of dead people's accounts, especially those who died that had no living relatives. Some of those credits that were tagged to a cryptocurrency, had a time stamp of creation. As it was there were numerous credits obtainable that had time stamps from five hundred years ago. Hence, they could cherry pick the credits they wanted to use that would show up as bona fide currency at the time Tinougl arrived. Because of all the unknown exigencies, Tinougl was provided substantial amounts of credits in the event he had to bribe individuals to ensure mission success.

"May I help you?" The clerk asked as Tinougl approached the reception counter, carrying his backpack like device that had a change of clothes and several personal items that would not be out of the ordinary for any individual in the event he ran into law enforcement and was searched. He also had a cover story built that would show up legitimate on any inquiry just in case.

"Yes, I would like a room for a few days."

"How long do you intend to stay sir?"

"I'm an author and meeting with my publisher, I'm not sure how long it will take, set me up for three days and if I need longer, I will tell you."

"Not a problem. May I charge your credits to reserve the room?"

"Sure. Here you go."

Tinougl moved his communicator next to the credit reader that created the transaction for those Cloud Crypto Credits.

In a short period of time the transaction machine sucked those

Cloud Crypto Credits out of Tinougl's communicator. Nobody on the planet would know these credits were archived five hundred years ago from a wealthy individual who passed them down to his grand kids and great grand kids who then passed them on to their future relatives as the fortune was never fully spent. Because of the nature of crypto currencies born out of the distrust of governments, they could never be traced back to the actual owner.

Around this time frame many merchants would only take such Crypto Credits and hotels and restaurants preferred them as a form of payment. The Crypto Credit vaults were stored in scattered satellite clouds further prevening any one government from confiscating wealth. The Space Business would never have exploded in size and scale if it were not for Cloud Crypto Credits such as Tinougl was now using to pay his hotel bill with added credits that entitled him full access to prepaid meals in the Cuìlù Resort Hotel Restaurant. Each day until he checked out of the Cuìlù Resort Hotel, his Cloud Crypto Credits would automatically be charged to zero the new balance.

"Our resort is exclusively wired for facial recognition. You do not need a key to your room as our security system will unlock your door as you approach it."

"That's good to know."

"We are a resort hotel and when you go to our restaurants, your meals are part of your room fee and that includes tips to the waiters."

"Does that include drinks at the elixir bar?"

"Yes. We are a cashless resort. You will have no need for any form of credits as you enjoy the resort. All your expenses are assigned to your room."

"That makes it nice and handy."

"Yes, all our customers agree."

"I suppose I need to get up to my room and plan my day."

"Your receipt and your room number are on your communicator now. Elevators are to the left."

"Thank you."

"Have a nice day and feel free to call the front desk with the communicator and appliance controller that's in your room if you have any questions or concerns."

"Alright, thank you," Tinougl replied and turned left to walk to the elevator.

There were no floor selections inside the elevator, but there was a message behind a clear plate, "The elevator knows the floor to stop on. If you wish to go to a friend's room, state the name of the person and the elevator will stop on their floor."

The elevator ride took some time and near the ceiling was floor indicators. When the elevator reached the 14th floor it stopped, and the door opened with a verbal message. You have reached your floor.

I wonder what happens when multiple people are in the elevator, Tinougl thought.

As Tinougl walked down the hallway, he heard a soft chime and a hotel room with a small light above the door turned green which indicated his room. Tinougl approached the door and just as he reached the resort hotel door to his room, he heard another chime and a solenoid sound that conveyed the door was unlocked.

The door opened to inside the room and Tinougl walked in and visually looked around. As part of his lengthy training, he assumed never assume there is no bugs or secret video cameras in the room somewhere. He had to play the role all the way and deal with the curiousity as he blended in with his cover story as a writer. During his lengthy training, he was sent on simulated missions where he dealt with the public just as he had to now act. If he somehow unexpectedly stumbled into surveillance, by acting the role all the time and never letting his guard down, he would not find himself as a suspect to some investigation.

A writer was an excellent cover story for Tinougl because it would easily mask his real purpose of fact finding. The information and target of his mission was not important in the present time. That would come into play long after he was gone. The key to finding out the information he sought would explain why certain things in the future ended up the way they did. Once he took that priceless information back to the future, then a huge decision would have to be made if they would act on it and send another time traveller back. There would be great debate because if they screwed up the fabric of time, there could end up some consequences they never planned on.

Motion sensors in the room picked up his movements and after he sat his backpack down on the bed and sat down in a chair observing an entertainment console, a primative Holograph was suddenly displayed at the entertainment console, "Tinougl, welcome to the Cuìlǜ Resort Hotel. I'm your personal valet. My name is Tondron so if you want anything just start talking and if you call my name Tondron I will know you want me to do something for you."

"Thank you Tondron. How about give me a little demonstration of the room amenities."

"Tinougl, you are looking at the world's best entertainment system for hotels and resorts. I am just a holograph as you can see, but I do have a robot helper named Guāiqiǎo tucked away in his storage room where he goes when his services are no longer required."

"Have Guāiqiǎo come out so I can see what he looks like."

Tinougl knew the robot would look terribly inferior but was curious as to what the Cuìlǜ Resort Hotel Resort used.

Since the Cuìlù Resort Hotel Holograph personality Tondron had wireless links to Guāiqiǎo the robot was directed to come out of his storage room and to walk over to Tinougl so he could observe the robot.

The robot was dressed like a human and the aesthetics were not bad. It wasn't the metallic robot Tinougl assumed would be provided. The resort obviousy wanted their clients to have a more natural feel with their clients.

"Hello Tinougl," the robot Guāiqiǎo said with very decent acoustics.

"Hello Guāiqiǎo, I'm glad you can communicate."

"I will do my best to communicate with you. My internal computational equipment is not very robust, but through Tondron, I have a vast computational system that provides me in situ any type of information or intelligence I need to complete the task I'm assigned."

"What kind of tasks do you normally do?"

"My primary task is to assist with your comfort. I'm your personal assistant and I maintain the room, do any cleaning required, and make your bed usually while you are out of the room or taking a shower if necessary. If you want one of the drinks in the refrigeration unit, tell me which you would like, and I will provide it for you. If an item is depleted, we have robotic deliveries for replacement of whatever you consume."

"What kind of elixirs do you have in the refrigeration unit?"

Tondron quickly responded, "Let me give you the names of the elixirs and their characteristics."

"Sure."

Tondron read off 30 elixirs and their characteristics, then suddenly Tinougl said at the last description of a Guavastrian Elixir, "Serve me one of the Lǐzǐ Guavastrian Elixir's."

Guāiqiǎo walked over to the refrigeration unit, pulled out a Lǐzǐ Guavastrian Elixir, walked to the adjacent area that had a counter, opened a cabinet door, pulled out a serving tray, and a glass and set them on the counter top, then opened the drink container and poured it into the glass sitting on the serving tray, then walked over to Tinougl and sat a napkin down on the table next to him and the glass of the elixir on it and said, "Tinougl, there is your drink. Is there anything more I can get you?"

"Do you have any snacks in the refrigeration unit?"

"Yes, we have some snack packs that go well with the Lǐzǐ Guavastrian

Elixir."

"Let me try one of them."

"I will get it for you now."

The robot walked over to the cabinet where he just left, pulled down a serving dish and a snack pack and opened it and dumped the contents into the dish, then walked back over to Tinougl and sat the dish down on the table next to Tinougl and said, "Here is your snack, I hope you enjoy it."

"Thank you."

"Anything else sir?"

"That will be all for now Guāiqiǎo."

Guāiqiǎo walked back to his robotic storage cabinet opened the door, stepped inside, and shut the door behind him. He had a chair he sat down on to help reduce the power drain associated with standing. Guāiqiǎo's left hand pulled the power cord out of his side and plugged it in to the power socket a six inches away where his power modules would now get a trickle charge until he reached 100%.

Tondron then asked, "Tinougl, is there anything else you would like?"

"Can you put on a news channel?"

"Certainly."

Tondron disappeared and a Holographic News Network broadcast started in three dimensional. There was a mix of local, international, and intergalactic news items. Even though the reality of what Tinougl watched dated 500 years prior, since the Empire had multiple planets and thousands of news stories, it would be like trying to find a needle in a haystack to find the coverage a person wanted to see, unless they searched the content to target areas of interest. A person watching this often could get neurologically addicted to the content.

Tinougl had to be careful in what he requested to see. He could not afford to leave breadcrumbs that some investigator might pick up on. His searches had to be more generic and even though he knew some of these things because they were ancient history he studied in preparation for the mission, he had to appear like it was new news for him. One thing he was trained to look out for was the potential of another time traveller showing up and presenting an issue for him.

The drink and snacks were quite satisfying. In a way he wished he had more, but he didn't want to spoil his appetite for a meal later.

After watching local and intergalactic news for a while, Tinougl said, "I think that's enough news for me for now. I think I'm going to recline and rest for a while. In case I fall asleep be sure and wake me up in a couple hours so I can make sure I get down to the restaurant and a decent time for a meal."

"Are you finished with your drink and snack Tinougl?" Tondron asked.

"Yes, thank you."

Just like on clockwork, Guāiqiǎo came out of his storage room and walked over and removed the dish and glass that had been sitting on the tabletop. He then walked back to his storage room that had a miniature elevator in it and sent the dishes down to be cleaned and copies of the exact drink and snack were sent back up and in less than two minutes, Guāiqiǎo restocked the refrigerator unit and the snack cabinet, then returned to his chair inside his storage room awaiting further instructions.

Guāiqiǎo was more than just a maid type robot. Even though it had a male like appearance, it could be a female model. When a customer checked into the Cuìlǜ Resort Hotel, during the check-in process they were given a room with a robot matching whether they were male or female. Half the rooms in the Cuìlǜ Resort Hotel had male Guāiqiǎo's the other half had female robots named Mǎshāwáwá.

Aside from the cosmetics once you took the robot apart it was the exact same model just with different programming to take on the role it was designed.

These robots were also part of the security apparatus. These robots were programmed in martial arts, had video and sound sensors, links with the Cuìlǜ Resort Hotel's computational and communications systems where it might get redirected as more surveillance on the issue at hand might dictate otherwise. It had a special provision in it's coding that stipulated the normal three rules for robots designed to not harm humans with a fourth robot rule: *If a person was attempting to harm a Resort Guest, the robot was directed to protect that person.*

If there was an altercation and they were both Cuìlǜ Resort Hotel guests, then the person who rented the hotel room was considered the protected.

Reprogramming was always ongoing as the robots were slowly developing much greater capabilities. Thanks to the mini elevator in each robot storage room, there were no external maids. The robot cleaned everything as soon as the guest departed. When the sheets needed changing, while the person was taking a shower or freshening up, the robot would remake the bed usually in 90 seconds with robot efficiency. Normally the only thing that went inside and out of the Cuìlǚ Resort Hotel rooms were resort guests.

The combination of the snacks and the elixirs made Tinougl slightly sleepy so when he laid back to rest, he soon fell asleep in the most restful doze he felt in a long-long time. The only other time he felt so restful was when he went through some surgery to repair some serious wounds, he received in mortal combat with an enemy spy trained and equally capable. One split second made the difference between living and death.

At the two-hour mark he heard some nice chimes and soon a sound coming from Guāiqiǎo standing over him softly saying, "Tinougl, you asked to be awakened in two hours. Do you need any assistance getting up?"

Tinougl's espionage mind quickly spun up and he did his 5 second automatic situational awareness scan to see if everything in his surroundings were normal and no exigencies existed.

Part of his training was when awakened during a new assignment anywhere, you must obtain situational awareness in five seconds or less because your life may at risk until you find out.

Tinougl quickly looked around and surmised there were no threats, so he stood down his next layer of defensive actions taken if his perimeter had been compromised and the enemy was nearby.

As soon as Tinougl made the "all clear" decision, he sat up and put his feet down on the floor and counted to twenty silently then stood up and walked over to the bathroom to take care of business. By the time he finished and washed his hands, Guāiqiǎo was parked back in his storage room waiting for his next assignment.

Tondron, the Cuìlǚ Resort Hotel room holograph personality then appeared and asked, "Tinougl, what do you wish to do now?"

"I think I'm going to go down to the Resort Dining Hall and see what they offer."

"What would you like us to do with your backpack while you are gone to the restaurant?"

"Just leave it where it's at. I'll deal with it when I get back."

Part of Tondron and Guāiqiǎo's training was:

Do not touch a resort guest private property unless they ask you.

However, they would guard it and protect it including storing it out of site in Guāiqiǎo's storage room. As the Cuìlù Resort Hotel security system that had real time trackers on all guests, detected Tinougl returning to his room the backpack would be placed back on the bed in the exact location it was placed earlier.

Tinougl walked to the elevator, and it opened shortly for him. When he walked inside and turned around, he noticed a placard that stated: "The elevator is an information provider, just ask a question."

"Can you give me directions to the Dining Hall?"

A holograph popped up with a detailed diagram that showed how to get to the restaurant. There was a voice as well that said, "When you exit the elevator, turn right in the hallway and 50 feet from the elevator is the entrance to the Dining Hall."

As the elevator descended to the lobby a quick video was shown demonstrating how to get to the Dining Hall.

As Tinougl exited the elevator a voice said, "Tinougl, please enjoy your stay."

This adventure had already given Tinougl an impression: *these people were not so backwards five hundred years ago, afterall.*

The walk to the Dining Hall was brief and the closer he proceeded to the front entrance the more people he observed in their holiday attire wearing all types of smiles. *Obviousy, these people are happy.*

Tinougl arrived slightly early for the dinner crowd. There was music being played by several performers, including the large black instrument with an apparent keyboard, that didn't seem relevant in modern times. Perhaps it's because it was too large and bulky. The music the performer made with the large horizontal instrument nevertheless seemed rather pleasing. The other instruments being played only looked remotely like what existed 500 years later, also produced interesting oscillations that added positively to the music. The performers were dressed well and in the center of the stage was a female singer who had been standing there and as if on cue, she started singing.

The singer's voice sent shivers up Tinougl's spine. This woman had an incredible sound that resonated well with Tinougl who enjoyed it immensely.

As Tinougl walked up to the Maitra d', he was informed, "Please chose where you would like to sit, there are a lot of open tables."

"Thank you, I think I'll go over by the window."

"Please make yourself comfortable." The Maitra d', then smiled and Tinougl made his way to an empty table by the window where most of the tables around there were currently empty.

Tinougl had a direct view of the attractive female singer and took it all in. A waitress then appeared with a menu and a glass of water and said after sitting the water and menu down on the table, "My name is Madalyn bon Donkers and I will be your waitress for your meal."

"Thank you, Madalyn, you can call me Tinougl."

"Would you like a drink?"

"Yes, I would like a nice elixir that will put me into a great mood. What do you recommend?"

"Everyone's taste is different of course, but if I had my choice and wasn't working now, I would consider the Trombocante del Sporbosa."

"Thank you for the suggestion, that's what I'll have."

The bartenders didn't have a lot of drink requests because it was still slightly early and were able to create that Trombocante del Sporbosa that contained an elixir that had psychoactive drugs, a wine like substance, and a distillate potent in alcohol.

Within just a few moments, Madalyn bon Donkers the waitress was back and served the concoction that would not quite inebriate Tinougl but would place him in a hyperextended mood that would allow his mind to maintain situational awareness at the same time unwind from the time travel and the possible implications it would bestow upon this mere mortal.

Madalyn then walked away to give the customer some privacy and time to look over the menu to determine what he would like to eat. In a short while after enjoying the Trombocante del Sporbosa, Tinougl was mildly shifted into a different psychological domain, where his emotions were equalized, and any pent-up demand eased off a notch or two.

Madalyn bon Donkers observing the customer from afar giving Tinougl space so that he could enjoy the entertainment, also was keenly observing the fact he hadn't checked out the menu.

Madalyn bon Donkers had a thin tablet like device that had voice analysis as well as a data terminal to inform staff such as any meal orders they were dealing with. At the point artificial intelligence determined a verbal interaction would soon follow as the guest looked over the menu, the tablet device informed the waitress who the customer was and any important facts that might blend into a social engagement or trigger a pathway to a conversation and subsequent information change, food requests and basic socialization.

Based on the facial recognition and the unusual name, the galactic wide search engine determined the guest Tinougl was a writer who lived on one of the other empire planets and was visiting. Since they could not track travel documents or and sort of transportation reports, it was assumed he arrived in this city via private transportation means, which a well-paid celebrity could easily afford. The instructions to the waitress indicated, to not pester the person who was traveling incognito, and no doubt cherished his privacy.

After the waitress Madalyn bon Donkers observed the customer look at the menu and sit it back down again, the tablet gave instructions to the waitress who had already determined she needed to approach the customer and take his order.

Madalyn carefully approached Tinougl smiling as directed from her tablet and asked, "Sir, have you decided what you would like to eat?"

"Yes, I would like the baked Plastybalkan served with Coefetty-fries."

"May I get you a refill of Trombocante del Sporbosa?"

"That would be delightful, thank you."

With clocklike precision, another drink arrived, and the empty glass removed. The water glass remained untouched.

Tinougl sat enjoying his drink and the lovely singing that put an exclamation mark on the small music group. *It seems like they went through a lot of extra effort to get that large musical instrument in here.*

The sounds that instrument created outshined the other instruments, but they too added magnificently to the oscillations and reverberations that had a positive effect on Tinougl and the audience.

Tinougl was a handsome man though dressed down for such an

exquisite resort. *If I stay here longer than I planned, I might need to purchase some more elaborate clothing,* Tinougl thought.

As the Dining Hall slowly filled up with happy vacationers on well-deserved holidays, it was not long before one of the tables about 20 steps away was filled with wealthy Barracuda's looking for strays and a means to find pleasure their neglectful husbands failed to do.

The pack leader had her radar locked on Tinougl and warned the other hungry Barracuda's keep your hands off my quarry. I plan snag that trophy before the night is done.

When Tinougl first arrived, there were virtually no food orders in. His order of Plastybalkan and Coefetty-fries were already cooked and ready to serve as they normally had at least 20 similar orders early in the evening when the older diners usually showed up.

As Tinougl was halfway done with his second Trombocante del Sporbosa and feeling a good buzz, Madalyn bon Donkers arrived pushing a little cart with her that had a sealed food warmer so the customer would get the meal at the same temperature as if the chef just placed it fresh on the plate.

As expected, the Plastybalkan had a leg and a thigh, and part of the breast, cooked to perfection with some type of gravy on it. The Coefetty-fries had a orange appearance and was crunchy and tasted really good with all the spices cooked with it. This was a throwback to the past when food still had some taste.

In the modern era 500 years later with all the medical and chemical applications to the food, it rarely had this smell and soon Tinougl surmised, taste as well. His speculation was right on the mark on how pleasant it was.

The Barracuda's left Tinougl alone while he was eating. Soon after he finished eating, Madalyn bon Donkers came by with a small cart and removed all the dishes and tablecloth and put it in separate compartments of her cart and laid down a new tablecloth without dinner settings as it was assumed the customer would have a few more drinks and listen to the performers and then leave. They wanted Tinougl to feel grand and well taken care of as their motive was customer service and lavishly spoil their guests in many ways.

"Would you like another Trombocante del Sporbosa?"

"No, I would like something not as strong so that I can casually walk out of here a little less lightheaded."

"I would suggest you try Chamboree del Pàrà Měilì. It gives heightened alertness, reduces drowsiness, and still gives you a great feeling."

"All right, I'll have one of them."

No sooner than Tinougl received his Chamboree del Pàrà Měilì, the musical group took a break. One of the Barracudas was just about ready to strike on the unassuming gentleman she knew looked like the kind of guy that could give her all night long passion, the singer passed her greeting all the customers along her path through about one half of the customer seatings on this side of the Dining Hall and eventually approached Tinougl's table.

"Hello, are you having a good time."

"Yes, I had a fine dinner and drinks and your singing made it all that much better."

"Well thank you, I'm glad you liked our performance."

"Are you taking a short break?"

"Yes, we've been at it for a while, and we need a break now because our next set will happen just about the time the Dining Hall fills up."

"Would you like to sit down and have a drink with me?"

The singer Wánměi de Mòlìhuā looked at the man who still had some youth left in him and was dressed casually and not stuffy like many of the resort clientele often showed up at the Dining Hall often acting pompous. Wánměi thought *it would be refreshing to spend some time with this laid-back simple person.*

"Sure, I wouldn't mind, I have about fifteen minutes before I need to be back on stage."

Tinougl stood up walked around the table and pulled the chair out for Wánměi de Mòlìhuā who took the perfect gentleman's lead and sat down allowing the fine person to extend to her the curtesy she expected.

Madalyn bon Donkers keeping her eye out for customer dynamics observed the unusual sight of Wánměi de Mòlìhuā sitting down with a customer. She knew the famed singer was on a break and needed her drink, a watered down Lǐzǐ Guavastrian Elixir.

Madalyn approached Mòlìhuā and asked, "Would you like a drink?"

"Yes, can you please give me on of your special Lǐzǐ Guavastrian Elixir's?"

"I would be delighted." Madalyn responded and briefly left and went directly to the bartender who was observing all they eye candy and waiting for his next surge in drink requests.

"My name is Mòlìhuā."

"Pleased to meet you Mòlìhuā. My name is Tinougl."

In less than three minutes Madalyn returned with a tall glass of the exotic substance that was watered down. Tinougl from his own personal experience in his resort hotel room thought: *Madalyn should be ready for prime time after drinking all that.*

"Are you enjoying your stay at the Cuìlù Resort Hotel, Tinougl?"

"I just arrived her today, just getting settled in."

"Will you be staying for a long period of time?"

"It could be as short as three days, but if I have issues with my publisher, I might have to stay longer to get things wrapped up properly."

"What are you publishing."

"A Novel."

"Oh really?"

"Yes."

That's why he looks so laid back and non-assuming, Wánměi thought.

"How long will your band be performing here?"

"We are under contract with the resort for two years. We have one and a half years left on our engagement."

"Did your group write all those songs?"

"Yes, we wrote most of the songs, but we had some professional producers work with us on the content and commercialize them far better than we could have on our own."

"The end result seems to be rather nice."

"Thank you for the complement."

"You are welcome."

"Are you from this planet?"

"No, I've spent most of my time living on Argecibo."

In the future Tinougl grew up in Argecibo, so it would be easier for him to sustain interrogations because of his familiarity with the planet. He did however have to take a strong history course to make him residual in knowledge about the time era he was trasported to Visluvia for his mission. Argecibo was located at the far end of the empire and most Argecibo inhabitants knew little about the distant solar system and planet. The likelihood of Tinougl meeting someone from Argecibo were very slim and thus worked out for his cover story quite well.

"How about yourself?"

"I grew up on the planet Konhagar and trained to be a musician and a singer. I can play all the instruments you see."

"I've never seen that big flat instrument before. What's it called?"

"That is a piano?"

"Are they made on this planet?"

"No. most of them on this planet were brought in by black marketeers who run the gauntlet and get into the rears of our enemies in order for them to do trade with the distant solar systems outside the Empire."

"Will we eventually build them on this planet?"

"I've asked that question and the general answer is they are very complicated instruments and it's far cheaper just to import them and give credits to black marketeers."

The conversation lingered for a few more brief minutes, then the rest of the music performers went to the stage and were about ready to start again.

"I'm sorry, but I must go rejoin the band now," Mòlìhuā said in a reluctant tone.

Tinougl was warned that if he stayed at the time traveled zone for long his body would go through something like jet lag. The combination of the food, drink, and soothing music was creating a sleepy sensation which after a couple more songs made Tinougl think it was time for him to return to his Cuìlù Resort Hotel room. Just as Tinougl stood up so did one of the Barracuda's who followed him. Tinougl saw her out of the corner of his eye and made no assumptions about what her intentions were and exited the Dining Hall.

It was a short walk to the elevator and in the span of less than three minutes Tinougl entered his room noting the backpack was on his bed where he left it and notified Tondron the room's artificial intelligence that he was going to lay down and take a nap.

The Barracuda had watched Tinougl get into the elevator which provided her with the essential information that he was a resort guest. She would be lying in wait for him the next day.

These Barracudas were wives of wealthy intergalactic bankers and businessmen. They often traveled to this resort together as their husbands were absent a significant amount of time on other planets wheeling and dealing with unsavory characters such as black marketeers, criminal enterprises, and credit laundering cartels and revolutionaries in places like Konhagar. Their husbands were naïve to think their spouses with unlimited disposable income would not hire spies and private detectives to find out what their husbands were really doing. Part of the Barracuda modus of operendus was to school new members of their exclusive club the necessity of spying on their husbands and the contacts to who could accomplish it.

Since the Barracuda's got revenge by conducting soiree's of their own, they also gave one another nicknames and alias' as to not leave behind scandalous information to third parties. Estele bon Stoffengar who laid claim to this new stranger she planned on meeting and manifesting a salacious relationship, had the nickname "Spicey." One of the other ladies in their group was "Sparky." The third one had the nickname "Schemer." Behind her back the other two Barracuda's called Schemer "Screamer" because of comments some gentlemen said when one of the Barracuda's aced Schemer and the men informed them why they didn't feel comfortable having sexual relations with a woman who woke up the adjacent rooms in the middle of the night.

It would not be unusual for one of the Barracudas to say to the other:

"Here comes Screamer, anotherone bites the dust."

Sparky and Schemer were of course surprised that Spicey had returned so abruptly.

"What happened to your quarry?" Sparky asked.

"He went up to his room." Spicey replied.

"Why didn't you go with him?"

"I didn't have the chance to meet the nice-looking man. The elevator was ready for his entrance, and it departed before I could get in and introduce myself."

"The night's early, I'm sure you can meet another?"

"I'm sure I will run into him tomorrow. This man looks delicious, I'll hold out for him."

Estele bon Stoffengar stayed at this resort frequently as her husband was gone the most and she already had a three-inch-thick dossier on him and knew he cheated every time he left the planet. He had an appetite for green and blue skinned women, and if some of the hearsay was valid, there these women were sexual goddesses. Estele's sexual relationship with Bertrand bon Stoffengar, her husband was lackluster at best and mostly seldom. She knew she was in her period and extremely desiring copulation with the stranger.

Estele bon Stoffengar got to know several important staff members of the resort she also knew took bribes. One of them was a security detective whose charter was to keep resort guests safe and organized crime from infiltrating and placing prostitutes into guest rooms. The security man, Balger could easily identify any resort guest. Balger was gone for the day, but Estele knew where to find him the next day if necessary.

Tinougl was going to sleep and wake up when he desired, but Tondron said, "Master Tinougl, before you go to sleep, let me pour you a bath and put in some salts that will help you rest better, then you can change into sleeping clothes and feel much better."

"I didn't bring any sleeping clothes with me."

"That's not a problem, while you are taking the bath, Guāiqiǎo will obtain the correct size sleeping garments for you."

"Sure, not a problem."

"The bathtub is now filling with water and Guāiqiǎo will be adding the bath salts momentarily. I think by the time you get undressed it should be ready."

"Alright."

Just as Tinougl sat down to remove his shoes, Guāiqiǎo left his waiting room holding a container and went into the bathroom dumping the contents into the nice warm bath computer controlled for ninety six degrees.

Guāiqiǎo came out of the bathroom holding an empty container and walked over to Tinougl and asked, "Tinougl, would you like me to put your backpack in the closet to give you more room on your bed?"

"Sure, that would be fine."

Guāiqiǎo walked over to the backpack on the edge of the bed, picked it up and walked to his service counter, sat the empty salts container down and walked over to the closet and sat the backpack down on a folding platform that was currently engaged to accept packages or luggage, and sat the backpack down on it, then closed the closet door, then walked over to the service counter and picked up the empty container and went into his waiting room, closing the door behind him.

Briefly, Tinougl undressed and went nude into the bathroom and hopped into the very large bath. Inside the bathroom was a small holographic projector so that Tondron could communicate with the resort guest if necessary.

As soon as Tinougl was situated in the bathtub already feeling the effects, Tondron's holograph appeared and stated: "There are waterjets in the bathtub to help massage you. Would you like me to turn it on?"

"Yes, sure."

Soon Tinougl was feeling the thrust of the water pumps creating complicated water patterns and vibrations. It felt like a massage and his muscles were quickly feeling great.

"Just what the doctor ordered," Tinougl said as he laid back with his head on a pillow like device with his body partially floatin from neutral buoyancy created by the additives as will as the water jets shot under him.

After approximately fifteen minutes, Tinougl assumed Tondron was always listening and said, "I think I want to get out of the bath now."

Tondron's holograph reappeared and said, "Tinougl, please stand up and you will be rinsed down with a cleaning and rinsing solution to add to your comfort."

As Tinougl was standing up the water in the tub was draining and a splash guard came out of the wall and wrapped around the tub, then water started shooting out of a nozzle that had a pleasant scent to it.

The shower wash and rinse lasted about five minutes leaving Tinougl feeling particulary good. Then it stopped, the splashguard retracted and went back into the wall and a cover closed automatically.

Guāiqiǎo then walked into the bathroom holding some towels and asked,

"Would you like me to help dry you off?"

"Sure"

Guāiqiǎo wrapped on towel around Tinougl and then took the second towel and softly dabbed the moisture on Tinougl's hair and face. Suddenly a device came down out of the overhead which Guāiqiǎo controlled and blew warm air to dry Tinougl's hair. By then all the water had drained from the tub and Tinougl took the towel that he had used to dab the hair and face and laid it on the floor and said, please step on here and I will get your undergarments and sleeping attire.

Tinougl stepped out of the empty bathtub and shortly after he was standing with a towel wrapped around him, Guāiqiǎo entered the bathroom and handed Tinougl his under garments one at a time which Tinougl put on and then the sleeping attire. His hair was dry, his skin felt fresh, and he was feeling drowsy as there were sleep inducing additives in the bath salts. Once Guāiqiǎo felt assured that Tinougl was ready to walk to his bed, he opened the door and they both exited and Tinougl followed Guāiqiǎo who walked over and pulled back the sheets so that Tinougl could lay down. As soon as Tinougl was in the bed, he pulled up the sheets and a thin blanket over himself and Guāiqiǎo casually walked over to the bathroom and picked up the towels and carried them into his waiting room and put them on the small elevator to send to the resort's laundry and dry cleaning.

The combination of time lag (jet lag) and bath additives helped Tinougl quickly transcend to an unconscious state where he entered a dream world.

The beautiful part of staying in a resort is you woke up when you dam well pleased. If it had not been for the fact Tinougl had to use the bathroom, he could have easily slept a few more hours. But the rest he did receive was substantial.

After relieving himself and walking back into his room he noticed all his belongings were on the table next to his bed and just before he asked where his clothes were, Tondron asked, "Would you like to get dressed in your clothes now?"

"Sure."

Guāiqiǎo walked to the closet and brought back Tinougl's garments fully dry-cleaned and pressed.

"We didn't want to disturb your backpack, so we dry cleaned these clothes for you."

"Thank you."

"I wasn't planning on staying here too long, but I do have a change of clothes in my backpack."

"Would you prefer we press them and wear them instead?"

"How long would that take?"

"About 15 minutes."

"Sure, go ahead."

Guāiqiǎo walked over to the closet and retrieved the backpack and took it over to Tinougl and handed it to him and said, "We are not permitted to open any of your private luggage or backpacks without your direction to do so. Would you like to pull out what clothes you want us to prepare for you to wear today?"

"Sure, not a problem."

Tinougl pulled out his only change of clothes thinking he would not need much more because as soon as he discovered the information he was sent to retrieve, he would get back to the time Machine and go back to the future.

Guāiqiǎo took possession of the clothing articles and went to his storage room and sent them down the small elevator and with wireless communications gave directions to the robot on the other end that would quickly drycleand and press the garments, making them look like new.

Tinougl was happy his change of clothes looked so good, and it would save him some time he didn't have to go purchase new clothes for another couple of days.

After Tinougl dressed, he casually said to Tondron, I think I'll get something to eat at the Dining Hall, then go for a little walk.

"We'll be waiting for your return, Tinougl"

Tinougl left the room, took the elevator down to the Dining Hall and in a repeat of yesterday was soon sitting down being serviced by another waiter he had not met before. He fortified his appetite with a brunch like selection, then he went back up to his room to freshen up and later decided to go out for a walk.

"Tondron, I'm going for a walk to get some exercises. Where do you recommend, I go?"

Tondron's holograph popped up and he replied, "Master Tinougl, the front entrance of the Cuìlù Resort Hotel is located on one of the busy streets of our Tartarnite Empire Capital City Santorini de Shénshèng. It goes by our Central Park which is the pride of the Empire. There is a lot to see there and a vast area to walk around. Let me show you some video we have filmed for resort guests who want to take a trip there."

"Sure, let me see it."

The holographic three-dimensional video with nice sound started playing. There was a very attractive female narrator. She was dressed to perfection and her makeup was as nicely done as many entertainment videos, that Tinougl enjoyed in his own time before traveling to the past. The luster of her voice was equally pleasing.

In some ways, the narrator seemed similar in appearance to the Singer Wánměi de Mòlìhuā which gave Tinougl added influence to want to go back and hear the wonderful singer perform again today.

The narrator introduced herself as Táozi and was filmed in three-dimensional holographic video leaving the Cuìlù Resort Hotel and turning right as she's discussing what to expect on the way to the park.

When Tinougl arrived the day before he was walking at a time that was not the rush hour of people coming and going to their employment and shopping. Since a lot of resort guests would head for the park this time of day, they would be confronted with what the city might be like during the busy time of day. There were far more transportation devices and pedestrians. Santorini de Shénshèng the Tartarnite Empire Capital City had ever reason for such a busy atmosphere as people throughout the empire would have reason to come to this planet.

The intergalactic banking cartels had headquarters here and the banksters tended to breed more and more Barracudas by their absence and infidelity. Organized crime and spy networks flourished. In reality, Santorini de Shénshèng hosted a cesspool of twisted and intertwined allegiances. Bankers, Spies, Organized Crime Syndicates, and others knew that not everyone was on their side, even if there was the outward appearance there was. The tendrils of all interested parties created a witch's brew that kept everyone guessing. Amid all this complexity was just one piece of information the time traveller spy needed.

His orders were precise: "Do not take any actions other than find the information and come back as soon as you get it."

Most resort guests would only watch this presentation briefly and head out and discover the central park on their own, but Tinougl was a curious and careful operative. This was an additional briefing as far as Tinougl was concerned. He watched it in depth with curiousity as well as concern because, it would definitely fill in a few blanks of his training. As detailed as his training had been, it was 500 years later when spatial distortion and time filtering blurred or created uncorrelated reality.

Even now going back 500 years, it was quite evident the Empire was huge and complex. Even though more modern science and equipment was engineered as society and technology advanced, the fact remains in this era 500 years before he lives and only saw it because of time travel, it still is well advanced.

As Táozi the narrator for Central Park video continued with her presentation she clarified public transportation, schedules, and intangible items that would be very ubiquitous for Tinougl pursuing and discovering the golden nugget so he could hustle back to that time machine and get back to the world he lived in.

Tinougl also made another astute judgement; if he made it back alive, he would never volunteer to time travel again. He also understood the obvious, *if his time machine malfunctioned and left him marooned 500 years before his time, he would make the best of it.*

The video took a while to watch, but at the end of it, Tinougl was happy he invested the time in it because it clarified some training shortfalls and boosted his situational awareness by knowing where he was going and what to expect.

"Thank you for showing me the video, it was very informative," Tinougl stated as the video ended, and the holograph disappeared.

"I'm glad you received some worthwhile information from the Holograph," Tondron replied.

"I'm going to Central Park now; I'll be back later."

"Enjoy rouself, Master Tinougl."

CHAPTER FOUR

SANTORINI DE SHÉNSHÈNG CENTRAL PARK

Tinougl left the Cuìlù Resort Hotel and followed the route laid out by the narrator Táozi. The traffic density and the pedestrian swarm was about the same as in the holographic presentation. Nothing in his training before the time travel mission provided as good a detail as Táozi's briefing. If he made it back to his own time in the future, he would make comments about how in some areas the training seemed weak. But as he rationalized it, he realized; *trainers cannot really put together a really accurate training scenario for a time frame five hundred years earlier, as it now obvious some of the information was lost or distorted in time.*

Very few people would walk the distance because public transportation was frequent and efficient. Most people would have taken public transportation to the Central Park. But in doing so due to the compressed time and reduced visibility, a lot would be lost.

This walk served two purposes, first he would spot egress routes. Even though he was a Tartarnite citizen, if for some reason he became a suspect and was thoroughly interrogated by planetary security personnel, he would wind up treated as a spy since he had very little footprint in this era to vet his presence. And if they applied the levels of torture that was used during this time era, they would not be impressed if he claimed he was a time traveller. His only way home period was to get back in the time machine as quickly as he discovered what he was sent here to find.

When you are of another time or another world, but you blend in, the personal psychology of knowing anyone who saw you had no idea who you really were, gives that sense of seclusion. It felt strange to know no living person at this time knew you.

Shops and cafés passed along the way looked interesting, well kept and not as grimy as they would be in 500 years. Population growth eventually catches up with the esthetics of society.

As he got closer to the Central Park, the pedestrian density seemed to thin out. Nevertheless, when he arrived at the park entrance, the public transportation unloading park visitors, quickly refilled the volume of people.

There were a few security officers at the park entrance, mainly to protect the crowds and prevent any nefarious activities of the criminal elements who might otherwise apply the crafts of their trades.

As Tinougl passed the two security officers, he had an eerie feeling. The public and nobody around him knew that he was a spy or that he traveled through time to get here. By all appearances he was simply just another Tartarnite walking into the park entrance.

There were many paths he could take but based on watching the video and determining how much time he would take the circular route around the park. He would complete this walk and do some more information search before he needed to get back in time to partake in another session of hearing the singer Wánměi de Mòlīhuā perform just as the Dining Hall would open for the evening meal.

Tinougl's walking velocity was quite brisk, he was in great shape even though he was still suffering from a little time travel lag that was no different than jet lag. The distance covered would equal walking at four miles per hour.

After a few hundred yards he passed children playgrounds and noticed the numerous birds flying around and some of them floating in the pond in the center of the park.

A few people sat at park benches reading and some engaged in conversations. The landscaping gave the impression of greatness the Tartarnite Empire would want to convey to visitors in the capital city and central business district that Santorini de Shénshèng exhibited.

Five Hundred years in the future, this park had none of the luxurious decorum Tinougl now observed. Sadly, most of this would be destroyed in a hundred years in a gigantic fireball.

As Tinougl made his way around the outskirts of the park, he had several pleasant sites and beautiful women to look at strolling around enjoying themselves usually with someone special or just a friend.

Tinougl wasn't going to exist in this time domain to worry about relationships. Even if he passed women who semi-flirted, he would just smile and continue along his own business.

The park was excellent and struck an emotional tendril just thinking about how in the span of 100 years it would disintegrate when that horrific fireball ignited directly overhead in one of the most fratricidal incidents in Empire history. Tinougl took solace in the fact none of these people he observed would be living by the time of that fateful day into the future.

The wildlife was far more abundant than it would be 500 years from now. If he knew which of them would become extinct, he would seriously think about bringing some eggs back with him to incubate. But in his training bringing back anything except himself was a big no-no.

Everyone he passed who were casually enjoying their day had

no idea the emotional stimulus all this played on Tinougl since he knew how much of it would be irrevocably lost in the future.

In his vast training he knew they warned him he would be tampering with the fabric of space time if he did anything to change the future with unpredictable results. As an example, if he delayed the inevitable demise of Santorini de Shénshèng for two hundred and fifty years, then perhaps when it was finally destroyed the devastation would be far worse. He understood he would not know the consequences of his actions until he returned possibly with huge regret.

The lake in the middle of Santorini de Shénshèng Central Park, was long but narrow. It was easy to visualize when he reached the end of the lake as the nice sidewalk train bent around the far end. Also, the sunlight was now against his back and instead of his face. He made the mental note to wear sunglasses and a hat the next time he walked in Central Park.

Walking along the lakeside, he saw there was another outer path that had some mechanical devices people rode and self propelled. The riders of these devices looked happy with no care in the world. He made the mental note to try one of these if he had the chance.

The walk was taking about as long as he predicted, though his fine physical shape had no difficulties in completing the long walk around the park in about one and a half hours. As he was walking by the park exit, he looked at a detailed map and pulled out his communicator and photographed it to study at a later date. Perhaps his controllers back in future time will be interested in what it was like. He instinctively spun around and took a couple photographs using his communicator he believed would preserve the images during the time travel back to his future.

He now exited the park and went back in the opposite direction from when he arrived. In a seemingly short while as he passed by retail establishments, he stopped and went inside and quickly discovered hats and sunglasses to purchase which he did mindful of picking items that appeared to be popular at the park.

With the sunglasses and hat, he wore after paying for them, his appearance remarkably changed. Like all good spies he was happy how easily he could change his appearance. Sewn into some of his clothes were temporary masks and makeup kits to further enhance a change of appearance if he needed to. He soon passed by a store that sold reading materials. He went in and looked around to see if there were any items that would benefit his search for information he was sent to discover.

Just like the holograph back in his room, there was a tremendous selection to sift through without arousing suspicion. He couldn't stay long if he wanted to get a table with a direct view of the Singer Wánměi de Mòlìhuā who would be performing in a short while. He picked out a couple books that were in the ballpark of what he was searching and a daily news source he could be reading at the same time Tondron put up a news holograph back in his resort hotel room.

He was soon back out on the city walkway edging back towards the Cuìlǜ Resort Hotel. Even though he was on the opposite side of the street, there was a pedestrian crosswalk in front of the hotel with streetlights to provide safe crossing. Moments later he was entering Cuìlǜ Resort Hotel.

CHAPTER FIVE

DINNER IS SERVED.

Simultaneously as he got to the elevator, one of the Barracuda's who saw him the day before named Sparky stepped out of the elevator but did not recognize Tinougl. She soon found her way to the Dining Hall and sat down next to Estele bon Stoffengar (aka Spicey).

"You looked dressed up."

"You do not look so bad yourself."

"The resort makeup artist and hair designer, did their magic."

"If your husband was here tonight, he might want to cuddle up with you later."

"I doubt that. He's too busy dipping his pen in company ink on the planet Rèqì Téngténg de Jǐngdiǎn."

"He's an intergalactic banker, what do you expect?"

"If it wasn't for his money and my ability to find some satisfaction elsewhere, I would leave him."

"Like the gentleman last night?"

"He slipped out of my grip, but I know more about him now. I'll eventually get him the way I want him."

"And what way is that?"

"All night long."

"The three Barracudas all giggled together, because it was their modus operendus since these bankers' wives all had similar problems: *when the cat is away the mice will play.*

Tinougl could not go into the resort Dining Hall with all the items he purchased and was on his way up to his room and dropped them off.

The hotel surveillance could not validate Tinougl with the hat and sun classes on and informed him, "please remove your hat and sunglasses so we can be sure who you are."

He removed the hat and sunglasses and the elevator door quickly opened, and he got in. No other words spoken were necessary and he was promptly delivered to the floor where his room existed.

He figured the room security would have the same problem so before he got near the door he removed had and sunglasses again and did not putting them back on that night.

When he deposited the items on the table, Tondron asked, "Tinougl, what would you like to do now?"

"I'm going back downstairs to the Dining Hall."

"Is it enjoyable for you?"

"Yes, there is a singer performer there named Wánměi de Mòlìhuā and I like her style and music, I'm going there mainly to hear her sing, but I'll get something to eat there while I'm at it."

"I hope you enjoy your time, Tinougl."

"Tondron, let me ask you a question."

"Sure."

"If I got lucky and Wánměi de Mòlìhuā agreed to come up to my room and do some boom-boom, would that be a problem?"

"What's boom-boom?"

"Romantic intercourse."

"Tinougl, what happens at Cuìlù Resort Hotel, stays in Cuìlù Resort Hotel.

We do not inform anyone of your private matters."

"No issues with bringing her or another woman into my room for some boom-boom?"

"She can come to visit you as long as you bring her here, nobody is allowed to enter unless you invite them in."

"That works for me."

"Good."

"I'm heading down to the Dining Hall now, don't be surprised if I have company later tonight."

"If that makes you happy, then I'll be available to assist by providing music, drinks or anything else you wish to share with your guest."

"I appreciate that."

"See you when you get back."

Tinougl didn't bring a lot of clothes with him because he knew to get the job done and get out of there as quickly as he was done. Unfortunately, nothing in the realm of what he was looking for was obviousy available and he couldn't do a big drilling down for it without arousing much attention, so he might be forced to go slow a couple days until he got the right source.

It was a short walk and took very little time to get to the Dining hall. Tinougl was delighted to see his table from the night before as immediately available. And just like the precision of a well-oiled machine, Dining Hall waitress Madalyn bon Donkers was there to immediately provide service carrying a glass of water that would no doubt be wasted.

Good evening Tinougl, may I get you something to drink?"

"You know I wouldn't mind another one of those "Chamboree del Pàrà Měilì like you served last night."

"Coming right up," Madalyn bon Donkers said and smiled affectionately.

Madalyn just like Spicey the night before was mildly impressed that a beautiful singer like Wánměi de Mòlìhuā would sit down and spend time with this stranger. He obviousy had some class and attraction to him. Although Spicey was irritated the singer got in her way. Hopefully that would not be the case tonight. Plus, Spicey had her own plan, the barracuda would attack while Wánměi de Mòlìhuā was singing if necessary.

Just like the night before, the crowd had not fully showed up. The bartender was standing there idle enjoying the music and was happy to mix the concoction for the resort guest, which he did quite efficiently.

Spicey wanted her new quest, Tinougl to loosen up a bit before she attacked her victim and eventually used him like a cheap gigolo later in the night. She was delighted to see Mr. Tinougl take a nice deep swallow of that drink to help matters along.

Estele bon Stoffengar (aka Spicey) was a frequent resort client and spent a lot of credits here. She also bribed employees often for information. The money she paid out was chicken feed for her. The information was priceless, and she got it very cheap because the employees all had their price, and an innocuous request seemed trivial compared to the nice tips given. In the few times she had to go directly to the resort hotel security manager himself, she had to do two things, one is explained why she wanted the information as well as pay the handsome bribe.

Spicey knew after several dealings with the security manager, she had complete confidence in his ability to be very discrete. After receiving the dossier on Tinougl, she knew he was the ideal target:

a young man, single from an offworld planet, and obscure author who was ostensibly at the Tartarnite Empire Capital City Santorini de Shénshèng for a professional meeting with an entertainment company representative who might further his success along quite a bit if they were able to strike a deal.

Who knows, if the young man could please her, Spicey would be able to bank-role the project. But the young man would have to sell his soul to the devil herself, if he took such generosity.

The music was playing, Tinougl was enjoying it and Dining Hall waitress Madalyn bon Donkers approached him and asked "Tinougl would like to order a meal?"

"I'll order after the band takes a break."

"Are you interested in talking with Wánmĕi de Mòlìhuā again?" Madalyn asked and smiled after observing the two the night before the conveyed there was a subtle attraction between the two.

"Yes, I enjoyed talking with her."

Madalyn was a beautiful woman and could have her way with men if she wanted but knew the rules she knew best: *do not fraternize with the customers, because you do not know them well and it could be more trouble than what it's worth.*

Having watched Wánmĕi de Mòlìhuā perform for several months,

Madalyn knew she didn't open herself up too many strangers like the night before, which surprised her. But she could see Tinougl was a nice looking male and had a sweet disposition.

After several songs, Tinougl finished his drink and Madalyn was right there to get him a refill if he wanted. During this interchange of conversation, the musicians took a break. Madalyn shortly was heading to the bar tender with another order of the Chamboree del Pàrà Mĕilì.

Spicey was almost ready to approach her conquest when Wánměi de Mòlìhuā walked past her and went directly to Tinougl's table where she was immediately offered to *please sit here.*

Wánměi de Mòlìhuā was surprised to herself that she had taken a liking to this man so quickly. She didn't know why but there was some attraction there.

Knowing what the two drank together the night before, Madalyn brought them both a drink which interlaced the ambience in a rather remarkable period.

"I'm glad you came to see me sing again tonight."

"I enjoy your singing, I'm glad to be here."

"Thank you."

"I arrived at the perfect time. It looks like the place is starting to fill up."

"You certainly did."

"I timed it just right."

"Did you have a good time today at the resort?"

"Actually, I went for a walk at the Santorini de Shénshèng Central Park and a little shopping."

"Did you enjoy yourself at the park?"

"Yes, I enjoyed watching all the happy people and all the birds flying around or swimming on the lake."

"A lot of people do not like the birds, consider them a nuisance."

"If they lost most of them like people experienced on some planets, they would quickly wish they were back."

"I agree with you. I like watching the birds too."

"I love your dress tonight. Black is one of my favorite colors."

"It's nothing really just another one of my performance clothes."

"It looks impressive to me. But I must admit your singing fully inspires me."

"Thank you I appreciate your feedback."

Tinougl could not help to imagine how Wánměi de Mòlìhuā would feel in his arms if he got so lucky to have a romantic encounter with her that resulted in splendid euphoria.

Wánměi de Mòlìhuā on the otherhand was very appreciative that Tinougl did not come on to hard, he was a true gentleman and kept a pleasant demeaner. It was men like Tinougl that could win her over because she wanted to oversee her own heart and take the matters where they needed to go on her terms and not some artificial schedule manifested by gratification seekers. Plus, she knew the reality was she might not ever see Tinougl again in her lifetime. That's how it was in the entertainment business, especially connected with hotel resorts.

Tinougl was a successful spy, and by second nature was looking for someone looking at him. In the case of the three Barracuda's his assessment was spot on. They were not a threat, nor the source of any interest. But like all good spies, all matters required vigilance and flexibility to respond in ways that might be beneficial to success of the mission, even if it meant doing something slightly distasteful, such as producing the gratification he knew the desires three Barracudas radiated.

Spicey's fire control radar was locked on and tracking Tinougl. Her almost computer like artificial intelligence in her brain was constantly calculating her next move. The performer was starting to become a pest to her. But as the queen Barracudas, she was patient and subtle and would apply her tradecraft at appropriate moments.

Spicey could tell by the body language and the flirtatious element between the two, there was some covalent bonding going on. That would not deter Spicey in the least bit because Spicey knew the facts of life: old age and treachery would overcome youth and skill.

It wasn't much longer before breaktime ended and the music played on. Just when Spicey was going to make her move, the waitress visited Tinougl's table and the way she was shaking her head knew it had to be something about a food order.

The Barracudas were all getting hungry, and Sparky no longer could hold out for Sparky's machinations spoke first, "I'm getting hungry, us order something to eat, we can watch Spicey go in for the kill after we eat."

Before Spicey could pitch a fit and counter Sparky, Madalyn bon Donkers was delivering the food order to the Chef that was just now starting to pick up activity. Tinougl's order was in ahead of most of the crowd so he would be served quickly.

Madalyn sent Tinougl's order via her electronic touch pad and walked over to the Barracuda table to take their order. It would be an ordeal because she dealt with this gaggle of Barracuda's that make Cougars blush. Usually by the time she finished taking in all three orders, one or more had already changed their minds.

As a result, Madalyn knew better than to send in the meal requests to the Chef, until the three-minute rule had lapsed, just in case. Today since Spicey was in a sassy mood because her plan had not manifested the way she intended; she made the ordeal even more time consuming. Finally, after the three-minute rule procedure was complete, Madalyn sent the request to the Chef and was alerted almost coincidentally to come pick up Tinougl's order.

The meal was already placed in the heater compartment of the cart with a folding glass top so anyone could see the contents which helped other customers get ideas of what to order. All Madalyn had to do was go over by the Kitchen entrance and pick up the cart and push it slowly and safely to Tinougl's table where he was patiently waiting and soon quite happy the order was filled so promptly.

"Here's your meal, would you like a refill on your drink."

"Yes, I would, thank you."

Tinougl didn't wait for the drink, he started eating the food that tasted better than about anything he had to eat before his time travel.

A lot of things had changed since the great cataclysm that wrecked the planet and almost destroyed the Empire. If it were not for a few pre-positioned security forces to take control of the Ruins, it's doubtful the Empire would have survived nor the Emperor. Most of the Emperor's enemies and the coup members were killed in the savage fighting. But in modern times it appeared slivers of the original anti-government forces had escaped the consequences of initiating the coup.

The Time Travel directorate believed that small group managed to get away to some very far distant solar system which left no traces of where they went. It is believed that at the time Tinougl arrived, the coup was already being engineered and safe houses and safe planets were slowly and quietly established. A lot of Tinougl's mission was to discover, if possible, the coup members that survived destination by obtaining where it was being created in utter secrecy.

The food was more than pleasant. Tinougl would be considered rude and crude if he ate like that in a formal dinner somewhere. He didn't care, he was hungry, and the taste and the quality of the food was second to none. He wasted no time in enjoying it the way he wanted which would expose his poor manners and lack of sophisticated social skills.

Spicey observed Tinongl's behavior which did not impress her, but she didn't care, she knew he would handle his sex the way he did his food and consume it whole heartedly. The thoughts of getting it on with an uncultured man made the sexual attraction even greater. Some women have an attraction to seedy characters. Spicey was one of them.

Halfway through gobbling the meal down, the delightful Dining Hall waitress Madalyn bon Donkers served his drink refill. If satisfaction had an image, it would be written all over Tinougl at that moment.

Right about the time Madalyn removed all the dishes off Tinougl's table and replaced the tablecloth, the Barracuda's meals were just served. The three Barracuda tore into their meals with equal vigor and after about three or four bites, the band was taking another fifteen-minute break and the lovely Singer Wánměi de Mòlìhuā had regained her seat at Tinougl's table.

The band was fed before the performance and given time to freshen up so observing all the people eating would not affect their performance.

Spicey was perturbed once again the singer beat her to her conquest. But she consoled herself with the lovely aroma and taste of her meal. She knew the night was still young.

"I enjoyed the last song immensely," Tinougl stated as he smiled passionately to Wánměi de Mòlìhuā.

"Thank you Tinougl."

"You are most welcome."

"I know etiquette makes people use my full name, but when I'm alone with you, just call me Mòlìhuā."

"Sure, thing Mòlìhuā, it's a lovely name."

"Thank you. My mother gave me the name of her grandmother."

"I see. Where did her grandmother live?"

"My family lives in Konhagar."

"Where is Konhagar?"

"It's in a very distant solar system. it's considered the most distant solar system from our Tartarnite Empire Capital City Santorini de Shénshèng."

"No other's further away?"

"No, none have ever been explored or discussed in any manner."

"What was it like living on Konhagar?"

"It was a great childhood. That's where I learned music and did a lot of reading."

"Is Konhagar anything like Santorini de Shénshèng?"

"It's nothing as glamorous as this city, but it has the Colonial Government and lots of pomp an extravagance especially with the drills of the Colonial Color Guards."

"What do you mean by drills?"

"You know, changing of the guard and exhibiting military marches when they have visiting dignitaries."

"You have observed all that?"

"As a child growing up my parents showed me such presentations on my home world so that I would know about the culture of my people." "What was it like for your parents living on Konhagar?"

"Most people that live in Santorini de Shénshèng have little or no awareness that Konhagar even exists. Living standards are not as good there as it is here. The Konhogers workers are made up of mostly former Konhoger slaves captured from imperial domain disputes."

"How does that relate to we Tartarnites?"

"Tartarnites were the taskmasters and the slave owners."

"So, there is probably lingering resentment and possibly hate?"

"If I took you there you would not want to openly admit you are a Tartarnite. You might risk your life in doing so."

"The resentment is that strong?"

"Konhogers view the Tartarnites as a roadblock for their independence."

"Well, they are part of the Empire."

"Only by coercion and brute force."

"You live on this planet now."

"Yes, I now view Santorini de Shénshèng as my home."

"You support the government then?"

"Absolutely. My parents feel privileged to live on Konhoger."

"What made that possible?"

"My parents were well educated and were permitted to travel to Santorini de Shénshèng to extend their knowledge and become scientists. They met each other here while attending their studies. But they knew they belong on Konhoger and gave up science to become farmers."

"Do you have any notions of moving back to Konhoger worlds?"

"I'm not sure, but anyone would enjoy living near their parents but also I think there are too many people willing to wreck that world out of the arrogant notion they could live better as an independent Empire."

"Why do you feel that way?"

"The Tartarnite Empire has significantly improved Konhoger worlds by applying many types of development and assistance."

"How would independence play into things?"

I think if the Tartarnite Empire granted the Konhogers independence, they would slowly decay back into a fiefdom ran by feudal lords who would be far more oppressive."

"What forces would cause that?"

"Before Konhoger's became a Tartarnite Empire, Colonial Government and provincial capital, corruption ran deep. Without the Tartarnite Planetary Security Services, the black marketeers and the social engineers would take over the government and corruption and misery would become part of most Konhoger's lives."

"That's very insightful. I had no knowledge of any of this. Perhaps since I came from a backwards planet, I was shielded from many such things."

"Where did you grow up Tinougl?"

"I was born and raised on my home world: Argecibo."

"What was Argecibo like?"

"It was mostly an agricultural world. Everyone is farmers on fishermen."

"What are your cities like?"

"We do not have many Cities. The only reason why we have any cities, is they are the transportation hubs and the location of the Empire's Planetary

Security Forces."

"Did you live in one of the Cities?"

"For a while, but I moved out to the countryside where I can write Novels without a lot of distractions."

"What is it like living in the countryside?"

"Most homes now have all the modern conveniences as any home in the city, but I chose to live off the grid."

"What does that mean?"

"I provide all of my own necessities such as water, electricity, or anything else I need."

"How's that working out for you?"

"I have an abundance of what I need and have no personal debt as a result."

"I do not have any debt either, but I have to work hard to keep it that way."

About that time the band members walked back on stage and Mòlìhuā who was enjoying the conversation said, "I'm sorry but I need to go back to work now."

"I need to get back to my room and do some work. I'll see you tomorrow if I'm still here."

"Alright looking forward to seeing you."

Mòlìhuā stood up and walked back to the stage where the band commenced more of their wonderful entertainment.

Madalyn bon Donkers was clearing the Barracuda table and obstructed Spicey's view and hence Spicey missed her quary leaving the Dining Hall.

Tinougl made his way back to his room. He had some new knowledge his trainers never mentioned. The solar system that was the furthest away from the center of the Empire might be the location of the secret base built for the revolutionaries. This was a lead to follow-up on.

After he arrived in his room he sat down and was looking at the news document he purchased at the store. It had a lot of Empire news in it, but nothing stood out that got his attention. So, he folded the flimsy paper and grabbed one of the books he purchased.

Spicey was upset she missed her quarry, so she got up and walked out of the Dinning Hall to chase after Tinougl to make her move. She had just missed him as from a distance she saw him step in the elevator and the door close.

This time however, Tinougl wasn't going to get away. Thanks to her little bribe to the security manager, she knew what floor and room he was staying. If you are a resort customer and know a floor and room number attached to the name, the elevator will let you proceed to that floor.

Spicey informed the elevator when she entered and the door closed, "Take me up to the 14th floor. I want to visit Tinougl in room 1414."

The elevator security system had fully vetted Estele bon Stoffengar (aka Spicey) and her request was fully legitimate under normal circumstances.

Moments later Spice approached the room and the door answer system asked, "May I be of assistance?"

"I would like to talk with Tinougl."

"One moment please."

Tondron's holograph suddenly popped up and informed Tinougl, "There is a woman at your door that would like to speak with you."

He then showed the image of her standing outside the door. Tinougl instantly recognized her and responded, "Tell her I've gone to bed and do not wish to be disturbed."

The last thing in the world Tinougl wanted was to have some Cougar interfering with his plans. He had work to do and had no desire to become a 'cub' for this brazen woman tonight.

The door answering system relayed the information to Spicey which really irritated her, so she turned and went back to the Dining Hall and was not going to divulge to the other two Barracuda her miserable failure.

Spicey was not going to give up. She would try again tomorrow. She knew through the valuable INTEL she received from the security manager, Tinougl was staying an indeterminant lengthy stay. He would not be leaving until he finished up his business. She would find a way into his business and bribe his associates if necessary to keep him her longer until she was finished with him and received an ample amount of gratification, she felt she deserved from this man who had no idea how wonderful she could be in the sack. Plus, she knew how to make herself irresistible if necessary.

Tinougl took a nice long hot shower then put on his sleeping attire and crawled in bed with one of the books and started reading it. The drinks he had created a drowsiness and soon he put the book aside and said to Tondron, "Please shut off the lights, I'm going to sleep now."

Chapter Six

Time for Swimming and a Massage

The night passed so quickly and Tinougl woke up at dawn and decided he would take a morning walk before engaging in any meals. He got up discovered all his clothes were dry-cleaned and hanging in the closet which allowed him to pick something else to wear today. Since he was coming up with no tangible leads except for the fascinating story that the beautiful singer Wánměi de Mòlihuā said to him, he might need to stay a little longer and probably needed to buy some additional clothes.

"Tondron, do you supply swimwear in case I decide I wish to go to the pool today?"

"Yes, master Tinougl, the resort can supply with whatever you need."

"Alright after I finish my walk, I think I might want to lay in the sun and do a little swimming."

"Master Tinougl, everything you need to go to the pool will be here when you return from your walk."

"Thank you."

Tinougl then left the hotel and walked to the park again. Today, he went in the opposite direction around the lake in a clockwise fashion. All his observations were about the same as they were the day before.

The tourists and the residents were all smiles. The weather was perfect and when everyone is happy and smiling it's infectious in nature. Today, he stopped by the edge of the lake and watched the waterfowl swimming aimlessly around. It was picturesque in nature and snapped a photo and hoped when he traveled back into the future 500 years those photos would still be on the device he could share with the researchers.

He looked at his ancient time piece that helped give him the appearance of someone that would exist in that era. He could probably skip a meal and go right to the pool. Most likely he could order snacks there if he got hungry, so he continued along his walk and made a loop around the park and headed back to the Cuìlù Resort Hotel. On his way, he passed some retail stores and liked the fashions of one and walked inside.

"May I help you sir?" the employee asked.

"Yes, I'm just visiting Santorini de Shénshèng, and I probably didn't bring enough clothes along because I'm staying longer than, I planned."

"We can certainly try to help you obtain some additional clothing to help your stay."

"I'm from a distant planet that is kind of backwards, I might need your help in selecting clothes that would be appropriate for me. I'm staying at the Cuìlù Resort Hotel and a lot of the patrons seemed to be better dressed than me."

"Not a problem sir. I'm a fashion consultant and I've had many customers come in here from the Cuìlù Resort Hotel when they realized they arrived unprepared."

"Alright, fit me up in a couple outfits and if I have to stay longer, I'll come back and get some more."

"Certainly. Why is your stay not scheduled?"

"I'm a writer here meeting with my publisher and you sometimes negotiations take a while. I had to make a long trip to get here and I'm not leaving until all the contracts are signed and I no longer need to be here."

"You are a writer?"

"Certainly."

"What do you write about?"

"The future. Technology shifts, galactic insights."

"Very interesting, I'll have to check your works out."

"You will soon have my name with the bill when I pay for the garments with my credits."

"I will."

"Thank you."

"Us go over to some clothing racks that I think will serve you well if you are mingling with the clientele at the Cuilù Resort Hotel."

"All right."

In the span of an hour, Tinougl was fitted with a couple more changes of clothes and the fashion expert convinced him he also needed separate shoes to go with each wardrobe item he selected.

After paying for the Merchandise that was now in two large shopping bags, Tinougl said, "If my departure is delayed, I'll have to come in here and pick up some more clothes."

"Not a problem sir. You were very cooperative, and your actions made this a far more efficient operation than we often deal with clients. You can be sure to know I will be most happy to assist you again. Here is may card. Please call me in advance so that I can prepare for your visit and think about what I should advise you on."

"Thank you. I certainly will."

The store employee really liked Tinougl. The way he engaged him, and the conversations and activities were a refreshing change to a lot of customers that come in and gave him pure aggravation.

Tinougl almost asked to have the purchase delivered but he realized he was only a block or two away, so there was no point.

Back to the hotel took little time and Tinougl was back into his resort hotel room and when he came in with the two large garment bags, Tondron swung into action.

"Can we help you with those Tinougl?"

"Sure, hang them up in the closet and put the shoes under the clothes that are in each bag."

"Certainly."

As expected, Guāiqiǎo came out of his storage room and approached Tinougl. "Let me have those two garment bags so I can take care of it."

"Thank you."

With robot efficiency the clothes were on hangers and the shoes in each garment bag were positioned directly under the clothes Tinougl brought back to make sure he put on the right shoes for the correct outfit.

With all that done, Tinougl said, "I want to go down to the swimming pool now, can I have my swimming attire."

"Certainly, master Tinougl. We have it all prepared for you."

Moments later Tinougl was trying on his bathing suit and noticed the crotch area was bubbled out somewhat.

"Why is this area padded and sticking out so much?"

"Master Tinougl, the resort is concerned about the appearance of some men who do not have a good shape for swimming suits. This is designed to make you appear as if you are about the same as other men so those men who are now endowed as well as you are will not feel so self conscious if they happen to be standing near you."

"I see. That's probably a good thing."

"Tinougl, people come in all kinds of shapes and sizes. We try our best to make everyone feel as if they fit in."

"Great thinking."

"Here is your swimming robe and sandals so that when you leave the pool you will not be cold and can protect your feet."

"I appreciate all this."

"We are here to make sure your comfort is taken care of."

"You guys are doing a great job in doing that."

"Thank you Tinougl, the management of the resort will appreciate such feedback."

"You are most welcome."

Tinougl slipped on the sandals and put on the swimming robe that had the resort logo on it, grabbed one of the books he bought, and walked out of the room and continued to the pool area.

Even though it was late morning, the pool was semi deserted. Tinougl wasted very little time and took off his swimming robe and sandals and approached the pool and dove in. He was expecting a temperature shock, but the majestic pool was heated nicely, and he felt a neutral temperature differential and no shock like he usually felt. *This resort really knows how to please their customers.*

Tinougl started swimming laps. He knew anything was possible including a possible run for his life, so he worked out with conviction. The staff rarely saw their clients swimming with such conviction.

Estele bon Stoffengar (aka Spicey) paid good money for INTEL. The security manager had provisions in their verbal contract to earn more money by feeding Spicey critical information.

The communicator rang about eight times before Spicey with a slight hangover forced herself to answer it.

"Hello?"

"Estele bon Stoffengar (aka Spicey), your friend is at the resort swimming pool swimming laps."

She immediately recognized the voice.

The person on the other end suddenly hung up. She knew what she needed to do. She stood up, walked over to her purse and pulled out a small plastic container that had a couple pills in it. It was hangover medicine on steroids. After she popped a couple of those pills and took a nice deep swallow of her water bottle, she immediately started filling better.

The Female Hotel room robot Măshāwáwá asked, "Madam Estele bon Stoffengar, is there anything I can help you with?"

"I need a bathing suit and a robe and sandals so I can go down to the pool right away."

A moment later the female robot walked out of her private room carrying all the items Spicey requested.

Just like clockwork, Spicey was feeling better and dressed for the occasion and left the room on her way to the pool with a mission. The other two Barracuda would be severely disappointed they didn't receive a heads up so they could watch the Cougar devour her Cub.

When Spicey got to the pool, Tinougl was still swimming laps.

Few other people were around, and it was obvious the soft reclining chair with a robe that had the Cuìlù Resort Hotel logo and their standard sandals had to belong to the young Cub Tinougl. She thus picked the soft recliner next to Tinougl's that he could not escape her view and sat down there, wearing her swim robe and sunglasses to prevent glair so she could keep a good eye on her snair.

After 20 hard laps, Tinougl swam to the edge of the pool and climbed out. As a spy who had a rigorous exercise routing before this mission, his muscles were the cat's meow for the women. His six pack abs left no doubt this immaculate example of a man could fullfill the wildest imagination of any woman that had an overflowing bank account like Spicey. She now felt even more desire for her future well built Cub.

A well-trained spy could not help but notice the person from the security monitor the night before. He suspected she was just a wealthy woman with too much time on her hands and not enough gratification from her mate.

The Cuìlù Resort Hotel had placed a couple towels on Tinougl's soft recliner which he grabbed and immediately dried off including his hair. Then he put on his swimming robe and sandals and sat back in his recliner waiting for the soon to be expected greeting from this woman that was bird dogging him.

Finally, Spicey thought it was time to break the ice and said, "Hello, my name is Spicey. What's your name?"

Tinougl viewed this moment as a mission element and understood how his training directed his next actions. He had to establish himself as legitimate and reasonable to remove all unusual and undue interest."

"My name is Tinougl," he replied acting to script he had practiced many times over. This was part of the game where deception would be counter productive even though the woman was starting to become a *pain in his butt.*

"Nice to meet you Tinougl," Spicey said lying on the charm and exposing as much of herself to enhance any possible inquisitiveness.

"Thank you."

"Are you enjoying your vacation."

"Very much so."

"I've not seen too many resort guests put the effort forth to swim as hard as you just did."

"I remind myself one thing: how bad do you want it?"

"Why do you think that?"

"I find staying in good physical condition helps my thinking and allows me to be more successful in my daily routines."

"Does that include avoiding pretty women?"

"I never avoid, I just wait until the time is right."

"The time could never be more perfect."

"That's right the sun is coming out nicely now so I can work on my tan."

"I want that too. Tinougl, you have nice looking hands, would you mind putting some suntan lotion on my back and my legs?"

"If that is what you would like, I am sure I can help."

Spicey handed Tinougl a new tube of a special suntan loation loaded with cannabinoids which made her skin feel so much better and had an analgesic affect.

Tinougl grabbed the tube out of Spicey's and she immediately flipped onto her stomach and undid the back of her bikini to to expose all of the area of her back.

Tinougl's hands were nice and strong, and he put on the suntan lotion with some finess and when he got to her thighs Spicey was in heaven. Tinougl was a very brave and cunning man, he would now do some things that would make the woman idolize him for life as his hands worked inside her thigh's and applied appropriate pressures that reverberated through the area and sent shock waves through her pelvis greatly intensifying the satisfaction. Spicey had to control herself. She had never come this close to an orgasm in public. Tinougl's hands were magic. She felt so blessed she was able to spot him first and lay her dibs on her before Sparky could get her fangs into him.

Towards the end of the lotion application and sensual massage, Sparky and Schemer who received a message from Spicey that she went to the pool, came down abruptly not expecting much of anything because it was kind of early and there, he was rubbing her thigh! They didn't know if they should scream or giggle.

They sat down at a good distance in a couple padded chairs to observe and take it all in. Had they watched Tinougl swim those laps earlier, they would feel starved about now. One thing they did see as he was applying his magical formula to her in the oscillations, he was creating in Spicey's body, was those incredible muscles and six pack abs. They knew why Spicey was the queen of the Barracuda's. She always spotted the best first. She had a nackt for it. But what they didn't know is she was the most desperate and neglected of the three.

"Thank you that felt so good."

"My pleasure."

Tinougl wiped his hands off on one of his towels and moved it aside and grabbed his book he wanted to read and laid back in his padded recliner that felt so good and started reading.

Spicey lay there in an almost post orgasmic condition feeling better than she had in a while. The combination cannabinoid laced suntan lotion and those strong hands that sent oscillations through her body and vibrated her most sensitive area left her almost spellbound. It was such a comfortable feeling, she just laid there for the longest time simply feeling grand and robust until the sensation slowly died down and she then reached behind her and reconnected the strap on her bikini so her breasts would not flop out as she turned around.

Spicey then laid back and was almost in the same posture as her new friend Tinougl and even though she already had Tinougl's life history (she thought) from her private detective, she had to play dumb and coy with him as to not spook him and lose him. it's better to have a fish in the hand than one you let get away because you jerked on the pole too eagerly.

Tinougl was soon absorbed in the book he was reading and was not paying attention much to the seductress lying beside him.

Sparky and Schemer were eyeballing the two holding back because they didn't want to accidentally screw it up for Spicey who was going in for the kill shot. If Spicey, had it her way she would be doing the horizontal in Tinougl's bed getting filled full of passion at this moment.

After speed reading 50 pages Tinougl put the book on his face using it as a sunblock and laid-back resting for an unknown amount of time. Spicey thought she had Tinougl all jacked up and ready to go and he didn't pursue it. She was disappointed and at the same time started feeling a little hunger pains.

"Are you hungry Tinougl?"

"I was just now thinking about food."

"Would it be ok if I call over a waiter?"

"Sure."

All Spicey had to do is look around for her frequent waiters and gave one of them a nod who came right over.

"May I be of assistance?"

"Yes, can you please bring us a couple menus?"

Behind their reclining chairs was a canopy table reserved for the people using those recliners. Spicey knew that and said, "Let's move to the table and have a snack there."

"All right."

"Soon they were repositioned at the table taking it all in as more people were arriving."

The waiter brought menus and waited and took their orders.

Food provided pool side was designed for snacks and not full course dinners to give the guests a happy hour like environment. The two ordered sample plates which gave them examples of the chef's wonderful concoctions.

"What would you like to drink?"

Tinougl recalling the drink the singer Wánměi de Mòlihuā ordered decided to try it. "I would like to try a Lǐzǐ Guavastrian Elixir."

Spicey looking at the drink menu could not make up her mind, so she simply stated, "I'll have what he's having."

The waiter went away and the two continued their conversation.

"Tinougl, when we finish our meals, I would like to invite you to my penthouse. I would like you to give me a massage like when you put on the suntan lotion."

"I'm sorry Spicey, after I get back to my room, I need to do a little work."

"All right, I suppose we can catch up with each other later?"

"Yes, most likely."

The meal and the drink fortified Tinougl and replenished his reserves from the rigorous exercise of swimming.

Spicey wasn't happy with the way her Cub was working out for her, but she would pave the way with other incentives soon enough.

After the meal and drinks were cleared off the table, Tinougl feeling a slight drowsiness as the elixir he wasn't used to hit his system. He then excused himself and gathered up his belongings.

"It was nice chatting with you Spicey, I'll see you again."

As soon as Tinougl was out of sight and most likely up the elevator and too his room, the other two Barracuda, Sparky and Schemer made a bee line to Spicey.

"How did that work out? Did you plan a rendezvous?"

"He was only nibbling on the bait; I didn't hook him."

"We saw the way he was putting the suntan lotion on, we assumed you had reached an arrangement."

"The only understanding we have is he's terribly aloof."

"I more or less offered it to him, and he backed away. I'm not sure what his motives are."

"He's a younger man, perhaps he takes time to kindle a relationship?"

"You might think he's inexperienced, but the way he massaged me while he was putting on the suntan lotion seriously excited me. He knows what he's doing."

"Do you think he's just playing with you before he decides to seek gratification?"

"I'm not sure, but I do know he knows how to please women the way he massaged me. I'm quite sure he knows he worked me to to almost an orgasm."

"What are you going to do about it?"

"You know those tickets I bought for us attending the concert tonight?"

"Yes?"

"You girls will have to get another set of tickets because I'm going to take Tinougl with me and I do not want you sitting too close to me."

The women all giggled as if they were cued to do so.

Tinougl went back to his room and said to Tondron, "I'm going to take a shower to wash off all the chemicals from the swimming pool, then I think I want to take a nap."

"As you wish Master Tinougl."

"The nice warm shower felt great and after Tinougl dried off, his handy robot Guāiqiǎo handed him sleeping garments and said, "Master Tinougl, you will feel better taking a nap wearing these sleeping garments."

"Thank you, that's a good idea."

In a few minutes Tinougl was sound asleep having the best dream he could remember thanks to the effects the Lǐzǐ Guavastrian Elixir created. Unlike the watered down Lǐzǐ Guavastrian Elixir the lovely singer Wánměi de Mòlìhuā, Tinougl drank the full natural content that had a way of making people drowsy like he now experienced.

CHAPTER SEVEN

LET'S GO TO THE CONCERT

Tinougl slept for several hours in a nice and quite resort hotel room. He didn't know it but all his communicator calls were silent. Tondron didn't need to make sound in the room as he could answer and talk to all callers silently using his electronic exchanges that would create artificial video and sound. Hotel security notified Tondron who the caller was when he silently responded using his electronic answering service.

Each time it was Spicey calling, "Hello, may I speak with Tinougl."

"I'm sorry but Tinougl is not available."

Spicey knew the holograph image of the valet was artificially created and it infuriated her each time. She wasn't used to being held back. She didn't know if Tinougl was purposely ignoring her or if he wasn't truly available such as would be the case if he left his room. She knew it would be pointless to ask about his whereabouts because the hotel security would not allow her to know if he was in the room or gone.

Finally, after a two-hour delightful nap, Tinougl awakened on his own and started getting up and grabbed the book he was reading.

"Master Tinougl, while you were sleeping, Madam Estele bon Stoffengar (aka Spicey) called four times."

"I'm not sure I know Madam Estele bon Stoffengar."

"You were with her at the pool today."

"You mean Spicey?"

"Yes, that is her alias."

"Alright."

"Do you wish to call her back?"

"Some thing tells me she'll call again. I'll just wait until then to find out what she wants."

"As you wish Master Tinougl.

"Tondron, can you put on the galactic news. I want to see what's going on in the world."

"It will be my pleasure."

The galactic news was on and Tondron watched it looking for any hints for what he was searching. It was almost a futile search since so much information was flowing. Nothing out of the ordinary stood out and there were no obvious points of tension. *I wonder if I arrived in the wrong time too early?*

Tinougl continued reading his book and listening to the news at the same time. When something picked his interest, he would glance up from the book to the holograph. Today appeared to be another bust as far as discovery, but he had one lead, thanks to his accidental meeting with the lovely singer Wánměi de Mòlihuā, which enlightened him about Konhagar which is a possible lead for him to follow-up.

All of Tinougl's briefing information for the mission was wrote to memory. He could not risk being caught with an extensive brief without giving the impression that he was involved in some nefarious activity, including possible espionage. He knew he arrived back in time during a period of dynamic evolution in political and Tartarnite Empire changes that resulted in the most five-hundred-year tumultuous period in history. Even though the strife appeared to be over, there was lingering unsettled business, and to finish it required to discover the source. And now since he was almost at a dead end, his only recourse might be to take a trip to Konhagar. He would probably stand out as an Empire agent if he went alone. What if he went there with Wánměi de Mòlìhuā to meet her family? Would he be willing to use her and break her heart to ensure mission success? It was a long shot but hanging out in this resort wasn't giving him a lot of options.

Spicey was about to give up her quest for the young buck, but something drove her to try again. She was the last person willing to accept defeat.

With great trepidation Spicey attempted contacting Tinougl again. The resort hotel communications had instant answering since they were always going through the artificial intelligence.

"Hello, may I help you?"

"I would like to speak with Tinougl."

"One moment please while I connect."

Tondron's holograph suddenly appeared and asked, "Master Tinougl, Madam Estele bon Stoffengar wishes to communicate with you. Would you like to show her your current image or a synthesized image when you were dressed?"

"Can you show me the synthesized image?"

"Certainly." Tondron then projected Tinougl's image recorded at a prior time sitting at the table with his street clothes on.

"That image looks ok, go ahead and show it."

Madam Estele bon Stoffengar's image then appeared. She was

wearing some very provocative and beautiful clothes that only a very wealthy lady could afford. Her choice of clothing was a matter of seduction, she was the least bit modest, and a couple of her attributes were slightly exposed with a manner of taste and resplendence.

The holograph was lifelike, and the size was scaled identical to her real being. Holograph technology five hundred years prior had advanced to the stage where granularity of the image was already greatly diminished. A person who was unaware this was a holograph from a primitive society would think it was the real person.

"Hello Tinougl, how are you?"

"I'm doing fine thank you."

"I tried calling you earlier to invite you up to my penthouse, but you were unavailable."

"I'm sorry I could not take you communication."

"It's getting kind of late, but I have tickets to the concert tonight. If you would like to go with me, it starts in about two hours."

"I didn't come prepared to attend events like concerts, and wasn't planning on staying here very long, so I didn't bring a lot of clothes with me. I didn't bring anything I could wear to the concert."

"That's not a problem. I routinely use the fashion consultants here at the resort to provide me clothes and attire for special events. If you would like to come up to my Penthouse, I'll have them send up the fashion experts and we can have you dressed in time to attend the concert."

"I suppose I could. How do I find your Penthouse?"

"When you go to the elevator just tell the elevator that will hear your voice, you want to go to Spicey's Penthouse. It will stop on my floor and give you directions."

"All right, I suppose I could."

"Come right away, they will get busy soon and we need to get your clothes changed in time."

"All right, I'll be there soon."

While Tinougl was putting on his street clothes spicey contacted her fashion consultant and had them send up a tailor, hairdresser, makeup artist, and selection of clothes.

While Tinougl went up the guest elevator, the crew went up the freight and staff elevator. The crew made it into Spicey's Penthouse before Tinougl arrived.

Thanks to artificial intelligence, Tinougl did not have to announce his arrival, the door automatically opened, and he went into the Penthouse and was quickly greeted by the group of people.

The fashion coordinator said, "Hello Tinougl, I'm Marifay, the fashion coordinator, and all these people will help me get you ready. First thing we want you to do is follow Ballenda into the bathroom as she needs to wash your hair and prepare it for the hair stylist."

"Sure."

Tinougl dutifully followed Bellenda into the bathroom that had a large tub that could easily fit six people with jets to massage the bodies and temperature controlled like a hot tub as hot as you wanted.

"Please take off your clothes and get into the bath, I will put some additives in the water to make you feel better while I wash your hair," Ballenda stated professionally with all due authority.

"All right."

The water filled very quickly with a six-inch pipe, digitally controlled from a microprocessor. The additives had some psychoactive elements that would help Tinougl improve psychological strength through the night as he was in the public eye. In a brief period in the nice warm water, the sensation grew nicely.

Bellenda washed Tinougl's hair and placed some enhancements in the wash that would help the hair designer create a masterpiece.

"All right you can get out of the bath now. I'll help you dry off."

Bellenda was very pretty and loved to feel Tinougl's muscles. There was more to the man than people realized. Ordinary people were not built with such exquisite muscles. There was now no doubt in Bellenda's mind of why Spicey had such an attraction to the young man.

Spicey had been taken to another portion of the Penthouse which had multiple bathrooms and she herself was getting her own treatments. She too had hair wash, body treatment, hair style, makeup, and everything to pamper a woman. Her toenails looked as exquisite as her fingernails when they finished with her. Spicey was smart in one regard, she trusted the fashion coordinator to pick the clothes for her that would do the best. Left up to herself she might look like a hag. The fashion coordinator dressed her like a living doll that Tinougl would be proud to be seen in public with.

Tinougl was led into the next room while the bath was draining. With just a towel wrapped around him they sat him down into a portable chair brought up designed for the hair stylist. Tonight, Tinougl would wear the *Cosmic Wave*, a new fad in hair style that had elegance as well as debonair appeal. To his utter surprise he would also wear male makeup. After trimming his eyebrows and adding the cosmetics he slowly transformed from a neophyte appearance to a sophisticated and cultured man exemplifying confidence. The makeup served another vital purpose. The makeup between he and Spicey gave them the appearance of not such an age gap. He would not look like her "cub" tonight. Instead, he would give the appearance of a man who can dominate a woman and make her cry from cauldrons of love. It might also have served to save his life because once he washed off the makeup later that night, Spicey's husband a philanderer that didn't want someone else touching his wife, would have spies looking for the wrong person, as his facial recognition had changed so substantially.

Once the hair design, shave, and other extraneous activities concluded, the moment of truth began. His undergarments were designed to inspire a woman watching him undress that no later might lead to splendid euphoria with Spicey later that night if he let his guard down.

The cost of all this was substantial. Common people have no idea what a male cosmetic makeup cost for such an extravagant event cost. It was chump change for Spicey.

The fashion coordinator now selected a very sexy white shirt with an open collar that would tantalize the ladies with his upper chest muscles and golden-brown hair that was subtlety exposed. The black trouser and matching suitcoat with short tails, created a spectacular image. He had to leave a mark the time travellers could find in the future. Tonight, there might be some gossip column in a media report that captures the moment.

Tinougl's travels also saved his life, he went to where nobody expected and not having a good facial recognition, and a complete disappearance foiled the most dangerous passage in his life.

Had Frederick bon Stoffengar been able to capture Tinougl, he would have ended up bound and dropped into a Gradvolchin Hog Farm. Gradvolchin's had two inches long extremely sharp fang like teeth designed to tear the flesh from their opponents and kill them. A Tartarnite bound person dropped amid a hundred such annimals would be torn to threads in moments and die excruciating pain. Organized crime sometimes dealing with banking issues handled clients in that manner.

The fashion consultant had a full-length mirror and when Tinougl makeover was completed, she had him stand before it and look. Tinougl transferred his communicator to his new clothes and thought this would be a great time to record an event for his trip.

"I like what you created with this effort. Here's my communicator, take a picture for me so in the future I can show fashion consultants this image to help them get an example for their work."

"I would be delighted to." The fashion coordinator then snapped a couple pictures on the communicator which looked amazing.

Women take a little longer to prepare so some of the fashion workers were leaving and taking their equipment such as the portable chairs and boxes of equipment and a closed clothing rack that prevented people from observing the contents.

In a few minutes, Spicey was ready to go out and the fashion people all left.

"I think if we go down to the front entrance of the resort, a limo will be ready to take us to the concert. We'll arrive just with a few minutes to spare."

"I'm ready if you are," Tinougl responded.

The two headed to the elevator and the front entrance. Sparky and Schemer were at the front entrance mainly to see the couple come down and were wondering if Spicey already got a taste of her cub.

When Spicey came out the entrance with her immaculate escort looking possibly ten years older, the two Barracudas were taken back. That *Cosmic Wave* hair style Tinougl wore certainly created an image they would never forget. The extra sun Tinougl had received walking at the park and at the pool, blended into the makeup quite extraordinarily. Sparky and Schemer knew one thing: all the ladies at the concert would be jealous of Spicey tonight.

The limos were lined up to take Cuìlù Resort Hotel guests to their evening affairs. Half of the guests leaving were going to symphony hall to hear the concert.

Skycars were still somewhat rare, but they did exist for the military, intelligence agencies, and upper echelon law enforcement. That would certainly change in 500 years in the dimension and time Tinougl came from.

As they approached the limo the resort attendant opened the door for them and Spicey stepped in followed by Tinougl. Tinougl didn't know what to expect, but he appreciated good quality music and assumed if the upper crust of society were attending, they would most likely put on a great performance.

The Limo drove past the Santorini de Shénshèng Central Park that Tinougl had grown accustomed the last few days and in a short while entered back into more congested building areas and came up to a majestic building with exceptional exterior lighting and lots of security and well-dressed concert goes getting out of Limos and walking up the shallow staircase towards a wide opening. Spicey had her eTickets in her small stylish purse with a holster strap more suitable for a young woman, but with her dress and makeup, she was a young woman tonight.

The security people knew she was ticketed and motioned for the couple to move into the venue. Spicey had been here many times before and in fact had reserved these seats. Sometimes it was for the three Barracudas when they were without dates and other times when she found her "cub" for the night.

These were semiprivate seats in the balcony that only performers could observe who the audience included in those sections. People sitting in the main concert hall directly in front of the orchestra could not see in the slanted balcony. The acoustic dividers on the balcony seats also minimized reflections and modulation of the music so that people throughout the concert hall would hear the uncorrupted music.

By the time they were seated in the private balcony section, half of the musicians were in their seats making last minute adjustments and tuning to their instruments. Moments later most of the other musicians appeared and took their seats and sat down and copied the actions of those who came before. In a small span of time, the conductor came out to his stand and the crowd gave applause and he bowed towards the audience. He then turned sideways and a lady in a luxurious dress walked out onto the stage and stood next to the large black instrument that Tinougl recalled was called a piano. *Tinougl then asked himself the question: I wonder why we do not have pianos in modern times?*

The glamorous woman with sparkling reflections on her dress sat down and adjusted her seat and nodded at the conductor who then turned directly towards the center of the orchestra and began hand movements that resulted in the lights dimming and the music now starting.

Tinougl reached into his pocket and hit a flush switch on his communicator that would secretly start recording this music he decided he would want to take back with him to show his sponsors something in their past he did not know existed.

This was a very pleasant experience. Tinougl experienced more interesting things today than he typically did before his time travel. He now realized the obvious: Some of the time travellers might not have wanted to go back to their time if they experienced days like this. *Is that why they never came back?*

The woman on the piano created exquisite sound. The 95-piece orchestra backing her up with their own roles in the music added magnificently to the sound. The beauty and the luster of the charming pianist now resonated a sense of radiance that engulfed Tinougl's passions.

Spicey was equally gratified by the performance. She was feeling slight tingling sensation because looking at Tinougl and herself in the mirror before she left her Penthouse, she felt like a doll, and she knew that later that night Tinougl would give her reverberations in his love making on a theme from Paganini.

From time-to-time Spicey would look up on her cub and feel the exquisiteeness. Knowing how his hands gave her dazzling reactions as they got very close to her most sensitive area, added splendidly to her thoughts now and she felt the moistness and knew it was happening. But before she had her way with Tinougl, she would pamper him with a dinner at an exclusive restaurant where she personally knew the owner well. And she knew he would oblige her.

The music played for approximately 45 minutes, then they had an intermission. People could use the restroom and the people in the main concert hall below could go to the lobby and get glasses of elixirs and concoctions to help improve the ambiences.

In the private balconies, people also had private bathrooms. They were small like airliner bathrooms, but they did the trick as in most cases it was just men needing to urinate. Waiters came into the balcony seats to serve drinks. The second performance would be elixir enhanced as Tinougl chose a Chamboree del Pàrà Měilì to enjoy. Spicey on the otherhand requested a glass of sparkling ferments that was created by a grapelike substance and laced with chemicals that were highly controlled due to their narcotic effect.

With the lights turned back on Spicey faced her prince charming and smiled lavish like. Her smile had an element of adventure to it because she knew what her intentions were. She was going to take her cub on the ride of his life.

In twenty minutes, the orchestra was all set. Surprisingly there was a different pianist that came out. The first pianist played a very physical performance and probably had no strength left to do it again. The second performance had a piano like concerto equally physically taxing and it was quite evident the first performer could not have endured the second piece back-to-back even with a twenty minute break.

Spicey knew these orchestrations quite well and about a minute before it was going to finish, she said, "Us leave now and avoid the crowd."

"Sounds good to me." Tinougl smiled and quickly stood following Spicey.

As they reached the front entrance, the applause began that would last several minutes before much of the concert goers would leave. As such a string of Limos were lined up and the first one had it's door open which Spicey walked directly towards and hopped in with Tinougl in tow.

The concert hall staffer shut the door to the Limo and the driver through the intercom asked, "Where would you like to go?"

"Take us to the *Top of the World Restaurant.*

"Right away Madam."

CHAPTER EIGHT

SITTING AT THE TOP OF THE WORLD RESTAURANT

In a few minutes they were delivered to this interesting building that appeared to be not much than a large lobby with a half dozen elevators that went high up into the sky to a disk like device several thousand feet in the air. Tinougl paid the Limo with his credits which didn't matter because Spicey would gladly have paid. They were well dressed so the security people at the entrance allowed them to pass. They had strict dress codes so that only those who could afford the price would be allowed in and not some tourist gawkers needing a thrill.

A staff member standing besides the elevators pressed a button and smiled and it opened, and they went inside and soon were enjoying the view from the glass front of the elevator as they quickly rose to the restaurant so high up in the air, it was stabilized by cables to other buildings and anchors some distance away. Without the cables the wind would blow it away.

The Maitra d' at the entrance to the restaurant knew Spicey well and figured out the man with her was her next cub she would soon be devouring.

He led the couple over to a table with a view next to the large plate glass window. Tinougl figured he could see lights 50 miles into the distance, and he wasn't too far off the mark. Another interesting fact was in modern time this tower did not exist. Nor did anything like it. *Was that progress?*

The wonderful restaurant had a piano and live dinner music.

Each table had a candle which created a flickering wave action that painted Spicey's face. The makeover took her back ten years in time from when they were sitting at the pool.

Spicey and the Barracuda's might have thought Tinougl was a cub or a neophyte. He was to avoid killing anyone as to not change the fabric of time during this time travel mission. But if he had to save his own life or kill someone to get back vital information, screwing up the fabric of time was something he might have to take the risk.

Spicey had no idea she was sitting across the table from a lethal killer sent here 500 years from the future. His muscles were so great mainly because he had to maintain exemplary physical conditioning to deal with his tradecraft that might place him in peril at any moment.

Tinougl was also aware that Spicey was virtually in heat and wanted that big "A" as one of his former lovers termed it. At the current moment big "A" wasn't in his itinerary as he wanted to get closer to the singer Wánměi de Mòlìhuā to discover more about the Konhagars which may be the target of his investigation. He would nevertheless find out more about this wealthy woman because she might be the source of some interesting findings leading toward his mission completion allowing him to go back to the future.

"Did you like the music?"

"Yes, it was very nice."

"Do you have orchestras like that where you came from?"

"Nothing that grand. I'm not even sure the music is that good."

"What's the main difference?"

"We do not have a lot of pianos."

Their discussion which was only serving as a time space to get the meal over and get back to the resort to see how things unfold.

Tinougl enjoyed the view but didn't feel like wasting a lot of time up in the restaurant was pleased that ordering and serving the food was so efficient. It was definitely very delicious.

Spicey was not the least bit hungry for the food. She wanted what was sitting across from her and the sooner they got back to her Penthouse and worked out her desires, the better it would be.

Tinougl didn't want to overeat and enjoyed portions of his entrees.

Spicey saw Tinougl was not eating much of what was left and she figured out the best thing to ask was, "Would you like some desert?"

"Actually, I'm kind of full, I would like to skip desert."

"Alright, then us leave."

"Let me ask the waiter for the bill."

"That's not necessary. They know me quite well; my accountant will take care of it."

"Alright."

Spicey stood up immediately and turned towards the entrance of the restaurant and the elevators and started walking. Tinougl followed like a puppy dog almost.

Spicey pressed a button on her communicator that immediately contacted one of the Limo drivers she used often and knew by the time they walked out curb side he would be waiting. Just like many other nights as she led her cub out of the entrance out to the sidewalk her Limo pulled up and another couple was eyeballing it waiting for the restaurant staff member to open the door for them and the driver rolled down his window and informed the staffer, "the lady in the purple dress is my customer."

"All right sir."

The staffer turned towards Spicey who was approaching and confusing the other couple and the staffer said to the other couple, "The lady in the purple dress called this Limo, your Limo will be arriving shortly."

The staffer opened the door and Spicey got in followed by Tinougl and the staffer then shut the door and the Limo drove off.

The trip back to the resort was rather quick.

As they pulled up to the resort, Spicey said, "Tinougl, I don't know what your schedule is, but would you mind coming up to my suite for a nightcap?"

"I suppose I could."

Chapter Nine

Dancing the Tango with a Cougar

They went right up to Spiceys room where Tinougl discovered something interesting. Spicey didn't have a holographic servant and robot. She had a real person. A female butler named Svetkat.

As soon as they stepped into the Penthouse, Svetkat asked, "Would you like me to take your jacket so you can be comfortable, Tinougl?"

"Sure, thank you."

Svetkat helped Tinougl out of his impressive looking suit coat. She then took it to a closet and hung it up and came right back and asked, "Can I get you two something to drink?"

"Sure,"Tinougl responded and Spicey said, just give me the usual.

Perhaps Tinougl would like to try it as well."

Tinougl smiled and shook his head in agreement.

Svetkat had already been instructed what to serve Tinougl. She wanted him so horny he couldn't refuse her advances. And she wanted him physically poised to go a long time.

Moments later Svetkat came back with the duplicate drinks. The drugs would not affect Spicey as much as they would Tinougl, but it would help her to some extent. It would not matter if they mixed up the glasses, the doses were the same.

Svetkat knew to leave the lovebirds alone and went back to her private room to wait until Spicey called for her. The holographic system in the Penthouse would notify Svetkat to serve Spicey.

Spicey invited Tinougl to sit next to her on the sofa while they consumed their drinks. Spicey knew not to spook him by coming in for the kill too quickly, plus some men like to make the first move.

They drank and smiled and didn't carry on much of a conversation. Tinougl knew Spicey wasn't interested in conversation she was interested in him taking care of business. Spicey wanted him to finish his drink to get his libido at maximum launch profile before moving forward, it was only a matter of a short time now.

Tinougl knew he was feeling funny and as a trained spy knew not to ever discount drugging as it was part of the business. Spicey didn't know anything about him, he knew she was only interested in "big A."

Tinougl knew the fastest way to get done with the evening is finish the drink and find out exactly what Spicey wanted. He downed the drink and sat the glass down on the coffee table.

Spicey knew now was the do or die time and stood up and held out her hand to Tinougl who instinctively knew what that meant. She led him to her bedroom and after he entered, she shut the door to make him feel he had some privacy.

Tinougl had no doubt what she wanted. And he needed practice, so he used this as a training session.

Spicey knew by Tinougl's actions he was ready for "big A", so she helped unbutton his shirt, unbuckle, and unzip his trousers and remove his shoes and trousers and in the process saw the wet spot on his under garments which means he already started some secretions of his magic nectar.

Spicey wearing Corture clothing had on no undergarments,

that's how they are designed to accentuate the woman's body better. The fashion consultant/designer explained to her by the fashion designer was to simply "lift it all above the head and you can be out of it in a dozen seconds."

And the designer was correct, she was standing nude near Tinougl in a dozen seconds.

Spicey had a very nice body. She never had children, so her breasts and legs remained like a younger woman. Because of her dieting and physical workouts her tummy was nice and flat, and her hips were perfect. But because her rich banker husband neglected her far too often, she had to seek gratification elsewhere. She hoped one day one of these young studs would knock her up.

Spicey grabbed Tinougl's hand and led him over to her super size bed, large enough to hold six people. It was time to enjoy the celestial feast and Tinougl knew just what to do. Spicey wasn't dealing with an amateur, she was dealing with a galactic scale spy living 500 years into the future who was trained by the best sexual advisors to the intelligence service on how to please women because sex is one of the major tools in a spy's tool chest.

Once they were mingling their bodies Tinougl went to work exploring her body in ways she wasn't ready, and the intense pleasure soon erupted. Tinougl would give her orgasms one right after the other until he decided it was time for him to reach the crescendo, then he entered her and furled all his manliness into her in ways he was trained to cause her to have the greatest possible reaction imaginable.

Tinougl seemed to have far more energy and stamina than ever before. As a spy he was always analyzing the situation. He realized he had probably been drugged, so he would make the most of it and continue to give her orgasms until she couldn't take it no more and begged to stop because she felt she was going to die.

In another thirty minutes, they reached that point and said,

"Tinougl, can we just lay here a bit and hold each other?"

"My pleasure, Spicey."

They were now embraced and Spicey was passing out to the point she started snoring.

The drugs, drinks, and sex had finished Spicey off for the night. Tinougl knew she was done for the night and slowly eased out of bed and put his clothes back on. He didn't know what to do about his jacket, but as he walked through the Penthouse by himself, the holographic security system notified Svetkat who came out and saw Tinougl.

"Are you leaving?"

"Yes, I think Spicey is sleeping."

"Let me get your jacket."

"Thank you."

Svetkat walked to the door and opened it and said, "I hope you and Spicey had a good time."

"I think she's quite satisfied she met me."

Svetkat smiled and Tinougl walked out of the Penthouse and went to the elevator on his way back to his room.

When Tinougl arrived at his room, Tondron reported, "The clothes you left at Spicey's were sent here and I had them sent to the dry cleaners, and they are now back in the closet."

"I have these clothes I wore from Spicey's residence."

"We will take care of them for you. We will send them to the dry cleaners and the fashion consultants will receive them when they are cleaned unless you want to keep them."

"No, I have no use for them."

"What would you like to do now Master Tinougl?"

"I'm going to take a shower then go to bed."

In a short period of time, Tinougl was freshened up, in his sleeping attire and in bed slowly easing into the sleep domain.

It was late in the morning when Tinougl awakened and as he was getting up Tondron gave him the full report.

"Master Tinougl, I received communications from Madam Estele bon Stoffengar while you were sleeping. She wanted to talk to you, but I informed her that you had not given me any instructions to be awakened if any person called. She then wanted me to give you this message. Do you wish to hear it now?"

"Sure, go ahead and let me hear it."

Spicey's holograph appeared. She was well dressed and looking good as if she were ready to go somewhere.

"Tinougl, I wish I could have seen you again before I had to leave, but I've been summoned home on important business I must attend. If you are still here when I get back, I would like to see you again. I had a glorious time with you, and you gave me great satisfaction. I want to be your friend and stay in touch in the future."

The holograph ended.

CHAPTER TEN
EVEN A SPY NEEDS A MASSAGE

The Cuìlù Resort Hotel Room Holograph personality Tondron then made another announcement.

"Master Tinougl, while you were sleeping the designer clothes you wore last night were sent to the dry cleaners and back to the fashion designers. Your clothes you left at Madam Estele bon Stoffengar (aka Spicey) Penthouse and shoes were also returned. The clothes were dry cleaned and the shoes shined.

The fashion designers were happy at the prompt return and would like to hear what you thought about the work they did for you."

"Let them know their work was excellent and proved to help have a very great enjoyable evening."

"They have been notified."

"Thank you."

"What do you wish to do now Master Tinougl?"

"I'm going to freshen up and take a shower. I think afterwards I will go for a walk."

Tinougl noticed on his communicator it was down to about 50% power storage so he went to the closet and pulled out his charger and took it into the bathroom with him where he could charge it up simultaneously with checking connectivity to world applications. During the charge process, as he linked up with the global communications grid.

One of his objectives was to determine inner connectivity to the global communications grid five hundred years ago.

This would be a major milestone if it worked.

He would start small then expand.

He got a link-lock on the communication signal which was most likely a nearby antenna and possibly within the Cuìlǜ Resort Hotel.

Tinougl quickly discovered some search engines he would use to find information. Since he was in a resort hotel, it would not create any suspicion if he checked out tourist information. The beautiful thing about tourist information is it also provided a spy like him a lot of information, not only on the attractions but a lot of other information that would work into a MACRO to size up an enemy.

Tinougl's first search was Tartarnite Empire Capital City Santorini de Shénshèng. He was immediately swamped with information about some of the things he already observed like "Top of The World Restaurant," Santorini de Shénshèng Central Park and the illustrious Cuìlǜ Resort Hotel and other attractions. There was also a quick getaway holiday to the moon Plexis de Chiveltros.

Like most of the more successful galactic spies, Tinougl was always planning and designing evasive manuevers in the event misfortune struck him. As he pondered his possible lead to a revolutionary outpost on Konhagar, he knew the easiest way go get there without raising any suspicion would be to travel with Singer Wánměi de Mòlìhuā ostensibly to meet her parents because a relationship had started between them.

Tinougl knew Wánměi de Mòlìhuā was a special young lady full of beauty and talent and he felt sinister to use her like he planned, but he reconciled it in his mind *he would not have been sent on a five-hundred-year time travel if the information wasn't of importance.*

Spies sometime must do distasteful things to create the situation that allowed them to operate in nontraditional manners to achieve almost impossible success. Compared to many other missions of enormous importance, this too was really a mission impossible.

Tinougl put a bookmark on the 48-hour tourist package link for the package deal to the moon Plexis de Chiveltros. It was most fortunate Spice departed on important business which would allow Tinougl ample time to seduce and get Wánměi de Mòlìhuā where he could really pour on the charm and sweep her off her feet to synthesize a relationship to get him to the provincial Konhagar worlds to discover how they all fit into the pending history.

Tinougl then pursued social links and gossip columns of social media without triggering search algorithms looking for the rich and famous. He didn't find anything related to Madam Estele bon Stoffengar (aka Spicey), but with a photograph memory he did spot one of the Barracuda that hung out with Spicey. According to the gossip column in a major social media outlet, the woman Vicky Bon Adenauer (aka Sparky) was an extremely wealthy banker's wife.

Having studied probabilities and seen artificial intelligence drill down to discover important information, Tinougl operated mentally in a similar manner and produced the obvious conclusion, Spicey's husband was probably a rich banker and bankers wives hung out together mainly because they had lots of money to spend and similar gripes about their husbands. The fact the three of them were together staying at the resort looking for action clearly gave Tinougl the impression hubbies were neglecting their wives who came here like Cougars, looking for a cub to give them a good time like Tinougl gave Spicey last night. And now he had a new crib. By reading up on Vicky Bon Adenauer (aka Sparky) he would soon discover her husband's friends or associates.

Perhaps it was his modern way of training to get data without leaving too many bredcrumbs behind for INTEL people to discover him, allowed him to go through the discovery process in a rather successful manner. Before long he found Sandstrum and Vicky Bon Adenauer. They were definitely the tops of the public figures in stature and wealth. And now by finding out who Sandstrum and Vicky Bon Adenauer's friends were he slowly drilled down in a lot of gossip pages and finally hit paydirt. According to all the gossip columns they were socially connected to Frederick & Madam Estele bon Stoffengar.

It also raised an alarm inside Tinougl. He had been seen with Spicey and she was just vectored home for some important reason. Perhaps her husband wanted to confront her about her infidelity. Another reason could be he could not afford any scandals in the position he was in and probably already received reports from his spies. Tinougl had not detected any surveillance, but if his intuition served him right, there indeed were spies here and he needed to be extra careful to not project any public images with Spicey. More reason to brew and affair with the beautiful singer Wánměi de Mòlìhuā who was not connected to that crowd in any manner due to her standing in life.

Tinougl realized he had already screwed up once but was grateful the makeup artist had disguised him so well putting on at least another ten years probably on purpose to make sure Spicey didn't stand out like an odd duck.

After freshening up and taking a nice shower which removed any traces of the makeup and hair styling solutions, Tinougl was back to his normal self looking ten years younger than the night before. Also, his plain hair style in no way looked anything like the *cosmic wave* hair style. With his sunglasses and hat on, nobody from the night before would recognize him.

Tinougl's assessment of spies was well placed, but they were not coming from the direction he thought. In the most bizarre twist of things, he would soon discover others had interests and he had stumbled into a vortex.

"I'm going for a walk, Tinougl informed Tondron and soon left the Cuìlù Resort Hotel and headed for the Santorini de Shénshèng Central Park. Today he took an alternate root, not out of fear of someone following him, but to break up the monotony of going the same direction every day. He crossed the street in front of Cuìlù Resort Hotel and took a little dogleg in the direction opposite of the park. He walked down this street which he originally came the day his time machine arrived. During the arrival a few days prior, Tinougl wasn't extremely interested in what all these buildings were about because he was navigating primarily for the interest in locating his new base, which would be a room in the resort hotel.

Now curiousity and practicality entered the picture. Each day he remained added to a mathematical formula of diminishing returns if he didn't strap on that time machine and come back. Tinougl hadn't come across anything to give him a sense he was onto the discovery of the information he was seeking. And now the only possibility might be a far distant planet he might need to get to do an on-sight investigation without getting into trouble and make it back to return to his time domain five hundred years from now.

By window shopping and entering a few establishments looking around, gave him the opportunity to clear his baffles. He was indeed a spy, had to operate as a spy and could not let his guard down because he was caught in a strange situation.

More window shopping and store visits cleared Tinougl's concerns there were no trailers and then worked his way back in the opposite direction to visit Santorini de Shénshèng Central Park.

A spy with a photographic memory eventually sees through subtleties. The old men at the park bench were in the exact same location in the two previous days. Normally they would be innocuous and expected in such a place. In the spy craft elderly people were sometimes used as watchers given simple defined roles. If they were watchers, they would report a situation when it was safe to do so by several ways such as meeting an associate somewhere like a coffee shop, library, or toilet. They could also at a convenient time send a message via their communicator everyone had to pay for their purchases. The odds these elderly men would sit at the same exact park bench in the same order every day seemed a little strange. *Perhaps there was a reason for it?*

The waterfowl were charming and self assured. If there were any threats that got close to them, they would simply fly away. Their colors and feathers were majestic. These were different birds today which demonstrated the diversity of life on the planet before the big convulsions in one hundred years or more.

Tinougl photographed these birds to add to his collection. When he went back to the future, he would take time to seek birds to see if any of them still existed.

He continued his walk knowing the elderly men were staring holes in his back. He consumed their interest and picked their curiousity to a stranger that acted far differently than all those around him. He didn't know what to make of it, but he knew they could be part of an INTEL aparatus that is complex and quite sophisticated. A lot of the INTEL associated with this period was lost with all the damage that was done in the great haemorrhage that this planet would experience after their lifetimes. *In some ways they should be grateful to be gone when it happens.*

The walk gave Tinougl some good exercise, but it wasn't enough. He decided a swim would be good and he could then order food poolside after swimming.

Today he walked down the side of the road the Cuìlù Resort Hotel was situated on. As he did before he took time to do some window shopping and entered a few establishments to check for surveillance. He didn't spot any, but that did not mean none of it wasn't there. No doubt he was on surveillance cameras government agencies could monitor. If they had a vested interest in him there would then be the trailing person following him around monitoring his activities and, in some cases, they could be planted like the elderly gentlemen at the park.

Tinougl eventually made it back to his resort room and changed into swim attire like he did the previous and headed down to the pool and SPA.

There were a lot of empty soft recliners as it was still kind of early in the day and Tinougl picked one right in the middle near the entrance to the pool. He sat his robe down and took of his sandals and walked over and stepped down the stairs into the pool and began his laps. Today he pushed himself a little harder and did 25 laps. When he got out of the pool his muscles were tight. In the spa he knew he could get a nice massage, but he had some slight hunger that grew from his exercises. He motioned towards one of the waiters standing back waiting because they knew the orders would start to slowly manifest as more people came to the pool area.

Tinougl picked out his snack and ordered a Chamboree del Pàrà Měilì drink which quickly quenched his thirst. The food that came out had meat strips in a pouch like bakery item with some incredibly wonderful tasting sauce. *Just what the king ordered.*

During his snack the remnants of the Barracudas arrived at the pool and sat down at a table about twenty feet from Tinougl. He didn't quite yet know who Schemer was, but he now knew the essence of Vicky Bon Adenauer who was probably out looking for some male flesh like her comrade Spicey scored the night before.

When Tinougl was thrusting into Spicey giving her the ride of her life, he was merely doing kinematic enhancement for his own purposes

Tinougl made an asserted effort to not make eye contact with the two Barracuda's. After he finished his snack and drink, he stood up and put on his swim robe and sandals and walked directly to the SPA.

The spa had heated baths, steam room, massage rooms, and private baths and dressing rooms.

The resort employees could see through the large windows Tinougl swimming the laps beforehand and speculated he wanted a massage.

"Hello sir, what would you like? We have the steam bath, public hot baths, and private hot baths and dressing rooms?

"I would like a massage."

"Please follow me to a room where we'll do that for you."

The attractive woman led Tinougl to a private room and another scantily dressed woman followed them in.

The hostess said, "This is Denettk who will be giving you a massage."

"Please to meet you sir."

"Likewise."

The hostess then left the room shutting the door behind her.

Denettk looked at all those glorious muscles on Tinougl and was inspired to massage him, and knew he had on swim attire and had just climbed out of the pool.

Denettk asked, "What is your name?"

"I'm Tinougl."

"Tinougl, I really do not like the smell of the chemicals in the swimming pool water. I have a hot bath that is part of my massage clinic, would you mind going into the hot bath with me so I can wash your hair and get off all that smell before I start working on your muscles?"

"Sure, no problem."

"This way please," Denettk said and led Tinougl into the adjoining room where an empty tub existed. Denettk went to a control panel and pressed a couple switches and the hot tub started filling up quickly with water from a large diameter pipe.

"Please undress and get in the water."

Tinougl took off his swim clothes and stepped out of his sandals as Denettk took his robe and hung it on a robe hanger stand. He walked down into the hot tub that must have been four feet from the bottom to the surface and found a seat that allowed him to set and be submerged up to almost his neck.

The computer-controlled heat set the temperature almost perfect for Tinougl. The temperature would slowly rise after he was sitting comfortable allowing the chemicals Denettk put in the water to absorb more effectively.

Denettk followed him also nude into the pool carrying a couple containers with her.

She had beautiful breasts and an excitedly trimmed pubis that conveyed desire. One of the containers she dumped into the water was a muscle relaxer that would enhance her work soon. The other container had a sweet-smelling hair application that would make his hair look shiny and healthy. She then started applying the hair application and messaging his head. Her breasts were merely inches away from Tinougl's face. He had a slight urge to reach out for her and put her breasts in his mouth and applying his magic.

"Keep your eyes shut for a few moments."

She then grabbed a silver metallic flexible hose with digital controls on it to make absolute water temperature to ensure the clients felt comfortable. Out of habit Denettk squirted the water in the hot tub for a moment until she felt the perfect temperature and used it to rinse Tinougl's hair.

Tinougl didn't know if she was toying with him, but she rubbed her breasts against his face as if she was taunting him to latch on. The more he ignored her the more she pushed against him until he finally did what she wanted knowing it would excite him. And as he was enjoying that spectacular moment feeling her nipples in his mouth, she was messaging his arm muscles feeling the exquiseeness of this human being. Normally she massaged fat or disgusting excuses for a man. Occasionally she would get one of these perfect specimens and let herself go. She felt she was entitled to enjoy them for all the gratification she gave them.

Denettk was already well paid and tipped fabulously so money was not an issue for her. Denettk then took Tinougl's hand and placed it on her femineity and at the same time grabbed him and confirmed he had an erection. Those circular chairs in the pool were perfect for her body and what she would do next. To Tinougl's great surprise, she sat down on his lap with her legs over the sides of his and took his manliness and put it inside her.

Tinougl was feeling a great satisfaction as he continued sucking on her breasts. Perhaps it was the fantastic feeling of this incredible man and his muscles, Denettk reached a spontaneous splendid euphoria and subsequent lingering orgasms. She had a unique ability she trained herself from advice from sex specialists on how to please a man, her future mate, and she now applied that to Tinougl and quickly caused him to respond which she instantly felt as the warmth of his contribution triggered additional gratification. They were then expended and Denettk held Tinougl with her arms around him as they slowly spooned and let the feelings linger. Tinougl felt the strange satisfaction of her hug and he reciprocated. The feelings were genuine, though shockingly not expected.

After a few minutes it was time to get professional again.

"Now that we got the preliminary's out of the way we can concentrate on the massage. You pleased me so much I will now give you the special massage."

"Please climb out of the tub and I'll dry you off."

Tinougl complied with Denettk's instructions and soon found

Denettk lovingly drying him off with super soft towels. She then quickly dried herself and put on a skimpy outfit she wore during her work. She then led him back into the massage room.

"Please lay down on the massage table on your stomach."

Tinougl complied and soon Denettk was applying a very nice smelling oil all over his backside. It gave him quite the tingling sensation as there were tree chemicals and cannabinoids mixed with an analgesic. After all the oils were applied, Denettk started messaging his entire backside. Denettk was a very strong woman and just the perfect masseuse for a man with such strong tense muscles.

Denettk said she would give the special massage and Tinougl was now starting to feel why. This woman knew her business and would be the perfect spy as she could seduce the hell out of men.

"Turn on your side."

Tinougl did that and now she showed her real expertise as she bent his arms and legs around like he never felt before. At times it was intensely painful. But soon the pain was replaced with pleasure.

"Tinougl lay on your back now."

Tinougl complied and soon witnessed the most incredible sensations as she worked over parts of his body. Denettk had not oiled his front side and that was now becoming apparent why as she demonstrated parts of the special massage as she performed fellatio on him while simultaneously making his muscles in his chest and legs feel incredible. He felt hard as a rock, and she did some strange things with the fellatio, and he then exploded in her mouth with an incredible release. *Now he knew what special massage meant.*

Denettk walked over and spit Tinougl's magic seed into the sink and took some mouth wash and cleaned out her mouth and took a drink of some strange looking blue liquid. She then came back to the massage table and applied oils to his front side and milked the residual out of him that gave him another nice rush. Then to Tinougl's profoundly unexpected surprise, she reached down and kissed him on his mouth with the lovely taste of the substance lingering in her mouth she had just washed out. The emotions were real and legitimate and the two hugged with the kiss.

Denettk was one of the best in her business as she now went to work on Tinougl sometimes tormenting him with tremendous pain that quickly turned into pleasure as his body slowly reconditioned like it hadn't in years. Then it was all done and Denettk said, "Lets go back into the bath so we can wash all that oil off your body, so you don't feel sticky."

"Alright," Tinougl said as he followed her into the next room, and they walked down into the bath once again refilling with fresh water.

Denettk had another container in her hand that she emptied into the hot tub water that gave Tinougl another sensation. His body was now feeling heavenly with no soreness anywhere and he was fully gratified almost not believing he could do all this once again so soon after Spicey seduced him.

After a while of rubbing him down and getting any last bit of oil off his body, Denettk saw a little green light near the ceiling which indicated her next client with a reservation was now here and she now had to cut this short.

"Tinougl, I have another client I must attend to now, so would you please get out of the tub and get dressed."

"Sure."

"Tinougl, I'm sorry I must leave you now. I kind of like you, but we can meet again in the future."

"It will be my pleasure, Denettk."

After they were both appropriately dressed, Denettk walked Tinougl to the entrance. He felt divine and walked past the Barracuda who looked bored and went back up to his room to ponder a few things as well as do some more research.

As he was sitting there thinking, Tondron asked, would you like to take a bath or a shower?

"I just had a bath; I was bathed by the lovely Denettk who gave me a massage at the resort SPA."

"She is very popular, but men who attempt to date her always get turned down,"Tondron stated.

"How do you know this?"

"The artificial intelligence that integrates all resort security briefed me on Denettk because it thinks you are interested in her."

"She is nice, I kind of like her."

"Tinougl, may I offer you some advice?"

"Certainly."

"Denettk is well liked by everyone at the resort. She's good friends with everyone. She's a nice girl and doesn't sleep around and never dates resort guests. If you like her and enjoyed your time with her, you should send her a tip, she might appreciate it."

"How much do you suggest?"

"You have a very considerable credit limit as your deposit was very substantial. 10 credits would mean very little to you, but it would mean a lot to Denettk."

"Can you send the credits."

"Yes, as soon as you authorize it."

"I authorize it."

"It is done."

"What would you like to do now Tinougl?"

"I feel so good I think I want to change into some sleeping clothes and take a nap. Wake me up in two hours."

"I certainly will."

Guāiqiǎo came out of his storage room carrying the change of clothes for Tinougl who put them on and crawled in his bed. Thanks to all the substances he received as well as the sexual gratification, Tinougl went to sleep very abruptly and didn't feel like wakening up, but Guāiqiǎo gently shook him until he snapped out of it and became alert.

"Master Tinougl, you have slept for two hours and wished to be awakened."

"Yes, thank you."

"Would you like to change your clothes?"

"Yes, thank you."

Guāiqiǎo walked over to the closet and brought Tinougl a change of clothes and assisted him change.

"What do you want to do next?"

"I want to watch Empire news, then go down to the Dining Hall and listen to some entertainment."

Soon a holograph was showing all the latest news headlines. Again, it was a dead end, nothing stood out.

"Alright, I think I saw enough, I'm leaving now for the Dining Hall."

CHAPTER ELEVEN

THE GREAT TÓNG CANYON

Once again Tinougl arrived before the crowd. The musicians were performing and there she was out in front, the glamorous singer Wánměi de Mòlìhuā showing her gracious demure and resonating the few guests present with oscillations of passion.

People might say that when Tinougl sat down, Mòlìhuā as she preferred Tinougl call her, improved her performance as if his presence motivated her to a great extent.

The pretty Dining Hall waitress Madalyn bon Donkers, quickly approached Tinougl with a smile that matched her attractiveness.

"Hello Tinougl, what would you like to drink?"

"I think I would like the Chamboree del Pàrà Měilì."

"Would you like a menu?"

"Yes, after the musicians finish their break."

"Certainly."

Madalyn walked to the bartender who was not busy at the time and quickly produced the premier drink Chamboree del Pàrà Měilì. Madalyn returned to Tinougl's table in a brief period and said, "I hope you enjoy your drink."

"Thank you."

Tinougl enjoyed the effects of the drink which set the mood and the quintessential effect while hearing Mòlìhuā singing. The chemical equilibrium developed by spontaneous eruptions of emotions manifested by the singing and the Chamboree del Pàrà Měilì blanked much of his remarkable experience with Denettk. But he suddenly had a flashback and subtle reflection of the event.

The relationship with Denettk was a spontaneous mutual attraction that led to an outlandish explosion of passion only because Denettk chose the person and the time. *Why did she choose me?*

Denettk was no fool and knew her sudden release of pent-up passions would not result in anything of permanence with Tinougl. Nonetheless, she enjoyed seeking the gratification of a man with such a fabulous body. She would do it again if he wanted and she had no expectations from him. And even if he wanted more from her, it was not in the plan nor in the mission. It was simply an anomaly of the mission.

The real issue at hand stood in front of Tinougl. A beautiful and talented woman probably with a heart of gold, that he would have to use. Spies sometimes must take from the unsuspecting. It might seem moral and reprehensibly wrong, but a mission so essential that his sponsors sent him back five hundred years made the casualties of the heart just a collateral function that was unavoidable.

As the music played on and the singing resonated with Tinougl, the Chamboree del Pàrà Měilì soothed his emotional state without impacting his situational awareness. The Dining Hall slowly filled up with resort guests and inevitably Sparky and Schemer arrived dressed for an adventure. They were definitely traveling in a safari to snare a wild beast and ride him all night long.

From time to time, the Barracuda's gazed at Tinougl. They were not as subtle in their gaze as they should have been. To a spy trained to observe and analyze, he knew what their inquisitive gaze amounted to. The *squad* had no doubt discussed him at some length. They might have even conspired and made suggestions to Spicey who might have already discussed her trophy with them. If his hunch was right, they too wanted to experience a *trophy cub* of their own and the sooner the better.

The music continued for a few lingering minutes and during their breaktime, their singer Wánměi de Mòlìhuā stepped off the stage and made a direct flight to Tinougl as if she was eager to see him again. *Perhaps since he didn't show up last night?*

"Hello, will you please join me?"

"I'd love to."

As soon as Mòlìhuā sat down, Madalyn bon Donkers approached her and asked, "Mòlìhuā, would you like something to drink?"

"Yes, I would like a Lǐzǐ Guavastrian Elixir."

"I'll be right back with your drink."

Madalyn walked up to the bartender who was making drinks for another table, and she said, "Make a Lǐzǐ Guavastrian Elixir for our singer."

The bartender knew the musicians and singer only had a brief break time and it was important to take their order ahead of the guests who were not under time constraints.

In a minute Madalyn approached Tinougl's table with a slightly watered down Lǐzǐ Guavastrian Elixir so that it would not impair her singing.

"I missed you yesterday."

"Yes, I'm sorry, I went to the concert and listened to the performances of two fantastic pianists."

"I wish I could have gone with you."

"Do you get any days off?"

"Yes, I have a few days off coming up real soon."

"Do you have any plans for your days off?"

"Not really, just stay home and relax and rest my voice."

"How would you like to rest your voice on Plexis de Chiveltros?"

"You mean the moon?"

"Sure."

"You would take me there?"

"Most definitely if you wished to go. And if you are nervous, I'll even make sure you have your own private room at the resort."

"I'll think about. But I will tell you something you need to prepare for."

"What's that?"

"If I agreed to go with you, I would not desire a private room."

"Why would you want that?"

"I know you would keep me warm and safe."

"That I would."

"What are the things you want to do on the moon?"

"Besides staying in a lovely resort, there are a few interesting things to explore."

"Is it dangerous?"

"No, they accommodate elderly tourists at each of the places I would want to visit."

"I suppose if an elderly person is going to these places, then I should not be concerned."

"Not at all."

"They have some amazing lava baths there."

"What's that like?"

"They have crushed lava flows materials they make a mudlike substance you bathe in that gives you a lot of health and vitality."

"That sounds like something I would like."

"The sightseeing is rather incredible, from strange rock formations to primitive jungles you ride over in suspended gondola's and look at rare animals that do not exist anywhere else."

"Don't spoil the fun by telling me too much, I would rather you surprise me."

"Let me know you want to go, and I'll definitely surprise you."

By the time Mòlìhuā finished her drink and the short conversation tailed off in anticipation of her departure, the band members were back on stage.

"I'm sorry to leave you now, but I'll talk to you during the next break."

Sparky and Schemer were carefully observing the couple talk and could not resist the comments to each other.

"Spicey would not be too happy watching that singer go after Tinougl."

"She's going to be gone at least a week. Apparently, her husband is taking her somewhere. Maybe he wants to rekindle the affection."

"I think he's waited too long. Spicey was beaming at the concert."

"I've never seen her look that good in ages."

"Yes, it was rather remarkable."

"Tinougl seemed to look older and more mystique about him last night."

"Maybe it was the clothes he was wearing."

"I'm still fascinated by his hair style last night. Someone professional worked on getting him ready."

"If I were in Spicey's shoes last night I would have said the hell with the concert, us go up to my Penthouse."

The two women chuckled, then Sparky gave Schemer a little INTEL.

"Spicey called me this morning a short while before she left."

"What did she have to say."

"All those things we speculated at the swimming pool together today was more than speculation."

"What do you mean by that."

"I didn't tell you before because I didn't want Spicey to get mad at me for being a blabber mouth."

"But you are."

"I know but I can't help it."

"Go on tell me the juicy details, I want to hear all about it."

"They had a lovely dinner at the Top of the World Restaurant, then she took him back to her penthouse."

"She did?"

"Oh yes. Her maid following her instructions drugged Tinougl?"

"Why did she do that?"

"For more sexual output."

The women chuckled some more.

"How was he?"

"She said her "Big A" was the longest and best she ever had."

"He does kind of look cute."

"Don't go thinking what I think you are thinking, you know Spicey claimed dibs on him first."

"Well, if she's going to be gone a week or longer, I don't want the poor man to be dormant too long. Plus I wouldn't drug him. Just a few minutes is fine with me."

"I wouldn't advise it."

"I'm going to go talk to him now while his singer girlfriend is busy. We are best friends; I do not want you to let Spicey know what I'm doing."

"I'm not going to get in the middle of it. Spicey can be a *vindictive bitch*."

Madalyn bon Donkers walked up to Tinougl and handed him a menu and to her surprise, he already knew what was on the menu thanks to his photographic memory and said, "I'll have the roasted Anas Platyrhynchos."

Tinougl then handed the menu back to Madalyn who said, "That's a really good choice. The Chef prepares it very nicely."

"Thank you."

"You are most welcome."

Madalyn walked away with the food order and about fifteen seconds later,

Schemer approached Tinougl's table and asked, "May I join you for a little bit?"

"Sure, why not."

Schemer sat down and began, "I'm a good friend of Estele bon Stoffengar (aka Spicey)."

"Alright."

"I saw the two of you at the concert last night."

"The music was very nice."

"You looked so handsome; I was impressed.

"Thank you for the nice comment."

"In the future if you have the time, I would like to take you to a concert or other entertainment."

"I suppose I could go sometime."

Schemer handed Tinougl a thin object and said, "If you would ever like to contact me, here is my personal card."

"Okay."

Tinougl looked down on the card. Schemer's name on it stated Sěphámy bon Cǎoméi.

"Sěphámy bon Cǎoméi is a beautiful name."

"Thank you, just call me Cǎoméi."

"I watched you swimming, you performed quite a few laps."

"I needed a good workout, I've had it too easily lately, need to get my body back in shape."

"Why such effort?"

"I find that when I'm in tip top physical condition, I'm able to write better."

"You are a writer?"

"Yes."

"What do you write?"

"Novels."

"Maybe that's why Estele likes you so much."

"I've not really discussed my writing with her."

"Well, I can think of a lot of other reasons." Schemer gave Tinougl an evil smile.

The conversation slowly decayed from there and suddenly the Dining Hall waitress Madalyn bon Donkers shoved a meal cart next to the table and started lying out a full setting and Schemer got the massage with the stares and said, "I better let you eat your meal, I will talk to you later."

"Alright, thank you."

Madalyn was glad to see the Barracuda leave and get away from the table. She knew the Barracuda's quite well and knew their modus operendus and their reason to stay at this resort, to harvest their fair share of *cubs*.

Madalyn laid out the entrée and everything Tinougl needed to enjoy his roasted Anas Platyrhynchos.

Tinougl was glad he received a portion that had a leg and a thigh on the serving as that part he liked the best. The breast meat was usually too dry for his taste, though there was some of that on the serving as well. Later as he enjoyed the meal,

Tinougl discovered the Anas Platyrhynchos breast meat was so nicely prepared it melted in his mouth. The entire meal was a masterpiece and quite a glorious exhibit of the prowesss of the chef.

The meal was completed, and the dishes were taken away and tablecloth replaced about the time the band had their next break.

Mòlìhuā observed Schemer make her play on Tinougl, and when the break started made her way quickly to his table to anchor her position in the affair.

"I really enjoyed your singing."

"Thank you."

"You are most welcome."

"How was your dinner?"

"Fantastic as usual."

"I always eat dinner here before the show."

"Then you know how good it is."

"Yes, I do."

The conversation meandered around irrelevant topics then suddenly Mòlìhuā surprised Tinougl, "My next days off start in a couple days, and I'm leaning towards going to the moon with you."

"That's wonderful, I would enjoy your company."

"I'll let you know tomorrow what my decision is."

"Good."

The conversation continued in anticipation the music would soon start again. Eventually the musicians all returned to the stage and Mòlìhuā said, "I hate to go back to work now, but I must."

"That's okay, I'm leaving soon to go to bed. I'm kind of sleepy."

"Alright then, I'll be looking forward to seeing you tomorrow."

"Likewise."

Mòlìhuā a few moments later started singing and the band started playing while Tinougl enjoyed the remainder of his drink and before Schemer had a chance to enter his midst, Tinougl stood up and walked out of the Dining Hall and proceeded to his resort room.

His drinks had prepared him for a good night rest, but he wanted to make sure he slept well, so Tinougl asked Tondron when a few minutes after he arrived, "Do you have any good sleep inducers?"

"Master Tinougl, yes we always have a lot of items people might need and forget to pack in their luggage before they travel."

"Good, can you provide me one and a glass of water?"

"It's on the way."

A moment later, Guāiqiǎo came out of his storage room with a tray holding a glass of water and a small container holding a dark blue liquid and approached Tinougl.

"Drink this and you will be sleeping in a few minutes. You can drink the water to remove the taste from your mouth."

"Thanks."

Tinougl consumed the contents of the small container which tasted rather delightful and washed it down with the water to clear the taste out of his mouth which wasn't bad. He then put on the sleeping attire that Guāiqiǎo immediately provided and entered his bed. Just Tondron promised in five minutes he was sound asleep.

During his sleep, Tinougl had vivid dreams like he never experienced before. He was sure it was all real until he awoke in the morning. The sleeping inducement must have created a *psychophysical response*. He felt well rested even though he thought he was living a life in his dreams.

"I think I'll get up and go for a walk, he notified Tondron, then went to the bathroom and did his morning routine, then changed into some of the new clothes he had previously purchased and went back to the park. As he strolled around the park everything seemed to be about the same as it was just yesterday. And as expected the elderly men were sitting on the park bench in identical order as the previous day. Tinougl ignored all that and completed his walk and went back to his room to put on swimming attire then went down to the pool and swam laps.

Today, Tinougl pushed himself and did 30 laps. Right around 15 laps, Sparky and Schemer arrived at the pool and took up their positions in the soft recliners they most often took command of because of the view to the pool. They didn't know how many laps Tinougl had already done but enjoyed observing his final 15 laps.

The pool was the perfect place to get a snack and a drink which he soon was consuming when Schemer came over and sat down on a chair facing Tinougl.

"Good morning Tinougl."

"Hello how are you Căoméi?"

"I'm okay thans for asking, but I would be in a much better mood this morning had you called me after you left the Dining Hall last night."

"Well, I was tired and wanted a really good night sleep, so I went back to my room and got a really good night of sleep in."

"That sounds so boring, you could have been having fun up in my Penthouse."

"I'm glad I had the good night sleep. I feel so much better today."

"What are you going to do after the swimming pool today?"

"I'm not sure, I haven't thought about it."

"Would you like to go up to my Penthouse so I can please you and then take you on a nice short trip somewhere."

"What do you have in mind for a trip?"

"I have my own private stratospheric transport; I can get us to the Great Tóng Canyon area in about an hour and we can take a tour there and be back in time for dinner."

"I was planning on getting a massage after I finish eating. My muscles are a little tight after swimming."

"I can give you a nice massage up in my Penthouse."

"I'll tell you what, I'm about done with this snack and the drink, I'm going to go get that massage from a professional, then I can visit you."

"All right I'm going to my Penthouse to get ready for you. Just tell the elevator you want to go to Căoméi's Penthouse, and it will direct you to the right place."

"Alright, see you then."

Tinougl got up and walked to the SPA wondering what Căoméi had in mind. *No doubt Spicey bragged, and she wants some of the action too.*

The nice and sexy receptionist was there again today and said, "Welcome back Tinougl."

"Thank you."

The receptionist demeaner was kind of strange. Perhaps Denettk informed her he received the "special massage." In reality, all the financial transactions go through the receptionist who transfers the tips to the massage technician. She saw that Tinougl had been very generous with Denettk. And Denettk had spoken fondly of this gentleman, the kind of clientele they preferred.

The receptionist knew Denettk would be highly disappointed if she took Tinougl to any other room and Denettk was not with a client at the present time, so she took him right there.

Denettk smiled broadly when her prince charming arrived.

She was more than happy to do another special massage and was somewhat disappointed he didn't want the special massage and said a flimsy lie he was still full of gratification from yesterday. Had she known he was saving up his load for Schemer, she would have been highly disappointed and made him pay for it by roughening him up while messaging.

The massage took half as long because of the truncated sexual tryst. Tinougl though gave Denettk a very romantic hug just before he left to go back up to his room to change back in his street clothes.

As expected, as he walked through the pool area on his way back inside the Cuìlù Resort Hotel, Schemer was gone, and Sparky gave him a wicked smile as she knew what Schemer had in mind for the young lad.

Sparky wasn't bad looking herself. Tinougl thought he would never turn her down. Very pretty face and a splendid body. She took good care of herself and had a neglectful husband who preferred the green skin women on the planet Azorelles.

Tinougl did not react to Sparky's obvious flirtatious gesture and marched smartly to the elevator and went up to his room to change.

After he arrived in his room and took off his swimming apparel, Tondron asked, "Master Tinougl, would you like to take a shower and freshen up?"

"No, I got cleaned up really good while I was getting a massage."

"How was your massage?"

"It was wonderful, my body feels like new."

"Would you like me to send Denettk a tip again?"

"Yes, I would appreciate that."

"What are you going to do next?"

"Sĕphámy bon Căoméi has asked me to join her. She wants to take me to the Great Tóng Canyon."

"How long will you be gone?"

"Just for the day."

"Alright, I hope you enjoy yourself Tinougl."

"I certainly will, I love sight seeing."

Tinougl left his resort hotel room and walked over to the elevator that opened in expectation of taking him to the bottom floor and front entrance. Before the elevator door shut, Tinougl said, "Please take me to Căoméi's floor."

The elevator quickly scanned new orders and found the invitation for Tinougl, and immediately lifted him up to the top floor of the resort and alerted him, exit the elevator to the right and you will see Sĕphámy bon Căoméi's Penthouse in about 30 steps."

Tinougl followed the elevator voice instruction and just like it stated, about 30 steps was a double doorway with a green light lit above it to indicate guest was arriving.

Schemer had a male butler named Vangrelle who stood just inside the double doors that each slid sideways under pneumatic power and invited Tinougl in:

"Please come in Tinougl, Madam Sĕphámy is waiting for you, please follow me."

Vangrelle led Tinougl through this front entrance room through another set of double doors into a very plush room with astonishingly decorated furniture bristled with artwork all around. Statues, paintings, sculptures, and countless art images abound.

Sĕphámy bon Căoméi's was indeed dressed for the occasion and said,

"Vangrelle, that will be all for now."

"I will be waiting in my room if you have any requests."

"Thank you."

Vangrelle departed through the double doors which shut behind him giving them privacy.

Căoméi as she liked to be called stood up and now her scantily clothed lingerie that didn't leave much to the imagination exposed the essence of her expectations. She walked directly over to Tinougl and put her arms around him and smiled and looked into his eyes for a few minutes and said, "Thank you for coming."

"It's my pleasure."

Căoméi showed absence of restraint and pulled Tinougl closer. Since they were almost the same height, she spontaneously put her lips on his lips and gave Tinougl a gentle but effective kiss. Tinougl knew what she wanted. It was quite evident the *bitch was in heat*, and he was there to satisfy her curiousity to find out what she missed out on when Spicey beat her to this fine gentleman.

Tinougl pulled Căoméi closer and wrapped his arms around her and pulled her stiffly against him. He had on a thin summer shirt and could easily feel her breasts through the material. She responded to his firm grip by kissing him even harder. It was a foregone conclusion of what was going to happen next. Even though there were drinks already poured on the guest table about four times larger than a standard coffee table, it was obvious they would skip that part as Căoméi (aka Schemer), suggested, "Come with me into the other room where we can get more comfortable.

Căoméi then grabbed Tinougl's hand as he released her, and she led him into the bedroom through a door that automatically opened and closed behind them. She led Tinougl to a foot away from the bed and dropped her negligee, then unbuttoned Tinougl's shirt and pulled it off him and tossed it aside on top of her negligee then undid his quick release shoes that he stepped out of. Căoméi undid his trousers and slipped them and his undergarment off

Cǎoméi then glided into the bed pulling Tinougl along with her and laid down on her back exposing it all and said, "You can do whatever you want to me."

Tinougl took those instructions wholeheartedly and moments later Cǎoméi was feeling those incredible muscles she quickly loved and felt ecstatic that Tinougl was well endowed and knew how to make a woman feel appreciated.

Tinougl was no five-minute wonder. In his vast training as a spy, he was taught to properly utilize all the items in his psychological and sexual toolbox in ingenious manners to create a synergistic effect that produced predictable results.

Innovation was sometimes required, but as he gauged Cǎoméi he analyzed she was very conventional and if he stuck to the basics and his Round Robin approach, Cǎoméi would succumb to his magic and receive the gratification she so eagerly sought.

In less than two minutes Cǎoméi was in orgasmic heavin as Tinougl was efficiently stroking her G-Spot and worked her clitoris to the point of almost a nervous breakdown. But as a professional in the line of duty, he knew when to let off a bit to allow Cǎoméi to regain her composure before he did his next sequence of the Round Robbin.

Cǎoméi thought she knew the essence of "Big-A" especially after group discussions with Spicey and Sparky, but she knew now why Spicey was such a changed woman after just one encounter with Tinougl.

Tinougl, knowing they needed to finish and dress for the trip to the Great Tóng Canyon, determined after 15 minutes it was time to stroke her hard so she would remember this for the rest of her life. He then used his athletic prowess and thrusted into her like she never experienced before. It was mildly shocking and unnerving for her until she reached a new type of gratification she never felt before.

Căoméi's Alpah, Beta, Gama, Theta, and Delta brain waves were all super active as her entire body physiology was in a total synchronization with every move Tinougl made when he gushed inside her and gave her the splendid Euphoria. Then it was done. They collapsed in each other's arms leaving Căoméi in a sweet mental condition she never felt before in her lifetime. And in her thoughts, she surmised she knew exactly how Tinougl had made Spicey feel who would be extremely agitated and jealous if she discovered the two of them got it on.

She would lie to Sparky and said they just went to the Great Tóng Canyon because she didn't want to harm Spicey's relationship with Tinougl. When the time came, Sparky didn't believe a word of it but went along with the ruse.

Căoméi (aka Schemer) knowing they had to make their presence at the Great Tóng Canyon, or the lie wouldn't work suddenly said, "Let's get up and take a quick shower and get dressed so we can go on that trip to Great Tóng Canyon."

"That sounds good."

Soon they were getting soaped up and cleaned and then blow dried with a body drier. Căoméi put on a bath robe and said "Why don't you get dressed and wait in the next room for me because it will take me a little longer to get ready.

"Sure."

Tinougl put his clothes back on and went into the glorious next room. While sitting there, a very pretty young lady who could not have been more than in her mid twenties passed by and said, "Tinougl those are drinks for your consumption. I'm going to help Lady Sěphámy get ready for the trip."

She then walked right on by and entered the next room and that door then shut.

Tinougl picked up one of the drinks and took a taste. It was familiar to him, and he quickly determined it was Lǐzǐ Guavastrian Elixir. After his physical workout a few minutes prior, the Elixir quickly hit the spot. He was curious and pulled his communicator out of his pocket and searched for this Elixir to find out what it cost. When he saw the price, his eyes almost popped out. One bottle of this Elixir cost almost as much as he earned in a month. Then he started analyzing inflation and what money was worth 500 years ago and realized it was exceedingly expensive. But to these rich people it was another trivial matter.

The ladies only took fifteen minutes to prepare, and it was definitely worth the wait when Cǎoméi came out of her bedroom looking beautiful and glamorous. The young woman was a movie producer makeup artist of great talent that spent a lot of time between filming at the resort, making the clients look as good as the movie stars she made up and did makeovers. She even had vast knowledge of hair and now Cǎoméi was the full package any man would love to be seen in public.

Cǎoméi said, "It's going to be a little hot and sunny where we are going, I have a hat and sunglasses for you."

"Thank you, I appreciate that."

"Our transportation is waiting for us at the front of the resort, shall we go now?"

"Sure."

The three walked into the next room and there was Vangrelle by the front entrance and as they approached, he bowed and gestured to the double door that was now sliding open.

"Have a wonderful trip Madam Sěphámy."

"Thank you Vangrelle."

The couple left the Penthouse with the young woman and Vangrelle standing in a respectful pose wishing them off to happiness.

They were quickly down to street level and exited the elevator and exited the front entrance of the Cuìlù Resort Hotel and right in front of them in the Limo pickup zone was a Limo to take them to Santorini de Shénshèng Transportation Center where Tinougl got the next nice surprise, a ride on Madam Sěphámy bon Cǎoméi's private stratospheric transport.

This super zippy craft was large enough it could carry thirty passengers, if necessary, but instead there was a cabin with seating for only six as the extra space was designed for personal cargo and extra fuel to go much longer destinations with no need to ever have a fuel stop on any round trip to anywhere on the planet.

People flying on private stratospheric transports did not go through general transportation terminals, instead had private terminals on the other side of the transportation center. Check-in took as long as it required for you to walk from the street curb sidewalk, through the building and into the hanger where the boarding took place. People could travel incognito because nobody saw who got on the transports.

Madam Sěphámy bon Cǎoméi's private stratospheric transport had a Four-engine cluster in the back of the transport and the delta shaped wing ended at the back of the plane surrounding the four powerful rocket assist propulsion engines. In just twenty years prior those engines were top secret military prime movers but now were used on private transports as the military now had much greater technology.

The wheels of the transport had electric motors and did not require a tug to pull it out of the hanger. Once the two were on the transport with the door shut, the hanger doors opened, and the electric motors slowly eased the transport out of the hanger and after it cleared the hanger, the hanger doors shut.

One of the prime movers came online and the craft made the

trip around the side of the runway on a service ramp, and when given permission, moved onto the active runway and all four prime movers came online and the transport took off. Tinougl was pushed hard against his seat and the transport quickly gathered speed and rotated upwards to about a 45-degree angle where it quickly gained altitude on it's way up to 150,000 feet where it would glide to it's destination. In an hour they were on a landing approach to the Tóng Canyon Regional Transport Center.

The private stratospheric transport pulled into a hanger that unloaded private transports and they were soon stepping down a ramp off the plane.

Madam Sĕphámy bon Căoméi led Tinougl out to the sidewalk curb in front of the building and waiting transportation for them was ready to go as soon as they got into the Limo.

Chapter Twelve

A Time Travel Spy and a Lover on the Train

Without saying much because Căoméi was still feeling an incredible post love making sensation, the Limo made it's way to a train station, where they were going to get on the Great Tóng Canyon Express, an elegant train that took tourists and well to do people up on a circular path around the Tóng Canyon. They would not take the entire trip which normally took several days including several stops along the way so that passengers could get off and purchase souvenirs. The trip Căoméi planned for them was an hour up the mountain and some sight seeing along the rim of the Canyon, then stop at an Alpine like resort have a glorious meal, then return to Cuìlǜ Resort Hotel later that day.

The sunglasses and the hat did a great job of concealing Tinougl's identity which might have preserved his life. The three Barracudas didn't know their husbands had killed several of their lovers, that's why they never called again. In most cases they were still alive when they were dropped out of a rotary transport into the middle of a large Gradvolchin Hog Farm with their arms and legs tied together in thick plastic restraints they could not undo. To make the Gradvolchin Hogs get even more anxious to rip into them, the boyfriends were cut in a few places and their blood smeared which the hogs smelled and knew they were getting an extra treat to eat that night.

Căoméi reserved a private cabin that had it's own entrance from the train platform and a very large glass window that opened to the side of the Canyon with most of the majestic sights. The sofa seat faced the window and this car that contained eight private compartments, had it's own staff waiters who responded to calls from each cabin. All the passengers had to say was "I want a drink," or a snack and the waiter would soon be at the entrance to their cabin and the artificial intelligence would ask the passengers, would you like the waiter to enter the cabin. As soon as they replied yes, the door would open using compressed air and the waiter would take their orders. All expenses associated with drinks, meals, or snacks was charged to the cabin and the person who reserved it.

The train got underway very smoothly. At first there wasn't much to see. The train sped across flat land for a while exposing the urban sprawl and slowly the train slowed down as it took an angle upwards into the mountains.

Tinougl looked at Sĕphámy bon Căoméi. Her makeup artist turned her into a living princess and easily took off 10 years of her real image. Tinougl knew if he woke up with her in the morning after she cleaned off all the makeup, she would not look so glamorous, but for the time being he enjoyed being with this very delightful woman of means.

When Tinougl smiled at Căoméi her heart raced. She was quickly growing fond of Tinougl. She also knew the obvious. If Spicey discovered, she had a tumultuous sexual relationship with Tinougl they would probably have a *bitch fight* where one slapped the other that resulted in a hair pulling contest. But Schemer was a smart woman, she would not go there and instinctively knew Tinougl would not divulge his inner secrets. However, if he fell in love with her, she would stand her ground. But she also knew a venomous woman like Spicey would send spies to inform her husband and poor Tinougl would end up at a Gradvolchin Hog Farm. After Tinougl pleased her so much, Căoméi would do what she had to protect him. The best way would be to conceal this *Soiree on a Theme from Paganini.*

The train slowed considerably and soon was only making thirty miles per hour because of the grade of the track was so great. Thanks to the horsepower and tractive effort the locomotives on this train delivered, it would continue up the grade at least 30 miles per hour. The slower speed added a level of comfort due to less bumps and sways of the train.

"This is quite beautiful, what do you think?" Căoméi asked.

"Yes, this is very inspiring. I never saw something like this before. it's breathtakingly charming."

Căoméi was thinking four chess moves ahead and in the privacy of this rail car decided to warn Tinougl on a few matters.

"Listen Tinougl, in case you do not realize it yet, I truly do like you."

"Thank you. I like you too."

"You are an outsider and do not know how things work around here."

"That's for sure."

"What I'm going to tell you now is because I care for you. You have touched me in ways no other man has before, so I think I want to protect you."

"What does that mean?"

"I will do whatever I can to protect you, but you need to know what you face."

"Well, that's obvious I would think."

"Tinougl you are pure from an off-world planet. You have no idea the level of corruption and greed that exists on this planet.'"

"I realize I'm at a slight disadvantage because I come from more meager beginnings."

"Tinougl, you pleased me like no other man before today. I know you are special. I do love you and I know I need to protect the man who gave me a great awakening."

"Alright explain to me, what I must do."

"Before I suggest what you need to do, you need to know a few things."

"Alright, what is it?"

"First of all, Spicey, Sparky and I are married to the richest and most powerful men in the Empire."

"How does that fit into all this?"

"As I said before, now I have an emotional attachment to you, I do not want to see bad things happen to you."

"What am I supposed to do?"

"You now know we are the richest women in the Empire, but you also need to know Spicey is the most *vindictive bitch* that ever walked on this planet. Our special time this afternoon must be a very guarded secret because if Spicey finds out I made love to you, she might have you killed."

"What can I do?"

"I can handle Spicey, she can't touch me but if she decides you must die, you will not live another day."

Tinougl was starting to understand the gravity of the situation he got himself into.

"What should I do?"

"I'm not sure when Spicey will come back. Usually, she's only gone for a week when her husband wakes up and decides to pester her. When she gets back, she will feel like crap dealing with that poor excuse for a man that's her husband. Act like you and I never had anything going and treat her like the love of your life. It will save your life and prevent a lot of damage."

"I'm sure I can do that."

Tinougl, I will be honest, you have seduced me like no other man could. I want to experience you again in the future. There will be opportunities for us to enjoy our friendship again. I promise you."

"Thank you for caring about me and protecting me."

"I'm glad to do so because now I've felt you. No other man has ever turned me on like you did. I will remember you for the rest of my life. And I want to experience that again with you one day in the future. I will protect you as much as I can, but you need to know, you live in a dangerous world because of your encounter with Spicey."

"I'll be ready that day when we can again celebrate our friendship."

"So will I."

Tinougl just realized he received the biggest INTEL briefing of his lifetime. As a spy he knew how to act upon it. Thanks to Căoméi he was three steps ahead of Spicey, though now he worried about how he could best protect Denettk and Wánměi de Mòlǐhuā from such powerful forces.

He hoped he would be on the Moon before Spicey returned.

His only real significant lead he's discovered was the singer Wánměi de Mòlǐhuā's home world. He needed to get there and do an assessment. That might be his ticket home, get the INTEL there and travel back to the future.

Tinougl knew that the Barracuda Căoméi started out as a vamp that just wanted a good sexual experience. But in the course of events, he had somehow pollinated her heart to the point she had a secret affection in him. A spy can always use good friends. Tinougl also felt some compassion to Cǎoméi. He knew she was honest and the real deal. For that he could cherish her, even though due to his disposition, he would have to leave her and all the rest behind when he traveled to the future. Though in the meantime he would give a few precious moments to her that she had more than earned.

"Cǎoméi, there is something I wish to tell you."

"What is that."

"I do feel affection towards you. I understand everything you are telling me, and I want to take this moment to give something back to you, so you know where my heart is."

Cǎoméi investigated Tinougl's eyes not knowing what to suspect, but she was eager to hear what he was going to say as it appeared he was being fully disclosure now and exposing the essence of his soul to her. And not knowing what to expect, she observed his face moving closer to her and it now became apparent as he kissed her with love and compassion.

This meant a lot to Cǎoméi as she knew in her heart, she would follow Tinougl to hell and back. No man had ever touched her like this before. It was truly an extravagant event in her life. She was kissing one of the most successful spies in Empire History five hundred years from now and didn't know it. The kiss created an auspicious moment and it exemplified how spies achieve in the most subtle manners possible.

The kiss resonated Cǎoméi. She knew that Tinougl had achieved great gratification by the deposits he left inside her she needed to clean out. And here he was, with no motives to further the sensation applying an exclamation on her eager emotions.

Cǎoméi knew Tinougl wasn't faking it. He already achieved his gratification to the most extent possible. He didn't even have to go on this trip. He was an eager volunteer, for reasons she could not understand, but his apparent emotions and his mannerism were undeniably from a person that had a significant bond that made her fill fulfilled in many ways. She knew this was her greatest feeling in her lifetime and the kiss electrified her soul. She was so grateful Tinougl reached out and touched her heart when he did. He was a young guy fully innocent, yet lovely. He had all the options in the world and here he was kissing her like his great love.

That kiss alone made the trip worthwhile nothing else mattered after this. It was gratification in a different dimension as it intensified Căoméi's affection and ultimately saved his live.

After the kiss there was a long period where the two consummated their covalent bonding with simply holding each other in their arms as if they were a couple watching TV together. Observing the Great Tóng Canyon together as a couple affectionately embracing watching TV together was no different. It was precious moments that could never be repeated by any other means possible.

As Căoméi reconciled her situation with Tinougl, she knew there was no future between them because who she was and the biggest vamp on the planet had utter lust for this strange individual who had muscles completely unlike males from the Tartarnite Empire Capital City Santorini de Shénshèng. She would take her gratification when she could to protect them both. But for the time being, her rationalization gave her a dozen hours of happiness that she would hold dear for the rest of her life.

Căoméi viewed her few crumbs of life, even if it was for a short time, was better than none. She would give Tinougl back to Spicey when she returned, but she also knew Spicey wasn't the only possibilities for Tinougl who was charming and built so heavenly, no doubt he would grow fond of a much younger woman, like the singer back at the Cuìlǜ Resort Hotel.

As many liberal bleeding hearts who believed there was ethics and morals in everything, there are no real rules in wars and espionage because the failure to secure victory affected everyone and the liberals the most. A spy knew this the best.

Căoméi's observation of the interactions between the singer and Tinougl gave her reason to believe there was a growing relationship between the two. The singer exposed the essence of her willingness to be seduced by Tinougl. As far as Căoméi was concerned, she knew Spicey was a fool to think she could control this man because she was certain that once he tasted the singer's forbidden fruit, there would be no turning back the reality of what it would spawn.

If Căoméi knew who Tinougl really was and what he was willing to do to ensure success in his mission, then she would know how much he was more than willing to seduce the singer Wánmĕi de Mòlìhuā since that's exactly what he planned and the longer Spicey stayed away the better.

The train slowly made it's way up in altitude and soon they passed a sign that said, "Altitude Four Thousand Feet.

Tinougl knew all about the Great Tóng Canyon from his Geography training as well as his own visit to this area before, but he had to play dumb and let Căoméi play tour guide as his cover story of him coming from another planet required an apparent lack of knowledge. It would be kind of interesting to see how much the Great Tóng Canyon had changed in five hundred years.

"Would you like something to drink?"

"Yes, I would thank you."

The artificial intelligence analyzing the cabin conversation summoned the waiter who quickly appeared and asked, "What would you like to drink?"

Căoméi responded, "I would like a Lĭzĭ Guavastrian Elixir."

"Sir, what would you like?"

"I would like a Chamboree del Pàrà Mĕilì."

"I will be back in a few moments with your drinks."

"Thank you."

One item that indelibly etches in a man's memories for special moments like this is the smell and scents surrounding the event. Căoméi was wearing a very special perfume, loaded with pheromones that Tinougl recalled from his future time. The perfume was rare and extremely costly. One ounce cost as much as some people's yearly salary. He was trying to remember the scent and he suddenly recalled it's fragrance, *Cofa de Coma.*

In one of his missions a few years before the time travel, he had to seduce a female Spratan Diplomat. He was so impressed with her perfume he asked her the name of it. Sadly, the lovely diplomat died from collateral damage. Her security force was attempting to kill Tinougl, and he made a desperate move to avoid the lethal laser shot from the assailant's blaster and when his body moved behind the diplomat the shooter was following him and made a predictive shot that he didn't see the diplomat before he pulled the trigger. She took the full blunt of a two second laser shot which gave Tinougl enough time to get one shot in to kill the assailent and escape by jumping out the window of the third story of a highrise building, landing on an awning to soften his drop that prevented any injuries allowing him to get away. He liked the Spratan Diplomat and wished she had not been killed in the incident. And here today, Căoméi brought back those memories by wearing the same perfume.

The waiter interrupted Tinougl's daydream when he suddenly arrived with the drinks and after serving the drinks said, "please enjoy."

After the waiter left the private cabin, Căoméi raised her glass and said,

"Here's a toast to you and your fabulous love making today."

"Thank you and you gave me great satisfaction," Tinougl responded.

The drinks were perfect to help enhance what was about to be bestowed on the two happy sightseers. Căoméi said, we should be coming up on Krakatori Falls soon.

"What is it like?" Tinougl asked to create an element of ignorance to help bolster his disguise as an *off worlder*.

"It's one of the largest waterfalls on the planet and creates clouds, especially on a warm day."

By the time Tinougl finished half of his Chamboree del Pàrà Měilì drink, he was starting to feel the good buzz it created. This coincided with Căoméi's comment: "I think I can see the Krakatori Falls coming into view."

Sure enough, even though they were only traveling approximately thirty miles per hour going up the grade, there was some cloud cover starting to appear from the water vapor given off from the waterfall. The train was in a curve and as it swung around to the left in it's curvy travel, the spectacular sight of Krakatori Falls came into view. The majestic panorama always left and impression with anyone not familiar with it. The view was reassuring to Tinougl in that it appears like it does five hundred years into the future.

The combination of the view of Krakatori Falls, the scent of *Cofa de Coma* perfume, the lovely made up Sěphámy bon Căoméi, and the effects of the Chamboree del Pàrà Měilì together created a surreal effect on Tinougl's psyche.

This was a rare moment in his life, where the rewards of being a spy and experiencing targets of opportunity made it's mark.

A spy with a photographic memory would indelibly etch this moment in his mind. He could easily fall in love with Căoméi, but the lessons learned from his experiences with the female Spratan Diplomat quickly helped him overcome such notions. He could not afford in his own conscious to make a victim out of Căoméi plus as soon as he discovered what he was looking for, he would be leaving her behind forever. One thought he had though was when he want back to the future was to see if he could find out any information on these women and what happened to them?

In about five minutes they went over a railway bridge across the Krakatori River and curved around to the right. They would now get to see the Krakatori Falls from a different angle. The sunlight was now to their backs and when they came up to that other view of Krakatori Falls, they witnessed the most incredible rainbow. Such a renowned vision added to the illustrious sensation.

Before long as the train hit a level grade and straighter track it sped up. Tinougl guessed they were doing sixty to seventy miles per hour and covered some distance before the train slowed down due to curvier mountain track. The time of day was perfect to be where they were at this point because the sunlight bathed the Great Tóng Canyon which exposed the color's and exquisite tapestry of this rather unusual area exhibited.

They finished their drinks and before Tinougl could suggest another round, Căoméi explained, "In about Fifteen minutes the train will stop at a mountain village. We'll get off the train there, have a nice meal and get a local tour, and get back on a train going in the opposite direction in about three hours."

"Sounds fun."

Tinougl skipped ordering a new drink since they would soon be in a restaurant.

The train eventually pulled into that mountain village where several dozen tourists exited the train. The artificial intelligence notified Tinougl and Căoméi,

"This is your destination. It is now safe to depart the train."

All they had to do is step towards the door of their private cabin and step out on the train platform.

Căoméi had been here many times before and said, "I'm going

to take you to one of my favorite restaurants."

"Sure, lead the way."

Căoméi grabbed Tinougl's hand and guided him through the thinning crowd and out the front entrance of the train station to a public sidewalk that led to the crowded downtown area and the dozen or more restaurants that dotted the landscape.

All the restaurants that were vying for tourist credits, were handsomely decorated. One could get the feeling they were walking in a fairy tale by the looks of things.

In the midst of the more grander looking restaurant establishments was the "Dà Yǎnjìngshé" restaurant. There were numerous snake ornamentations on the architecture of the building.

Soon they were inside the restaurant seated when Căoméi said, "This restaurant specializes in snake and reptiles."

"Interesting."

"I know it sounds kind of icky, but the food is really nice with spectacular spices. I'm sure you will like it."

"I'll try anything once."

Căoméi offered to order for the two of them because she was most familiar with their dishes. Tinougl was soon enjoying the taste and aroma of Yǎnjìngshé steaks marinated in some of the galaxie's best chef's spiced sauces.

There he was eating farm raised vipers that would be extinct in 500 years. It tasted pretty good too, just like some farm raised birds he liked.

The drinks that Căoméi ordered was a fermented local fruit that tasted superb and the fifteen percent alcohol and psychoactive drugs that laced it wasn't noticed because of the marvelous taste.

The meal and the drink hit the spot and when Căoméi realized they were finished, suggested: "Let's grab one of those tourist Terrain Followers and have them take us for a quick excursion around this town and area."

"Let me grab the waiter to get the check."

"That's not necessary, they use facial recognition billing and I'm one of their routine clients. The bill and the tip are already paid."

"That's nice."

As soon as Căoméi stood up, the waiter quickly approached and said, "Thank you Madam Sěphámy for stopping in today. I hope you enjoyed the food."

"Let the chef know it was terrific."

"I certainly will."

The two exited the restaurant and along the street were several Terrain Follower tour guides ready to provide a spellbinding jaunt to the nearby wilderness.

Terrain Followers were a hybrid combination hovercraft and helicopter. They were restricted to fifty feet above any terrain or building as to not interfere with air traffic.

The body of the Terrain Followers were enclosed and quietly air conditioned and soundproof because the hovercraft and helicopter mechanisms were noisy.

In a lot of communities, the noise from the Terrain Followers would not be tolerated. The locals knew the reason why the restaurants that employed half of the towns people existed only because tourists came out to ride on the Terrain Followers and see the spectacular countryside that only had the railroad connection to the outside world. Without the railroad and Terrain Followers there would be no town.

To help mitigate the noise and make the locals slightly happier, the Terrain Followers did not engage the helicopter lift until they passed the outskirts of town. Until then they only operated the hovercraft mode. Once the Terrain Follower was about one quarter of a mile away from the town on an access road to remote homesteads, the helicopter mode was activated, and it lifted off into the air and made a 90-degree turn heading down into the deep canyon.

In modern times 500 years later, the town and the Terrain Followers no longer existed here. During the upcoming major conflict in 100 years, all the Terrain Followers were confiscated by the military to use in Alpine operations, and none were ever returned because most of them were destroyed by drones and shoulder launched kinetics and powerful lasers employed off enemy scout ships.

The Terrain Follower would stay in the helicopter mode when necessary and switch to only the hovercraft when unobstructed level ground was traveled.

Because the Terrain Follower had a great drop to experience, winglets were deployed, and the helicopter blades went into a neutral lift mode that had little impact on the Terrain Follower due to the acceleration caused by gravity. Down into the valley they went and in a brief period sped up past 100 miles per hour then the Terrain Follower leveled off traveling above treetops along the rim of the canyon where they got a bird's eye view of nature and the uninhabited area.

They could see wildlife of all types, from four legged mammals to countless numbers and types of birds, some nesting, others flying. The pilot slowly added pitch to the propellers as the Terrain Follower slowed from wind resistance and gravity.

The sight was awesome and even though the canyon had a similar appearance as it would in five hundred years, one thing was clear. A lot more animals lived in the valley before the grand global strife that was coming in one hundred years. Patches of rock formations appeared as outgrowths from the valley's vegetation.

The Terrain Follower dipped down and they went deeper down into the valley and soon approached a lake and landed on the lake switching to the hovercraft mode pushed along with the pusher propeller in the back. They traveled near the shoreline where they could see furry animals at a stream depositing water into the lake and those animals were expertly grabbing fish and eating them. They kept on going and it appeared they were heading for the edge of the lake where it abruptly ended, and the pilot casually flew off the end of it switching back to the terrain following mode with helicopter blades and there they were flying over the Krakatori Falls!

The Terrain Follower flew out and slowly curved back slowly lowering down the sides of the gigantic water fall where they observed it at a safe distance but significantly closer than what they could see on the train. They curved around again and flew right into a huge rainbow, larger than they had seen in their lifetimes.

The Terrain Follower slowly came down to the lake that formed at the end of the waterfall, and they were soon surrounded by a dozen boats and other Terrain Followers as people were there, sight seeing and enjoying the afternoon. Now back in the hovercraft mode, they followed the big circle of sightseeing craft taking it all in.

After a couple laps looking at the waterfall and the unique plant life that existed in a tropical rainforest created by the Krakatori Falls, the Terrain Follower soon went airborne again and flew down the canyon a few more miles gaining altitude and slowly flew up the opposite side of the canyon from the railroad tracks that was now bathed in sunlight taking it all in. The majestic sight created almost a spiritualistic feeling as they were enjoying something most people never would and in five hundred years, none of this infrastructure existed. As a result, Tinougl felt privileged.

At the area of the Canyon where it started expanding into the larger canyon in front of them, the Terrain Follower changed course going back to the other side and soon they were flying one hundred feet above the railroad tracks and followed it back into town. As they reached the edge of the town, the Terrain Follower edged down onto the access road and took it's passenger back to the area they left from and stopped there to let them out and pick up the next passengers.

Tinougl asked, "How much we owe you sir."

"The lady has already paid; you are good to go."

"Well thank you for the excellent ride."

"The pleasure was all mine."

After they exited the Terrain Follower, Căoméi asked, "would you like to go into some of the shops? We have a little time before we need to board the train."

"Sure."

Tinougl was thinking this might be a good place to pick up something to take back to the future with him to show his handlers as an artifact of his trip. He still didn't know what he could do to leave something they could find in the future in five hundred years.

It would be important the object be small simple and light and something he could carry with him and not have to worry about packing in the event he had to bug out quickly. It would be his source of memory to Căoméi, a gorgeous creature with an inner glow of luster of a woman that should not be neglected the way she is by her husband. Rich men like her husband grow tired of their mates because they get a constant stream of young gold diggers and only keep the spouse as a status symbol. But in the end, it was a mutual agreement. Tinougl assumed and he was very astute that Căoméi wasn't much of a performer and if he never touched her again the rest of his life, she would be ok with that too.

Eventually Tinougl found what he was looking for a small medalian that had an image of Krakatori Falls with the current year stamped on it.

"I'm going to get this, so I will always have something to remember you by."

Căoméi was very touched by Tinougl's sentiments, and each growing moment was learning more about him. "Let me get that for you," Căoméi said feeling it was an important item that linked them together.

"If you wish."

In a few minutes after Căoméi paid for the gift, the two left the shop. Căoméi said, "We can walk back to the train station now, I know a nice way to get there where we can go past this home where an elderly lady has the most beautiful flowers I'd like to see."

"Sure, if that's what you want."

CHAPTER THIRTEEN

CRIMINALS VERSES TIME TRAVEL SPY

Crime was starting to become evident in this tourist town and this route Cǎoméi was turning into an area where the criminals were accosting tourists to rob them and the police which were limited, didn't put enough priority on it, hoping passengers would just walk directly from the downtown area to the train station a short walk away.

In this rather auspicious moment, the two well dressed people were closing in on the home Cǎoméi wanted to see. As a good spy, Tinougl always paid attention to sound. It was like a sixth sense as such attention to detail had saved him times before. When he heard the footsteps that were quicker than a leisurely pace he knew a group was approaching quickly and turned around and saw the three men approaching at a pace that indicated they had nefarious activity in mind.

"Cǎoméi, keep walking we have trouble approaching us from behind, go as quickly as you can to the train station. I'll be there shortly."

Cǎoméi looked at Tinougl with horror in her face then quickly turned around and saw the trouble approaching about 10 feet away and closing fast.

The criminals didn't think the couple would hear them and respond so decisively. They noticed the woman kept walking and that's okay because it would be easier for them to rob her as one of the guys would break off and get her.

Tinougl knew the men were probably armed so he had to act fast. The element of surprise creates the advantage. The surprise was the hoodlums didn't know they were facing a galactic level spy who had dealt with far worse.

Tinougl knew the man stepping aside would accost Căoméi so to the surprise of the other two, that was his first target of opportunity and by the time the two other criminals were close enough to do any damage, Tinougl did a fast side step and delivered a lethal Karate Chop to the neck of the assailant which temporarily disabled him for a while then jerked back in the path of the other two troublemakers who saw how fast he disabled the other one and stopped dead in their tracks.

"You will regret doing that," one of the criminals stated as he pulled out his weapon and the other started to brandish his as well.

The only weapon Tinougl had the nice small medallion he felt in his pocket and grabbed it. Tinougl knew how to weaponize that medallion and immediately used it on the first criminal poking his eye causing him great pain and immediate loss of the ability to respond and then received a good kick that finished him. The second criminal now lunged at Tinougl and was quickly flipped and landed hard on the sidewalk suddenly feeling a lot of pain in his back. He also received a kick to disable him so that Tinougl could calmly walk by the beautiful flowerbeds and enjoy the incredible talent of the elderly woman who demonstrated the essence of Botany.

Căoméi looked back and saw half the action. She already knew how strong Tinougl was by feeling his muscles and his thrusts during love making and now she saw how quickly he disabled those criminals and she then knew there was more to this man that she didn't know about. That observation quickly triggered a fascination she now held towards Tinougl. Căoméi already developed an attachment towards Tinougl but watching him risk his life to protect her created a bond that would last forever. She now knew she had love for this marvelous stranger.

Tinougl walked briskly to Căoméi who wasn't wasting any time looking at the beautiful flowers and the two of them quickly made their way to the train station and moments later boarded their return train to Santorini de Shénshèng.

The woman who planted the beautiful flowers called the police who quickly descended upon the crime scene and discovered the three disabled criminals. Based on surveillance video they were able to corroborate with the elderly woman's statements, they arrested the three criminals and took them away and started looking for the two involved in the altercation.

Based on the police investigation the train was held and since the surveillance video showed the couple coming at a time expected to the train station from the location of the altercation, the police boarded the train and immediately went to the cabin where Tinougl and Căoméi had reservations. The police entered the passenger car and asked for identification.

"I'm Sěphámy bon Căoméi and if you do not leave my private rail car immediately, I will contact my husband and you all will lose your jobs."

Before there was any aggressive movement the lead detective directed the other police force to exit the train and he would discuss the matter with the two.

"I'm sorry for intruding but there are three guys we just found that have serious injuries and we need to know what happened."

"My husband is going to be extremely upset that we were attacked today by those criminals because you police are not doing a good enough job to protect the public, if I didn't have someone with me who could protect me, I might be dead now."

"I'm sorry what happened but I need to ask you a few questions."

"I've already explained what happened. We were accosted because you do not police that street effectively and my husband will be contacting the governor of this province to find out why I was almost injured by those three criminals."

"I'm very sorry Madam, I only wanted to ask you a few questions."

"Here are your answers in advance: three criminals attacked us that you should have prevented. You need to figure out why that happened. It gets back to your negligence and failure to do basic policing."

"I'm very sorry all this happened." The police official said as he started reading his personal communicator which said this woman is a VIP, get off the train immediately."

The police detective then said, "I'm sorry about your experience here today, we will take care of the matter."

"Thank you."

"You are welcome."

The detective left the train private cabin and moments later the train started moving. Tinougl now knew he was in serious trouble as he would soon be discussed and exposed in ways he could not control. It was now more essential than ever before to leave the planet, get to the moon to seduce the Wánměi de Mòlìhuā and get to the Konhagar planet to verify his hunch.

Once the train was underway, Căoméi looked in a fearful manner at

Tinougl and asked, "Who are you really?"

"What do you mean by that?"

"Those three guys were very bad guys. You stopped them so quickly. No normal person could do that. I've felt your muscles as we made love. I know you are not a normal person tell me who you are. Your secret is safe with me."

Tinougl knew he was trapped by a very powerful woman who could hurt him if he didn't answer the questions appropriately and thus offered a statement. "Căoméi, if I confessed the truth, I seriously doubt you would believe it."

"Tinougl, my fair love, you have awakened me to many things I never knew in my lifetime already, I assure you I will not disbelieve you. I want to know, and I think you owe me an explanation."

"There are some things in life you really should not know."

"But I want to know."

"Alright, will you keep this confidential?"

"The fact I'm married to one of the most powerful bankers in the galaxy means you do not need to worry about me keeping it confidential."

"Alright but it may cause you a lot of grief."

"I need to know."

"Alright, I will tell you but first I must admit I've developed an emotional bond to you."

"Tinougl I already know that. I know you love me. Don't worry about that, I want you to tell me."

"This may sound rather bizarre, but since you insist on the truth, I will give it to you."

"I insist."

"I'm a time traveller."

"What does that mean?"

"It means I came her from five hundred years in the future."

"So, you know what's going to happen to our worlds?"

"Not fully, there is a lot of lost details."

"What's going to happen to us?"

"During your lifetime, not much, it will be business as usual."

"Then what?"

"Your offspring will have a difficult life."

"Why is that?"

The future is subject to change. In due time they will discover why."

"If it's true that you are a time traveller and my love, why will you not tell me what's going to happen?"

"Enjoy your life. You will not experience the negative things that develop that occur."

"I've enjoyed you and when the train takes us back, we will have to act as if nothing happened for our mutual protection because Spicey is a *vindictive bitch*."

"I understand. Would you like to do it one more time now on the train?"

"I've never done it on the train before."

"Let me show you how."

"Please do."

Tinougl stood up and said, "Get up on the sofa on your hands and knees."

Căoméi did as he asked. There was plenty of room on the sofa. Tinougl positioned himself behind Căoméi and lifted her dress and slid her under garments down. then the undid his trousers and dropped them down enough to

get them out of the way. He was instantly invigorated observing her womanhood and his erection immediately followed. He then checked her to see if Căoméi was well enough lubricated or he would have applied some saliva.

Tinougl was delighted to discover additional lubrication was not necessary and slowly entered her and very slowly pushed the full length of his manliness into her and felt the tip of his penis hit her cervix. He now knew how far to thrust as to not cause her any pain. Then he went to town giving her strong thrusts.

The pleasure Căoméi now felt was unsurpassable. She was with this handsome man who she really loved who had saved her life from those three criminals in a rather spectacular manner. She saw some of it as she turned around in sheer terror and saw how efficiently he dispatched three very tough guys who made the mistake of attacking the wrong person.

One of them had to be airlifted to a hospital to save his eye. The other two had the greatest pain they felt in their lives and one of them lost a testicle. The police knew who had injured them gravely, but since that person was with this VIP's wife, they assumed he was her security detail and knew better than to press the point because her husband might investigate their negligence in policing the area. Plus, the merchants in the town were not happy with these three criminals that had a material impact on tourism. All three men were subsequently sent on a train back to the city with instructions to never come back.

Căoméi quickly reached an orgasm. In the manner Tinougl was performing he was rubbing her G spot and vibrating her clitoris in the most pleasing fashion. Tinougl could feel her orgasm as her vaginal muscles tightened in a manner that increased his own gratification and could not hold back and gave her his full load. For a while he just held his position as the vaginal muscles were oscilating in a psychophysical reaction to the large deposit now adding another layer of pleasure to the event.

Căoméi's endorphins were spinning around in her head in ways she was unaccustomed. Her surreal experience made this adventure one that she would never forget. She would cherish Tinougl for the rest of her life. If for some reason her crappy husband divorced her to make way with one of those twenty-year olds he often had affairs with, she would seek out Tinougl and propose marriage and offer her fortune to him if he stayed with her. She knew she had fallen in love with this man, but she also knew the great danger she put him in. Either her husband or Spicey could find out and then bad things might happen.

Tinougl pulled out and pulled her underwear back up into position and he then reassembled his own clothing as if nothing happened.

"I need to use the restroom," Căoméi said as she knew she needed to clean herself up as she felt Tinougl's load was extreme, unlike any she ever experienced in her life.

After she took care of business in their private bathroom she came back and saw her lovely prince sitting there enjoying the view facing the canyon. All the passenger cars had their picture window always facing the Great Tóng Canyon while traveling in both directions.

Căoméi sat down next to Tinougl and put her arm around him and said, "No man has ever pleased me as much as you have today. I will never forget you."

"I will never forget you either. The gift you bought me saved our lives today." Tinougl didn't elaborate how and Căoméi didn't want to know as she saw briefly him besting the three men very spontaneously.

It was a special moment as the train wound it's way down the hill going almost as slow as when it was climbing through the canyon. The train was dynamic breaking, and the speeds were kept down for a couple reasons. First was to give the passengers a nice view of the scenery, especially as they were passing Krakatori Falls, but also to prevent derailments from dangerous speed if the dynamic breaking failed, they could hard break the train and keep it from reaching derailment speeds.

The time passed too quickly for Căoméi. She savored every minute of the remainder of the trip, and then while they passed Krakatori Falls again, she indelibly etched the moment into her thoughts, of viewing such a sight while holding her prince charming. She intuitively could feal Tinougl reciprocating the splendid emotions and she knew she had just done of the best things in her lifetime. She would now think differently about trains. In future years as she traveled again up past Krakatori Falls she would have sorrowed the minute she saw the falls because Tinougl was not with her. Nobody would ever touch her in ways this fine gentleman had. Tinougl set the bar for Căoméi's romantic heart.

Eventually the train reached level ground and sped up and took a short while to get them to the train station so they could return to the Cuìlù Resort Hotel.

When they arrived at the resort, they went their separate ways. Căoméi went to her penthouse and Tinougl went to the Dining Hall and hoped to see the beautiful singer Wánměi de Mòlìhuā.

Căoméi would not be coming down to the Dining Hall this evening in case Spicey returned and Sparky had a big mouth. She would find in the days to come, Spicey would not be coming back until after Tinougl vanished.

It was still somewhat early. Tinougl wasn't the least bit hungry for food or sex, but he had to contact Wánměi de Mòlìhuā to further his plans. He wanted to leave the planet before Spicey returned or she possibly could spoil his plans.

Tinougl quickly found his preferred table and the musicians were already performing with Wánměi de Mòlìhuā singing with her beautiful voice. She perked up the minute she saw Tinougl and was looking forward to her break time that was coming up in just a few minutes after they finished this last song in a series.

Meanwhile, the Dining Hall waitress Madalyn bon Donkers was serving Tinougl another Chamboree del Pàrà Měilì. The visual gave Wánměi de Mòlìhuā the notion, everything was in order, and she would soon be enjoying her prince charming.

Eventually the break time occurred and Wánměi de Mòlìhuā joined Tinougl for a drink and a short conversation.

"Nice to see you."

"Thank you."

"Are you working tomorrow?"

"No, I have the next four days off. What do you have in mind?"

"I would like to take you to a resort on Plexis de Chiveltros."

"Do you promise to be a gentleman and not do something I don't let you?"

"I always prefer the woman make the first move."

"That's what I like, to be in control of the situation."

"I'll reserve you a private room so you will have no fear of me placing any demands on you."

"That will not be necessary, but I will want my own bed, so you need to get a room with two beds."

"Absolutely."

The two talked about trivial things, as nothing could be as exciting as the expectations for tomorrow.

Soon it was time for Wánměi de Mòlìhuā to start singing again.

"I'm going to go up to my room and pack up for tomorrow and get some good sleep. In the morning when you are ready, could you meet me out front of the resort?"

"Sure, that sounds good. What time would you like?"

"Come when you are ready and call me on your communicator and I'll come right down."

"Okay Tinougl, see you tomorrow."

Sparky just took her seat at the Barracuda's table and was wondering where Spicey and Schemer were. She observed Tinougl get up and leave. She never saw him again for a long time and sometimes wondered what happened to him and why Spicey and Schemer never discussed Tinougl.

The three Amigos would have to discover new targets of opportunity.

Tinougl returned to his resort hotel room and notified Tondron, "I'll be checking out of the resort in the morning."

"Are you finished with your work here?"

"Yes."

"Will you be returning home now?"

"Yes."

"Do you want me to make travel arrangements for you?"

"No that will not be necessary but thank you anyway."

"Your bill for your stay has been settled, you may leave tomorrow when you are ready."

"Thank you."

"Master Tinougl, you may think of me as just artificial intelligence, but Guāiqiǎo and I are programmed by the greatest computational and communications experts that ever existed. We have emotional subroutines to help us better deal with customers. I want you to know that during your stay here I learned a lot from you and determined I like you. I hope that one day in the future you come back to the Cuìlǜ Resort Hotel for a visit so that I can see you again and enjoy you as a friend."

"Thank you Tondron, the feeling is mutual."

"You are most welcome Master Tinougl."

"I'm going to use the bathroom then take a nice long hot bath afterwards."

"We will be ready to help you."

While in the bathroom sitting on the throne, Tinougl went to transportation reservations and booked tomorrow's flight for two around lunch time to the moon Plexis de Chiveltros under his name. He still possessed far more credits than he could ever use, but the reason to have all that wealth with him was to buy his freedom if necessary or bribe someone for critical information. After checking the half dozen resorts on Plexis de Chiveltros, he selected and reserved a room for four days with double beds. After taking care of his business, Tinougl started filling the bathtub and undressed and began enjoying a nice hot bath to wash off the residue of todays events. He reflected on it all and knew he had touched Cǎoméi's heart who would soon grow melancholic when he disappeared.

Spicey indured her terrible husband for a week and feared what kind of deadly diseases he might have picked up from those green skinned women and gave her. She really had no idea why her husband even wanted to have sex with her since she knew he had returned from multiple orgies where no such thing as protection was used.

After the few sexual encounters before her husband departed again, she cleaned herself out with some of the best pharmaceuticals available and hoped no deadly pathogens were left behind. Finally, after a week, she was able to travel back to Santorini de Shénshèng where her second home in a long-term lease existed in the Cuìlǜ Resort Hotel Penthouse near the other two Barracudas.

It never dawned on her that Tinougl had fled. The other two Barracudas were strangely silent about the young "stud muffin."

She first met up with Sparky and a few days later, Schemer showed up in the Dining Hall, and the two didn't have much to say. There certainly weren't any men that arrived for a while in the same stature of Tinougl. Sparky knew quite a bit more than what she was willing to reveal, because her omissions alone would put her at odds with Spicey, the terribly *vindictive bitch*. She suspected Schemer had probably tasted Tinougl's forbidden fruit, and it seemed rather strange Tinougl departed the day after Schemer ostensibly had a romantic soirée with him.

The fact the other two women never discussed Tinougl left Spicey to believe the man had probably finished his work here and simply returned to his planet. In a way she was furious that her neglectful philander husband had insisted on some happy time with her, because it prevented her from establishing some permanent relationship with Tinougl. And now she had no way of tracking him down without possibly triggering interest in her husband's spies who got paid lavishly to deal with anything that could erupt in scandal. They were already checking out leads on a possible soirée at the concert and the "Top of the World" restaurant. Unfortunately, all leads ended because whoever it was disappeared and left no breadcrumbs behind to follow.

Another interesting development was the singer that seemed to be infatuated with Tinougl disappeared about the same time he did. When Spicey confronted one of the Musicians about *what happened to the other singer?* They simply did not know why, but at the end of her four days off she simply quit the group and they hired a new singer. None of them had any idea where she went nor did their manager. But it was not uncommon for a talented singer to simply leave and travel to another planet and pick up a new gig. But it did add to the mystery that the two seemed to have disappeared at the same time.

Chapter Fourteen

Take her to the Moon!

After Tinougl's bath he said he wanted to sleep now, and he would pack his belongings in the morning.

During the night, Guāiqiǎo dry cleaned the clothes he wore and since he now had more clothes that could fit in his backpack, he received some of the benefits for resort guests that ran into this situation and provided him with new reconditioned luggage.

What happens is some guests leave behind luggage and never come back to get it because they live off world. The luggage and contents are stored for a while, but after several months when the guest does not contact them to forward the luggage and contents, the resort must dispose of it. They make note of the contents in case there was something of value which was typically not the case. The luggage is cleaned and prepared for future guests who needed extra for new purchases and the lost and found clothes were typically given to charities, and they often were not of much value as they did not adhere to local customs.

Guāiqiǎo who liked Tinougl as much as Tondron selected luggage that fit the size of what Tinougl needed for his extra clothes. All his dry-cleaned clothes and laundered under garments were staged for packing in the morning sitting besides his backpack.

In the morning after a really wholesome sleep, Tinougl awoke happy knowing he was entering a new phase of his mission and getting closer to the answers that would allow him to go back to the future.

It was late morning before Wánměi de Mòlìhuā contacted Tinougl who was starting to get worried they would be late for their flight and be stuck on the planet an additional day.

"Hello, this is Mòlìhuā."

"Are you downstairs?"

"No, but I will be arriving in Ten minutes."

"Okay, I'll be there waiting for you."

"See you then."

Tinougl then said to Tondron after he hung up his communicator, "All right guys I'm ready to leave now. Thank you for all you did for me."

"It was a pleasure, Master Tinougl."

About that time Guāiqiǎo walked out of his storage room and said,

"Tinougl, I really enjoyed you being here. I will miss you."

"Thank you for all you did for me."

Guāiqiǎo an inquisitive robot was always studying humans held out his hand to Tinougl to shake it. Tinougl thought it was kind of strange but grabbed Guāiqiǎo's hand and shook it. The robot was pleased this human treated him more than just some existential being. It gave him hope for the future of humanity.

"May I help carry your backpack to the door?"

"Sure."

Guāiqiǎo grabbed the backpack and walked to the door and opened it. As Tinougl got outside the doorway he turned back towards Guāiqiǎo who then handed him the backpack.

"Goodbye Tinougl."

"Thank you Guāiqiǎo. I will miss you guys."

"We shall miss you as well Master Tinougl."

Tinougl turned and walked towards the elevator and soon was outside the front of the resort taking it all in and reflecting on all the events for the past few days. He had as much activity as he had on almost any other spy missions and just like the rest had to deal with danger and risk when the three criminals attacked him.

While he reflected what seemed like a small eternity, the very chipper Wánměi de Mòlǐhuā traveling semi light since she was only going to be gone four days and knew she could buy what she wanted at the resort if she didn't bring enough.

"Hello."

"You look well."

"Going on a vacation tends to make people look happy."

"Shall we go?"

"Certainly."

Tinougl walked to a waiting Limo parked for the next guest to depart which now was Tinougl and his lovely friend Wánměi de Mòlǐhuā. He got a clean getaway. There was no Spicey or Schemer to soil the departure, and he knew how vindictive women could be cruel and make Wánměi de Mòlǐhuā feel terrible including calling her names like "Tramp."

The resort bell hop waiting by the Limo asked, "Would you like me to put your luggage in the trunk?"

"Sure."

The limo driver heard the statements and flipped the switch that opened the trunk automatically. The bell hop put the luggage in the trunk then opened the passenger door and the couple got in and he shut the door for them.

Having been through this ritual many times the bellhop who personally knew the driver nodded at him and he flipped the switch to close the trunk and then drove off.

"Where to sir?" the driver asked through the intercom."

"Take us to the Space Transportation Center."

Even though the Limo ride took fifteen minutes, it seemed shorter they were soon at the entrance to the Space Transportation Center. They had plenty of time so there was no rush, they could simply walk along with their luggage to the departure counter where the space transport employee immediately got facial recognition of the couple with different names. Otherwise, she would not have had to ask the question: "Are the two of you traveling together?"

That answer immediately qualified the reservation prepaid and their names were then electronically tagged to their seats.

"The flight is on schedule and will be departing out of gate 11."

"Thank you."

"I'll take your luggage now."

"We appreciate that."

"Your luggage will be provided to you at your destination."

"Thanks."

Since the transportation company took everything including the backpack,

Tinougl's hands were free and as they walked through the Space Transportation Center, he grabbed Mòlìhuā's hand, and they walked as if they were a couple. In reality, they were a new couple.

The two leisurely walked to gate eleven exhibiting no care in the world. The reason why it took Mòlìhuā to get ready is her best friend worked hard with her makeup to give Tinougl an impression. Mòlìhuā had very nice physical features and probably didn't need any makeup, but the added effort would indelibly print this image of her in Tinougl's thoughts.

It increases a man's self-esteem when he's with a beautiful woman.

Strangers looking at the couple would think it was a lovely combination. If Tinougl was wearing a tank top and shorts, the women would know why this beautiful lady had a liking for him. But Tinougl's magnificent body was one of those mysteries that were yet to unfold for Mòlìhuā.

By the time they reached gate eleven, passengers were boarding. The flight attendant simply looked for a green light that indicated the passenger could board the space craft. If a red light turned on there would be an inquiry of sorts.

Tinougl gestured Mòlìhuā to go first through the entrance and the flight attendant simply said, "Have a nice flight."

Tinougl stepped through the entrance and the light turned green and the flight attendant repeated, "Have a nice flight."

They walked horizontal through a hallway that led up to the doorway of the space craft and as they entered the space craft the flight attendant informed them their seat numbers, all based on facial recognition software.

Moments later they were seated, harness strap clicked in place and ready to go. It seemed like a short while all the passengers that were going taking up more than half the seats were aboard, and all the flight attendants were in the spacecraft and the door shut.

Moments later the captain said on the intercom, "Ladies and Gentlemen, thank you for choosing Plexis Space Lines. Your flight will take approximately one hour."

Moments later they could feel movement as the space launcher and space craft pushed away from the terminal. Electric wheels did all the movement on the ground saving fuel.

The Space Launcher traveled down the runway access to the end of the runway. The six large jet engines would get the jet airborne to about 60,000 feet then it would launch the space craft, then return to the airport or catch another space craft returning. On a return flight the space craft would dock on the back of the space launcher that would land and take it back to a gate to prepare for the next flight.

The Space Launcher flew straight for 20 minutes before it reached the launch altitude. As soon as the rocket engines were ignited and ready to throttle up the Space Launcher released it and the two craft separated. People inside the Space Craft could feel the G Forces as the rocket engines throttled up and in two minutes reached max-Q. There was no main engine cutoff like a standard rocket, it would just throttle down to maintain minor thrust for navigating precisely to the lander.

The moon landers were different. They were electric catapults that launched and landed the space craft on a runway several miles long. As the space craft approached the electric lander in the precise geometry, robotic gripers would attach as the lander matched speeds with the spacecraft. Once the attachment was affirmed and interlocks closed, electric magnets like maglev would slow the space craft down and at the end of the ramp, the electric landers would turn off the landing strip and with the use of electric motors in the wheels drive over to a terminal to unload the passengers.

In one hour, Tinougl and Mòlìhuā exited the space craft and walked to the baggage claim area where supervised handlers handed each luggage item to travellers all based on facial recognition.

Tickets and baggage receipts were a thing of the distant past.

Having received their luggage, they were soon at the front

entrance noticeably feeling the difference in gravity, but the air seemed the same. This was a vegetated moon that had ample plant growth to rejuvenate all the oxygen they needed. The biology of the planet was very constant, however development was limited to keep it that way. The only construction allowed was in relation to supporting the resorts on the moon.

The electric Limo soon had them on their way. About a mile parallel and East of the space port was the "Strip."

The Strip is where all the resorts are located. This was zoned in accordance with environmental ordinances to limit this area for development to make sure the flora abounded to maintain the atmosphere and climate of the moon. Settlements around the moon were sparse and highly regulated and mostly to support park rangers. Ninety Nine percent of the population lived on the Strip.

Just like the Cuìlù Resort Hotel, the Grand Plexis de Chiveltros was all facial recognition and when Tinougl approached the check in counter, the receptionist simply said, "Your room is ready, the elevator will take you to your floor and direct you to your room. Do you need any help with your luggage?"

"No, that will not be necessary."

"Enjoy your stay Tinougl and Wánměi de Mòlìhuā."

"Thank you."

The beautiful receptionist had seen many flings arrive in her day and assumed in fifteen minutes Tinougl would have Wánměi de Mòlìhuā screaming with the perfect coitus. Her assumptions were wrong, because the last thing in the world Tinougl was going to do is spook the girl that may be his only means of getting the information he needed so he could return to the future.

The two went up to their Grand Plexis de Chiveltros Resort room. The elevator stopped on the proper floor and announced, "you room is three rooms down on the right with the green light now lit above the door."

The couple entered the room with their luggage which wasn't that much and closed the door behind them.

As requested, they had a double bed, and the curtains were open exposing the beautiful view away from the Strip and the Space Port. Tinougl had been here five hundred years into the future, but the Grand Plexis de Chiveltros Resort no longer existed, and the moon was now totally different having been a garrison for a few years during the great war that left it's ugly mark. Half of the vegetation was burned off the planet with all the combat, however, society was working hard to restore it's previous splendor, but unfortunately half the animals were extinct and gone, from the consequences of war.

Chapter Fifteen

Swimming on the Moon

"After we unpack is there anything you would like to do?" Wánměi de Mòlìhuā asked.

"Maybe we can go down for a swim. When I booked the resort, I looked at the amenities, and their pool is advertised as the best on the moon."

"I didn't bring a swimsuit with me."

"I'm sure our room host can fix you up with something."

As expected, the artificial intelligence listening to the guests to determine what they needed to enhance their happiness of the visit suddenly appeared in a holograph.

"Hello Tinougl and Mòlìhuā," the AI said understanding how people from Santorini de Shénshèng liked to be referred to as a matter of custom.

"Hello," Tinougl instinctively responded.

"My name is Milton. I am your personal aid for your stay. We also have a room robot for you named Yuánběn."

Just like back at the Cuìlǜ Resort Hotel, a robot came out of it's storage room and appeared looking slightly better esthetically than Guāiqiǎo. The Grand Plexis de Chiveltros was a premier resort hotel for newlyweds and lovers going on a quick getaway to allow them to exercise their romance in the privacy off the planet where few people they knew would spot them. They raked in so much profit they could afford to have better facilities than down on the planet and the striking difference in the robot was amazing. Guāiqiǎo didn't look too bad, but Yuánběn appeared to be as human and real as anything Tinougl had seen in the world of robotics even five hundred years into the future. He was quite amazed with what he saw, and this of course would be articulated in his reports on his adventure.

"Pleased to meet you Tinougl and Mòlìhuā."

"Thank you."

"Mòlìhuā, I understand you need a bathing suit?"

"Yes." Mòlìhuā responded.

"Tinougl do you also need a bathing suit?"

"Yes, I do thank you."

"Milton will now show you choices of bathing suits to pick from which we'll provide you with a bathing robe and slippers."

Milton's image vanished and soon there were a series of models wearing male and female bathing suits in a high-resolution holograph.

Mòlìhuā was quick to respond, "I'll take the one in red."

Tinougl soon afterwards said, "give me the one in black."

Yuánběn quickly responded, "Your bathing suits are on the way."

"You didn't ask for my size," Mòlìhuā stated.

"Mòlìhuā, I did special computer imaging of your body. I can see in wavelenths you cannot see and just like an X-ray machine I have the exact dimensions of your body. Your bathing suit will fit very well."

"Oh really, thank you."

Tinougl already experienced such treatment at the Cuilǜ Resort Hotel and knew it would fit and didn't bother mentioning it.

Thanks to the wireless network Yuánběn and Milton shared, Milton quickly said, your swimsuIt's will be available momentarily. Yuánběn went into his storage room, and like other similar resort hotels had the miniature elevator that sent up the swimsuIt's from the support staff which he retrieved and took them to the two resort guests.

Tinougl suggested, "Mòlìhuā you can go ahead and change first in the bathroom, I'll change out here."

"Alright."

Mòlìhuā took the bathing suit and went into the bathroom and changed. Meanwhile Tinougl changed standing next to the table by one of the beds. By the time Mòlìhuā completed changing and walked out into the room Tinougl was changed and ready to go to the pool.

The robot Yuánběn handed each of them a swim robe, then walked back into his storage room promptly and came back with swimming pool sandals that would prevent them from slipping and falling thanks to the non-skid on the bottoms. "Here are your sandals."

One size was obviousy larger than the other which he handed to Tinougl.

Milton said, "Have fun at the pool," as the two guests wearing their swim robes walked toward the resort door.

In about five minutes the couple found a nice soft recliner near the pools edge. There were approximately twenty guests there and most of them were younger than Tinougl, either honeymooners or off on a holiday to engage in *rarefied pleasures on a theme from*

Paganini.

After getting situated, Tinougl said, "I'm going to swim some laps. Want to join me?"

"Perhaps when you are almost done. I want to get some suntan first."

"Alright."

Tinougl walked down the steps of the pool and decided he needed to ensure his physical conditioning and made a goal to swim 30 laps around the large pool.

Mòlìhuā knew these expensive resorts had everything and saw some waiters standing by to provide services to the clientele and she signaled one lady who came promptly.

"What can I do for you dear?"

"I didn't plan ahead and didn't bring any suntan lotion."

"Not a problem I will get you some. Would you like some soft hands to help put it on?"

"Perhaps on my back."

"Alright." The woman left an in just about three minutes came back with this very pretty, and a young lady carrying suntan lotion and a towel.

"This is Lunsaree who will assist you with your suntan lotion."

"Thank you."

Lunsaree being obviousy intuitive about guest etiquette issues and handed Mòlìhuā the suntan lotion and stood by to assist. After Mòlìhuā got the suntan lotion everywhere except the back, handed the lotion back to Lunsaree and asked, "Could you please put this on my back?"

"It will be my pleasure Madam."

Lunsaree gently applied the lotion all over Mòlìhuā's back including behind her bikini strap and down near her buttocks.

"Thank you very much," Mòlìhuā stated when the effort was completed.

"My pleasure, Madam."

Lunsaree then placed the suntan lotion on the table next to Mòlìhuā's recliner and said, "Let us know if we can do anything for you. I'm leaving the lotion on the table in case you want to put more on after a swim."

"Thank you."

"You are welcome."

Lunsaree then departed and went back inside the resort where she was probably on call for many other similar tasks.

Mòlìhuā then set back and started watching Tinougl swim the laps. His wakeup calls the day before with the three criminals gave him reason to rethink his physical fitness.

He wasn't showing off to Mòlìhuā. He was doing what he felt was essential for his own survival.

Amazingly this resort had many attributes similar to the Cuìlù Resort Hotel, including a SPA by the swimming pool.

Mòlìhuā subconsciously counted the laps that Tinougl swam. After about twenty laps she thought he surely must be done so she walked over and started swimming. She could not swim nearly as fast as Tinougl and made no attempts to do so so she just leisurely swam from one side to the other and back, about a quarter the distance each lap Tinougl swam. Mòlìhuā was still counting and as he was nearing thirty laps, she was slowly becoming stunningly amazed.

After thirty laps, Tinougl got out of the pool and laid back in his soft recliner feeling a lot of pain in his muscles.

Mòlìhuā followed Tinougl out of the water and joined him. His muscles truly ached, and he knew Mòlìhuā had no way of knowing how much it hurt.

In the back of his mind, Tinougl kept on thinking about Denettk and her massage and so he felt he needed it badly and said, "I want to get a massage, would you like to come with me and get one at the same time?"

"Sure, if that's what you want."

"Us walk over to the SPA, I'm sure they do massages."

"Alright."

In a little more than fifty steps was the entrance to the SPA.

Just like the Cuìlǜ Resort Hotel, there was a beautiful receptionist who asked, "May I help you?"

"We would like to get a massage. Can we be in the same room together and get it simultaneously?"

"Absolutely, we have several rooms set up for couples."

"That's what we want."

"Do you want a male or a female massage specialist?"

"Female of course. I don't want another man to touch her," Tinougl said with a poker face.

"Alright, please come this way."

They were led into a room with several massage tables and a moment later the female massage technician arrived, and the receptionist introduced them. She already knew who they were based on facial recognition software and said:

"Janelle, this is Tinougl and Mòlìhuā who want a massage together."

"Alright, Jessicar will be here in a moment, so we'll have two people doing the work."

"Alright. Enjoy your massage," the receptionist said then left the room."

Moments later Jessicar entered the room and Janelle introduced her to the couple.

"Before we get started, we want you two to come with us in the next room where we have a bath that we will bathe you first so you will not feel too much pain when we massage you."

This was going to be a stressful moment for Mòlìhuā who now knew Tinougl was going to see her body for the first time. She was mildly apprehensive and hoped he didn't reject her based on what he saw. She clearly underestimated herself.

Tinougl had been nude in front of women and female spies in the line of duty, so this did not phase him in the least bit. He could care less how Mòlìhuā appeared because he was going to seduce her irregardless and his motive was to get to her planet where he could dig for critical mission information.

The water started filling automatically and after Tinougl took off his swimming attire, he stepped down into the large bath that could easily accommodate 6 or more people and sometimes it did.

He purposely did not look or stare at Mòlìhuā who appreciated his gentlemanliness. She knew if he wanted, he could turn his head and see the full essence of her nudity.

Even though it was assumed they were a couple, Jessicar still gave Mòlìhuā a small tow to cover up her privates. Her breasts would be exposed but she realized in a day or so Tinougl would probably engage her in romantic splendid euphoria, so there was no point in hiding her breasts from him knowing what ultimately was going to transpire.

Just like at the other resert there were multiple underwater solid chairs that allowed the person doing the massage get close, wash their hair, and do some preliminary messaging. Janelle dumped the contents of a plastic container into the water and the jets that turned on quickly spread the substance that soon gave the two a nice tingling sensation. The two women were almost nude only covering their bottoms and in a brief period their breasts which were nicely shaped were rubbing up against the two clients. And they didn't care because they had to get close to do what they needed to do.

Each person got a hair wash which was mainly to get the swimming pool chemicals out of the hair, so the technicians didn't have to smell it. After so many massages of swimmers it gets old fast smelling the chemicals.

After the hair wash and some messaging Tinougl and Mòlìhuā were invited to get out of the bath where they were dried off and towels put around them. Meanwhile Janelle and Jessicar dried themselves and when they toweled themselves, Tinougl got full body looks which the women didn't mind and would have invited a private session under the most auspicious occasion had Tinougl not been with Mòlìhuā.

Both women were somewhat dazzled at Tinougl's muscles which were even more apparent after the stress of swimming. Swimming did a great job of pumping up his biceps and his six-pack abs. They were led into the other room and the massage tables with fresh linen were waiting for them. "Please lay on your backs on these two massage tables so we have plenty of space to work and do not bump into each other," Janelle directed.

The two complied and Mòlìhuā could not help but show her body to Tinougl as she climbed up on the table. Tinougl liked what he saw and was relieved that he would not have to seduce a woman that wasn't appealing.

The two massage technicians went to work covering them with an oil like Tinougl experienced back down on the planet. Then they started working the muscles. Thanks to the bath chemicals laced with opioids and cannabinoids, the rough treatment the women gave them only caused pain for a brief period. It was an oscillation between pain and satisfaction repeatedly.

Almost like the perfect choreography the couple was shifted to one of their sides and more work continued. Tinougl knew his muscles were sore when he arrived in the SPA and was already feeling the results and was now only fifty percent tight. Jessicar working on Tinougl wished she had been alone with Tinougl because his body was a masterpiece she rarely saw. If his girlfriend wasn't there, she would have aroused him then mounted him and pleased the two of them. But such activity was not going to happen today.

Janelle worked over Mòlìhuā really good who felt the pain almost to a frightening level, but thanks to the bath came down from the pain after a brief period of time. Soon they were flipped on their other sides and stretched like they never experienced before. It was a killer pain for a while, but it quickly subsided with the help of the opioids and cannabinoids in the massage oil. The oil also helped the massage technicians and prevented pain in their hands. One thing was certain, these two women had very strong hands from their occupation.

Finally, they were put on their stomachs and the most enjoyable parts of the massage now happened even though there were spurts of seriously painful episodes. And just as they were reaching the point of almost fearing terror, the massage technicians then said, "Alright we need to go back into the tub and wash off all that oil."

The second body wash was for two reasons. They received more pain relievers through the skin and the resort didn't want people taking that oil back to the swimming pool where it would mix with the chemicals and cause the need to replace the chemicals more often.

During the bath Mòlìhuā showed no modesty whatsoever and made no attempt to cover anything up because she knew Tinougl and her would soon consummate the friendship and he had seen her nude already, though he was very polite about it.

When they were all done, the massage technicians said, "We'll walk you to the receptionist."

"Thank you."

As they approached the receptionist she asked, "How was it?"

"Very good," Tinougl responded.

"It's what I needed," Mòlìhuā stated in a very friendly manner with an effectious smile.

The couple left the SPA and Tinougl suggested, "We probably need to get something to eat. I do not want to eat pool snacks, us go change and find a restaurant to eat."

"Great idea," Mòlìhuā responded as though she wondered if he planned to deflower her after they went back to the room."

They went up to the room in their bathing suits and Milton asked, "Would you like to take a bath or shower?"

"No, we just had a bath at the spa after we received a massage."

This time Mòlìhuā didn't bother going into the bathroom to change, she took off her bikini and handed it to Yuánběn who was suddenly standing there to take care of their wet bathing suits.

In a brief period, they were dressed and ready to go out. The bathing suits were on their way to the laundry to be prepared for their use again if they wanted.

The couple then left the room and took the elevator down and walked out the front entrance to explore the strip.

They were not in a hurry to find any restaurant, they let their curiousity drive them.

They eventually found a restaurant that seemed appealing to Mòlǐhuā and went inside. The Maitra d' set them by a window where they could have a nice mountain view with an artificial duck pond about 50 feet in front of them to add to the image.

Tinougl always kept situational awareness as almost second nature survying everyone around him. About twenty-five feet away was a gentleman with a glamorous lady, obviousy lovers. With a photographic memory, Tinougl immediately knew who the man was. It was none other than the intergalactic banker, Frederick bon Stoffengar (Spicey's husband). Frederick bon Stoffengar had no idea what Tinougl looked like, but he was a person of interest Frederick was investigating over the allegations his wife might have done the horizontal tango with him. Frederick didn't even know the alleged person's name or what he did, and the person seemed to disappear while he had Madam Estele bon Stoffengar (aka Spicey) on ice.

Tinougl saw all he needed to see to grow sympathetic with Spicey. It was now clear how that hole situation existed. Tinougl wondered, *why don't they just get divorced and go their separate ways?*

The problem is an intergalactic banker could not afford to have the appearance of a scandal with his wife. His business partners and clients didn't mind him banging the bimbo he was with, but they feared a vindictive wife and worse yet one that might have pillow talk with her lover boy. Frederick bon Stoffengar had to nip it in the bud before there was and suggestions of scandal.

But then when loverboy disappeared suddenly and had not been around in a few weeks the fear subsided as it was now viewed just an opportunistic hit and run. And if that's all it was, Spicey getting her rocks off which was seldom, he didn't care.

Tinougl knew not to get observed by the man which meant he could not spend too much time analysing him and instead turned to the duck pond and made casual conversation with Mòlìhuā.

The dinner menu was excellent, and they each settled on lunar cuisine made from the best native animals and substances the moon Plexis de Chiveltros had to offer.

The food came exactly at the right time when their bodies were recovering from the workout and the massages. Hence it satisfied any hunger really good. Halfway through the meal, Frederick bon Stoffengar and his bimbo exited the restaurant which was fine for Tinougl. Less chance of drawing any sort of attention that way.

After the meal it was time to take a post dinner walk and do some sight seeing. Most moons have a face that always points to the planet. Plexis de Chiveltros spun but was slowing down very slowly. When it arrived in the solar system it was spinning a a much higher rate and experts thought about a billion years ago, the moon glanced the planet a got semi trapped in the gravity and due to it's spin rate and direction, it got locked into an orbit spinning quickly, but slowed the spin rate since. At the present rate it would slow ten minutes every thousand years and eventually slow to a very slow spin and end up facing the planet just like most of the other moons in the solar system.

When it started to get dark and the temperatures were declining, they went back to the resort and decided to get some rest to help recover from heir experiences today. Tinougl wanted to get horizontal and rest his aching body. The last thing he had on his mind was sex. In due time, Milton provided them sleeping attire for their comfort and they each got into a bed by themselves and soon slumber hit them.

Tinougl didn't quite remember it but halfway through the middle of the night, Mòlìhuā got up and walked over to his bed and got in with him and put her arms around him. It felt really good, and it simply made the restful sleep even better for the two of them.

In the morning, Mòlìhuā was still holding onto Tinougl almost in a romantic fashion. There was definitely a feeling of romance attached. Tinougl completely forgot his recent romantic encounters and enjoyed every minute of it. Eventually Mòlìhuā awakened and realized she was in Tinougl's bed. But she didn't care, she liked the feeling of companionship and safety.

Chapter Sixteen

Mòlìhuā Performs a Hit Love Song

Tinougl knew instinctively this was not quite the time to begin the next phase of the relationship. He wanted solid bonding to make sure the seduction was strong enough to withstand headwinds in the future, whatever they may be. He did kiss her on her lips, and she felt a tingling sensation and enjoyed the fact he wasn't rushing things. He gave her time to think about what she wanted to do on her timeline and not his. For that she appreciated this kind gentleman, but she was growing in the realization that eventually if not today, maybe tomorrow they would reach the point where the absence of restraint would usher in what they instinctively knew was coming.

Tinougl suggested, "Let's get dressed and go down to the resort Dining Hall and get something to eat and while we are eating, we can check out some of the things to do."

"That's a good idea."

Soon they were dressing in front of each other and got ready in a brief period and went down and found the Dining Hall that was just as luxurious if not better than the one in Cuìlù Resort Hotel. Soon they were spoiled with a galactic class chef's creation that hit their pallet really good.

Tinougl discovered something while eating and checking his communicator for things to do at Plexis de Chiveltros. It turns out there was two major tourist attractions: Terrain Follower tours and jet ski tours on a nearby lake.

After the brunch Tinougl suggested, "Let's go up to the room and freshen up then we can go on a Terrain Follower tour.

"Sounds good to me." Mòlìhuā said because she didn't want to feel bloated on the Terrain Follower tour. She also did not rule out the fact that Tinougl might want to have sex at that time. She was willing to do it, but she would let him make the first move.

When they got into the room, Tinougl being the perfect gentleman suggested, "Mòlìhuā, you go ahead and use the bathroom first." He didn't want to leave behind a foul stench when he freshened up that might turn her off.

Mòlìhuā took care of business and then gave the bathroom to Tinougl where he was happy to offload some breakfast before the tour knowing the Terrain Follower could have several sudden movements. Tinougl knew he could probably have sex with Mòlìhuā now, but wanted to wait for the right moment, like after dinner and drinks and some romantic entertainment.

As soon as he was ready, they left the room and the resort and quickly found some of the Terrain Follower businesses specializing on taking tourists to some of the most enchanting locations nearby. And soon they were airborne going up the sides of mountains and down into vallyes and across lakes and many unsettled wild areas designated game reserve to preserve the species. During the trip, they shifted from helicopter mode to hovercraft and spent time on some nice lakes with magnificent landscape. After a couple hours it was time to get back to the resort/hote on the Strip.

Mindful of his need to keep in shape, Tinougl said, "I would like to go to the swimming pool and swim a few laps. Not as hard as yesterday, but just to keep my shape."

"Sure, I'll be happy to go with you." Mòlìhuā stated with a nice smile.

Soon they were changing into their swimming attire, and it was clear Mòlìhuā was fully exposing herself as she felt secure with Tinougl. She sensed he wouldn't do anything right now because the moment wasn't right.

They went back to the pool and Tinougl swam 20 laps and layed down on the soft recliner and said, "Maybe we should get a small snack and drink to hold us over until dinner?"

"That's fine with me."

Tinougl signaled for a standby waiter who soon approached the table and asked, "What can I get you sir?"

"We'd like a couple menus and drinks."

"What would you like to drink?"

"I would like a Chamboree del Pàrà Měilì."

"How about you Madam?"

"I'll have what he's having."

"Let me get you some menus and I'll put your drink order in immediately."

The woman walked over to the bartender and gave him the drink requests and grabbed two menus.

The two settled on a couple small servings of decapod crustaceans called Bongo Bongo and cephalopods called Dragon Dúcì they could dip in the sauces provided and eat with delicious crackers baked with savory spices. It wasn't any of a substantial meal, just slightly enough to hold them over for dinner that would not happen for several hours.

Mòlìhuā wasn't a plane Jane, but she didn't bring any expensive clothes with her, probably because she had to dress up every night she was singing. But as Tinougl analyzed the situation made a command decision to get them each dressed up for the dinner and entertainment later that night. So, after they finished their quick snack and went back to the room, Tinougl informed her, "The resort no doubt has a fashion designer and I'm going to have them prepare us for the dinner tonight because I want us to look really good."

"Sure, I can do that." Mòlihuā responded with an evil grin.

"Milton, will you please contact the resort fashion designer and have them come up and fit us for dinner?"

"Master Tinougl, it will be my pleasure."

By the time the fashion people showed up Tinougl and Mòlihuā were dressed in their street clothes, but they had not bathed to get rid of the swimming pool chemical smell.

The fashion designer said, we need to have Mòlihuā take a bath so we can wash her hair with some special products to make her ready for the hair designer, then Tinougl will have to do the same for the same reason."

Mòlihuā was soon scrubbed and pampered by a couple ladies and soon exited the large bathroom with a bathrobe and her hair in a towel.

"It's your term Tinougl."

He too was put in the bath and pampered, and the women fell in love with his body. One of them got super horney looking at his muscles and when he had an unscheduled erection which happens sometimes, both women wanted it but knew it was an impossibility under the circumstances. But they enjoyed the view.

Mòlihuā received holographic introduction to various garments available and was advised which one would look best on her tonight, and it was a short black dress that would reveal some cleavage and a lot of leg. The fashion designer knew her makeup girl would make Mòlihuā look smoking hot. And the work was in progress with her makeup and hair style. They did not want Tinougl to see the magic they were performing so like in many cases, they brought up dividers so the husband could not see the preparation on the wife until they were finished. They wanted the husband to see the final product and have the great surprise to make it all worth while.

The hair style suggested Tinougl get a *Cosmic Wave*, but Tinougl suspected people were looking for a guy like that and knew better, so he opted for a *duck wing* style where the hair came back on both sides of the head and met at the rear into a rising cluster of hair.

And he too was given a holographic presentation of clothes and suggested his attire to match the lady with a sexy hot black dress on.

Thanks to bathing and preparing Mòlìhuā first, the couple was finished approximately at the same time. The fashion designer had Tinougl stand looking right at the temporary room divider and said, "Behold."

The assistants took the room divider and twisted it 90 degrees fully exposing the smoking hot Mòlìhuā.

Tinougl had no idea Mòlìhuā could receive such a substantial makeover that would elevate her stature stratospherically. It hit him very hard because he instinctively knew tonight would be the night, they consummated their friendship and he seduced her for the sake of the mission.

Mindful of the time, the fashion designer knew they needed to leave now to get good seats for dinner because there was an excellent music group performing.

"I suggest Tinougl you take this lovely lady to dinner now because it will fill up quickly. We'll clean up and remove everything while you are gone."

"Thank you I appreciate this."

"You are most welcome. How do you like the way Mòlìhuā looks?"

"She looks stunning. I absolutely love the way you created such a glamorous woman."

Mòlìhuā had looked into the fashion designer's full-length mirror brought in and she knew she was smoking hot looking that night. There might be some women give their husbands elbows to the rib cage tonight!

The couple made their way to the resort Dining Hall and got there early enough to get a decent table and there were musicians already playing nice music and a singer, not nearly as beautiful as Mòlìhuā tonight. One of the musicians knew Mòlìhuā and instantly reacted quite apparently. He knew who she was but also recognized she's the last person in the world he would ever expect meeting up here and she looked stunningly attractive. The musician also observed her date thought he looked suave and rarified.

The couple sat down and was soon joined by a beautiful waitress with a name tag that said 'Xiǎomāo.'

"May I get you something to drink?"

"May I have a Lǐzǐ Guavastrian Elixir," Mòlìhuā asked as she was thinking how nice she would soon start feeling without the watered-down version she usually took while singing at the Cuìlù Resort Hotel.

"I'll have the Chamboree del Pàrà Měilì," Tinougl added.

The waitress left the couple some menus and went to place their drink order.

Instinctively, Mòlìhuā had picked the chair with her facing the musicians at about a 45-degree angle. She had to turn slightly to see the entire band but focused her attention on her prince charming that was starting to show his class and his respectful gentleness.

Tinougl was a man quite different than anyone Mòlìhuā had ever met before and now sitting in front of her this wonderful specimen of a being charmed her with his mere presence. The great awareness that slowly grew included her fascination towards his immaculate body. She had never seen a man with muscles so incredibly formed. She knew that had to be the results of many years of working out. When she caught glimpses of his tool in a semi erection state, she knew how good it must feel and felt her own moistness in anticipation.

The drinks arrived just in time for her to take her mind off sex before she got herself into trouble as she felt a strangeness develop in her womanhood. She knew her nipples were hardened and the dress she was wearing could expose them if she wasn't careful, so she had to calm herself down. The Lǐzǐ Guavastrian Elixir instantly helped Mòlìhuā's psychology, and it calmed her before she might have made a fool out of herself by suggesting they leave now for something she urgently felt she needed to do.

Tinougl didn't understand yet why the one musician was focused on him and Mòlìhuā, but that all soon was to unfold. The sensation Tinougl received with the imagery of Mòlìhuā, the lovely sounds of the musicians and the lovely singer, and the effects of the Chamboree del Pàrà Měilì gave a euphoric sensation. If Tinougl went to the restroom now, he would find a wet spot in his undergarments from the significant influence Mòlìhuā had on him right this minute. If he was not conditioned as a spy with the lengthy coercive persuasion his masters did over many years to indoctrinate him on mission necessities, he easily could have decided to stay with Mòlìhuā forever. Compliance reliability is the primary reason why he was picked for this mission.

They were here a little early and were not yet quite hungry and would wait a while to order. Xiǎomāo observed the couple and knew they had not picked up the menus, so she gave them space as she knew a lot of couples listened to the music for a while before they got interested in ordering.

As the musicians performed there was a slow but steady movement of resort guests arriving and filling up tables. Xiǎomāo was suddenly busy getting in their drink orders and new the couple were enjoying the music and would probably not order for a while.

In another ten minutes just about the time their drinks were half empty, the musicians took a fifteen-minute break, and Tinougl observed one of the musicians approach their table. Mòlìhuā looked up and saw the musician, whom she worked with in the past and hit on her a few times, but never made it to first base.

"Hello Mòlìhuā, I didn't recognize you at first, you are looking very nice this evening."

"Lǎoxīng, let me introduce you to my friend Tinougl."

"Lǎoxīng bowed towards Tinougl and said, "It's an honor to meet you sir."

Tinougl somewhat a sophisticated social engineer knew it would be wise to discover as much information about Mòlìhuā as he developed his relationship with her for the soul purpose of exploitation to support his mission. He knew the obvious thing to do was to invite Lǎoxīng to join them for a drink.

"Would you like to join us for a drink?"

"I would be delighted."

Tinougl gestured towards and empty seat which Lǎoxīng took that allowed him to simultaneously face Mòlìhuā and Tinougl.

Tinougl looked over towards the waitress Xiǎomāo and signalled her to approach.

Xiǎomāo a sophisticated waitress knew the singer was socializing with the couple and walked up and asked, "Lǎoxīng, would you like something to drink?"

"Sure, I'll have what he's having."

"I'll be right back with your drink."

True to her promise in three minutes Lǎoxīng was enjoying the effects of the Chamboree del Pàrà Měilì.

Lǎoxīng knew the couple was probably lovers because there were no causual friendships that came all the way to the moon to hear their band. He instantly was jealous of Tinougl assuming he had already had his way with Mòlìhuā who appeared to be in full blossom. The signs of love were quite apparent.

"Tinougl are you from Santorini de Shénshèng?"

"No, I live on Argecibo."

"What brings you here, that's a long distance?"

"I'm a writer and my publishers are in Santorini de Shénshèng."

"What do you write?"

"Novels."

"I'll be honest I do not read very many Novels."

"That's alright, I seldom perform music."

"Maybe we can get Mòlìhuā sing you a song tonight."

"I would really enjoy that."

Lǎoxīng turned towards Mòlìhuā and asked, "Do you remember the song Dǎkāi Wánměi de Liánhuā [Opening the perfect Lotus]?

"How could I forget that song, I sang it for three months."

"We perform that song here, I'll talk to my band members and let them know. Perhaps you can inspire our singer whose been acting kind of lackluster tonight."

"I'll do my best."

For a few more minutes the three sat there simply enjoying a conversation and as soon as Lǎoxīng finished his drink he said, "Okay, I need to get back to work. Get ready to sing real soon Mòlìhuā and he stood up and rejoined the other musicians and informed them what his plans were. Since he was the head of the band and their manager, they did what he asked.

The group performed the first song and predictably the female singer seemed to perform in a lackluster fashion and wasn't exciting the clientele very much. At the end of the song before they started the next song, Lǎoxīng grabbed his microphone and said, "Ladies and gentlemen, I have a surprise for you tonight. One of my former collegues and fantastic singer is with us tonight and she has agreed to sing a song for us. Please welcome the wonderful singer Wánměi de Mòlìhuā, who will now sing the song, "Dǎkāi Wánměi de Liánhuā."

When the gorgeous creature Mòlìhuā appearing as movie star quality stood up and approached the stage, there was an air of excitement. The other singer sat down at a table by the stage and didn't have a very happy look on her face because this surprise guest singer made her look tarnished and lacking the sparkle that now seemed to electrify the audience.

The pianist started the music that was slowly joined by the other instruments and after the lead in, Mòlìhuā started singing. Tonight, Mòlìhuā just wasn't singing like she had in the past at the Cuìlù Resort Hotel. Mòlìhuā was singing for love. She knew she was falling in love with that handsome man sitting out there directly in front of her. Her eye contact was with him only. She ignored the rest of the Dining Hall as she exemplified the essence of quintessential love transcending towards a new emotional spirit. She knew the lyrics well because after three months of singing it repeatedly, wrote it to memory.

Lǎoxīng who had performed that song with Mòlìhuā synchronized well, and his performance synchronized the rest of the musicians to where every single note and lyric hit precisely at the right time. The Diva was now electroying the audience, including the singer who was touched and inspired by it all.

Normally during a Dining Hall adventure like this, the clientele continue in their personal conversations so there is a little noise level because of it the singers and musicians ignore and carry on smartly.

Tonight, it was so quiet you could hear a pin drop if the musicians and Mòlìhuā suddenly stopped as all conversations had ended, and the entire Dining Hall had their focus on this singer. The manager of the Dining Hall which includes oversight on the musicians and the content saw this all unfold and was captivated by what he saw. He saw movie star quality in the woman and before the night was out make her a very generous offer.

Dǎkāi Wánměi de Liánhuā is a song that lasts a little longer than most as it took almost seven minutes. Tinougl was moved because he felt the performance direct at him and it was almost as if only, he and Mòlìhuā were in the room as all other sensory was filtered out.

The next thing the manager noticed was something that almost never happened in the Grand Plexis de Chiveltros Dining Hall, *a standing ovation*. There wasn't anyone in the Dining Hall that wasn't standing, clapping, and shouting lovely explatives.

Mòlìhuā felt the emotions and saw Tinougl's eyes water up. She knew he was emotionally struck by her performance, and those tears of joy resonated her heart. She felt the love. She had to force herself to say, "Thank you. Thank you. Thank you very much," as the crowd continued with their applause.

Mòlìhuā then stepped down off the stage and handed the microphone to the singer and said, "You have a lovely voice. I'm enjoying your singing tonight."

The singer startled by the gracious comment smiled and said, "Thank you for your kind words. You are so beautiful and talented.

I feel privledged to hear you sing that song."

"I'm looking forward to hearing your singing. Please sing something nice for my boyfriend."

"I will I promise."

The women shook hands softly as there was a sweet exchange of emotional bond that moment. The singer took a liking to Mòlìhuā and was now going to put maximum effort into her next song to pay back a great moment of satisfaction to this lovely woman that just enthralled her.

As Mòlìhuā approached their table Tinougl stood up and held both hands out to her which she grabbed whole heartedly and he said, "That was a very lovely song. Thank you for singing it for me."

"Thank you for making me feel special," Mòlìhuā responded.

Their drinks were almost empty, and the waitress Xiǎomāo approached their table and asked, "Would you like refills?"

"Yes definitely."

Xiǎomāo walked away and the musicians were performing their next song with an apparent shift in the singer's attitude and performance. Mòlìhuā had influenced the evening.

About that time a well-dressed man in a black suit approached the table and said, "Your performance was spectacular. I've never seen a singer fire up the audience like this before. Here's my business card. If you would ever like to come here to perform for a few weeks, please contact me and I would be most happy to schedule you."

"Thank you for the offer," Mòlìhuā stated as she knew in her world, she had to achieve such offers to have a livelihood and she didn't quite yet know where she was going with Tinougl. Their life plans had not yet developed. She was hopeful, but she was no fool. So, it was always good to have contengencies in case plans didn't work out.

Mòlìhuā looked down at the business card and noticed the businessman was named Thurston bon Hamerstein. His name sounded familiar, and she now realized he was one of the leading recruiters for the entertainment industry.

Here's the man who controlled the destiny of many of the top singers. He had a reputation for quid pro quo. But he usually wasn't the instigator. Desperate women attempting desperate measures often led to that quid pro quo and all he was doing was allowing them to act out their motives. After the fact the women embellished their stories to cover up the fact their personal behavior was the sources of the scandals.

After some minor chitchat, Thurston said, "I must get back to work. It was nice meeting you and please call me if you ever want to come back and perform full time."

"I will."

Thurston had a hand in placing women singers in many of the resorts on the Strip. And he knew when he saw a super star. Tonight, was a pleasant night for him because he felt he would eventually get a call from the young lady, and she would create a similar atmosphere like she did tonight with the Dining hall now showing countless smiling faces and bountiful happiness.

Tinougl picked up a menu and said, "I'm getting a little hungry should we order?"

"Sounds like an excellent idea to me," Mòlìhuā responded as she too was starting to develop an appetite.

By the time Xiǎomāo returned with their drinks, the couple had determined what they wanted to order and were soon waiting for their meal.

During the wait, a half dozen very well dress men and women approached their table and said to Mòlìhuā her song was very inspiring. She had never received this level of attention while performing at Cuìlù Resort Hotel. She felt a huge change in herself and knew that Tinougl had a big effect on her. She also knew if he broke her heart, she might consider suicide. He was all she wanted in her life now. She knew how Tinougl affected her feelings quite strongly.

But something in her heart told her that Tinougl, a soft and gentle person wore his personality on his sleave. What you see is what you get. She had a growing confidence that he would want to stay with her. Would he want to go back to his home world Argecibo? Could she tolerate the place if that's where she was taken? It was a complicated situation, but she knew also for the next year and a half she had job security at the Cuìlù Resort Hotel and could possibly do short gigs here if Tinougl abandoned her. Her mind was swirling with thoughts wondering how life was going to bestow upon the destiny she sought.

The food was soon served, and the meal was delicious, but that's not what Mòlìhuā wanted right now. She slowly wanted the man sitting in front of her to take her and the sooner the better. But she needed her nourishment and knew Tinougl was hungry, so she politely ate her meal and set aside her strong desires for the present time.

They finished their meal and as soon as Xiǎomāo cleaned away all the dishes and changed the tablecloth, she asked, "Would you like another drink."

This is where Mòlìhuā took command of the situation and responded before Tinougl had a chance and said, "No we are leaving now. Thank you very much for your service."

"It's my pleasure and I loved to hear you sing tonight. You have a beautiful voice and inspire people."

"Yes, she does," Tinougl said smiling very proudly at Mòlìhuā.

The two left the Dining hall with a lot of men checking out Mòlìhuā's posterior including the manager Thurston bon

Hamerstein.

"Where would you like to go now?"

"Let's go back to the room so we can freshen up first."

"All right."

The couple arrived at their room in a short while with Tinougl following Mòlìhuā into the center of the room and said, "You go ahead and freshen up first."

Mòlìhuā surprised Tinougl by saying that will not be necessary and approached him and put her arms around him and pulled him close. They looked into each other's eyes and slowly their lips met with a very soft but sensual kiss. Tinougl became aware something was happening when Mòlìhuā started unbuttoning his shirt and took off his bow tie. She then helped him out of his suit jacket and layed it on the nearby chair then bent down on her knees and helped him take of his shoes quickly then stood up and undid his trousers which he stepped out of. She could not help but see the wet spot in his underwear as it appeared he had already started having some reaction to her. She kicked off her shoes turned around and asked Tinougl to unhook her dress and as soon as he did, she was out of it now just wearing a seethrough bra and sheer panties. She then grabbed his hand and led him over to one of the beds and pulled the sheets back and climbed into the bed and pulled Tinougl in on top of her.

She knew he probably had the knowledge to take it from there and he did not disappoint her as he removed her bra and panties and soon started kissing her. He felt her wetness and soon proceeded to guide himself gently into Mòlìhuā as their emotional dam was breaking and the acceleration of passions exceeded light speed.

Almost immediately, they were encompassed into splendid euphoria as their psychophysical responses generated all their motions that were mechanically synchronized to their growing exquisitee feelings. Mòlìhuā's silky womanhood created a strange sensation that drove Tinougl into caldrons of pleasure that soon triggered the ultimate gratification as he flooded her with pent up desire.

Mòlihuā's gratification now reached a peak and lingered for several minutes as the mechanical actions continued while the sensation slowly declined, and they both slipped into a subconcious orbit around each other almost like in a different time and dimension. When it was apparent, they had completed the perfect coitus, Tinougl slipped to the side of Mòlihuā and held her dearly for what seemed like a small eternity.

Mòlihuā's head was against Tinougl chest, and his face was near her head where he gently kissed the top of her head and smelled her fragrance. The scent was very similar to Cofa de Coma perfume, something that would help him remember this moment in the future. And when or if he came across a woman wearing Cofa de Coma perfume, he could not help remembering the magic spell that Mòlihuā placed on him.

After a nap the two slowly awakened simultaneously. Tinougl remembering an experience he had five hundred years into the future while being on Plexis de Chiveltros during a clandestine operation where he held another woman in his arms about this time during the twilight said, "Let's get dressed in our street clothes, I want to take you down by that little duck pond near here and show you something."

"Alright dear."

In ten minutes, they dressed and outside the resort doubling back around behind it. There was a nice large gazebo where sometimes musicians would play during the daytime to people liezeruly enjoying the music in a park like environment watching the waterfowl and enjoying a carefree moment for a few hours. The resort had employees there to serve drinks and snacks during such days.

They walked up to the temporarily abandoned gazebo where they had complete privacy. Once they were up on the platform, Tinougl said, "Close your eyes Mòlìhuā, I'm going to reposition you and keep your eyes closed for a few minutes, I have a surprise for you. Based on his memories it would happen shortly.

After Tinougl got Mòlìhuā in position he put his arms around her and held her in the most loving fashion and waited for that magical moment and when it happened, he said, "Okay you can open your eyes now."

Mòlìhuā was feeling the warmth and the gentleness of Tinougl slowly opened her eyes, and there it was in all it's glory, the Tartarnite Empire world Tartar rising above the horizon. The light reflected from Tartar was much brighter than looking at the moon on the planet and the size was significantly larger giving it such a surreal look. The image coupled with the loving embrace gave Mòlìhuā a sensation as if moon beams were striking her like Cupid's arrows.

Mòlìhuā felt so good in the arms of a man she loved, and the way he held her and kissed the top of her head now filled her heart full of joy. Her emotions overflowed and she suddenly had the urge and quickly rotated around and looked at the reflected sun rays striking Tinougl's face giving barely enough illumination to clearly see his face and she put her arms around his neck and shoulders and sought his tender lips and kissed him like he never felt before. The electricity between them flowed.

Tinougl now knew clearly, he was quickly becoming a casualty in time travel. This could not be undone. He had just warped the fabric of time and space with his actions. He was almost to the point of no return now. His actions were clearly slowly eroding that fabric and he was changing history as a result. He couldn't know what damage he was creating, nobody could. It was far too complex. But he knew he felt a tantalizing love like never before. He had felt some strange pangs of emotions for Cǎoméi which as a good spy he was able to compartmentalize and not allow it to endanger the mission or tamper with the fabric of time.

Tinougl had to seduce this beautiful woman as a means to carry out his most daring expedition in his lifetime, but in the process, he became the victim of his own making. He now realized he might not be able to complete the mission and one minute after he launched an empty time machine would return with no knowledge of what happened to him. *But was that so bad?*

The kiss and the embrace lasted a while and then Mòlìhuā turned back to the image and wrapped Tinougl's arms around her again to feel his warmth and savor the moment. Tinougl was still an enigma and a stranger, but the sensations of her emotions felt like finding a long-lost friend. Perhaps in other dimensions they had experienced this before, and she was simply receiving the reverberations of multi-dimension intersection to an unforgettable moment?

In about thirty minutes the optical illusion of Tartar slowly evolved, and the planet appeared to shrink and lose some of it's majestic appearance as the moon's gravity was no longer distorting the image of the planet. Tinougl knew it was time to go and suggested, "Let's take a walk down the strip and get a little exercise."

They set off on foot and walked past other resorts and adult entertainment venus designed to entertain newlyweds and people arriving for just a quick holiday to have an affair far enough away from home to avoid a scandal. As they were walking along and talking and enjoying each other, Mòlìhuā unwittingly set up the next phase of their journey by simply making statements that ordinary people would make under the circumstances. Perhaps she was testing his true motives, Tinougl didn't know but it dovetailed nicely into his plans as he started thinking mission again.

"Tinougl, I would like to one day soon introduce you to my family. I'm sure my parents would like to meet you."

"I would love to meet your parents and I'm willing to go there with you any time you wish to go."

"Would you consider going after we get back to Santorini de Shénshèng?"

"Yes, my schedule is very flexible now. I've recently published my next Novel and I've not started another yet, so I can go anywhere now and do anything I want. If you want to go visit your parents, I can go with you now."

Mòlìhuā now knew this was the real deal and not just someone seeking gratification from a pretty lady. The emotions flooded her as she turned around and threw her arms around Tinougl and said, "I really love you."

"I love you too." Tinougl articulated those words with the deepest sincerity.

Mòlìhuā now broke down and started crying as her emotions overflowed. Tinougl knew what he had just done. The seduction was now complete. But he also knew he too was a casualty because he allowed himself to be seduced as well. He could no longer compartmentalize his emotions from his mission and as a spy had just failed. Regarding his career in espionage, this was the biggest failure in his life, even though it wasn't quite painful. But he knew the truth, as a spy he had just failed because he allowed emotions to overcome his will and strength and his formidable ambitions.

The rest of their stay at the Grand Plexis de Chiveltros was much like it had been including some time on a Jet Ski on a beautiful lake, except the morning of the last full day. Mòlìhuā said she wanted some time alone and wanted to go somewhere and would tell Tinougl about it later. She suggested he take a swim and get a massage and she would be done by then. Tinougl assumed she would probably be shopping for souvenirs or even a gift for him, but he was wrong. She wasn't purchasing a gift; she was making a gift.

When Mòlìhuā was by herself she contacted Thurston bon Hamerstein.

"Hello."

"Mr. Hamerstein?"

"Yes, what can I do for you?" Thurston replied to the nice, lovely voice.

"My name is Mòlìhuā, I'm the singer you met a few nights ago and you gave me your card and asked me to contact you if I ever wanted to sing at this resort."

"Oh yes, I remember you. Do you want to come here to sing for a period?"

"Actually, just tonight one song."

"You mean like the other night?"

"A different song, I want to surprise my boyfriend."

"I'm sure we can work something out."

"I've broke away from my boyfriend for a few hours and if you can contact the musicians and meet for a practice session, we can work the song out and have it ready to perform tonight."

"Will it be as good as the one you sung the other night?"

"It will be better."

"Nothing can possibly be better."

"If you would like to come to the practice session, I can show you something can be better."

"I would certainly love to find that out."

"Alright, how soon can we get together?"

"The musicians all live in the resort and have their private rooms here.

They should have been awake for a while; I'll contact them and ask to meet you at the Dinning Hall that is currently closed between meals, and you can do your practice session there."

"How soon do you expect?"

"Meet me there in half an hour and I'll see if I can hustle up the musicians."

"Also, I recommend you bring the singer because after I'm gone, she can perform the song."

"Excellent idea, I like the way you think."

"Thank you."

"See you soon."

Chapter Seventeen

Practice Session for a New Love Song

In thirty minutes, the musicians and the singer were at the Dining Hall, all perplexed at this sudden and strange meeting and when they witnessed Mòlìhuā there, it got even more strange, and the singer was fearing for her job.

Thurston bon Hamerstein then explained what was going on.

"You all remember Mòlìhuā who sang that beautiful song the other night. She is going to sing a different song tonight and we will perform that song in the future in sets, but she will be gone so she will help us quickly master it for tonight's performance only and from then on, we'll perform it without her."

The group shook their heads in kind of strange contemplation, but as musicians they were all interested in hearing new music, especially if they are going to perform it.

The group's singer looked on and evaluated it as a nice gesture and an inspirational time for her. This woman was going to teach her a new song to sing, and she would pour her heart into it and make her proud. She viewed this as a very positive opportunity and was already liking it.

Mòlìhuā could play the piano and knew all these musicians were very talented and could play by ear and pick it up fast. She said, "I'm going to play the melody on the piano first and I've written out the lyrics for you to use later."

Mòlìhuā went to the piano and sat down and shortly started playing the beautiful melody she had created. Everyone listened and knew it was a spectacular melody that would capture the audience attention real fast. The song was a little more than six minutes long. When she finished, the musicians all unanimously all indicated, "That's really good."

Mòlìhuā had the lyrics memorized and did not need to read them and handed them to the other singer to study and she played it again this time singing the lyrics. The musicians were stunned and one of them said, "I do not think you need us; you can just play the piano and sing that yourself."

"No, I want you guys to play the music because your sound will add phenomenally to the acoustics."

Then she turned to the other singer and said, "See where I underlined the words?"

"Yes."

"I want you to sing with me those words. Your voice backup will help resonate those words and add to the performance. You will stand next to me during the performance. She also had some rough sheet music she handed to the pianist and asked, "Can you read this well enough to perform it?"

"Let me try, I think so."

"Okay shall we give it a shot?"

They all agreed and soon the pianist led the group with the opening chords, and they all joined in.

Thurston bon Hamerstein patiently stood there taking it all in. The first time the group performed it, no doubt it sounded like they needed to work on it. They immediately performed it again, and now it was starting to show it's magic. He knew he had a winner on his hands and if he could convince Mòlìhuā to stay, he would end up with the hottest show on the strip. None of the others ever had standing ovations like she created and he knew Mòlìhuā could pull it off every night.

By the fourth time they performed the song, it was now professional recording quality. The regular singer was very pleased with her participation, and some how felt Mòlìhuā was improving her singing and her motivation. The entire group was happy they had put together a very successful piece in such a short period of time. The reason for the success was the genius in the composition allowed it to be performed so elegantly because the pleasing sound and lyrics had an arousal to it.

The musicians eventually said, "I think we got it, we'll be able to perform this very well tonight."

Thurston bon Hamerstein knew he would be having another standing ovation tonight and if the band continued performing it well in the future, even without Mòlìhuā's presence, they would have a motivational piece for the audience.

"Alright everyone, thank you for coming in and getting this ready on such short notice. You all will be given a bonus because of your efforts. I'm very proud of you and tonight, I will be pleased to see how you inspire the audience."

The group adjourned and Thurston went back to his office wondering what kind of inducements he could offer to get Mòlìhuā to stay.

When Tinougl went to the pool, he had a lot on his mind. It wasn't that he couldn't handle the situation, it was more of soul searching to analyze what he had done and what he was doing going forward. He didn't feel bad that he failed as a spy, most of the spys who failed usually ended their lives in a very painful situation in swimming pool, or a crematorium, or something else that made them wish they were dead to end the suffering.

Tinougl swam the thirty laps hard and at the end of the workout his muscles were bursting in pain. He pushed himself to the ragged edge with barely enough energy to crawl out of the water. He knew better than to sit down on the soft recliner because he might not be able to get up for an hour, so he grabbed his robe and put his sandals on and went directly to the SPA to get that massage to bring him back to life.

The delightful receptionist took him into a room for a single massage since Mòlìhuā was not with him.

Jessicar was in the room waiting for her next client that happened to be Tinougl.

"Hello again."

"Good to see you."

"Just finished another swim?"

"Yes, I had to come here right away, I pushed myself really hard, I'm not sure I have any energy left."

"You know the drill, us go into the other room and hop in the tub before your muscles tighten up too badly."

"My thoughts exactly."

Today it was a little different since it was just the two of them and Jessicar loved this man's body and admired his tool.

She helped Tinougl into the bath as she could tell he was semi cripled as his body was recovering from the high energy exercise associated with the 30 laps. Other resort guests watching Tinougl were in awe watching him and when he climbed out of the pool with his muscles all nice and tight, his image was beyond a body builder.

Tinougl sat at one of the circular chairs and was feeling slightly better as the warm water soothed him slightly. The additives that Jessicar dumped into the water slowly had their affect.

Today, Jessicar took everything off. She wanted to enduce Tinougl to engage her in ways that would allow her to feel his manliness. As she gave him a preliminary massage, she was almost shocked at how hard all his muscles were. He was as hard as a brick. She was taunting Tinougl slightly even purposely putting her nipples at his mouth hoping he would engage. She sat down on his lap and bounced around a little hoping for an arousal as she worked on his shoulders and moved from one breast to the other onto his lips. Then she got really brave and reached down and grabbed his tool and felt it was getting nice and hard and asked, "Do you want to put that inside me?"

"Yes, I do, but I'm going to save it for Mòlìhuā. If I wasn't with her, I'd have you on the massage table now giving it to you nice and hard."

"That's the way I like it."

"Mòlìhuā will get it all tonight."

"You are close to her?"

"Yes, more than I should be."

"What do you mean by that?"

"When a man puts a woman into his heart and she starts to control his thoughts by the feelings she gives him, he becomes vulnerable."

"You do not feel vulnerable with me?"

"I know you are a professional and will do your best to treat my sore muscles and you you want to make sure I leave here healed. If I didn't have that woman in my heart and my mind, then I know I would want to enjoy your body."

"It's a shame you do not want to enjoy it now."

"You are very beautiful and desirable, but I have a situation that precludes me from enjoying you in that manner."

"Tinougl, do you realize you are the only man ever that has turned me down to make love."

"I do not doubt that."

"I admire you. You have extreme willpower."

"Perhaps it's the power of love."

"You are such a sweet man. I know why Mòlìhuā wants you so much."

"Thank you. I like you and you are a sweet woman."

"If it doesn't work out between you and Mòlìhuā, you can come back and get me any time you want."

"We never know for sure where we are going in life until we get there. But on the journey through life, I'm glad I met you and if it were not for other circumstances, we easily could have become lovers."

Jessicar through her arms around Tinougl and embraced him very effectionately and wished he would let go and put himself inside her. But even though she was disappointed he didn't go there, she still enjoyed hugging this glorious man whose body was unreal.

His arms and legs were so tense from lactic acid building up and exhaustive workout. Jessicar went to town messaging his arms and legs to prevent cramps. The cannabinoids and opioids in the water obsorbed through the skin was helping to reduce the inflammation and loosen his muscles a bit. She reached down and felt his tool again. He was rock hard, and she almost wanted to grab it and stuff it inside her, but she realized that's not what he wanted so she slowly disengaged those thoughts and concentrated on the therapeutic efforts she applied.

"All right, us get out of the bath and I'll dry you off."

In a few minutes they were back in the other room with Tinougl lying on his back getting the special oil applied to his body. She even oiled his tool and kissed the tip of it and smiled. And when she saw the minor excretments she was happy knowing she had stimulated him and respected him for his great control he exhibited. Jessicar knew she was a very attractive woman with a fantastic body and knew few if any men could have maintained such self control. Little did she know she was dealing with a deadly spy, a killer, and someone who had done things in his lifetime that would put great fear in her.

Thirty minutes prior as Tinoungl climbed out of the swimming pool, he didn't know if he could make it and certainly would be laid up for most of the evening without this massage, a super time saver. He was responding nicely to the treatment and wished Mòlihuā was here because he would have made love to her immediately after the effects he now felt.

Jessicar knew her business and soon turned Tinougl on his side and stratched his muscles back out. Between the cannabinoids, opiods, and the oil that had tea tree and other substances in it, his body was quickly healing with the help of the physical agitation Jessicar provided.

Jessicar rolled him on his stomach a put great pain into him which he quickly recovered, loosening up more muscles, and then she rolled him on his other side and stretched him out some more. And soon they were done and Jessicar said, "Let's go back to the pool so I can wash off all that oil."

"Alright."

Jessicar washed his hair again and cleansed his body and again sat on his lap and grabbed his tool and rubbed it against her womanhood and even inserted it momentarily and said, I just wanted to feel it a little. She did feel a small deposit but knew she had to let Tinougl save it for Mòlìhuā and finished cleaning him and led him out of the tub, feeling great and relaxed.

He put on his swimming attire and swim robe and sandals, and they walked to the entrance. As they got in front of the receptionist, Jessicar turned to Tinougl and said, "By the way I want to thank you for the generous tip you gave me the other day."

"My pleasure. I'm sorry I couldn't give you the special tip." He then smiled and so did she.

Tinougl then departed and went back to the resort room where Mòlìhuā was with the fashion designer getting prepped and a room divider was in place.

"You must have read my mind."

"Thurston bon Hamerstein sent them. He wanted to pamper us since this is our last night and we made him very happy when I sung the song at the Dining Hall."

"Works for me."

The fashion designer said, "Tinougl, you need to take a bath now so we can also get you ready."

"Sure."

A couple cute girls were soon bathing Tinougl and one of them joked, "If you and Mòlìhuā ever break up please come and visit me, I want to try that out."

The other girl tapped her on the shoulder, and they giggled. One of the benefits of a fashion designer assistant was to get to see all the beautiful bodies. But they also got to see some ugly ones that needed a huge makeover.

The hair conditioner made his hair very soft, but it had already been washed twice previously. The scent added to his bathwater made Tinougl smell very seductive.

His body aches were gone, and he was feeling very good from the massage and the baths and soon after he had on his under garments and in a bathrobe, the hair stylist was working on him and molded him into a rather handsome man. *I could easily get used to this,* Tinougl thought. The fashion designer selected the wardrobe and matching shoes. Tinougl was now just about the sexiest man on the moon and was feeling especially good too.

No sooner than he was fully dressed and ready to go out, the fashion designer had her helpers twist the room divider sideways to let Tinougl observe the creation they just finished. One glance at Mòlìhuā and he was glad he didn't let Jessicar take him to the finish line. He now had saved up in him Mòlìhuā's reward for her exquisite beauty that she now bestowed upon him.

"You should leave now to get a good seat. The manager thinks the place will be packed tonight so you want to arrive early," the fashion designer stated. "Thank you again for making me feel so lovely," Mòlìhuā stated in the most respectful manner.

"It's been my pleasure to work with you. I can usually do a good job if the client is cooperative like you are. Part of my success is the help you gave me in the mannerisms you work with me."

"I'm very pleased."

"We'll clean up everything here you can leave now."

"Thank you."

The couple went to the Grand Plexis de Chiveltros Dining Hall in about five minutes.

The attractive waitress Xiǎomāo came to them immediately all smiles because the manager had informed her privately of the big surprise coming up. She was so happy for this lovely couple and the other night when the lovely diva Mòlìhuā sang, the music resonated with her.

They had great seats again and the band members had a unique smile on their faces because they knew about the big surprise that was just about to unfold.

The manager was right. The place was filling up fast. He sent out via his special operatives the communiques they would give to their esteem clients which get alerted when important events happen on the strip they don't want to miss out on.

Tinougl noticed there were a lot of eyes on him. He really was jaw dropping handsome with the makeover he received. He looked movie star quality. His companion Mòlìhuā was no doubt the very best-looking woman in the Dining Hall tonight. The manager had instructed the fashion designer he would pay extra to make her look the very best. Mòlìhuā didn't know this but she had the best makeup artist and newest fashions which nobody had ever seen before. She was also a fashion model tonight and didn't know it.

The manager had taken a few peeks as the evening developed and already phoned the fashion designer to congratulate her on the awesome work she had accomplished.

The two were enjoying their drinks and nowhere near hungry yet and the musicians were performing, and the singer was doing much better tonight. *Perhaps it was her anticipation of the big event soon to happen?* Mòlìhuā wondered.

The musicians had their break and Mòlìhuā's friend Lǎoxīng came to the table all smiles. He knew that Tinougl didn't know what was going to happen in a short while and he knew it was going to be an incredible surprise. Lǎoxīng had got to know Mòlìhuā while performing with her for several months. He knew the kind of woman she was and didn't suffer fools for long. The fact she would do this special song for Tinougl convinced Lǎoxīng that Mòlìhuā was in love with Tinougl, and they had traveled here together to enjoy the celestial feasts. As well as the couple looked tonight, there was no mystery behind why they would be attracted to each other.

"Enjoying your stay at the resort?"

"Yes, I got another good swim in today. Without the the massage afterwards, I'd probably be lying up in my bed in pain."

"How much longer will you be staying at the resort?"

"We are going back to Santorini de Shénshèng tomorrow."

The conversation lingered until Lǎoxīng finished his drink and said, "I'm sorry but I need to get back to work."

"Nice talking to you."

"Same to you."

The musicians started performing and it seemed to Tinougl the Dining Hall was filled to capacity. There was a lot of expectation in the air with lots of conversations going on. Tinougl also noticed a lot of wealthy people wearing unique clothing he knew was very expensive.

The more he looked at the crowd, the more he realized EVERYONE was staring at him. A good spy figures this out quickly. It troubled him that he was the focus of attention. It was almost an eerie feeling because they were all strangers. *Perhaps it's because I'm dressed up the way I am?*

The music was exceptionally good tonight. It was evident the musicians stepped up their performances a notch or two.

After a couple more songs, Lǎoxīng walked out to the side of the stage and said, "Ladies and gentlemen, we have a special guest tonight that has an incredible song she will sing. Please welcome the lovely Wánměi de Mòlìhuā."

Mòlìhuā gave Tinougl a wicked smile and stood up and walked to the stage where she stood next to the regular singer.

The piano started playing and soon the other instruments joined in. And after the prelude, Mòlìhuā started singing her heart out.

The other singer sang her memorized lyrics at the time Mòlìhuā had designed. The crowd was utterly astonished. And in the crowd was film makers and recording studio executives all incredibly impressed with what they were hearing. The crem da la crem of the strip was in the Dining Hall that night utterly spellbound. The only dissatisfaction the crowd had was it was just a little over six minutes long. And just like the night before a rowdious standing ovation while Mòlìhuā bowed with the other singer. All the musicians were smiling. A star was born. After several minutes of the standing ovation the crowd was yelling for an encore.

Lǎoxīng walked over to Mòlìhuā and whispered into her ear, "Would you mind singing the song you did a few days ago?"

She said, "Sure but I want to make a quick announcement."

"No problem."

When the crowd applause died down, Mòlìhuā looking directly at Tinougl said, "This next song is for a very special man in my life."

She then turned around toward Lǎoxīng and nodded at him and he started playing the piano and the music began.

This song was a little longer and Mòlìhuā whispered in the ear of the other singer, "Just sing along with me and help out."

The other singer smiled and was tremendously motivated because she had never experienced such loud applause before.

Just like the previous song, Mòlìhuā looked directly at Tinougl who was already in an emotional trance. Even his best preparation and indoctrination as a spy could never prepare him for this. Now he knew where she was today, preparing all this. The crowd was mesmerized and the other singer helped Mòlìhuā quite a bit as it added volumes to the song. By the end of the song a lot of women had tears rolling down their eyes as they felt and saw the interaction with the well-dressed handsome man. They were exposing their love to the world. And when a woman exposes it like this, that usually means it's well earned.

The manager was stunned. This Dining Hall nor any other resort on the strip had ever had this kind of audience response. The two singers bowed several times as the standing ovation was quite compelling.

Mòlìhuā then turned and hugged the singer and said, "Your voice was so beautiful tonight."

"You helped my singing a lot. I learned a lot from you."

As the applause died down, Lǎoxīng walked up to Mòlìhuā and said,

"Thank you that was wonderful."

"You are most welcome." Mòlìhuā replied and handed the microphone back to Lǎoxīng.

Mòlìhuā stepped down from the stage and walked back to their table and Tinougl stood to help her get comfortable in her chair and sat back down. He was utterly speechless. And he also knew every pair of eyes in the Dining Hall were burning holes in him. It was the most uncomfortable feeling any spy would have. But he also knew in situations like this the worst thing a spy could do is lose his cool.

The beautiful waitress Xiǎomāo approached their table and asked, "Would you like refills?"

"Yes, thank you, but I have a question."

"Sure Tinougl, what can I help you with?"

"Would you mind asking the chef what he recommends tonight?"

"I would be delighted to ask the question." Xiǎomāo then turned towards Mòlìhuā and said, "Your singing was very lovely it touched me and sent shivers down my back. I love your singing."

"Thank you."

A few minutes later Xiǎomāo returned with their drinks and said, "The chef is going to surprise you in a few minutes."

During the performance, the music is piped into the kitchen as the chef and his assistants liked to hear the performances. Tonight, the performance captivated the Chef so when his favorite waitress conveyed to the Chef the singer's boyfriend asked what you recommended, he said, I will bring that table my recommendation.

The chef ordered his two top assistants, put on your dress outfits for VIP's. They always had a quick change for such occasions. The Chef personally put his most prestigious concoctions as two samplers for the couple, and quickly switched into his VIP Chef's dress uniform and when everything was ready the three marched out of the kitchen to the VIP's table, one man pushing the cart and the assistant following and the Chef last. In the perfect choreography demonstrated many times before, the two assistants took their position on each side of the cart while the chef stood in the middle and made the announcement.

"My dear lovely singer, you have an exquisitee voice, and I enjoyed your singing immensely." He then turned toward Tinougl and said, "Tinougl, it takes an extremely capable man to motivate a woman to sing to her love like she has tonight. For that I congratulate you as few men have ever accomplished what you have."

"Thank you." Tinougl responded feeling the resplendency in all of it.

"My assistants will serve you some samplers of my best works that are not well known even though they do appear on the menu."

There were now many eyes on the table because the Chef usually was not involved in such activities unless it was a VIP.

The two assistants served their meals with great expertise of the best waiters on the Strip. After everything was in place, the

Chef grabbed the small vase with a flower in it and sat it besides Mòlìhuā's settings and said, "Please enjoy your meals. It is my greatest honor to cook for you tonight."

"Thank you very much," Mòlìhuā responded and then the two assistants then moved the cart back to the kitchen with the Chef following.

Once back in the kitchen, they changed back into their cooking clothes that sometimes took abuse from the sauces of the night.

The food was very tasty, and a sampler gave them a little bit of everything which was just right. The meal was an excellent diversion from all the stares. The meal was quiet and somber. Mòlìhuā hoped Tinougl appreciated her gesture in the performance. Mòlìhuā didn't quite no what to think because Tinougl was always soft, kind, and courteous, and always showed her romance when she least expected it. She thought *Tinougl seemed to have the nackt of doing everything exactly at the right time.*

They finished their meal and Tinougl was only thinking of exiting stage right and disappearing like a good spy would under the circumstances.

The music played on, the band was inspired, the Dining Hall was electrified, but their business was done here. Tinougl was seriously thinking about his exit strategy and figured out a strategy.

"It looks like you are finished eating, I'm feeling kind of romantic, can we go up to the room for a while?"

Mòlìhuā feeling alive with her emotional spike behind her was more than ready for romance and quickly responded, "I would be delighted."

While everyone was watching the musicians perform in the most spectacular manner with all the motivation bestowed upon them tonight, Tinougl and Mòlìhuā slipped out of the Dining Hall while the crowd was focused on the singer hitting some high notes of their current song arrangement.

They were long gone before the manager and some of the recording executives could get to them for a high-pressure sales pitch.

Up in the room they eagerly discharged their fantastic wardrobes and got into one of the beds.

Tinougl had his mind on the girl giving him the massage earlier and how she grabbed him and tried to insert him for her pleasure. He could not fully control it and excreted a small amount but shut it down as fast as he could. But now as he was entering Mòlìhuā he had that vision in his mind and it was as if he were actually doing it to the massage technician which added to his arousal.

Mòlìhuā felt his excitement and his quintessential transcending to that splendid euphoria that crowned the gratification. Mòlìhuā thought it was all about her and what she had done to manifest this moment. As such she was touched, and the intensity of her gratification grew abruptly into orgasmic passions as she wrapped her legs around Tinougl and bucked him like a bitch in heat.

The two of them reached an uncontrollable orgasmic plasma. And the pleasure centers of their brains were on overload until it slowly decayed into a void of physical reactions.

A good spy will never reveal the truth or expose the activity. Some secrets are so precious that they can never be disclosed. This fantastic orgasm would be one of those matters Tinougl would never reveal to anyone why he exploded in pleasure so powerfully. It was best the target of his enterprise believed that she influenced Tinougl's explosion of pleasure.

If Toinougl was truthful and informed Mòlìhuā what triggered his massive gratification, it would be highly damaging to the relationship including the possibility of the loss of a vital asset and his ability to get into Konhagar in a plausible manner that nobody would suspect was associated with a nefarious activity of a spy.

They laid there for the longest time and Tinougl suggested, "Would you like to take a shower with me and get dressed in our street clothes and take a walk around the Strip?"

"Sure, it might help me come down from all the excitement of the night."

They went to the shower and slowly washed each other kissing and hugging like they were on a honeymoon.

The shower soon ended, and they dried off and put on their street clothes and ventured out. While they were gone the robots took care of the clothes returning them via the small elevator in the robot's storage room and cleaned and remade the room as if it had never been disturbed.

Walking up and down the strip this time of day were many different people. Crime was very low because organized crime provided protection for all the tourist area for a price. Nobody ever lived to brag they ripped these places off. The banker husbunds of the three three Barracuda's Tinougl met all had investments on the strip. One of the reasons why Spicey's husband was here and saw the performance of the nice lady was nothing more than checking up on his investment. it's kind of hard for a resort hotel to say they are not making any money if all the rooms are full. Likewise, if the restaurants are always full of clientele and they are losing money usually means management is stealing.

CHAPTER EIGHTEEN

TIME TRAVEL SPY FINDS A WAY TO KONHAGAR

During the walk the planning discussion went on.

"When were you planning on visiting your parents?"

"Since we just had a lot of unprotected sex and will not know the results for a bit, I think we should go right away in case I'm pregnant."

"Does that mean you will take a leave from your work?"

"There is no other way."

"When do you want to go there?"

"It might be good that as soon as we get back to Santorini de Shénshèng I contact my manager at the Cuìlǜ Resort Hotel and let her know I'm going away for a while and need to go home to my parents for personal reasons."

"What about your home in Santorini de Shénshèng?"

"I live with another woman who's my room mate, she can take care of things while I'm gone."

"What if we decide we want to visit your parents for a long period of time, and you don't get back there any time soon?"

"She would have a financial hardship because she needs my rent money to pay the bills."

"I always like to be prepared for contingencies. I don't want to be at your parents' home enjoying the visit and must rush back to pay your rent. This is what I'm willing to do. We will meet your room mate and I will pay her years worth of credits, so that will give us plenty of time to get to know your family and not rush back."

"You really would do that?"

"I no longer have a family. My parents and siblings are all gone. Your family will be my family."

"With that attitude they would be more than happy to welcome you into the family."

"Mòlĭhuā, I hope you know we have gone past the point of no return. I want you in my life forever and I promise to always be kind and considerate of your feelings and tolerant of those we need to be for your benefit."

"That's very sweet to say such a thing."

"I believe once you commit to something, go get it done. Let it be the focus of your efforts and don't dilly dally around."

"You certainly have shown that to me on this trip."

"What you see is what you get."

"If you move in with my family, my father might expect you to work hard just like his farm hands."

"You saw me swimming 30 hard laps on that pool. I may not have a massage afterwards, so you will have to learn how to massage my sore muscles."

"It would be my pleasure, but I would expect you to massage me as well."

"Tomorrow morning our flight is scheduled for mid morning. Let's get back and make all those arrangements then hop on a long-distance transporter and go to your family."

"Sounds good to me."

"Will we have to spend a full day? Should I get an over night room at a resort?"

"Just in case it takes a while for me to get everything arranged, perhaps you should."

"Do you think I should go back to the Cuìlù Resort Hotel?"

"It's as good as any other place, and in case I get hung up in the morning, you can go for a walk and a swim."

Alright, we'll do that. One other thing. I'm not going to risk a delay with going to a bank in case we run low on time, I'm going to transfer via my communicator directly to your communicator which I can do just like making a phone call via one of my banking applications and you can transfer the credits to you room mate's phone so that there will not be any reason to go to a bank or do any extra activity."

"That works for me."

"How much is your yearly rent?"

"It's 2200 credits."

"Alright I'll send you 3000 credits since I only have 1000 credit tokens."

"No problem. I have some credits I can make the appropriate change."

As they walked up and down the Strip getting good exercise there wasn't much to do unless they went in and saw a show. But since they just came from the best show in town, they probably would not enjoy it, so they walked back to the Gazebo and hung out for a while watching the planet rise and then went up to their room.

"I'm sorry I requested the double beds; I feel kind of dumb now we could feel more comfortable in a larger bed."

"I like the smaller bed; I can just hold you close in my arms."

"I like that idea too."

Knowing that the couple were checking out in the morning, Milton had all their clothes dry cleaned and semi packed. There would not be much for them to have to do in the morning.

The couple was happy that Milton had done such a great job helping to get them ready to leave.

"Milton, thank you for helping with everything."

"Not a problem Tinougl, I enjoyed your company and hope one day you come back so we can visit."

In due time, the couple were changed into their sleeping apparel and Tinougl asked Milton to play some soft music. In a brief period, the couple were sleeping blissfully in their loving companionship while Milton and the Robot Yuánběn arranged for the last-minute dry cleaning and laundering of the apparel they wore late this evening.

By morning, all they had to do is put those freshly dry-cleaned clothes and shoes back on and they were ready to leave. Tinougl had excess credits deposited at the resort in case he needed something and was pleasantly surprised the manager of the Grand Plexis de Chiveltros Dining Hall paid for all the fashion consultations including the first one, so he had all those excess credits ready to be sent back to his communicator.

Tinougl appreciated how the massages helped him be able to train rigorously and yet be physically able to conduct affairs later in the evening, so he informed Milton. "Give the massage technicians the standard tip and add twenty percent."

The SPA was fully integrated with central billing of the resort and in a few microseconds, Milton responded back, "the massage technicians have received the tips in their accounts."

The couple were ready to leave and Yuánběn carried their luggage to the door and asked them: "Would you like a porter for your luggage?"

"No, we packed pretty light so we can take it."

The couple were soon at the curb hopping into a Limo Ride over to the space port where they were systematically boarded for the trip back to the planet.

When they arrived back to Santorini de Shénshèng, Mòlìhuā asked,

"Would you like to go to my home and take a look?"

"Sure."

The limo dropped them off at the high rise building where Mòlìhuā lived. In a brief period, they were inside the home, but the room mate was gone away to work. Tinougl quickly figured out one or both of the women are clean freaks as the place was well kept and spotless.

"Want to see my room?"

"Sure."

They went into Mòlìhuā's room that was well kept and it appeared she was a sophisticated woman with truly good taste. This was a pleasant surprise to Tinougl that he wasn't getting tied to someone he wouldn't enjoy being around because some women lived like pigs. And when a female pig marries a male pig, they always end up with a pig pen.

Tinougl mindful of the rent situation because he truly didn't want to come back here until he finished his mission, said, "Now that we are in Santorini de Shénshèng, I can safely send you the credits via the secure link in your home I'm going to transfer you the money. After validating the phone number and name the credits were transferred and Mòlìhuā verified she had the 1000 credit encrypted tokens. She also had lots of 100 credit tokens from her work and tips rich people often gave to the singers at clubs. And she had another big surprise, the manager at the Grand Plexis de Chiveltros Dining Hall was able to track her down via the manager of the band, Lǎoxīng who had her contact information from previous work together, and she had another 50,000 credits the manager gave her with the note:

"As you know being an employee at a resort, management has the exclusive right to record and sell the music performed in the establishment. I felt your two songs were exemplary and I sold them to a recording studio who will sell subscriptions of them to the general-public. These 50,000 credits are your current royalties for the work. You will also receive residual royalties in the future as more subscriptions are sold to the public.

"If and when you can get back here, we will gladly do more recordings of other songs and you will get paid in likewise fashion. You are truly a wonderful singer, and you now have a lot of fans you are unaware of. Please contact me when you desire to come back to the Grand Plexis de Chiveltros Resort as we will gladly book you and arrange for you to have a band to perform with.

"Best wishes,

"Thurston bon Hamerstein."

"You probably need to be here when your room mate comes home in a while. I do not need to take that suitcase with me. I'll just take my backpack and we'll leave from here tomorrow; I can pick it up then."

"Sure. What about tonight?"

"Maybe you can swing by the Cuìlù Resort Hotel. I'll make sure I have a large bed, so we'll be more comfortable."

"I'll come by as soon as me and my room mate work everything out."

"Alright, I'll wait for you. Maybe I have enough time to get a swim and a massage?"

"Sure, do all that because my room mate is not going to get home for a couple more hours."

"Okay Mòlìhuā, I'm excited to get to meet your family and see where you grew up."

"My family will be excited too because we'll beat the deep space transmission to them warning them, I'm bringing a visitor."

"What will we do if they do not have enough room?"

"My family lives a couple miles from a very nice hotel. We probably should stay there for a while until they get used to the fact you are making love to their daughter quite often."

"Does your home have bad acoustics?"

"They will know everything you are doing."

"Yes, the hotel sounds like a better idea."

Mòlìhuā smiled and said, "I'll do whatever is required to make you feel at home and satisfied."

"Alright I'm going to go check in to the resort. Try to let me know how soon we can leave tomorrow so I can do our reservations."

"There are about 10 long distance transports that leave here about once an hour that go to a hub where we switch to the long jump flights that have a couple a day leaving for Konhagar."

"All right if it seems we'll not leave until noonish, I can get in another swim and work on my physical fitness."

"I'll let you know as soon as we get it all figured out. I'm sure we'll leave before noon."

"All right, I'll be waiting for you. If I'm not in my room call my communicator."

"I will."

The two hugged and kissed and Tinougl was out the door and down the elevator to the street where he signalled a Taxi-Limo though an APP. In three minutes, the taxi-Limo was on it's way to the Cuìlù Resort Hotel.

Tinougl again was lucky in that the same day they left Plexis de Chiveltros, the three Barracuda were traveling there because Spicey's spies said that's where her husband went, and other spies said that's where Tinougl was with his smoking hot singer girlfriend. Spicey was going to kill two birds with one stone and the other two Barracuda were along for the ride. After spending a couple days up there looking around, they quickly figured out the birds had flown out of the trap.

Tinougl called from the taxi-Limo for a reservation at the Cuìlù Resort Hotel and was quickly confirmed. He asked for the same room and the receptionist asked why?

"Because I enjoyed my two room attendants."

"That's not a problem. Whichever room we give you, they will be your room attendants because they are linked to all your future accommodations."

"That's nice to know."

"Tinougl, your old room is available, do you still want to go there?"

"Yes, I do."

"All right, it's all set."

Tinougl knew the drill just walk up to the elevator, they knew him well.

The elevator using facial recognition confirmed the guest and said,

"Welcome back Tinougl, we are happy you rejoined us."

"Thank you."

When the elevator stopped on his floor it informed him, "You have the same room you had the last time you were here."

"Thank you."

"You are welcome."

Tinougl saw the green light lit above the door to his resort hotel room and walked towards it. As soon as he was a foot away, the door opened, and he went inside.

"Welcome back," Tondron the room AI said.

"Thanks, it's good to be back. Did you guys miss me?"

"Of course, we did."

"I want you to know I'm going to have a visitor later, Wánměi de Mòlìhuā."

"Are you referring to the singer with the group performing in the resort Dining Hall?"

"Yes."

"Very interesting Tinougl. May I ask why she's visiting?"

"She's, my lover."

"That is quite extraordinary Tinougl. How did this come about?"

"I took her to the Grand Plexis de Chiveltros for a few days where we became lovers."

"Did you have fun?"

"Definitely. While we were there, she sang songs for me a couple times while we were having dinner."

"Why did she sing there?"

"She wanted to make me happy."

"Did she succeed?"

"More than you can imagine."

"We will be waiting for Madam Wánměi de Mòlìhuā's arrival and we have inserted her on your list of contacts that will be visiting you."

"She should be the only one on the list."

"That is correct she is the only one on the list."

"Thank you."

"What do you want to do today Tinougl?"

"I'm going to go down for a swim then get a massage."

"Do you wish us to provide you necessary swimming attire?"

"Yes, that would great."

"It's on the way, since we already have your size and choice in your file."

"Thank you."

In fifteen minutes, Tinougl was in the pool making laps. He pushed himself hard again because he knew he would be traveling for a few days and miss out on the workout and didn't know if he could do that where he was going.

Tinougl was happy the three Barracudas were not at the pool

today as he didn't want them to approach him and knew that Spicey would demand some of his time. She hadn't got her rocks off since the last time they were together, probably and he wasn't going to be able to provide it and didn't want that rich woman complicating his life or screw up his relationship with Mòlìhuā. He was glad he would be leaving the planet for good until he traveled back to the future, unless he decided not to go back.

Tinougl now had a theory why others never made it back. They chose not to come back after finding themselves into a situation like he now experienced.

There were several people watching him swim sitting in the soft recliner chairs and sitting at the tables drinking and socializing. There were no less than a dozen attractive women watching the exhibition and when he got near the 30th lap and starting to have agonizing pain, he had already caused them great curiousity. They had never seen anyone swim like this before including during sporting events. Probably the championship swimmers only swam half as long and not any faster. It was truly a remarkable sight.

Just like Tinougl experienced the day before, his muscles were extremely tight, and he was in a lot of pain and exhausted. If he were attacked now, he would not be able to defend himself.

When Tinougl got out of the swimming pool and went to his recliner and put on the bath robe and sandals, a few of the women were in awe looking at his body. His muscles were even now more apparent than before because they had tightened up so severely during the long swim. His six pack abs absolutely appeared incredible to women gawkers, and the swimsuit dynamics exposed the essence of a well enowed male. Some of those women were ready for him right now and if he were to approach them, they would politely ask him to escort them up to their hotel room for some boom boom.

Tinougl did not give away the fact he was in severe pain and worried about cramping up. That's why he didn't sit down on the soft recliner as he feared it would take him over an hour just to get back up and walk over to the SPA.

Without knowing the women were checking him out had he not put on the swim robe, they would be utterly salivating over his man buns.

The delightful receptionist was in the SPA and said, "Welcome back Tinougl. We are happy to see you again."

"Thanks, I can definitely use a good massage now."

"Please follow me."

In a minute he was in the massage room facing the very pretty Denettk who was more than eager to work over his body today. She of course was hoping to get some side benefit from her well endowed client. She was already suffering from Tinougl withdrawl syndrome and knew the best way to cure it was to get another good dose of his silver nectar in the place that gave her quantum satisfaction.

When Tinougl walked down into the large tub he barely made it. His muscles were super tight, and he was extremely drained of all energy. Those were probably his best thirty laps he ever swam.

Denettk applied the chemicals with another special additive she hoped would enhance Tinougl's arrosual and propel him into transcending a different level of sexual enthusiasm. Looks were deceiving, Tinougl was half dead, and she didn't know it. Every ounce of his energy was depleted. He had nothing left and his body ached in ways she could not imagine.

Some of the success of the massage was done in the bathing where the preliminary massage was done which allowed the massage technician to feel the body of the client and determine which muscles needed the most work. All Tinougls muscles were tight as a brick. Denettk was quite perplexed. She had never felt a man like this before. Was he even human?

Denettk didn't understand why Tinougl did not respond when she pressed, her nipples up to his face. He sat there like a sack of potatoes hardly moving with a gaze as if he were drug enduced. In a way he was drug induced. He was going through a near death experience and his body was pumping endorphins through his brain at the maximum rate to which it could produce it. Endorphins act like morphine and reduced Tinougl's perception of pain.

While swimming at a superhuman effort, the adrenaline was pumping through Tinougl's body, especially as he was nearing the thirtieth lap. His brain was pumping Serotonin, Norepinephrine, BDNF, Dopamine, and Prolactin into his body at a high level during his last few laps swimming.

Denettk wanting Tinougl to give her another gigantic orgasm had a special chemical combination she put in the water with the cannabinoids and opioids to help the inflammation in his muscles. The skin would absorb the chemicals and help the brain produce more oxytocin and dopamine. Usually, it only took ten minutes but sometimes Denettk would have to do a little mechanical agitation to the love muscle to accelerate the effects.

Today as she sat on Tinougls lap doing every trick in the book to influence his trandscending to that spontaneous eruption of pleasure, she was surprised he wasn't responding. Tinougl wasn't in the mood and his body could not support any further stress at the moment. Even her intentional mechanical agitation of his manhood wasn't working as he remained lymp.

"What's wrong with you today, Tinougl?"

"I'm exhausted, I think I overdid it in the pool."

"Your muscles are so tight. This is the worst I've ever felt."

"I'm feeling a lot better than I did just a few moments ago, but I'll be honest I wasn't sure I was going to be able to even walk in here."

"My poor baby. I'll do my best to help you."

"Thank you."

"You might be slightly dehydrated. I have some special drinks with me I take that give me extra energy when I have a large client load. Would you like one?"

"Sure."

Denettk climbed out of the wash tub and walked 10 feet to a refrigeration unit she had for her drinks and pulled one out and loosened the top slightly to make it easy for Tinougl then rejoined him and gave him the drink he started consuming. The drink contained taurine, ginseng, B vitamins, glucuronolactone and guarana (another source of caffeine). The artificial sweetner and carbonation added nicely to create a very tasty substance he quickly consumed and started feeling better immediately. The bath water saturated with all the love making chemicals and pain reducers added to the combined experience.

In ten minutes, Tinougl could easily have mounted Denettk and made her cry out in utter pleasure with strokes she was unaccustomed to, but now he was preserving all his manhood for that special woman he knew he would rendezvous with later. As Denettk pleaded with him to grind her into utter pleasure, Tinougl stuck with the story, "I'm sorry, Im just too exhausted. I over did the exercise today. The sweet lie was very operationally effective as eventually the horny bitch pulled back her unsolicited sexual favors requests. Denettk assumed lover boy would be back tomorrow and she could then satisfy her desires with the flesh of this magnificent being unlike any man she had met before.

For now, she cared for this wounded animal just as if it were a precious bird with a broken wing. She was a master at massage and knew the cannabinoids and opioids in the bath water would slowly have their effect, but she also knew that if Tinougl was expired as badly as he claimed, it might take his body several hours to bounce back to normal, and by then the SPA would be closed and she would be long gone.

~~~

About the same time as Tinougl was avoiding being drained of his male essence he was saving up for Mòlìhuā, the room mate had returned home, and they had their girls talk sprinkled with giggling as the adventures to the moon and back were disclosed.

Mòlìhuā's room mate was happy to receive a year's rent in case she didn't come back for a while. Mòlìhuā being a pragmatic woman packed all her essential items she would want to keep in the case she didn't return and informed the room mate she could have all her belongings in the event she didn't return. The room mate would not have to go shopping for clothes for a very long time if that turned out to be the case.

After enjoying the conversation with the room mate for a couple hours, Mòlìhuā said, "I think everything is packed and ready. We'll swing by here in the morning to pick up the luggage on our way to the space transportation center."

"I'll delay going to work and see you off and meet this incredible man you met."

"Thank you I appreciate that."

"I've known you a long time and I've never seen you engage a man like this before. He must be extra special if you are interested in him."

"I know he's in love with me."

"How do you know that?"

"I made him cry a couple times. I'm in his heart and he is in mine."

"You have always been a good judge of character and it kept
~~~

you out of trouble. You've never had a disappointment in your life because you have good common sense."

"My mother didn't raise a fool."

"You must have a wonderful mother, because you are a classy lady, and you earned my respect many times over."

"Thank you. And I feel the same way about you."

"If you do not come back, I will miss you terribly."

"I'll make it a point to try and come back and visit you in a few years. By then we will be settled down and my family will be adjusted to Tinougl."

"You will always be welcome here and thanks to my recent pay raise, I can more than handle the rent by myself."

"That's good to hear."

"Okay, honey go see your boyfriend. I'm sure he misses you already."

"I know he does."

"See you in the morning."

"Thank you for everything."

"Thank you for being such a good friend."

"I'm very grateful to you."

The women walked to the door and there was one last hug and a few tears already forming on both women. It was a transistional period in Mòlìhuā's life and her friend and room mate were happy for her, but she knew she would greatly miss her. Good friends are hard to come by.

Mòlìhuā had a regular Taxi-Limo to take her to the Cuìlǜ Resort Hotel when she was working as personal security was important.

She had the company on speed dial, and they linked her up with her favorite driver who was sent to pick her up and take her to the resort. In three minutes, the transportation arrived, and the door opened automatically by remote control from the driver.

Mòlìhuā entered the vehicle which soon shut the door via remote control, and they were off to the resort. The driver didn't bother asking destination since he already knew.

In a short while, the Taxi Limo pulled into the circular driveway to unload passengers. The door opened and Mòlìhuā stepped out of the vehicle onto the sidewalk and proceeded inside the resort passing a few familiar faces that were quite surprised when she walked directly to the elevator that already had her programmed to go up to Tinougl's room. In less than three minutes she entered the room and there was Tinougl back in his street clothes and all smiles.

"What would you like to do Mòlìhuā?"

"I talked to the manager and explained tomorrow I was leaving to fly home to my family for personal matters and didn't expect to be coming back soon. He asked that I go to the Dining Hall tonight they want to give me a little send off."

"No problem. Should we dress up for it?"

Before Mòlìhuā could answer, Tondron spoke up and said, "I've been instructed to inform Mòlìhuā, her manager is sending fashion designers to prepare both of you for tonights festivities."

"How does he know I'm here?"

"Mòlìhuā, I'm sorry to inform you that you are now a semi famous person. Word has reached back to the Managager about your wonderful performances at the Grand Plexis de Chiveltros and he has since subscribed to your performances that are being sold in amazing volumes. Somehow the film and recording industry also discovered you would be here today and are sending representatives. You must look your best. Also, the manager Thurston bon Hamerstein at the Grand Plexis de Chiveltros is sending the entire band here tonight for your going away party."

"Why would he do that?"

"You made him a lot of money and gave the Grand Plexis de Chiveltros a lot of prestage."

Mòlìhuā knew these were powerful people and it was in her best interest to play along with them, or bad things could happen to her and Tinougl and she responded, "I suppose I might as well look good to see my friends off."

"They will be grateful to you because it's not every day they get to perform with a superstar."

"I'm not a super star."

"Mòlìhuā, a lot of things are happening now in the media concerning you. Your fame is shooting up to stratospheric high over night. With galactic communications, your performance is already selling on a dozen other planets."

Tinougl felt the sting, he knew that he would also be the focus of the media's interest. He was never happier about going to Konhagar than right now.

Predictably the fashion designer and her staff showed up in a few moments and they immediately went to work on Mòlìhuā.

The divider went up and after Mòlìhuā's bath and shampoo, and they were working on her. Soon afterwards, Tinougl was getting his own treatment and after he dried off and found himself getting a new hair design. In twentyfive minutes, the hair design looked incredible and his male makeup going on changed his looks to the point he was not recognizable as Tinougl. Anyone who might be interested in him would not make the connection in the Dining Hall which made him feel more comfortable.

The change in appearance was astonishing and Tinougl was lucky that Tondron loaded his new image into his security portfolio, otherwise Tinougl might have issues getting back in his resort hotel room. Suddenly all that was left for Tinougl to do was put on his dress suit for the evening.

The covered clothes rack was open, and the fashion designer pulled out what she recommended for the night, and they tried it on and it fit perfectly because they had his measurements from his soirée with the wealthy women.

As soon as he was dressed and checked, the designer said, "You are ready to leave now and Mòlìhuā's ready now as well."

The dividers then were swiveled out of the way, and there Mòlìhuā was standing in the full-length red dress evening gown that went all the way to the floor. Her shoulders were bare, and the top of the dress covered her breasts and nothing more. The high heeled shooes made Mòlìhuā look several inches taller giving the illusion her buttocks were a lot smaller and her figure immaculate. The image was stunning. The red dress went perfectly to match with Tinougl in his fabulous black suit and white silk shirt that gave an exhibit that would make women's knees weak in the Dining Hall. If they knew supplemental information such as his muscles and his tool, they would be drooling and quite jealous of Mòlìhuā.

"We'll clean up here, you should go down to the Dining Hall, they are waiting for you."

"Thank you."

The couple proceeded to their destiny. They were feeling good, but Mòlìhuā would admit she had a few butterflies in her belly from the latest news from Tondron.

As they approached the entrance to the Dining Hall there was a line already backing up. Two security men had been alerted the couple was coming down and were shown holographic images on their special heads-up glasses so they could identify the couple and as Tinougl and Mòlìhuā approached the long line, they approached them immediately and one said, "Tinougl and Mòlìhuā we are part of your security detail for the evening. We will escort you to your table."

People in line overheard the conversation and turned around to look at who it was the security guys were talking with and immediately discovered it was the new star they were coming to see and as soon as Mòlìhuā was several steps ahead of them she overheard one woman saying to the other: "There she is."

They walked into the very busy Dining Hall. It had never seen this kind of business, especially this early into the evening. The place was packed and right in the middle with a clear view of the stage at about ten feet from the band was a table with a beautiful bouqet of flowers and ornate settings with candlelight where the security men took them and then one said, "This is your table. We hope you enjoy."

"Thank you," Mòlìhuā responded.

One of the security men helped Mòlìhuā with her chair and the other security person who was also well dressed, helped slide in Tinougl's chair after he was seated.

The conversations in the Dining Hall were kind of loud and suddenly there was a major shift as it was evident the crowd was synchronizing their conversations based on the arrival of the VIP guest.

The normal band came out and started playing. It was kind of interesting the female singer who was performing tonight was the singer that performed with Mòlìhuā at the Grand Plexis de Chiveltros. She gave a wonderful smile and blew Mòlìhuā a kiss.

Mòlìhuā was wondering why she was acting so super pleasant. What Mòlìhuā didn't know because she hadn't checked her communicator since she was talking with her friend at their residence, all the band members at Grand Plexis de Chiveltros had received a gigantic bonus because the manager had sold a significant number of subscriptions. Grand Plexis de Chiveltros sent Mòlìhuā a second payment more than 10,000 credits. She was now semi rich at a young age.

The big boys of the film and recording industry were also there tonight and took good account of how lovely Mòlìhuā looked in that red dress, and ideas were already flooding their thoughts.

The musicians performed lovely music with the new singer and Tinougl's favorite waitress Madalyn bon Donkers appeared with their drinks she knew they would order out of habbit.

The evening was all staged. This wasn't really a going away dinner, it was actually a coming out celebration with more exposure to the entertainment industry now starving for a new Diva.

After the set finished and the musicians took a break, the lovely singer came off the stage and walked over to Mòlìhuā and said, "Mòlìhuā you have done more for my singing career than anyone ever did before. I owe you a lot. In the next set we are going to perform *Dǎkāi Wánměi de Liánhuā*, I know it would sound so much better if you would come up and sing it with me."

Mòlìhuā looked at Tinougl and said, "I'd be happy to perform it for my sweet love, if he says it's okay."

Tinougl was a little bashful, but managed to say, "I would love to hear her sing it."

The singer threw her arms around Mòlìhuā and hugged her and said,

"This will make me very happy. Thank you for singing it with me."

After drinks the musicians went back up on the stage and began performing again. The singer was noticeably better as if someone lit a fire. She knew this would result in another lucrative bonus, so she was thoroughly invigorated."

After several more songs, the musicians left the stage except for the singer and suddenly the band performers from Grand Plexis de Chiveltros walked up on the stage and took their positions. The singer then made an announcement:

"Ladies and Gentlement, we are pleased to have a special guest with us tonight. Just back from her devue at Grand Plexis de Chiveltros is the lovely Wánměi de Mòlìhuā. The singer held out her two hands towards Mòlìhuā urging her to come up on stage, and so Mòlìhuā stood up and walked over to the frontal stairway onto the stage next to the singer. One of the other musicians walked up and handed Mòlìhuā a microphone. The microphone wasn't necessary, it was a hold over from the old days to add a psychological element in the psyche of the audience by bringing back memories of those golden years of broadcasts.

The manager of the group was on the piano and by now had memorized the piece and refined it even further with his interpretation. The other band members performing their instruments added to the splendid cocophony of sound that resonated the audience even before the singer got started.

After the lead up, the singing began and the lyrics flowed. The Diva was resonating the crowd and casting a wonderful spell on them. The gratification and satisfaction were immense.

Looking at Mòlìhuā in the red dress had a profound effect on Tinougl. The surreal nature of what went on left an indelible mark in his psyche that for someone with a photographic memory would never dull.

The film and recording execs were mezmorized. This raw talent was more than they could bargain for. The manager of this facility knew the rules and procedures of marketing this performance and it was recorded using the best holographics money could buy. The performance was a lot longer than most spell binding beauties that charmed many audiences in the past, but too short for the crowd's taste. They wanted it to last a lot longer. *Dǎkāi Wánměi de Liánhuā* was quickly topping all the charts in the entertainment and recording industries. But with the made-up Diva sporting the splendor and the elegance tonight in that red dress, it created more enthusiasm. The bittersweet ending of the last note that Mòlìhuā sang created a firestorm in the audience that wanted more. The applause was gigantic and the film and recording exects knew what to expect from the performance at Grand Plexis de Chiveltros. Mòlìhuā's performances were now starting to get predictable: fantastic.

It took six or seven minutes for the applause to die down and the other singer whispered something in Mòlìhuā's ear, and she shook her head in the affirmative and the band leader knew what the question was, and the band anticipated it. Mòlìhuā then took a moment to say a few words before the band started playing. Looking directly at Tinougl, she said, "This is for you."

The next song they all knew well lasted eight minutes and filled a lot of people in the audiencee with profound joy and happiness.

Mòlìhuā reached a new stratum tonight and owed it all to Tinougl. He made her what he was by giving her the reason to perform in such a grand fashion. To be honest, she never tried so hard in her life to make those lyrics sound as good as she did. She did so for the love she felt for Tinougl to send him the massage how much me meant to her. The fact he wanted to be with her and be a part of her family touched her deeply. Her love was golden.

After all the applause died down, Mòlìhuā returned to her table and Tinougl stood to greet her and help her with her chair. In doing so he also put the spotlight on himself because the three Barracudas were observing all this on a big screen at the Grand Plexis de Chiveltros and knew damn well who prince charming was. Sparky wasn't going to divulge what she knew because she would then be a target herself of some of Spicey's vindictiveness. At the same time, she knew she had to protect Schemer for the same reason. They all had to play dumb and let Spicey stew who was adamantly upset the young singer had stolen her boyfriend and now appeared to be a rising star, the next super Diva. It felt unfair how she lost Tinougl. All she really could do about it now is go cry herself to sleep later.

To help keep the happiness flowing with the audience, they rotated the two bands all night long, so the variety of music was very broad and very successful. The Dining Hall had never seen such an auspicious day.

Tinougl knew they had a long day ahead of them and they needed to get a restful sleep so about two hours after they finished eating, he suggested, "Let's go up to our room and have our private celebration."

Tinougl stood up walked around and slid Mòlìhuā's chair out for her and she stood up and grabbed his hand and they walked out of the Dinning Hall with the two security guys directly behind. Some people tried to approach but suddenly there were two more security guys boxing them in and opening a pathway out of the buzzing Dining Hall and over to the elevator.

Two of the security men waited at the elevator while the other two went up with them to their room.

Tinougl knew what they were doing, as he realized his lover was now a super Diva and they required protection. The door to his hotel room opened and one of the security men said, "Two of us will be outside your door for the rest of the night. You do not have to be afraid of being disturbed."

"Thank you, I appreciate what you are doing."

"No problem, you definitely earned it."

As soon as they were in the room and the door shut, Tondron popped up and said, "Tinougl, the resort has initiated extra security for you tonight. The security detail will be outside your door all night long. Also, I want you to know in the event there is danger Guāiqiǎo is a martial arts expert with some special weapons and if there is any threat towards you, he will immediately be poised to deal with any threats if they make it past the exterior security men."

"Thank you I appreciate that."

"Because we are in a different threat condition for the room, Guāiqiǎo will be standing by the door tonight to give you an added layer of security."

"I do not think it's necessary, but thanks anyway."

"We always increase security when VIP's stay with us."

"We are a VIP?"

"No, Wánměi de Mòlìhuā is now a VIP and is now known on 30 planets in our Empire. We expect by morning that number will grow to 60. The next time you stay with us, we'll put you in a Penthouse at no additional cost."

"Interesting."

The two undressed and skipped the sleeping attire and Tinougl gave instructions for a wakeup in the morning and asked, "Please turn out the light."

The two lovers were nestled in the bed holding each other in their arms filled full of love but also reached a level of slumber together as they were both tired for various reasons.

Halfway in the middle of the night Mòlìhuā woke up feeling a strong desire and could hear Tinougls shallow breathing knowing he was sleeping but she wanted him now as she was feeling that unrequeted love at the moment. One of her hands grabbed his tool and started messaging it. The other hand took his hand and she spread open her legs to put the hand on her womanhood so that Tinougl would feel her silky wetness when he came too. At first

Tinougl thought he was dreaming about Denettk in what she was doing to him today which he did not solicit, but the mere thought of touching her like that caused him to feel great effects.

The combination of feeling the mechanical agitation on his tool with Mòlìhuā's hand and feeling the wetness between her legs, caused Tinougl's brain to start producing far more oxytocin and dopamine. It wasn't clear exactly when Tinougl passed from dreamland to reality and as soon as he reached reality and discovered what was going on he turned over and slid on top of Mòlìhuā and mounted her and was soon exreting his silver magic into her which triggered a significant orgasm in each of them that slowly faded into more sleep and a wakeup call in the morning.

Mòlìhuā was given the honors to use the bathroom first because Tinougl liked to take his time and didn't want to leave a sour scent behind when he finished.

CHAPTER NINETEEN

ON THE WAY TO KONHAGAR

In due time they were dressed and heading for a Taxi-Limo to go back to Mòlìhuā's home and pick up all their luggage for the trip.

Two hours later after saying goodbye to her room mate, the couple was on an interplanetary transport on their way to a transportation hub, where they would change space craft and take that lonely flight for a long distance to discover Mòlìhuā's family. When they eventually arrived, they beat the fame by several days.

The space flight to the intergalactic transportation hub took several hours. This hub anchored in space orbiting a planet in a nearby solar system was purposely built away from the Tartar planet to significantly reduce transportation flows down to a minimum of directions which provided additional security since space crarft were not expected arriving from other directions. If a spacecraft came to Tartar from an unexpected direction, it would be intercepted and possibly boarded well before it got within weapons range to the planet.

As the interplanetary transport got near the transportation hub, it was sequenced in a landing pattern of many space craft that lit up the pilots displays showing an electronic freeway in space of orderly precisely spaced transports that flrew through security buoys confirming their identity and purpose. Looking up to this formation of intergalactic spacecraft from the planet at night appeared like a long streak of light as their running lights created a colorful imagery of a multi-colored lines.

The transportation hub had dozens of slots on each side of a major arms protruding on sides of the large circular hub. Each space craft that required access to the hub was built to general specifications that conformed to the size of the slots it landed in. Each slot could stack up several space craft with independent access tubes for passengers to get on or leave. From the hub to the Tartarnite Empire Capital City, Santorini de Shénshèng, there was only a single electronic pathway which had several security buoys along the way validating the transports and their manifests. This also had an impact on reducing illegal black marketeers access but was not able to eliminate the black marketeers who employed ingenious methods to defeat the electronic gateway.

The interplanetary transport docked in one of the slots and in less than a few minutes the telescoping tube with built in air locks on each end attached to the spacecraft using robotic grippers.

The space transport company would transfer their luggage, they only had to exit the space craft and once they got into the terminal, ride the people mover to the central concourse and head for the gate of their departer. They had plenty of time since it wasn't leaving for two hours.

"Would you like to go to a café and get a drink and snack?" Tinougl asked.

"That sounds like a great idea," Mòlìhuā responded and dutifully followed to a café that they were coming up on.

The café hostest took them to a seat that had an excellent view of a nice portion of the transportation hub. From there they could see space craft come and go.

The hostess handed them menu's and asked, "Would like something to drink?"

Mòlìhuā knew she wanted something that would help her

relax more and one drink she discovered while performing was a particular Elixir, so she asked, "Do you have Lǐzǐ Guavastrian Elixir?"

"Yes, we do."

"I'll have one of them."

"How about you sir?"

"I'll have what she's having."

"I'll be right back with your drinks."

This café wasn't small, it easily seated 50 people and a lot of travellers had the same thing in mind.

After a few minutes looking around Mòlìhuā looked at Tinougl and asked,

"I wonder why all those people are staring at me?"

Mòlìhuā had no way of knowing the current situation with her nor did she know over Five Billion people had viewed her performances and subscribed. Shortly after their drinks were served and Mòlìhuā had a couple nice swallows of the wonderful elixir that was already calming her down, a well-dressed gentleman approached their table and he asked, "Are you the singer Wánměi de Mòlìhuā?"

Mòlìhuā made the fatal mistake of adhering to her mother's upbringing where she was taught honesty was always the best policy, responded in a very polite tone, "Yes I am."

The gentleman who watched the performances telecast from Grand Plexis de Chiveltros as well as Santorini de Shénshèng's Cuìlù Resort Hotel, smiled and said, "I must congratulate you. I must say your two songs were the best I've heard in my lifetime, and I've heard quite a few."

He then held out a business card and said, "I'm Reladondo bon

Scrafatorious the chief operations officer for Guānxīng Entertainment."

"It's a pleasure to meet you Reladondo bon Scrafatorious."

"Please call me Reladondo."

"Reladondo, this is my special friend Tinougl."

"Hello Tinougl, I saw you as well on the recordings, and it should be quite an honor to have such a Diva sing her heart out for you."

"Yes, it is. I'm blessed that I met Mòlìhuā."

"I hate to appear as a nosy person Tinougl, but you do have a nice sounding voice, what do you do for a living."

"I'm a Novelist, I write books."

"Are there any particular books you wrote you recommend I read?"

"Sure, my spy novel Sanctuary City."

"I'll certainly check it out and if I like it, I might offer you a movie deal if you could convince Mòlìhuā to play a role. Are there any beautiful women in the book?"

"Yes, in fact there are three of them."

"Which one would you recommend she play the part if we film it?"

"Obviousy the final woman in the main character's life."

"That statement seems to be so metaphoric if not outright presumptive."

"Perhaps it matches my life and my circumstances."

"If Mòlìhuā is the final woman in your life, nobody could do better."

"I agree completely."

"Enjoy your meal and I hope you contact me. I will read your book Tinougl and Mòlìhuā I'm ready to sign a contract with you that would be very lucrative when you feel you are ready."

"Thank you for the offer."

Reladondo bon Scrafatorious was very versed in the reality of movie stars and Diva's and knew this couple was in trouble and closer to being mobbed than they realized as soon as the terminal was made aware of Mòlìhuā's presence. He had no less than four well armed men in his security detachment, being one of the largest entertainment producers in the Empire and when he went back to his table he gave his security guys their marching orders, "See the lovely couple I was talking with?"

"Yes boss?"

"The woman is Wánměi de Mòlìhuā now suddenly one of the top celebrities rising in meteoric trajectory. Make sure they get on their tansport without being mobbed and molested and contact space port authorities for additional backup, I don't think you guys will be able to handle it when they finish and walk out of here."

"Right on it, boss," the senior security expert responded and stood up and walked out of the café.

As they enjoyed their drinks and ate a light lunch, Tinougl was at the perfect angle to see the entrance of the café and noticed a large crowd gathering outside. It dawned on them; they were in trouble now. This was a disaster in the making. They should have just schedattled directly to their space transport and avoided public exposure.

Then out of nowhere came some spaceport security people that were slowly moving the crowd out of the way. The noise level was intensifying, and a lot of pictures were being taken including with some old fashion flashes. All the meals were prepaid before served so the couple could depart when they wanted.

Tinougl said, "I think we need to get out of here. That crowd I believe is here because of you."

"Why me?"

"You obviousy have been seen by a lot of people from the recordings made while you were singing yesterday."

"I do not need to eat anymore, us just leave then."

The two stood up simultaneously and walked to the exit. Tinougl knew somehow the kind gentleman had arranged for the crowd control and bowed at Reladondo bon Scrafatorious who responded likewise as they exited the café.

As soon as they hit the entrance there was a wall of twenty security officers who evidently knew where they were going providing a strong wedge to split the crowd out of the way allowing them to proceed to their transport space craft. The good news was the boarding ramp to the space craft was only one hundred yards away which they made in no time. If Tinougl had looked behind he would have seen an astonishing mob following behind to get a look at the couple.

The security personnel escorted them through the tubular entrance to the space craft and sealed off the area to everyone except people with valid ticketed passengers with valid reservations.

"I hope we don't run into that at your parents' home."

"My parents live in an agricultural zone and there is an eight-foot-tall wall around the entire zone that helps keep the city folk out."

"Why do they do that?"

"If they didn't have the wall there would never be any crops to harvest."

"That sounds reassuring."

"You will be perfectly safe there. Only friends and relatives get into my parents' compound."

"I thought we were going to stay in a hotel for a while?"

"We might need to stay with my parents for a bit until all this dies down."

"Did you ever think for a minute, what if it never dies down?"

"You should have thought about that before you gave Reladondo bon Scrafatorious the name of your book because it will probably get turned into a movie."

"But would you want the role in the movie?"

"Absolutely if there's a love scene between the woman and the main character."

"There is."

About that time the flight attendant came up to the couple and spoke. "We have this open bay seating so that people can watch entertainment and be here during takeoff so we can be sure and account for everyone. I've talked with spaceport security, and we normally do not allow passengers into their private cabins until after launch and acceleration to transport speeds."

"We understand Tinougl responded."

The flight attendant then explained a sudden change in policy: "Because you are a VIP and the chaos that erupted in the spaceport when the public discovered you are here, we've determined that it would be best if you be in your cabin until we reach transport speeds because the passengers tend to go to the cafateria or their own cabins to rest and it thins out really good which will make it easier for us to deal with the passengers who might get rowdy otherwise."

"Sure, not a problem."

"Please follow me."

The two stood up from their chairs and followed the flight attendant back to their private cabin that had two births and a private toilet. There was a paper sticker across the toilet in the water closet area that said, "Do not use until after launch and artificial gravity turned on."

Tinougl locked the cabin door to prevent other passengers to enter uninvited.

There wasn't much to do at the moment but sit back and relax. Tinougl asked, "Would you mind if I turned on the holographic projector and see news updates?"

"Sure, no problem." Mòlìhuā replied.

After watching news updates which didn't provide anything of interest to Tinougl, he surveyed other channels and came across a series of entertainment channels and one of them was a music entertainment show. They were playing the top ten songs and Tinougl started watching with reasonable expectations. The music was extremely good which quickly conveyed to Tinougl how good these top artists really were.

After five songs, he was in for a huge surprise. The next two songs were performed by Mòlìhuā!

These were the two songs she sang at Grand Plexis de Chiveltros. The audio and the video holograph combined to create a surreal image for Tinougl, just as if he was sitting there in the restaurant. At the time he probably did not appreciate Mòlìhuā's beauty as much as he should have, but this recording did make him take notice. It was crystal clear Mòlìhuā had struck the nerves of the public and inspired them to a great extent. Here he was, a spy who wanted a low profile, with a very famous woman and it's clear the Empire knew about him too.

The real Tinougl he had stolen the identity simply went missing. Nobody knew what happened to him, but his literary works were definitely real, and his resemblance was eerily similar and with the cosmetic surgery for the mission made the facial recognition an absolutely perfect match.

One of the minor fabric-of-time distortions was caused by Reladondo bon Scrafatorious reading the book "Sanctuary City" and then producing a movie basd on it. Without the time travel, the real Tinougl would have simply disappeared as a nobody the public would ever remember him.

Mòlìhuā observed Tinougl watching the holographs and when they were done, he changed the channel to star watching video.

"Does my singing bore you?"

"No, it's good every time I see it."

"You really like it?"

"I love it."

Mòlìhuā walked over and sat down on Tinougl's lap and put her arms around him and hugged and kissed him.

After a few kisses, Tinougl said, "We better stop that before we get out of control and have to go further."

"I wouldn't mind that now."

"I want to watch us get up to transport speeds and see how the stars look then."

"All right, I'll let you relax until after all that, then this pussy cat may want to purr in your arms."

"You can stay here and purr in my arms while we watch it together."

"I think I would like that."

All the passengers were soon on board. The transport in the slot in front of them had departed so it was clear to leave now as the pilot-initiated undocking.

The passengers were warned, "Ladies and Gentlemen, we will be transiting from transport center artificial gravity to self gravity in a few moments. Take time wherever you are to fasten yourself with a harness until we transition between the two gravity fields."

The space craft then slowly edged through the slot and soon was fully discharged out and into open space. The acceleration was slow and steady until they were far away from the transport hub, then powerful propulsion engines added continuously to the acceleration in a satisfactory manner with the ships artificial gravity engaged.

The pilot then came over the intercom making an announcement, "Ladies and gentlemen I would like to thank you for choosing this spaceline for your transportation needs today. I have switched on our artificial gravity, so you are now free to move around and utilize restrooms and the cafeteria at this time."

The space hub they just left was the last real time communications with the Tartarnite Empire Capital City, Santorini de Shénshèng, also the banking center of the Empire. Mòlìhuā feeling comfortable simply staying in Tinougl's lap and huggin him, felt the silent buzzer go off on her communicator. She said, "I'm getting up, I just received a massage from someone I need to check. She wasn't expecting any communications. The communications were from the bank she used which alerted her to financial transactions that just occurred under the title, "deposits were made to your account. Click here to see details.

Mòlìhuā clicked on the icon and was soon reading the deposit information. She was downright startled. Her royalties from five billion subscribers appeared spell binding and sent chills up her spine. She didn't know how to take it and felt lucky to have Tinougl to help her keep her witts under the circumstances. Women who were in similar situations in the past didn't have a solid anchor and eventually had tremendous issues in their lives, often cut short.

Tinougl didn't know what Mòlìhuā was looking at, but she definitely had a mood change. In a few more seconds she put her communicator back in her pocket and went back and hopped on Tinougl's lap and threw her arms around him and held him very tight. She was evidently rattled. Tinougl was wise knew it would be best for her to convey to him the nature of it when she felt up to it. He sensed she needed him now more than ever. He was also analyzing his own posture and re-evaluating everything and what he must do.

He didn't like operating in this fashion but the spy in him kept on making him think, "How bad do you want it?" Perhaps it was part of his conditioning and his indoctrination, to complete the mission at all costs. He would eventually have to chose between two paths, either of which would impact his very essence. His mission might be more essential than he knew. Some of it was compartmentalized in case he was captured. His mission was still in progress and would not be a failure or a victory until he made that fateful decision and crawled back in the time machine and hit the blue button. *Would it still work then?*

Holding Mòlìhuā in his arms made that decision far more complicated and in time he knew it would get even worse. Nobody would ever understand what he was going through. He took solace in the fact he could at least temporaneously enjoy the worldly feasts and extrapolate the essence of happiness until that bittersweet moment.

Being in Tinougl's arms calmed Mòlìhuā down quite a bit. Also knowing she would soon be home and with her family added a layer of contentment she strongly desired to overcome the shock that presented her by the most recent revelations that affected her personally. She had no idea how fast this sort of thing could get out of hand and the recollection of the crowd back on the space hub scared her. She might have unwittingly altered her life in ways she wasn't planning. Going from basically a cabaret singer to a superstar Diva overnight was shocking to say the least. It was too fast and furious for her personality. She knew she wasn't ready for that stratospheric jump in society. Unfortunately, it was now out of her control. A person can't reach her level and simply back down. Powerful entities would never allow her to assume her previous circumstances. She would sooner or later have to learn how to deal with it and cope.

Thanks to the fact they were wearing their casual street clothes, they would not stand out in ways to alert travellers on the long-distance transport. Heading towards the most distant planet in the Empire was also a good thing since they were not such a cosmopolitan society full of social climbers. People would take them at a more low-key mannerism.

With Mòlīhuā's head lying against Tinougl's left shoulder, she did not block the view of the stars in front of them. As they jumped to hyper-velocities, Tinougl enjoyed the view for an important reason. It would look identical to 500 years from now. Some things would not change in time.

Without artificial intelligence now navigating the long-distance transport, they could never go this fast and this straight, and the journey would be prohibitively long. In just a few more days they would be arriving down on the planet Konhagar.

Mòlīhuā felt so relieved being held in Tinougl's arms that she succumbed to a stress nap. Soon she was purring and Tinougl could easily feel her pulse and knew she was resting and didn't wish to disturb her. Plus, she felt good.

In about an hour, they had been traveling high speed and over half of the passengers had made a trip to the cafateria, where food and drinks came with the fee. Actually, it was the transportation company's analysis that giving them the free food and drinks would eliminate several issues, including people carrying food and packages onboard that would add to trash disposal. By providing all that at no additional charge, they could design the packaging and content to such an extent that they could minimize trash storage issues as everthing was recyclable and easily converted in the trash shredders and easily sent through the nuclear rocket engines where it would be part of the plasma created by liquid hydrogen super heated by the nuclear reactors creating tremendous thrust.

In about an hour, Mòlìhuā woke from her nerotic fog created by stress emotions created by the shocking revolation of her recent banking transactions.

She then stirred and felt the need to use the restroom and slowly stood up and walked over to their private bathroom and drained her kidneys.

Mòlìhuā came out of the toilet smiling and said, "Let's go to the cafateria and see what they have to offer."

"All right, sounds good to me," Tinougl replied somehow thinking the food would not be as good as the resorts where he got spoiled.

They made their way to the cafeteria. The shipwide security system that operated off facial recognition locked their space cabin the minute they left even though there really wasn't anything left behind of value to steal.

Nobody paid attention to the couple as they transversed the open bay seating area where people went to watch the entertainment and socialize between films and holographic entertainment.

When they reached the cafateria there wasn't anyone there, which was okay with Tinougl. They checked out their options with the automated food preperators and it would end up only as snack time. Getting spoiled at resorts was not good this close to long distance transportation. *Perhaps in a day or two their appetites would return to indulge in more than a snack.*

They could actually get alcoholic drinks since the automated service was augmented with facial recognition. There were elixirs and entertainment drinks people could drink and enjoy company while injesting some of those concoctions.

Tinougl could not help but feel like he needed a concoction right now as he was almost in a mental zone that seemed surreal if not impossible. Once Mòlìhuā got the nerve to divulge what was going on with her bank accounts, he would only feel more melancholic. But he brought this on to himself seducing this beautiful woman. As he analyzed the situation, he knew there was no other way to get himself planted almost like a mole into Konhagar.

If he were to die as a spy in the near future, at least he had a rare opportunity to receive the love from a Diva. For that he was eternally grateful.

They each selected an elixir and tasted it. The conclusion after sampling the elixir, it tasted pleasant. Long distance transports were exemplary in beverage service because they had to deal with psychology of passengers, some of which could be claustrophobic and not know it. One of the flight attendants for this flight had full medical credentials and could just about perform any emergency service, but if it came to claustrophobic passengers that were losing it, they would be injected and sleep the rest of the trip in a special cabin under restraints if necessary.

The staff was very well trained in taking down unruly passengers. Other passengers certainly would not want to threaten Tinougl or Mòlìhuā because they would end up with a lot of pain with a knee in the middle of their back with arms fully disabled and painful.

A woman and her daughter came into the cafateria. The young lady looked somewhere between twelve and fourteen years of age and the very second, she spotted Mòlìhuā her face lit up like a Christmas tree. The mother wasn't paying attention, but the sophisticated looking daughter approached Mòlìhuā and asked, "Excuse me, are you the lady that was singing on the music video's last night?"

Mòlìhuā liked the young lady and replied, "I'll give you the answer if you promise to keep it a secret and not tell anyone."

"I promise."

"Yes, I'm Wánměi de Mòlìhuā singer and if you watched the video, you probably saw my sweet friend in the video as well," Mòlìhuā answered and gestured towards Tinougl.

The young lady was now super animated and had a dozen questions to ask and started by asking, "Are you going to Konhagar?"

"Yes, that's where I'm from."

"Will you sing while you are there."

"Perhaps I may, and if I do, I will invite you to the performance."

"I would love that if my mother would take me."

"I'm not scheduled to do any singing there; I'm visiting my family. But if somehow, I'm asked to do a performance, it will likely be at the Serintango Hotel and Resort. If it happens it will be on the local news reports. Have your mother bring you there if I perform. I will remember you and make sure you and your mother get nice seats."

"I will I promise."

"In the meantime, you must keep our secret, okay?"

"I will. I love the way you sing. it's so uplifting and inspirational to me. What happened to make you sing so beautifully?"

"That's another secret, do you promise not to tell anyone?"

"Yes, I promise."

"This gentleman cast a spell upon me. Without that it never would have happened."

The young lady looked at Tinougl who was very attractive with that actor's jaw and the residual hair design that would likely last another week or so. Her heart went pitter pat as she saw how awesomely handsome Tinougl was, and she too felt the magic spell.

The young lady's mother then urged her to get a drink and something to eat since that's why they came to the cafeteria in the first place.

The four sat there snacking, drinking, and having a good time. The young lady's mother took a liking to the couple who treated her daughter very nicely and acted nice themselves and not stuffy like a lot of entertainment people usually conduct themselves. The mother had seen some of the media reports on Mòlìhuā as well as the performances with her daughter and was so surprised she was so sweet and not condescending like most of the super Diva's turned out. *Perhaps since she was from Konhagar is why she's so down to earth?*

The woman asked Mòlìhuā, "What do you plan on doing while you are on Konhagar?"

"I've not seen my family in quite a while. I've been struggling as a cabaret singer and need a break."

"Anything interesting planned while you are at Konhagar?"

"We do not have anything planned. We just want to relax and visit my family. The time spent with them will be precious. I'm so happy to go home."

"Does you family know about your fame?"

Mòlìhuā replied, "My mother is far more concerned about my health and safety than she is my fame."

"As she should."

"Konhagar is nothing like Santorini de Shénshèng are you sure your friend will enjoy it?"

"He's proven to me to be very flexible. I think he cares so much for my happiness; it will not matter to him in any way if I'm happy."

"Well then you are lucky dear, because my husband isn't quite so accommodative, that's why we are going to Konhagar without him."

Mòlìhuā could see jealousy written all over the woman. Her dreams never came true and now here she is with a young daughter who would be very vulnerable in a few more years as she reached that age when women get frisky.

Mòlìhuā knew better than to ask any probing questions in front of the daughter because she already figured it out and there would be no point as she would unlikely see this stranger again after they arrived on Konhagar. Tinougl also was an expert social engineer and knew not to go there and believed as most spies do: silence is golden.

The daughter was somewhat disappointed the couple was not dressed up like they were in the videos, but she could see they were very attractive.

Mòlìhuā was learning fast and knew it was time for them to crawl back in their cave and ignore the passengers as much as they could for the remainer of the trip. Nevertheless, the daughter kept an eye open for them in case they reappeared, she wanted to pester them some more and wished her mother would let her go freely about the space craft so she could mingle with other passengers. She had seen several young men she thought would be charming and if they lived on Konhagar, it would be nice to meet them and get to know them for future trips. The young lady knew far more about the birds and the bees than her mother realized. Her mother would be in a state of shock if she heard the conversations her daughter had with other girls in her school!

"Enjoy your trip to Konhagar," Mòlìhuā said then stood up and gave a respectful bow to the mother and the daughter.

Toinougl knew to follow her lead and leave the mother and

daughter and go back to their private space cabin and see what they could do to enjoy themselves.

Once they got there, Mòlìhuā figured out what to do next. "We can lay on the bed and watch the entertainment together."

"Good idea."

"Take your clothes off first, I don't want you putting a lot of germs into that bed."

"Not a problem. Can I keep on my undergarments?"

"Sure, but I may want you to take them off later for other reasons."

"I'll be ready when you are."

In a few minutes they were situated and Mòlìhuā was selecting entertainment channels and scoping out what holographs to watch. When she asked Tinougl each time he was very agreeable. His modus operendus was just to get to Konhagar without a lot of undue risk. If he went alone, he would instantly be suspect. But going as the boyfriend of a local girl cleared the way real easy.

But the situation had significantly morphed since Tinougl first arrived and going back to the future wasn't necessarily in the cards right now. It would all unfold and at the moment of a singularity, a decision would be made, and his legacy would irrevocably be secured, one way or another. Least path of resistance is always the best course to take.

There were some over riding issues such as, is there any actionable intelligence or is this mission a wash?

What if he comes back empty handed, is the trip wasted?

What if he chooses not to go back to the future?

Is there a possibility they send someone after him to prevent him from altering history?

Tinougl wasn't naïve, he realized there were many aspects of this mission that were not totally clear to him. In ten or twenty years after his departure in the time machine the sponsors might have more degrees of freedom to determine future actions including sending a hit team to prevent his impact on the fabric of time.

Should Tinougl decide to stay, one thing is evident, he would have to keep a low profile and not get too involved with many things as to not leave a footprint for the time enforcers to detect and have a target. It truly was a complicated situation. Tinougl knew he wasn't any where near any conclusions or hints about the data he was seeking. But he assumed eventually he would stumble into a window of opportunity and make the discovery. He knew deep down inside; he might be compelled to journey to that time machine if he found the golden nugget. *But could he?*

The days combined with copious love making, snacking on substandard food, but enjoying the elixers that were in great supply since many people didn't care for the elixir buzz, allowed the time to pass seemingly quick.

Before they knew it, they were once again advised by the flight attendant to remain in the cabin until most of the passengers departed the space craft. They would be escorted off the spaceship and through the company offices and out to a waiting Taxi-Limo where their luggage would be staged. Their exit route was a good 50 yards from the main entrance of the space port where a growing crowd was gathering as passengers had sent images and massages via their communicators to friends and relatives about the Diva being on the longdistance transport. The crowd wasn't looking in the direction of the lone TaxiLimo and with the smoke glass windows as they passed the crowd nobody knew who was inside as they foolish waited to get their look at the hometown girl turned intergalactic Diva.

Tinougl was happy, to avoid that crowd and further exposure and the fact he was going to a remote location with Mòlīhuā also fit well into his plans. The isolation would be perfect until he got the lay of the land.

It didn't take too long to travel from the space port to Mòlìhuā's parents' home. The area they lived looked quite different than the city. It was far more compelling as the flora abound. The homes and farms were well maintained, and it was obvious society in the part of the world took pride in what they did.

In some ways the patches of trees that separated the settlements reminded Tinougl the Great Tóng Canyon. The only difference was it wasn't on a slope. Even though there were mountains off to the distance, this area was all flat for 30 miles in any direction.

Mòlìhuā's parents were not expecting anyone, and the news of their Diva daughter had not reached them or the local news stations. Only travellers who discovered them on the high-speed transport were aware of who she was and that she had came to this planet. Within hours of arrival, the news media was looking for her and trying to find out who she is.

The best actions the couple took was to stay at Mòlìhuā's parents' home for a few days since they had fulfilled a lot of their sexual appetite during the trip, they could hold off for a few days and give the appearance of a different situation.

Mòlìhuā's mother was a little surprised seeing the Taxi-Limo drive down their driveway a quarter of a mile from the main road. They had a large open area a vehicle could turn around and loop back to the road if necessary. Occasionally, strangers would get lost and do that. Friends and relatives would also do that out of habbit. Nobody knew who was in the Limo until it looped around and stopped. The door automatically opened, just like it would in the city and Mòlìhuā got out of the car. Her mother approached and could not believe who she saw. The women quickly embraced with the love of a mother and a daughter happy to see each other after a long absence.

Mòlìhuā's mother now had the next biggest surprise in a long time when Tinougl stepped out of the Limo and Mòlĭhuā instinctively said, "Mother let me introduce to you a very special man in my life."

The second shock was about as big as the first. The man looked clean and handsome and far more sophisticated than Mòlĭhuā's mother would ever think her daughter would end up with. She had no idea the extent she underestimated her daughter. However, if she knew he was a time travel spy, it would be an even greater surprise.

"Mother this is Tinougl."

"Hello, my name is Karenna."

"Pleased to meet you Karenna."

The TAXI Limo driver was removing all their luggage and it now hit her mother the significance of all this. The driver had been paid in credits as soon as they pulled into the driveway and as soon as he unloaded the last piece of luggage, he politely asked, "Is there anything else you need sir?"

"No that will be all, thank you for the ride."

"My pleasure. If you need any transportation, my contact information is on the receipt that automatically was sent to your communicator when you paid the fee."

"Good. I might be calling you soon."

"I have the coordinates logged into my navigation system so it will be no problem coming here if you contact me for transportation."

"What is your name?"

"Bustamante."

"Alright Bustamante, I will contact you when I need a lift somewhere."

"It's my pleasure Tinougl," which the driver knew based on the receipt his automatic transaction system informed him during the payment a few minutes prior.

CHAPTER TWENTY

GREEN ACRES

"Is father home?"

"No, he went to the bank to negotiate a loan. He may not be happy when he gets home."

"He's worked hard all his life providing for us. I think I'm in a position to help him now if he will let me."

"Talk to him when he gets home. He's having a rough time now, but you know how proud he is."

"Yes, I'm aware. I hope he isn't upset that I brought a man home with me."

"Let's take your luggage into the house and get a nice cool drink and talk everything about you and your friend."

The three of them had no problem toting all the luggage into the spacious home.

"We'll put Tinougl into the guest room which is available, and you have your room which is the way you left it."

"But what if I want to be with Tinougl at night?"

"I do not want to know what the two of you have done but give your father a few days to adjust to Tinougl."

"Mother, you might as well know now, the reason why I brought Tinougl here is you need to be aware, he's now a member of the family."

"Did you two go off and secretly enter a unification?"

"No, we wanted to wait until you and father could be there."

"What about Tinougl's family."

"He no longer has any relatives."

"I'm sorry to hear that."

"That's okay mother, we will be his family."

"How soon do you plan on going back to Santorini de Shénshèng?"

"We plan on staying a long time so you can get to know Tinougl. He's a writer and has no requirement to be anywhere, he can do his work wherever he is. Plus, I think some of the film makers will likely chose his book "Sanctuary City" to make a holographic movie."

"How certain are you of that?"

"Mother you need to brace yourself there are some things you need to know about and be prepared to deal with."

"Are you pregnant?"

"Not that I know of."

"Then what could be so pressing of an issue?"

"Mother I will explain after we get those cool drinks."

"All right."

Mòlìhuā's mother, Karenna stood up and proceeded to make them a very nice tea that had hemp and some cannabinoids in it. The instant chiller, doing the opposite of a microwave machine cooled the drinks down to just above freezing. The taste was great, and the effects were not too bad either.

"Okay honey, tell me what's going on with you."

"Mother I succeeded in a couple recordings. The two principal parties that published them have already sold five billion subscriptions."

"What does that mean?"

"That means I have so many credits I no longer need to work."

"How does Tinougl play into this?"

"He inspired the work and motivated me to perform as well as I did. He's the source of my success."

"Is that why he's with you now?"

"He was with me before I got lucky. Plus, he has his own wealth, he doesn't need my money."

"You are a couple now?"

"Yes mother, we have gone beyond the point of no return, and you need to know Tinougl, and I are lovers. There is only one thing left to do is an official unification. That's why we are here so that you and father can be with me when we do it."

"I hope your father isn't too stressed out when he comes home."

"Mother, when I hear his vehicle come down the driveway, I'm going out to meet him. You and Tinougl stay here so I can deal with him in my terms."

"Alright dear, you were always his little girl. He will no doubt listen to you better than he would me."

The three enjoyed their drinks for another fifteen minutes talking about some of the performances and then there was that unmistakable sound of a hovercraft coming down the driveway.

"Is he driving a hovercraft into the city?" Mòlìhuā asked with great curiousity.

"He is, he can tell you all about it."

As soon as Mòlìhuā's father turned off the hovercraft and there was silence she said, "Looks like he's home, I'm going out to greet him mother."

"Alright dear. Good luck I hope you work your magic."

Mòlìhuā rose up and walked out the home and out past the landscape of the home past a metallic gate to keep out the wild animals to the big loop open area her father pulled his hovercraft up to.

At first her father didn't believe his eyes. Even though he had a terrible day with the banker and a lot of unsettled things still existed, the sight of his daughter temporarily allowed him to escape all that negativity for a while.

"Hello daddy."

"Well, I'll be. I never expected to see you today."

"I had some good fortune so I'm taking some vacation time to spend with my family."

"That's good, us go inside and talk with your mother."

"First you and I need to talk about a couple things."

"Such as?"

"Mother informed me you had to talk to the banker today about your debt."

"Yes, unfortunately, I had to do that."

"Was that taken care of?"

"No, not really."

"Daddy, you don't know this, but I have a lot of money now. I want to go to the bank with you in the morning and pay off all your debt."

"It's a large amount of money, how can you possibly do that?"

"Daddy, your little girl now has more money than you need to pay off your debt."

"How did you get all that money?"

"I'm a recording star. I've recently made a lot of money. You will be hearing about me from the media in a few more days. Be prepared for a lot of things you are not aware of yet."

"Are you into a lot of trouble?"

"No, all legitimate. I made a lot of money singing."

"Really?"

"Yes, and I'll pay off all your debt in the morning so there is no reason for you to be upset tonight, okay?"

"If what you are saying is true, then I will be very happy."

"Daddy there is something else I want to talk to you about privately."

"What is that?"

"I'm in love with a man and I brought him home to meet you. He wants to be part of our family and be with me the rest of my life."

"Is he with you just because you have all that money?"

"No, he has his own money, plus he helped me earn it. I owe a lot to him."

"You are in love with this man?"

"Yes, he's the nicest person I've met in my lifetime and he's willing to stay here forever with us if you let him."

"This all rather astonishing."

"That's why I wanted to talk to you alone first. To make sure you know you no longer have money problems, and you now have a reason to be happy because your little girl is successful, and I have common sense. My mother did not raise a fool."

"Alright, us go inside and meet him."

"Not quite yet. Daddy, I do not want him to know I'm paying off your debt. Let's just play like you are taking me to the city to do some shopping and a few errands, can you please do that for me?"

"For what you are doing for me, that's the least I could do for you."

"I know for a fact he loves me very deeply and I love him too. You will find out he's a really great guy."

"Alright Mòlīhuā, you be the tour guide and I will humbly submit. Us go inside now."

Mòlīhuā threw her arms around her father and started crying.

"What's wrong now?"

"You do not know how happy I am, why should I not cry."

"All right dear, take a few deep breaths and you will get over it. Go in and smile for your mother and your special friend."

"Thank you, daddy, I'm getting it together, just give me a minute."

"Of course, dear. Take your time. We'll go in when you feel ready."

In a couple minutes Mòlīhuā regained her composure and dried off her eyes and put on a smile and said, "Alright, I'm ready now."

The two walked into the house and into the kitchen where Mòlīhuā's mother and Tinougl were sitting talking about trivial matters and nothing important in the world.

Tinougl the perfect gentleman stood and stayed into a respectful poise until Mòlìhuā introduced him. "Daddy, is my significant other, Tinougl."

"Glad to meet you sir," Tinougl quickly stated.

Mòlìhuā's father had sized up a lot of people in the past and was a good judge of character. The first thing he noticed was Tinougl was polished. He looked very professional and besides being very handsome, appeared to be well built. First impressions are usually correct. Tinougl was indeed a shining example of a well-prepared man. To the point Mòlìhuā's father had a sudden fear this incredible specimen of a man was far too sophisticated for his daughter.

Now was the time to unlock the mystery and discover what drew his daughter towards this man. She easily avoided men in the past. She by no way was ready to settle down, let alone be subjected to the machinations of a particular male when she had so much life ahead of her. But whatever the reason had grown very attached to Tinougl. He was of course curious as to what that attraction was. And he would take his sweet time figuring it all out.

"Nice meeting you Tinougl, please have a seat and I will join you."

The probing questions that Tinougl anticipated now started. Success was nothing more than anticipating what others were anticipating and take actual steps to achieve success by it.

"Tell me Tinougl, what do you do back on Santorini de Shénshèng?"

"Well sir, I actually live on the planet Argecibo. I was just staying in Santorini de Shénshèng to deal with my publisher."

"You are some sort of writer?"

"Yes, I'm a novelist."

"Are you successful at it?"

"I have all the money I need."

"Enough to take care of a family?"

"Certainly. I invested my royalties and multiplied my wealth. I can retire now if I want."

"But will you?"

"Probably not. I'll find something to do. I'm thinking about writing holographic screen plays."

It was getting close to mealtime so Mòlìhuā's mother suggested, "Honey why don't you take Tinougl in the other room and watch the news reports while your daughter and I make something for dinner to eat."

"Sure, that's kind of what I wanted to do anyway."

Mòlìhuā's father stood up and started walking to the other room and Tinougl followed him.

After they got into the other room there were four recliner chairs all at an angle so it's occupants could equally see the holographic projector screen. Mòlìhuā's father gestured to one of the chairs and said, "please have a seat."

Tinougl sat down and the Holograph soon started showing the local news report. Much of it was all Greek to Tinougl who had no real sense of foundation to this outwardly lying solar system and planet.

"My name is Morgan, by the way."

"Nice to meet you, Morgan."

"I suppose you already know my spouse's name is Karenna."

"It's a beautiful name like Mòlìhuā. Those names do not sound like any names I've heard before."

"The folklore goes something like this: many generations ago we had visitors from some distant solar system not part of our Empire called Earth. Those travellers left behing some artifacts with names on them that our ancestors decided to use to name their offspring."

"I see."

"Tinougl if I may, I would like to ask you what your intentions are with my daughter?"

"I want to spend the rest of my life with her."

"What if she decides she wants to live in this backwards community?"

"That's fine by me. We can always take a vacation somewhere if we need to do something different for a while."

"What's your passions and what do you like to do?"

"I like staying in good physical condition. I try to work out every day."

"I got some hard work around here if you want to get some good exercise."

"I'm sure if you are willing to take the time to show me what you want me to do, I can get it accomplished and if it helps me keep my daily vigorous routine, then I would be happy."

"What kind of exercise do you like doing the most?"

"To be honest l like swimming hard as it tasks my body like no other activity. Aside from that I also walk and run when I get a chance."

"If Mòlìhuā decides to remain here, you are good with that?"

"Mòlìhuā remaining happy would also make me happy. I find when she's happy I am also happy."

"My daughter is very precious."

"I know that and so do a lot of other people."

"What do you mean by that?"

"Your daughter is now a celebrity."

"How does that affect things and us?"

"Probably in about another week when word travels to this planet, you will probably feel some of your privacy has been stolen away from you."

"This is kind of a desolate area. Only us agricultural clans seem to ever travel out and about here."

"I predict that will soon change and you will have the personal annoyance of closing your gate out on the access road each time you enter to keep out the crowds."

"Think so?"

"Yes, you need to prepare for it. Hopefully tourists do not come here from other planets to scope out your daughter."

Morgan suddenly realized he wasn't being very sociable to his future sonin-law asked, "Would you like a drink or an elixir?"

"Sure, what ever you have."

"I have some elixirs I made myself out of some of the fruits I grew."

"Yes, please let me try one of them."

Morgan stood up and walked over to what would pass as a china cabinet and pulled out a clear glass bottle with some ornate design and a couple glasses and poured the brown substance half full in each glass and then put the cap back on and set it back into the cabinet and closed the glass door. He then walked over to Tinougl and handed him the glass of elixir and said, "Toast to your good health and happiness."

"Thank you, sir, and I wish you good health."

Tinougl tasted the concoction and quickly evaluated it as pleasant and powerful.

"This is as good as any commercial product I've ever tasted."

"I sell some of that elixir, based on referrals."

Tinougl was watching the news and there was some discussion about some militants that were again stirring up trouble in a place called Azure-Tiānkōng..

Tinougl was thinking Azure-Tiānkōng might just be a possible clue to what he was searching and asked, "Morgan, where is Azure-Tiānkōng located?"

"Azure-Tiānkōng is located just about 8,000 miles due West of here."

"What is the basis for their dispute?"

"They have always wanted autonomy. They were never proponents of globalization and claim it strips them of their identity."

"Well, that's what globalization does. It turns a planet into a single organism of sorts and reduces the tolerance for different points of view."

"You are definitely right about that. That's exactly how the Azure-Tiānkōng feel about it."

Tinougl planned from that minute onwards he would make it a point to watch the news with his prospective father-in-law.

About the time they polished off their elixir drinks, Mòlìhuā walked into the room and said, "Would you gentlemen please come into the dining room for dinner."

"I'm getting a little hungry, the news can wait." Morgan then stood up and followed Mòlìhuā into the dining room where the table was already arranged, and their entrees were already placed on their plates in a very professional manner.

The scent of the food seemed rather pleasant to Tinougl who was asked to sit in a chair that faced Morgan and Mòlìhuā sat down next to him facing her mother Karenna, who sat down shortly.

The preservings were an excellent idea on the part of Mòlìhuā that prevented any of them from the necessity of leaving the dinner table once they started enjoying their meal.

The drinks provided at the dinner table were a purple liquid. As Tinougl ate and drank the substance he commented. This drink is very nice.

Karenna responded, "That is a fermented drink we made here to help the palates."

"It's doing a great job at that," Tinougl replied.

"One of the benefits of being a botanist and a farmer is we can create our own beverages at significantly lower in prices than what the poor city folk have to pay."

"I'm impressed, it definitely tastes very nicely."

"Thank you."

Karenna was very curious about this man who sat across from her at the dinner table and asked, "Tinougl, what is your main desire for being here on Konhagar?"

"Mam, I am here because I want to feel Mòlìhuā close to me for the rest of my life."

"Tinougl, in life there is a slow decay in the intensity of emotions as we are with our mates for a long period of time. How do you see yourself ten years from now when that initial sparkle wears off and you are caught up with the simple of passage of time?"

"Life is obviousy a voyage in time and space. We never know for sure where we will end up. I learned a long time ago to take each day by day and discover where life takes you because the Empire is so complex, we have no idea what it will be like in 10 years."

"Yes, that's true. But let me ask you the question, what do you intend to do if you suddenly discover Mòlìhuā is pregnant and has a baby on the way?"

"I would try to do what I could to make her feel comfortable and make her feel as best as she could. I would do anything I could to help her."

"You would not run away and try to avoid your responsibilities?"

"I'm not running anywhere. My destiny is with Mòlìhuā. I will do as she asks me to do with great pride and happiness."

Tinougl was looking at Karenna and had no idea Mòlìhuā's tears were flowing down. Those tears suddenly caused Karenna to truncate her questions. She realized this was an extraordinary moment in Mòlìhuā's life and the two love birds had already gone way past sex and pregnancy was only a question of time.

Morgan was taking it all in and felt stress over the stress he felt Karenna was placing on Tinougl. Based on what Mòlìhuā said privately to him and what had transpired since, he already concluded Tinougl was a good guy and had honorable intentions. His daughter was truly lucky because Tinougl was such an intelligent and attractive man. He easily could understand why his daughter fell for Tinougl, but at the same token, he vividly understood Tinougl's interest in Mòlìhuā. She truly was a living princess and if it was true, they met before she became this apparent Diva that was good too because he knew her before the transition to a new life.

The rest of the dinner and following conversations went on

without such an emotional twist to it.

After it was apparent that everyone had finished their meal, Karenna got up first and Morgan followed her, and they started clearing the table.

"Let me help you," Mòlìhuā said.

"I can handlel this quite easily, why don't you and Tinougl go enjoy yourselves."

"Alright mother, thank you."

They went into the ajacent room and Mòlìhuā said to Tinougl, "Lets go for a walk, I'll show you around our farm."

"Sure, that sounds good to me."

Mòlìhuā's real motive was to talk to Tinougl alone and explain how they would have to act tonight.

When they were away from the house and walking along an irrigation dike, Mòlìhuā said, "Tonight, you will have to sleep by yourself. My parents are not quite ready to deal with us making love in the middle of the night."

"Sure, I can handle that."

"I'm sorry I'm doing this to you, but in time we'll be sleeping together, and I will reward you for being so considerate."

"You have already awarded me. I"ve received more from you than I desrve."

"But so have I."

"All right, I understand, I'll be in the guest room for a while."

"I promise to make it up for you."

"That's not necessary. I love you and if this is what you want, it's fine by me."

Mòlìhuā through her arms around Tinougl and hugged him very strongly. The love energy flowed through their bodies until they reached equalization.

From a distance, Morgan saw all this and realized, it truly was a remarkable situation between the two young couple. Whatever Tinougl said obviousy triggered a response which easily explained the situation quite well. It was now apparent that Tinougl was a fixture in the family now. Hence, Morgan needed to find out more about Tinougl. And he had the friends that could do it.

Soon the night came, and the family was sound asleep. Karenna wondered why the couple wasn't in the room together screwing like rabbits, but she understood her daughter was a little apprehensive and if she caused this arrangement then she knew it was probably the way it should be.

Chapter Twenty-One

Mòlìhuā To the Rescue

Mòlìhuā woke early in the morning, it was perfectly quiet.

She walked into her parents' bedroom knowing they were sound to sleep and woke her father and said, "You need to get up. I want to be gone before Tinougl wakes up in the morning. We need to go to the bank today."

"Honey, they do not open for at least four or five hours from now."

"I know that father, please get up and get ready so we can leave before Tinougl wakes up. I do not want to explain all this to him."

"All right dear, I'll be ready in a few minutes."

At the crack of dawn, the two went outside and Mòlìhuā's father started up the hovercraft, and soon they were on their way down that country road for the big city.

Nobody would know who this was. The Diva was in total disquise. Any Diva hunters would not be looking in this direction.

Morgan pulled his hovercraft into a very good parking spot since it was just about the beginning of commuter time, plenty of spots were still available. After he shut down the turbos for the hovercraft he turned to his daughter and asked, "Since we got a lot of time to kill what do you want to do?"

"Let's go window shopping and find some nice presents for mother and find a nice restaurant for breakfast."

"Sounds good to me."

The two trudged along dutifully and eventually came upon a restaurant that Morgan knew quite well as he went here many times before on his way to the bank and other places in the city for business.

"Let's go in here. I come here quite often; I like it."

"Alright father."

The two went inside a 24-hour restaurant that had different classes of customers depending on what time of day it was.

They were seated soon and one of the regular waitresses approached the table and said, "Good morning, Morgan, you are kind of early today."

"Yes, this is my daughter Mòlìhuā, we have some business to attend to in the city but are here early to avoid the traffic and do some shopping, before we go home."

"That sounds fun."

"It will be fun; I've not seen her in a while."

"Why is that?"

"She's been singing at Santorini de Shénshèng."

"Really. Where at?"

Mòlìhuā then jumped into the conversation and said, "I have a two-year contract with Cuìlù Resort Hotel. I was recently featured on a recorded broadcast done at the Grand Plexis de Chiveltros. You will probably see it on nationwide Holograph video in a couple days."

"Really."

"My daughter has a beautiful voice. You will be pleased when you hear her sing," Morgan said.

"Well, she is very pretty, I'm sure that helps too," the waitress said.

"Thank you, that is very nice for you to say," Mòlìhuā responded."

"Let me take your order, would you like a drink?"

"I'll have Gordrashian Tea," Mòlìhuā responded.

Morgan also said, "Give me the same."

After the waitress was away giving the chef their order, Morgan asked,

"What is Tinougl like? Does he treat you well?"

"Father, mother taught me to never let a man abuse me. If Tinougl ever did such a thing I would never have brought him home to meet you. He's always soft and gentle and speaks to me in the most pleasant tone."

"That's good to hear."

"Tinougl has a gentle heart. He's the sweetest man I've met in my lifetime. He's had to endure a lot with me lately because of my fame. He's handled himself very well. He's sophisticated and knows how to deal with the complexities of me being in the entertainment industry."

"Tingoul is a very handsome man, other women may offer themselves to him. Do you think he will maintain his commitment to you?"

"I've seen him in action and observed very wealthy women throw themselves at him. He ignored them and chose me. I'm confident I know how he will behave."

"What's his plans?"

"Tinougl is independently wealthy, he doesn't need plans. He doesn't have a family. I'm his family. You are his family. He will stay here indefinitely with you and me. You don't know this. I'm coming home to stay."

Tears were starting to stream down Morgans cheeks, and he had to ask, "Is this for real?"

"Yes daddy. We are his family. He loves me and he will love you. Give him time."

"I will I promise."

About that time the drinks appeared with the waitress who saw the tears on Morgan and served the drinks and thought it was in her best interest to serve the drinks and get away and not hear any of it.

Morgan always liked to be around his daughter and if Tinougl was going to bring her home for good, that meant he would truly like Tinougl.

The breakfast was mildly substantial and got the job done. Eventually they were ready to leave, and Morgan asked for the check.

"Father, I have a lot more money to spend than you, let me pay it."

"Okay if that's what you want."

In a few more minutes the waitress was utterly shocked and asked, "Is this tip correct, did you make a mistake?"

"In a couple more days when you watch me on a holographic entertainment report you will discover I have the means to give you such an elaborate tip. I figured it out you have treated my father well for many years. You earned the tip many times over."

"Thank you miss. I adore your father. He's a kind gentleman. Everyone here likes him."

Mòlìhuā smiled at the waitress who was totally humbled as her tip was more than a monthly salary. In a few more days when she saw Mòlìhuā on InterEmpire news she then was stunned. There she was with one of her best customers with a Diva who was now one of the top entertainers.

By the time the two finished breadfast, they still had about an hour to kill before the bank opened. So, they went window shopping.

"The stores will not be open for an hour, but I think we can come back after the bank and buy mother some nice things."

"Sure honey. Your mother deserves more than I can afford."

"Father. I'll pay for it, but you give it to her."

"That doesn't seem right."

"Oh, but it is. You are the reason why I'm successful. it's your money." Eventually it was time for the bank to open and the two went inside.

They walked up to a counter where clerks stood by to handle banking needs and the sweet lovely asked, "How can I help you sir?"

"I would like to talk to Mr. Qwestron."

"Alright, one minute sir."

The automated request went to Qwestron who looked at the surveillance video and wasn't too enthused to talk to the loser he met with the day before. He would lay down the law today and inform him foreclosure and eviction were his only choice unless he could magically come up with the minimum payment and interest!

A woman appeared from a side door and asked, "Are you

Morgan?"

"Yes."

"Please follow me."

The two were escorted to a conference room and the overzealous banker appeared a couple minutes later.

"Morgan, do you have the minimum payment?"

Mòlìhuā didn't like the banker's attitude but nevertheless knew to maintain professionalism and get it done then she spoke up, "Sir, I'm here representing my father my name is Mòlìhuā."

"Mòlìhuā, what is is you wish to say?"

"How much is my father's debt?"

"Let me check."

"Alright."

The banker touched a few things on his touch pad and said, "Your father's debt is 7500 credits and the minimum due is 1000 credits or by tomorrow or we will foeclose on him."

"Alright, I will pay the 7500 credits now."

The banker looked at Mòlìhuā with an incredulous look and said, "If the credits are good then fine."

"Give me a link to the payment." Mòlìhuā held out her communicator and said, "Send me the interchange number."

The banker was obviousy getting nervous and inside this conference room only Mòlìhuā could receive the interchange number alloweing her to do the transaction. A moment later she transferred the 7500 credits. Her father's debt was now canceled. The bank could no longer harass this gentleman.

Mòlìhuā asked, "Has the credits been applied, and the debt

eliminated?"

The banker said, "Give me a minute."

In a short time, the banker was astonished, the debt was resolved and said,

"Yes we received the payment."

Mòlìhuā was upset because she knew this banker had caused her father a lot of discomfort in the past and decided it was now time to give him some discomfort. She had that special business card with her and pulled it out and said, I'm sure my friend will come looking for you if you ever cause my fathter discomfort in the future. She then pulled out the business card of one of the most powerful men in the Empire. The banker took notice and instantly knew the name on the business card and responded, "Everything is in order now. Your father is in good standing with the bank."

"Keep it that way if you know what is good for you."

Mòlìhuā and her father then stood up and walked out of the conference room and the bank. Mòlìhuā in the span of a few minutes had resolved 35 years of her father's debt.

When the banker reported the incident to his superiors who then did a check on Mòlìhuā and the gentleman identified in the business card, recorded by secret video, the responded to the banker, "This is all true, we would not be able to protect you if she decided she wanted you to receive something very bad."

The banker was soon having nightmares because he had hastled this man for over ten years.

Mòlìhuā and her father retraced their steps to stores they passed on the way to the bank. After a few stops along the way and making the merchants happy with the purchases. Mòlìhuā and her father made their way back to the ubiquitous hover craft and made their way home.

~~~

Tinougl was awakened when he heard the hovercraft start up and leave. He didn't have a swimming pool to exercise in and thought he could run in the mornings to make up for lack of swimming, but he didn't have any running shoes or workout clothes. He knew what to do. He dressed and went outside the home and called the Taxi-Limo driver Bustamante who quickly recognized him on the communicator, "Good morning Tinougl, what can I help you with?"

"Would it be possible for you to come back here and pick me up. I need to buy a few things in the city."

"Sure, not a problem. I can be there in about twenty minutes."

Taxi-Limo driver was more than happy because he really liked people that gave him especially nice tips like Tinougl had done the day before. The vehicle pulled into the driveway less than twenty minutes later and Tinougl hopped in.

"Where would you like to go sir?"

"Take me to a good sporting goods store. I want to get some running shoes and workout clothes."

"I know just the place. My friend is a manager at a such a store, and they open early."

"That's great. Can you wait for me while I purchase a few items?"

"Not a problem, it will give me a chance to visit with my friend."

The ride to the sporting goods store was relatively quick and Tinougl was soon inside picking out the items he needed. By the time they got back to Mòlìhuā's parents' home less than an hour had elapsed. Mòlìhuā and her father were still in the city doing their business.

Karenna saw the Taxi-Limo pull in the driveway from her living
~~~

room window and Tinougl get out carrying a couple bags with him. She didn't even know he was gone.

Tinougl made his way into the home and Karenna asked, "Would you like me to make you something to eat?"

"I am going to change into running clothes and go out and exercise. Maybe afterwards."

Tinougl changed and was soon out the door and jogged to the front gate that was still open and he thought it would be a good idea to start keeping it closed, especially when Konhagars discovered one of the most famous singing Diva's lived here. The sanity could get out of control real fast. If the crowds opened the gate and came onto the property, they would be trespassing, and the authorities would have no choice but to remove them. *Will we have to hire private security* Tinougl wondered?

Tinougl headed down the two-lane country road running against traffic which was the smart way to do it so he would know when a vehicle was approaching, he could move to the side and let it pass. There wasn't much traffic this time of day which he was glad.

Tinougl felt good to run again. Swimming was a better exercise since it also worked his arms and upper torso. But running would have to do for now. He purchased an exercise mat he could lay down on the grass next to the home and do other workout routines. His communicator even though it was archaic compared to what was available 500 years in the future did have some exercise tracker capability including average speed. He would set his pace to fifteen miles per hour and run about two and a half miles down the road and turn around and come back. Anyone who watched his running would instantly assume this person was some sort of athelete due to proficiency of his running. Tinougl was down and back and just inside the gate when he heard the hovercraft coming down the concrete road built strong enough to handle the weight of heavy farm machinery. He then stood by the gate.

Morgan drove the hovercraft through the gate after turning into the entrance of the main road that went by, there was Tinougl to close the gate.

These actions surprised Morgan who would soon appreciate Tinougl in a few more days.

Morgan ran the hovercraft and circled around the driveway and pulled up to the sidewalk leading to the home and shut down the turbo and the two exited.

Tinougl jogged up to the hovercraft and saw they had several bags of purchases, and he said, "Let me help you."

"Thanks," Mòlìhuā responded and smiled looking at Tinougl who now appeared to have worked up a nice swet from running.

"Were you out running."

"Yes, how did you guess?"

"The swet gave it away."

"Yes, I had a good run and feel really good now, got a good cardio going."

"Did you have breakfast?"

"Not yet, I don't like eating before I run in the mornings."

"Would you like me to make you something to eat while you shower and clean up?"

"Sure, that sounds great."

Morgan was smiling and liked how the two young people seemed to get along. Mòlìhuā always seemed to have good common sense and while she was living in Santorini de Shénshèng, she never wrote home about meeting a man or showed any indications of having a boyfriend, so to see Tinougl suddenly show up was a great surprise. But he was a very handsome guy and the swet from his workout gave an indication he was disciplined, and another interesting aspect was his muscles on his arms and legs were not those of an amateur. Tinougl had a great athletic body. *Perhaps that's what turned on my daughter?*

While Tinougl was showering, Morgan announced to Karenna, "I suppose I should tell you what happened this morning."

"Yes, I'm kind of curious."

"There are things about your daughter you don't know about but will get to know soon."

"I figured when she showed up unexpectedly with a man I would be in for some surprises."

"We went to the bank today."

"Did you make any headway with that mean banker?"

"Your daughter paid off all our debt."

"She what!"

"Yes, it's true. She left that banker dazzled."

"That's a lot of money, how did she come up with all that money?"

"Mother I'm sorry but in a few more days you will find out more about me and you will lose a lot of privacy because of me. But there is no way around it."

"Alright dear, please explain it to me."

"Mother, there are a few things you got to know about me and Tinougl. First of all, I got wealthy really fast because I got lucky with my singing career. I owe lot of that to Tinougl because he put me into the position where I could be noticed by important people. And since I've made a fortune and it will complicate our lives. it's our intentions to be close to you from now on."

"Well, we like having you around."

"There are some other things you need to know. Tinougl and I are a couple. We have already consummated our love. I'm not going to sleep alone tonight. I'm going to sleep in his arms, and he will make love to me, so you might as well get used to it."

"Is he attracted to you because of your money?"

"No. We were making love before I got rich. He fell in love with me when I was just another simple cabaret singer without a lot of money."

"Are you sure he wants more than just your body?"

"He didn't come all this way to meet you and promise to live here forever if it were just my body and my money. He has his own money and can afford anything he wants. In fact, he spoiled me when I was still a poor girl."

"How did he get wealthy?"

"As you know, he's a novelist. He's very intelligent, and he invested his money wisely and grew it. He can retire if he wants, he does not need an income of any sort."

"What about you?"

"Well mother if you knew how much money I have you would be utterly shocked. And it keeps coming every day. I also have numerous opportunities to make a lot more with movies and music recordings. I already have the offers, and they will engage me in enterprises any time I want. But you see I already have more than enough money to live the rest of my life in any fashion I desire. I'm not going to jump on those offers any time soon."

"Why do you say that?"

"Well, if I have it my way, I'm going to make you a grandmother as soon as I can."

Mòlìhuā could tell her mother was in a state of shock about the revelations and felt bad she had to spit out the brutal truth. She walked over and put her arms around her mother who started sobbing and thus Mòlìhuā had to put the exclamation point on the conversation and let it end, "Mother I'm not your little girl any longer. I'm a woman in love and I have my prince charming. He is what he seems to be. You will find out in due time."

Tinougl felt the shower really hit the spot as he started drying off and had his under garmets and street clothes nearby to put on. His hair was slightly damp, so it held it's shape nicely after he combed it. Soon he was dressed and started smelling some cooking and it hit his senses really good, so he soon felt slight hunger as he opened the bedroom door and walked into the dining room.

There was significant quiet in the room as Mòlìhuā's parents were sitting at the table drinking their morning tea in a quiet fashion watching their daughter go to town fixing Tinougl something to eat.

"Have a seat Tinougl I have a place setting for you," Mòlìhuā stated.

There was only one place setting at the table and Tinougl figured the rest had probably eaten already. In a few more moments Mòlìhuā sat a plate down in front of Tinougl that appeared to have some type of fried potatoes, eggs, and a type of meat he had never seen before.

Mòlìhuā then sat a tea container down next to Tinougl and then sat down to the side of him facing her parents feeling like a naughty girl for exposing too much too quickly. But she knew one thing for sure. Her father was a business failure and had she not bailed him out, they would be forced to move off this nice agricultural holding with a bleak future.

Tinougl was hungry and dug into the food quite severely enoying it immensely. "This is wonderful, thank you for making all this."

Mòlìhuā put her hand on Tinougl's shoulder and said, "It's my pleasure honey."

Morgan had work to do this morning. He had to let his farm hands go because he could no longer afford to pay them especially since the banker had said no to any more loans. But he was going to finish his tea and visit with his prospective son in law while he ate, then get his sorry ass up and go to work.

"What are you planning to do today, Tinougl?" Morgan asked.

"I really do not have any plans now, was just going to enjoy the day and look at your agriculture settlement."

"How about you Morgan?"

"When I finish my tea, I was going to go out and work on replacing some fence posts that need replaced to keep the neighbor's livestock out of my fields."

"Perhaps I can help you. But I do not have any of those farmer clothes."

"We are about the same size. Karenna, can you get Tinougl some of my coveralls and a pair of boots, I think will fit him."

"Sure honey." Karenna stood up and went to the laundry room where she had several stacks of coveralls and then went to the shoe rack by the back door and picked out a pair of boots that she had cleaned that could be tried on in the house. She also had a blue farmer's shirt to go with the coveralls and one of the nice hats to keep the sun off Tinougl's head especially around mid-day when the sunrays got the most intense so he would not get a sunburn.

She then brought all the items into the dining room and sat them down on the little table near the dinner table where she sat food containers while serving meals to make them handy in case someone wanted additional servings.

"Tinougl, here's some farmer's clothes to try on, I think they will fit.”

The food hit the spot and Tinougl was soon finished and stood up and said, "Let me go try on all these clothes."

Tinougl was back in about five minutes dressed looking like a typical farmer in the area.

Mòlìhuā laughed and said, "You look like a farmer Joe already!"

Tinougl loved the way Mòlìhuā smiled and when she giggled and laughed, his heart went pitter pat. Mòlìhuā had a huge effect on him.

A short while later Tinougl was with Morgan in the hovercraft that pulled up to a pile of fence posts and they loaded a dozen along with several tools used in the work. With two people lifting they were easily manageable. Afterwards they began heading out along the fence leading North towards the end of the property which was out of sight because of a hill.

The agriculture operators had to systematically change out the fence posts because they only had a certain life span before they would deterorate and lose the strength. Tinougl who was a problem solver knew in modern times they dug big holes and encased the fence posts in concrete to prevent the degradation. Perhaps after they finished the work today, he would suggest that.

They came up to the first fence post that was obviousy in need to be changed. Morgan shut down the turbo and stepped off the hovercraft and grabbed a few tools and handed one of them to Tinougl and approached the fence post. They had to remove the wire holder to free up the fence post prior to pulling it out of the ground.

Tinougl had to act dumb letting Morgan show him everything, but in his formative years, Tinougl had done all this. Morgan demonstrated the techniques to free the post and left the wire holders on the ground because they were rusted, and he would install new ones on the new post.

During the demonstration, Tinougl had a flashback to his early years where he had some of the happiest days of his life. As a young man before he could legally drive vehicles because of his age, he had operated a lot of farm equipment including tractors, grain harvestors, and large trucks hauling the grain to companies that had grain elevators and driers as well as loading facilities for grain trains. He also had some nice memories of the Farmer's Daughter.

Once the fence post was free of the wires, Morgan demonstrated how he rocked the rotted post back and forth loosening it up so it could be pulled out of the ground.

"Sometimes I had to use my tractor front end loader to pull the hard to remove fence posts or drill new holes."

Morgan knew Tinougl was in great shape but had no idea what his body mass was. Thanks to the specialized drugs the spy agency gave him for body building and reaction time enhancements, his body weight was fifteen percent heavier because his vast muscle structures were far denser.

Morgan shook the posts a few times, but the fence post wasn't budgin.

Tinougl said, "Let me try it."

Morgan stood aside and Tinougl went to the fence post and shook it a few times with far greater effort than Morgan then simply lifted the fence post out of the hole by himself as if it were made of light weight material.

Morgan then pulled another tool out of the hovercraft and said, "This is a post hole digger. We use it to clean out the hole before we put in a new post."

He then demonstrated how it worked. Tinougl was more than adequately familiar with that tool and after a minute said, "Let me try it."

"Sure."

Morgan handed the tool to Tinougl who then slammed it down into the hole and brought up a tool full of dirt each time. Morgan didn't know this, but Tinougl's strength was such that he could put that digger down two or three times harder than his farm hands could.

Morgan said, "That hole is probably deep enough, us check it with a new post."

To Morgan's astonishment, Tinougl walked over and grabbed one of the new posts by himself with on hand as if it didn't weigh anything and put it down in the hole then optically sighted it looking over the top down the fence row to gauge the height and said, "It appears to be at the right height."

Normally Morgan would have to spend all day long doing this by himself since he no longer had farm hands. With Tinougl's help, they were back to the house in time for lunch.

"You guys decided to take a break?" Karenna asked?

"No, we are done. Tinougl is a very good worker, better than any farm hand I ever had."

Mòlìhuā was beaming at Tinougl who seemed to strike a chord with her father. She was extremely grateful for her father's attitude and wondered if *he wasn't embellishing it a bit to make his future son in law feel good?*

Karenna had done the basic preparation for lunch but did not start the bird fryer until the men were home to make sure it tasted fresh, because Morgan had a habit of working most of the day and skipping lunch, especially when he started running into financial stress and had to start letting go of his hired help.

Morgan's daughter had saved him in two ways, first by paying off all his debt he had accumulated over the past thirty years due to back-to-back crop failures due to unpredictable weather such as draught when his irrigation water was cut off by the water district, but also late freezes, hail, and severe weather.

The other thing she did was bring home a man who appeared to be eager and had good work ethics, if he continued in this mannerism. If he didn't have to pay out salaries to farm hands, his crops could help accumulate wealth over time.

There were a lot of changes ahead of them, and this was a small glimpse of what was yet to come.

The bird fryer took about fifteen minutes to cook the meat in an enclosed rotisary which had a positive pressure vent that exited the rear of the house in a small three-inch pipe that rose above roof top and had a ninety-degree bend and a flapper to keep rainwater out.

Even with the forced air system some of the smell leaked out and gave off a very nice aroma as the spices Karenna rubbed all over the bird created an exceptionally nice aroma.

"I'm glad you came back earlier for lunch so that we women didn't have to go hungry."

"The way Tinougl worked is what allowed us to come back early. Otherwise, I'd still be out there if I were working by myself."

Tinougl wasn't terribly hungry since he has a late breakfast, but the morning run and hard farm work did help him digest his food so he was ready he could eat again without too much difficulty.

The food was served, and the young adults sat together on one side of the dinner table while Mòlìhuā's parents sat on the otherside smiling and feeling happy.

If Tinougl knew what Mòlìhuā informed her mother while he was taking a shower, he would be more than self conscious and wonder if that was what the smiles were about. He assumed; *they were just happy to see their daughter again.*

The food hit Tiougl's palate nicely as there was nothing better than the taste of farm fresh food. Of course, Tinougl would be slightly depressed seeing all the bird feathers in the waste disposal bin behind the house where it was collected and given to another farmer that powered his alcohol still by burning the trash. He then powered his farm machinery with the alcohol and sold some to Morgan for significantly reduced prices since it wasn't taxed, and the tax collectors had no way of tracking it since the funds were trivial amounts and never triggered any curiousity. Farmers all throughout this valley did as much barter as possible which helped all of them and created a private economy nobody was aware of.

The meal was very filling. Tinougl said, "I think I need to go back to work to work off some of this meal. Want to go do some more?"

"I think we did enough for today," Morgan said.

"I want to do some more. You can come along and just give me company, I'll do the work."

"Well, if you insist."

"I insist."

"Alright you men can go do your thing. Mòlìhuā and I will take care of the dishes."

"Works for me," Morgan said.

The men stood up and walked through the house and out the front door. They hopped back on the hovercraft and Morgan started it up and drove back over to the pile of new fence posts and they loaded up another dozen and headed back out to work on the fence. The tools remained in the hovercraft. They were soon at mending the fence and talking about trivial matters.

Morgan was kind of interested in Tinougl's history. Tinougl

who had a photograph memory and thoroughly studied the man whose identity he had stolen. That man had perished but his body would not be found for almost another hundred years when the planet like most of the Empire was gripped in a devastating war that led soldiers to the area where his remains laid.

Tinougl was able to articulate a great description of the planet and his surroundings where the real Tinougl lived including people the person knew.

Morgan wanted to help more but Tinougl was so fast and effective he quickly figured out it was best to stay out of his way.

"I have a suggestion for these fence posts so they last a lot longer and will reduce your maintenance."

"What's that Tinougl?"

"If we made the holes slightly bigger and filled them with concrete after we put in the posts, it would protect the lumber and prevent the rot and damage."

"I thought about doing it but it's kind of expensive."

"Don't worry about the concrete. I'll pay for it."

"I do not think this hovercraft can deliver much concrete to the farm."

"You do not have a truck?"

"No, I had to sell all my vehicles to pay the farm workers salary when I ran out of money and the bank refused to give me any more loans."

"I have a suggestion. Us go back to the farmhouse and grab Mòlìhuā, I'm sure she would be very happy to buy you a truck, she has more money than she could probably ever spend."

"I suppose I could."

Chapter Twenty-Two

Every Farmer Needs a Truck

"Also, instead of taking your hovercraft into the city, I'm going to have my Taxi-Limo driver friend pick us up. We can drive your new pickup back."

The men drove back to the farmhouse and Tinougl called Bustamante the Taxi-Limo.

"Hello Tinougl, how can I help you?"

"I need you to come pick me up and take a few of us into the city."

"No problem. I'll be there soon," Bustamante replied and arrived 15 minutes later.

"Why are we going into the city?" Mòlìhuā asked Tinougl.

"You are going to buy your father a new truck."

"What's wrong with his truck?

"He no longer has one."

Mòlìhuā looked at her father and could see the look on his face. She knew it was embarrassing. People that have financial failures often are very distressed for a while. The activities of his daughter helped reduce the pain but would take a while to eliminate the torture he felt the banker did to him for the past ten years.

It was a quiet and somber ride to the dealership. The salespeople were slightly intrigued observing a limo pull up. *It obviousy was a rich dude who was an easy mark they could manipulate and screw them in a deal.*

"Can I help you?" the salesman asked looking condescendingly towards the two men with farm clothes on, but the sexy woman added a level of fascination to it all.

"Yes, we are going to buy a truck."

"Do you see one here you might like?"

Mòlìhuā then interjected, "Daddy, just pick one you like."

"I suppose that red one over there is about the size I had before. It was perfect for me."

The salesman said, "Will you plan on financing it?"

Tinougl then interjected himself and said, "I'm going to make the deal with you. She's going to pay for it."

"Who are you?"

"I'm her partner."

"I see."

"Okay mister, I'm sure you are a nice guy and a great salesman, so this is how we are going to handle it. We will talk to you on the deal we make, but if anyone else gets involved in this conversation, we will immediately leave and buy a truck somewhere else. Do you understand."

"Yes sir, I understand."

"Does that truck have automatic steering and global positioning navigation?"

"Why yes it does. It has all the latest features."

"Got a stylis and a piece of paper on you?"

"Yes, I do."

"Alright, write down the price as is, no financing required." Tinougl could see the salesman was now under great stress.

"Even if I quote you a price, I will still have to get approval from my supervisor."

"Like I said, we'll buy it at the price you write down if we agree. It will be that price, or we will buy one elsewhere."

"I need to go look at the sticker price, I don't remember the price."

"That's fair." Tinougl said as he already knew the markup was already on the sticker price so they could negotiate down from there if they had to.

The man walked over and looked at the sticker price and wrote a number down on the paperl and handed it to Tinougl.

"How long will it take you to get that truck ready so we can drive it out of here and home?"

"If it's a cash deal like you said, it will take us about thirty minutes to register it and prepare it for you."

"That's fair. I'm not going to send the Limo away until we are getting into the truck to drive it home." Tinougl walked over to the Limo and explained to Bustamante he wanted him to stay until the deal was done. He then walked back to the salesman standing besides Mòlìhuā and her father.

"Okay us get this done," Tinougl said.

"All right, please follow me into the office so we can start the paperwork after I get the truck serial number." The salesman walked over, pulled out his communicator and took a picture of the sticker that had all the details he needed.

"You don't want to test drive the truck?"

"I'm sure the truck is fine, and Morgan is an expert at driving a Truck."

"Alright sir, us go into my office."

When the paperwork was completed and registered in Morgan's name, the dealer asked, "How are you going to pay?"

"Bank transaction, I have the bank access on my communicator," Mòlìhuā replied.

Mòlìhuā had done one smart thing since arriving she put a lot of money into her local account which allowed her to pay off her father's debt and have a lot of money for whatever she needed, which eliminated the 3-to-4-day delay of dealing with her Santorini de Shénshèng bank account. The salesman took them up to the cashier with the pile of paperwork and handed it to the cashier. The cashier knew these were simply copies of what was now on her data terminal in front of her, but all the initials on the paperwork were customer validations to make sure there were no errors. Thanks to worldwide relational databases, the address to the registration and the future owner all passed a validation and verification which meant as soon as the transaction cleared the bank in a few minutes, Morgan would own the truck.

The dealership also knew a third party, the daughter was paying for the truck.

The nice woman asked, "Are you ready to do the transaction?"

"Yes."

"Have your communicator read in this link," the woman said as she posted it on a client screen next to her data terminal.

The terms of the sale were on the screen and when Mòlìhuā clicked on, "accept the link," it then prompted her on her communicator to send money.

That money went directly to the dealership and the customer screen noted:

"Transaction Complete balance due 0 credits."

The salesman said, "Why don't we go into my office and wait there. I will be notified shortly the truck is moved to the departure lane and you can drive away in it."

"Thank you."

"Would you like me to go with you on a drive around the block in case you have any questions about any of the controls."

"It has global controls, right?"

"Yes of course."

"My last truck had global controls, so I'm familiar with it. All the other features, I'll read about it in my spare time this evening."

"All right, sir."

A while later after a friendly discussion the salesman was notified, "truck is in the departure lane cleared to leave."

"Okay folks, us go to your truck."

They got to the truck, the salesman said, "This is a keyless truck. It does facial recognition, and your picture was taken as standard procedure on all new registrations and the facial recognition is based on that picture. The truck is fully voice controlled so all you must do is say start the truck, after you are sitting in it with doors closed and the breaks applied. It will not start if you are not engaging the breaks. That's a safety feature mandated by all new automobiles."

"Thanks, that helps out."

"Also, this truck is drive assist. Once you are on the road going in the direction you wish it will keep it in the center of the lane until you exit the lane by moving the steering wheel. It will also automatically break if there are cars in front of you."

"Alright, that is a nice feature."

"Since you paid cash and didn't waste a lot of precious time haggling on the price, you received a free tank of fuel. You got a reasonable deal on this truck because you paid cash. Had you financed it, we could not have given it to you this cheap because we must eat the finance charge the institutions place on us. A clean cash deal gives us far more flexibility."

Tinougl then electrified the salesman when he said, "I noticed a few vehicles out front that I'm interested in. I will be back in a few days to buy one of them. If you do the deal exactly the way we did this one today which I know is fair and decent, I will be driving that vehicle home the same way. Instead of her paying for it, I will buy it."

"Sure sir, I will be most happy to help you." The salesman named Jaswohn handed Tinougl one of his business cards.

"I'm setting up local bank accounts now. As soon as the bank is done setting up those accounts, I'll come back then so we will be able to do the transactions."

"All right, anything else sir?" Jaswohn asked

"In a few days from now you will discover who Mòlìhuā is. She's a celebrity. You will retain our future business and our trust if you keep the fact, she is one of your personal customers a private matter."

"I understand sir, we do not broadcast any client information in any manner."

"Thank you."

Then Bustamante the Limo driver was released, and his Taxi-Limo followed Morgan's pickup for a while as they slowly made their way through the city to a hardware store.

"We have to stop here to get a few supplies," Morgan said and the three of them went inside the store where they purchased premixed concrete sacks, a tub, and a water bladder they could put in the truck or hovercraft to mix the concrete with. They then made their way out of the city and back to the farm.

"I think I've had enough action for the day," Morgan said as they pulled up in front of the home."

As the men headed into the house, Mòlìhuā walked over to the unattached garage which was about 50 feet from the house and looked through the window and to her horror, she saw her mother's car was missing. Her daddy had sold it and many other things to scrape by. She almost wanted to cry. She felt so bad about this. She now knew she owed Tinougl much more because had he not developed the relationship at such a critical moment, her parents probably would have lost the farm and everything they owned and turned into poppers and beggars. It took her a while to regain her composure before she went back in the home.

The men were watching the news and the women were preparing the next meal. Karenna said to her daughter, "Your father said you paid for that new truck."

"It's the least I could do for him for raising me good and helping to prepare me for life."

"That's very sweet of you." Karena said then grabbed Mòlìhuā and hugged her very affectionately.

"We are going back to the dealership in the next few days."

"Why?"

"Tinougl wants a vehicle. He's used to driving around and doesn't like using Limo's all the time."

"He really intends on staying?"

"Why would he buy that automobile when he's from another planet if he didn't intend on staying?"

"He almost seems like a miracle."

"He is. I would not have made all that money had he not dressed me up and motivated me to sing that love song to him."

"I would love to hear that song, could you play it for us tonight?"

"It will not sound as good because we do not have an orchestra, but I'll play it, and when the subscriptions start selling in the city, I'll buy you one so you can hear how nice it sounds with a band and another back up singer."

"I would love to hear that."

"The piano is in direct sight of the dining room, maybe I'd like to surprise Tinougl and father tonight when they start eating."

"That will be so good to hear and watch their reaction."

"Our secret, ok? I want to surprise them. But what I want you to do is watch Tinougl closely while I perform."

"I will, that's what mothers are supposed to do."

"Also, I don't want you to hear the noise we make tonight, because I'm sure you know what I plan on doing."

"Sometimes I play classical music while I'm lying in bed with your father at night reading books while he's falling asleep and snoring. I'm sure I want to do some reading tonight."

A while later the meal was ready and Karenna walked out into the living room and said, "Why don't you guys come into the dining room. Dinner is ready."

The meal smelled especially good and Tinougl was ready to learn more about the local cuisines.

Everyone started eating. Mòlìhuā tasted a few of the items, winked at her mother, stood up and walked twenty feet directly to the family piano. It was a standup model like pianos usually sold on this planet. It had not been tuned since Mòlìhuā's high school days, but it was good enough.

Tinougl watched Mòlìhuā and was curious what she was doing then observed her sit down at the piano and raised the cover to the Keyboard, and with no delay started playing her love song that stole Tinougl's heart. Tinougl was touched. He didn't know what caused him to suddenly feel so emotional, he just could not help it. His eyes watered up and soon the tears were coming down. Morgan and Karenna had thought they had seen everything. And before their eyes was this incredible reaction. They now knew something extraordinary had happened between Tinougl and Mòlìhuā. If there was any doubt before this, those thoughts were utterly destroyed by this expression.

The music was indeed quite beautiful. Karenna was so proud of her daughter and now understood why the public ostensibly liked the music, and as she sang the lyrics, it also hit her parents and they could not keep dry eyes either.

Finally, after the six minutes. The song was finished and before they could applause or react, Karenna said, "I will now play the song I know caused Tinougl to fall in love with me."

In the next few moments, her voice resonated, and she sang like she was in front of a huge audience and wanted to entertain them. This song was totally detailed to Mòlìhuā's memory since she performed it a few times over a six-month period.

Tinougl's emotional spike was over, and he calmed down and dabbed his eyes with his napkin and hoped his future inlaws didn't catch his tears. He was very self conscious about it.

Karenna had no doubt now what Mòlìhuā planned to do to Tinougl tonight. It was also a good thing their bedroom was on the opposite side of the house from the guest room!

Mòlìhuā's parents didn't want the music to end and were grateful it lasted a long time, a full eight minutes. Her articulation while singing was starlet quality. It kind of put magic into this old farmhouse that had probably existed 100 years. This music did a lot to resolve a lot of issues, the biggest was simply: why?

After the song ended, Mòlìhuā closed the keyboard cover, stood up and walked back to her chair next to Tinougl.

"That was very beautiful," thank you for playing and singing that for us," Karena said.

"It was my pleasure."

"It truly was remarkable," Morgan said.

Tinougl was strangely quiet. Mòlìhuā's parents knew that Tinougl had gone through emotional spike and respectfully gave him his peace and allowed him these precious moments to unwind. That first song had definitely touched a nerve.

The conversation withered and as the food was mostly consumed, Karenna knew she needed to change the dynamics, stood up and said, "Why don't you guys go watch some holographs while I clean up here."

"I want to help you mother."

"Okay dear."

The men got the massage and went into the living room and were out of sight and the holograph audio blocked any conversations the women would have.

Karenna asked Mòlìhuā, "Is there something special about that song?"

"Yes, I sang it for Tinougl on the very first performance of it at the Grand Plexis de Chiveltros. That's also where the first recording was made that made me all this money."

"Oh, how sweet."

"I was a virgin until that night I sang it to Tinougl so that when we made love, he would know it was my special gift to him."

"I probably shouldn't tell you this, but as your mother I must. When you sang the first song, Tinougl got very emotional and actually started crying."

"I know how much it means to him. He had never been in love before. He's a very very strong man, almost to the point he's supernatural. Writing books are probably a cover story for him. I suspect he's been into a lot of things we don't want to know about. He's extremely wealthy."

"Maybe that's why he wanted to come here. To disappear?"

"I'm sure one day he will tell me a lot when he thinks I'm ready for it."

"What if you can't handle it?"

"My time with him has been precious. I'm grateful I got to do what I did, and I know he had a lot to do with my wealth. He might have even done some things behind the scenes I do not know about."

"What's going to happen with your room mate back at Santorini de Shénshèng?"

"Tinougl didn't want to have to go back to Santorini de Shénshèng if he enjoyed this place, so he gave me money to give to her, to pay my rent for a year. If we never go back, she can find another room mate and keep what I left behind, there was nothing left important to me."

After the women were finished making the kitchen spotless, Karena informed her daughter, "I'm going to grab your father and we are going into our room and catch up on some of our reading. Can you do me a favor and don't make too loud love noise tonight?"

"I'll try my best mother, but you know Tinougl turns me on so strongly I might have to scream. If you hear the screaming, please to not interrupt us."

The women started laughing and walked into the living room.

"Morgan can you please come with me; I have something I need your help with."

Morgan stood up not looking happy thinking his wife had some "honey do" for him to accomplish.

After Morgan and Karenna were out of the room and most likely in their bedroom, rearranging their evening, Mòlìhuā said, "Tinougl, please come with me I want to show you what we did in the guest bedroom today."

Tinougl like a good soldier marched into the guest room and Karenna followed him shutting and locking the door behind them. She didn't want an accident like her father coming in while they were engaged in transcendental celestial feasts.

The first thing Tinougl noticed was his exercise clothes had been washed and folded up and put on a nice pile on the middle of a desk across from the bed.

"I see you took care of my workout clothes, thank you. What did you want to show me?"

CHAPTER TWENTY-THREE

MÒLÌHUĀ'S SURPRISE

Mòlìhuā only had 3 buttons on the front of her sporty top and undid them and opened it up showing her breasts and said, "This." Then she walked over and put her hands on Tinougl's head and pulled his head to her lips and kissed him like a woman in love would do for a spontaneous eruption of passion she wanted to give to her lover.

Tinougl who loved her gorgeous body, kissed her back as if he was starving for love. He couldn't get out of his clothes fast enough, so Mòlìhuā helped him and then pulled him into the bed on top of her and expertly helped him quickly enter her as she wanted to feel him right away. She then wrapped her legs around him and he might have thought he would do all the trusting and soon discovered the covalent bonding created a synergistic action which drove his gratification into an explosive release. From the very beginning, it must have taken two minutes for them to reach orgasms precisely at the same time and that hot essence Tinougl pumped into Mòlìhuā at the most perfect moment added and multiplied her orgasm into a very sharp pleasure that she could easily have screamed but she knew to control it and struggled but maintained then pulled Tinougl down to her and started kissing his neck as they slowly spun down that ecstasy into a post orgasmic platue filled with love and desire.

Mòlìhuā mindful she didn't know everything about Tinougl that there was obviousy a lot of omissions, and those extremely strong muscles were not normal for men unless they were in a business that required extreme strength developed over time.

Mòlìhuā was a brillian A student throughout school, not only did she excel in music, but she also excelled in literature, chemistry, math, biology, and practically every other subject. She truly was a sophisticated woman to be able to travel by herself to a far away planet and establish herself as a musician and performed well enough to earn a living and have a nice apartment with a room mate in a decent residence that most single women could not afford.

As a book worm, Mòlìhuā read several books every week growing up. Hence, she knew there were only a few types of men that would have extraordinary bodies like Tinougl. She wasn't naïve and could easily catagoriize them into four possibilities including organized crime, law enforcement, military special forces, or spies. That was the only explanation. She would not pry and let him inform her when he was ready. In the meantime, she would play ignorant and go along for the ride and hoped he would not break her heart. The first love is always the hardest if it fails.

After Tinougl felt his erection shrinking he pulled out of Mòlìhuā and then moved to her side. Then he positioned them, so their chests were together, and his chin was on her head, and they simply adored each other. She could feel him kissing her head. Mòlìhuā knew those were love kisses and they were exposing his heart to her. His arms around her made her feel wonderful. It was the greatest satisfaction she felt in her lifetime. And to be able to first sing that song she created to him that night at Grand Plexis de Chiveltros just before she allowed him to deflower her meant a lot to her. She knew how it affected them and tonight the secret reports her mother gave her wasn't unexpected. There was something in Tinougl's life he wasn't admitting that caused that emotional spike, but she knew enough about him already to know when he felt it was time to tell her, he would. She was slightly fearful, especially if he was organized crime or a spy.

In due time they fell asleep and Mòlìhuā felt slightly cold and pulled a blanket over them and slept the best she had in a long, long time until in the morning she felt his movements and saw Tinougl get up. She played like she was still sleeping, as it was almost dawn. Tinougl quietly put on his running clothes and silently left the room without making a sound. She heard a small click on the front door as he left.

Mòlìhuā was curious and sat up on the bed and looked out the window. She saw Tinougl, go out the gate, closing it behind him and started running down the road. He was running hard, probably fifteen miles per hour or more. He knew the pace he had to keep and remembered the landmarks at where he turned around the day before to return back towards the farm. When he reached that landmark, he checked his communicator and verified he went two and a half miles, then turned around and ran back to the farmhouse.

Morgan was still sawing logs with his snoring. Karenna was once again mad at herself for not asking him to buy her some ear plugs when he was in the city. She would be sure and ask her daughter to get them as she anticipated she would be going with Tinougl soon when he went to go buy a new car.

Mòlìhuā was making tea and started cooking a meat she thought Tinougl would enjoy that came from wild hogs' hunters in the valley shot that were a threat to their crops. One would think it tasted like bacon. It gave off a nice aroma which did not escape Karenna who immediately hopped out of bed to see if the two love birds were up and not doing a morning bagalorian tyrist or horizontal tango.

Mòlìhuā was dressed in what she wore the previous evening but planned on changing her clothes after she bathed when the men went to work as she expected.

Her mother came into the kitchen and said, "That really smells good, can I help?"

Mòlìhuā said, "Sure mother why not make some toast and some Kratchen Eggs like you used to do for me."

"Sounds like a plan."

"Do we have any of that fresh butter you used to buy from the neighbors?"

"You better believe it. That is so wonderful. Also, Margol gave me a jar of fruit preserves yesterday, the kind you like to put on your toast."

That's wonderful. Tinougl will be in for a big surprise."

A short time later Tinougl came into the well lit up house drenching in swet.

"Honey, go ahead and take a shower and leave you workout clothes in the bathroom, I'll take care of them after breakfast," Mòlìhuā replied.

"All right," Tinougl said with a nice smile.

Tinougl went into the guest room and grabbed the farm clothes he was going to wear that had also been laundered and went into the bathroom, showered, and then put on his new *Green Acres* outfit.

By the time he made it back to the kitched dressed to go to work, Morgan was there sitting in his chair enjoying morning tea and waiting for breakfast to be served by the two lovely ladies.

Soon they were served and started eating the meal.

While eating Tinougl made an inquiry, "Are we going to cement some posts today?"

"Definitely if that's what you want to do. I kind of want to see how it all works out."

"It will make it a lot easier since we will not have to pound the dirt back into the hole."

"Yes, I can see that."

"This breakfast tastes really good," Tinougl commented.

"That's because you are eating real fresh butter and preserves. You can't find that in any stores."

"I'm impressed. What's the meat?"

"That's breakfast meat we get from wild bores, farmers and ranchers in the valley hunt and kill because they damage the crops."

"I've never had anything like this before. It is very delightful, thank you."

The Kratchen Eggs were cooked sunny side up and Tinougl noticed Morgan dipping the bread into the ege yoke and copied his technique and soon discovered the savory combination hit the spot fairly well.

Soon the meal was finished and Tinougl made a quick trip to the bathroom to freshen up then came back into the Kitchen and said, "I'm ready to start working on that fence."

Morgan said, "I'm a little concerned that water bladder will be too heavy for the hovercraft."

"May I suggest you drive the truck with the water bladder filled with water and bags of cement. I'll drive the hovercraft with the new fence posts and tools."

"Yea, that's probably a good idea."

The men proceeded to leave the house totally obsorbed in their fence mending mentality.

The women were left behind to clean up the dishes, do a little laundry and start working on lunch.

"With Tinougl helping, I suspect those men will be back at lunch time."

"I think so too."

"By the way, thank you for not making too much noise last night. Your father was on pins and needles."

"Mother you have no idea how hard I had to try to not scream. I never felt so good in my lifetime."

"You seemed to have picked a nice man who's not afraid to work."

"He has enough money; he could hire 50 men to work here full time if he wanted. But this is what he wants to experience."

"So, he has a lot of money?"

"Yes, he's very wealthy."

"How did he get all that money?"

"He invested his royalties wisely and grew it. He mentioned to me privately and please do not repeat this, he never has to work again or write another Novel. Plus, I'm a rich girl now too. It would scare you if you knew how much money I had just a couple days ago, and it's still growing fast."

"There are some things I don't want to know including your sex life."

"It's not a sex life. it's a love life."

"I hope you can keep it that way.

"So do I."

~~~

Tinougl followed the truck out into the field with the hovercraft. Morgan came up to the next post to remove and Tinougl pulled in behind.
~~~

Moments later after confirming that was the next fence post, Tinougl had the old post out of the hole and disconnected from the fence wire in less than three minutes. He then dug down deep cleaning the hole then he caved in one of the sides expanding the hole by at least thirty percent, just enough to encase the post with cement. In short order he had a tub next to the pickup truck and dumped a sack of cement mix into it then started putting water into the mixture from the water bladder and mixed it with a shovel until he felt it had the consistency he knew was required for the job.

Tinougl then surprised his future father inlaw by putting the post in and nailed the wire holders in place which then did a great job of holding the post perfectly in place while the cement cured. Tinougl knew that within 30 minutes the cement will have hardened to the point it firmly supported the fence post. He then said, "We need to pick a fence post at least two or three down the fence line so this post is fully supported while the cement cures."

"Alright let me walk ahead and take a look."

After about five more fence posts, Morgan said, "I think this will be it."

Good, I can just pull the tub down there with this rope. We have enough cement for one maybe two more fence posts before we must mix another bag.

Just like before that fence post was out of the hole in less than three minutes and Tinougl was running that post hole digger down good.

This work was sweaty and eventually Tinougl decided he was going to take his shirt off for a bit because he was really swetting badly.

That's when Morgan got an eye opener with Tinougl. Morgan had never seen a man with such incredible muscles. It also made him start wondering what that was all about. Few men could obtain this shape. He had to be an extraordinary person, and likely was involved in things in the past his wife would be very fearful of. Suddenly, the situation was now far more complicated when such a stranger arrives like this. Morgan started developing some fear because he knew only a few men with particular roles could have such a body and just like his daughter, Morgan had ruled out most of the possibilities within ten minutes.

The next morning as Morgan heard Tinougl go out for his morning run, Morgan got his pair of binoculars he used when he and his buddies went wild hog hunting and went out the back door and to the side of the house and watched Tinougl run. Morgan knew the wearabouts that Tinougl turned around about two and a half miles down the road and when he was back at the farmhouse in twenty minutes that meant he was clocking at least fifteen miles per hour over a five-mile distance. Even athletes would have a hard time keeping that pace. Morgan was now even more fearful as to what his daughter got herself mixed up with. Those were real tears when she played the piano. *Seeing this guy in action, those tears meant something. But what was it?*

Another day of replacing posts and the fence was really shaping up. The maintenance required in the future would be greatly diminished with this process. After a couple more days, Morgan said, "I think we need to take a break now. I'm kind of tired and need a day to rest up." He said that knowing Tinougl did about 90% of the work as if it was a trivial matter and he was tired.

"I could use the day off because I want to go buy car."

"Alright I can drive you there in the truck."

"Sure, I want Mòlihuā to come with us to help pick out the vehicle."

"Alright, we'll go after breakfast."

"That works for me. I'm looking forward to more Kratchen Eggs."

Every day Tinougl was knocking the rims off Mòlihuā's tires in the bedroom. He figured it was any time now that she would probably get pregnant. That too would be alright with him as he figured he would not be leaving to go back to the future.

After breakfast the three Amigos were in the truck heading to the same vehicle dealership that sold them the truck.

Tinougl had the salesman Jaswohn's business card but was met by several sharks who wanted a piece of the action.

"Can we help you sir?"

"Yes, I have an appointment with Jaswohn."

"Let me go get him."

The chief shark (aka King Shark) went to Jaswohn's office and asked, "do you have an appointment with someone?"

"No why."

"Don't worry about it."

Jaswohn was curious as to what the hell that was all about and followed the King Shark out the door and out of the showroom to the carlot. He saw King Shark come up to the three people, then he remembered who they were. He knew he was just about to be aced by the King Shark and abruptly approached the three.

Just as King Shark was going to feed Tinougl a BS story, Jaswohn came up almost in a panic and Tinougl saw him and said, "There he is thank you." Tinougl immediately stepped past King Shark and went toward Jaswohn.

"I'm ready to buy that car now, I verified this morning my accounts at a local bank are set up to transfer the funds to your dealership."

"Alright which one do you think you would like."

"This one over here." It was a four-door coup and a slightly larger than most vehicles these days.

As they looked over the vehicle, Mòlìhuā said, "It's a little too big don't you think?"

"I want your parents to fit in nicely when we take them somewhere."

"But this is a 5-seat car, surely it's a little big."

Tinougl smiled and patted Mòlìhuā on the belly and said, "I'm thinking ahead honey."

Morgan kind of thought that was funny, but didn't laugh, though he did smile.

"Alright honey, you know what you want."

"Good I'll take it."

"I'll start the paperwork immediately sir."

About that time Mòlìhuā said, "Tinougl, can I talk to you privately."

"Sure."

The two of them went to an area where they could talk privately.

"Yes dear, what do you want to talk about."

"This is kind of embarrassing, but since you are now part of the family, you might as well know about it, and we can deal with it."

"What is it Mòlìhuā?"

"My father got so hard up recently, he sold my mother's car. I feel very bad about it. She can no longer go visit her friends like she used to."

"What does that have to do with this car?"

"I want to buy two cars so we can give mother back her car."

"That's a very reasonable idea. I tell you what. I got plenty of money and I know you do too. So, you pick out the car for your mother and I'll buy them both."

Mòlìhuā through her arms around Tinougl and hugged him dearly.

The salesman didn't budge until they came back, he knew she might have just changed her husbands's mind and he did't want to waste his time changing the paperwork.

Tinougl approached Jaswohn the young salesman and said, "We have a change of plans."

"What is the change sir?"

"We are going to buy two vehicles, is that ok?"

"Definitely. Which other vehicle do you think you would you like?"

"She's going to pick it out." Tinougl nodded his head towards Mòlìhuā."

In due time Mòlìhuā picked out a vehicle very similar to what her mother had. She felt so grateful to Tinougl who accepted her failed family. *Perhaps had she stayed home and not ran after her singing career she might have helped them avoid all the negative they experienced the past few years.*

The car dealer Jaswohn was daydreaming about his bonus checks. These strangers paid full boat for the vehicles, the sticker price. No haggling, just a sincere *us get it done attitude*. Jaswohn liked the couple. They were good people.

In due time the cars were ready to drive home. One was registered in Mòlìhuā's name, the other in her mother's name. They formed convoy and drove home. Following Morgan home was good because it prevented them to get lost and he was a conservative driver and made it a comfortable drive.

The three cars pulled up to the garage but did not park inside.

Karenna observed three vehicles pull into the driveway and was curious and walked down to see what that was all about.

"Mother, we bought this blue car for you, and you will be able to visit your friends more often."

Karenna was slight emotional as once again her daughter had given her a big surprise. Later when they were alone together, she would let her know it was Tinougl who purchased her car for her. That added to her growing appreciation for her future son in law.

Since Karenna wasn't at the car dealership, they had a special camera in the car to photograph her with a set of keys and they would then program the facial recognition as soon as she started up the car with the keys and answered a few questions so the voice verifcation could be used to validate the facial recognition.

Karenna had not driven a vehicle in a year, but she had it wrote to memory, plus these new models had the self driving feature, her expertise was not required.

The four hovered around the cars for a while talking and suddenly Karenna said, "Morgan can you please put the cars in the garage. Then come in the house. Dinner will be ready in a few minutes."

Tinougl followed the women into the house and went into the living room and was watching the news looking for any leads for his original mission. If nothing else he could send a note back in the time machine, hit the blue button that had a five second delay and close the lid and get out of the way.

Mòlìhuā went into the kitchen with her mother to help out.

"Thank you for buying me that vehicle."

"I didn't buy either vehicle. Tinougl purchased them."

"Just like that?"

"Yes, don't you get it? You and daddy are now his family. He has nobody else."

"How do you know all this?"

"Mother I'm not dumb and naïve, I've done some things he doesn't know, and you would never suspect."

"And what is that?"

"I hired a private detective and paid half of all the money I had to verify who he is and what he is. All the way back to his hometown and friends. I know everything about him. But there are a few minor items I didn't get good answers on, and I don't want to investigate that."

"Perhaps that's exactly what you should have looked into."

"It's too late. We've gone to far now. I must accept him who he is and what he has done. The past is the past."

"You might need to rethink that."

"Mother I need to tell you something you need to think about. I'm now very famous. People here have not yet discovered I'm here and who I am. I need a very strong man like Tinougl to protect me. I can no longer afford to put my life in the hands of amatuers."

"What does that mean honey?"

"In a couple more days you will see it start to develop as I'm discovered here. You will probably have to hire private security. And that's not a problem. I'm sure Tinougl would be willing to pay for it all. So, could I. it's coming. Your little girl is now someone you and this planet do not yet know about. This is our hideout."

It was hard to gauge if Mòlìhuā was speaking from a fantasy. It all seemed so surreal.

Chapter

Twenty-Four

King Shark Blows Mòlìhuā's Cover.

At that same moment the manager of the vehicle sales company called Jaswohn into his office.

"Yes sir, what can I do for you?"

"Good job on selling the truck and two cars at full price to that family."

"Thank you."

"I have some eye andy for you. Do you know who those people really are?"

"Not really but they definitely have money."

"No kidding, take a look." He then showed the holograph that was now starting to show up on local news reports.

"Incredible."

"Do you think they will be coming back soon for more vehicles?"

"Good question."

A few minutes later after Jaswohn went back to his small office,

King Shark walked in and asked, "What did the boss want with you?"

Jaswohn pulled up the video on his world wide web data stream and said, "He wanted to show me a video of my customer that bought the three vehicles from me. Take a look."

"Jaswohn twisted the display terminal around so King Shark could see it."

After watching a couple minute, the woman made up singing her love song to her lover boy, the King Shark said, "I'll be god damned."

That video was many of more to follow. The news feed was ablaze with reports because the DIVA WAS LIVING IN KONHAGAR!

The King Shark did a dastardly deed and went into his office and called the tip line of one of the news channels and said, "I know where the DIVA Wánměi de Mòlìhuā lives."

The news screaner asked, "How do you know that?"

"My vehicle sales company just sold her family a truck and two new cars."

The news screaner asked, "All right where does she live?"

"I think this information is worth some money."

"How much?"

"50 credits."

"Alright where do you want to meet?"

"You know that Golden Dragon Bar on 4th street, it's a block away from the dealership. Meet me there at lunch, say 11:30."

"All right."

"I'll be setting at the bar. I have a white shirt and blue tie on."

"See you there."

~~~

Another day just like the previous with Tinougl running the five miles in twenty minutes.

After breakfast they were out working on fence posts again. Morgan said while they were working, "I have some bales of hay in one of my fields we need to hall and then I need to borrow a tractor so we can plow that field."

"You do not have a tractor?"

"I had to sell it to pay the farm hands."

"Is there a place around here that sells them?"

"Sure, several in the valley."

"I think this fence can wait. Us go get you a tractor."

"Alright," Morgan responded knowing damn well what Tinougl had in mind.

Away they drove and instead of stopping at the farmhouse, they went out to the road. Morgan drove the truck and stopped at the gate. Tinougl hopped out and opened the gate and Morgan drove through and Tinougl closed it behind them. Ten miles down this country road was some farm and ranch supply stores including a few that sold farm machinery.

One of the dealers that sold tractors, a gentleman named Garrot, knew Morgan and felt sorry for his financial stress. Most of the neighbors knew the bank had cut off his credit and was playing hardball. The banker wanted his land.

"Hello Garrot, this is my son in law Tinougl," Morgan embellished slightly and Tinougl felt he was all but officially that
~~~

role and didn't matter. That marriage was one of the minor legal actions they would soon wrap up as it was time to demonstrate his ultimate dedication to Mòlìhuā. Their journey had come to the point they needed to make it official. This was his new family and he enjoyed them more than they could ever imagine. *Or was this the calm before the storm?*

Tinougl knew the obvious. Morgan has lost most of his farm machinery, so he said, "Listen Morgan, I know you need more than just a tractor. I'm sure these guys can deliver what ever we purchase. Get it all now. Anything you need we will buy now before we leave.

Garrot looked upon Tinougl with great curiousity and just about could not believe what he was hearing.

"What kind of tractor do you want," Garrot asked.

"He needs a good size one with a front-end loader," Tinougl stated before Morgan could get the words out. And it was true that's exactly what he needed.

Garrot walked them over to a line of tractors that had cheaper models and more expensive models. Tinougl knew a lot about tractors from his teenage years and walked past the cheaper models that Morgan was eyeballing to one that was undoubtedly more expensive than most of the farmers around here could afford. "How about this one?" Tinougl asked.

Garrot was rather perplexed that a popper was in the market for one of the most expensive pieces of machinery on the lot. He though now would be a time to ask the most important question of the day.

"Sir, how do you intend on paying for it?"

"We'll pay directly credits from the bank. I have a local account that can transfer you the credits."

"If that's the case, we cans start the paperwork and the process."

"You will deliver everything we purchase, today?"

"Absolutely, we have equipment haulers and I know where Morgan lives."

"I'm going to buy everything, but I want it all registered to Morgan."

"Sure, no problem."

Morgan felt a very strange tinge. He also knew Tinougl was more than he let on to be and it frightened him, but he had let this go too far. His daughter was probably pregnant by now and there was no turning back, he would have to take the good with the bad.

Over the span of another hour Morgan selected everything he needed to get back to where he was twenty years ago before he fell on tough times and some very bad years of crop failures. Two hours later all the contracts were signed and Morgan and Tinougl received electronic copies of all the paperwork on their communicators. They went home, it was lunch time.

"We might as well stop in here and get something to eat."

"Works for me."

The men were soon enjoying the presence of the most wonderful women in their lives who out did themselves making a wonderful lunch. "We are going to have some equipment delivered today."

"Really?" Karenna's curiousity suddenly peaked.

"I needed some farm machinery. Tinougl helped out. I'll take the cost out of his salary."

Tinougl chuckled. All was good.

King Shark made his mark and pocketed the 50 credits after showing the billing information of Wánměi de Mòlǐhuā's truck purchase and said, "This is one of the three vehicles they purchased over the past couple of days."

He then had another doozie, a several minute video he spliced out of a security video and showed it to the reporter.

"This is amazing. That really is her."

"And you got her address."

"What do you want for the video, when I show that to my producer, they will immediately let me run with the story."

"I could get fired if my company knows I gave you that video. I'll let you have it to show your producer, but do not air it."

"Not a problem, now that we know where's she's at, we'll get our own video. I just want this to get my producer to approve the story I'm going to air."

"All right, I want another 100 credits."

King Shark walked out of the Golden Dragon, with as many credits in his pocket as Jaswohn made in bonus for the car sales he missed out on.

~~~

After lunch, Morgan said, "I think we need to hang out at the farmhouse and wait for the equipment delivery."

"I can go work on the fence posts by myself if you want?"

"It takes both vehicles to get everything we need down there."

"We can load everything up and go to that area we are working, and I'll drive you back to the farmhouse and go back and work."

"I think we can leave the pickup there with everything you need, and I'll just drive the hovercraft back myself. When the equipment shows up, I'm going to call you on your communicator. I would
~~~

prefer you be here when the equipment is delivered, and they will demonstrate how it all works."

"Sure."

Tinougl was soon at work replacing fence posts and filling in the holes with concrete. In a couple hours he made good progress and ran out of fence posts, so he put everything in the truck and drove back to the farmhouse. Morgan met him and said, "I was just about to call you. Garrot just called me and said the equipment is on the way."

"Good timing, I ran out of fence posts and our concrete supply is low.

We'll need to get some more concrete tomorrow."

"A short distance away from the tractor supply is a builders store that sells everything we need."

In 10 minutes, a caravan of equipment movers began arriving, driving into the yard. It was indeed handy that Morgan's farm had such a large driveway area they could all pull into and unload efficiently.

The women heard the commotion and left the house to see what all was going on.

It was a sight to behold, every item Morgan had to sell was now back, except it was all new, not wore out junk like he disposed of. One man's junk is another man's treasure, so he was able to offload it at reasonable prices. His wife helped quite a bit by painting a lot of the farm machinery, so it didn't look so old and wore out.

When Karenna saw the new tractor, she was dumbfounded. It was big and it looked expensive. Inded it was. Between her daughter and their new son in law, their farm had been put back together and hole again in the matter of a week. Tinougl's arrival was very auspicious. And the most pleasing thing was he always seemed so pleasing and never had anything negative to say.

Garrot was with the group because he wanted to make sure the customer knew all there was to know about the operation of the equipment. Tinougl with his photographic memory caught on real fast. One of the things Garrot learned over the years working with the farmers in the valley was to have them operate every aspect of the equipment so they would not pester him later about repeated training they should have done in the first place. It was evident that Tinougl quickly passed the Green Acres 101 course. Garrot was rather impressed how the young man picked up everything and asked astute questions.

Now there was only one other issue to deal with and that was fuel. Garrot made a killing on the sale and saw it only fitting he provided a tank of fuel, not only in the equipment but in the farmer's fuel tank he used to fuel up all his equipment and vehicles.

"Morgan, I brought a fuel truck with us. I'm going to give you a free tank of fuel to show you I appreciate your business."

"Thanks. See the tank on the side of the garage?"

"Yes."

"That's my fuel tank."

"All right, I'll have my men fill it up."

"Thanks."

"By the way we deliver fuel so in the future if you need a refill on your tank, call me and I'll have it delivered. Out prices are posted, and you can get them by calling us or getting the information on our datasite."

"That's great. I don't want to use my former supplier who became a PITA."

The equipment delivery trucks and personnel slowly left the

farm and soon they were gone. Tinougl and Morgan had moved the equipment around like the older equipment had been placed. Morgan had concrete slabs put in so he didn't have to worry about weeds and grass he would have to clean out around the machinery. All that new equipment sitting on the concrete slabs looked impressive.

While they were standing there just taking it all in, Karenna received a phone call from her friend Marjinoe, another farmer's wife that lived nearby."

"Hello Karenna."

Karenna recognized the voice and said, "hello Marjinoe."

"Karenna, I hate to be the bearer of bad news, but your daughter is on the holographic news channel 100 and they also have shown your address. It looks like they sent a vehicle past your farm and filmed it too."

"Thanks for the heads up. I need to talk with Morgan."

They hung up and Karenna said, "Morgan I think we are going to have some trouble. We better go inside and talk about it."

The two couples walked back into the house, and Karenna went directly to the holographic projector controller and selected the holographic news channel 100. There Mòlīhuā was, performing at Grand Plexis de Chiveltros one of the Empire's most exquisitee entertainment venus on the Strip.

The report was about over, but all holographic reports had the rewind icon that let someone who missed part of the report to see it all again from the start."

Everything that Marjinoe stated plus more was on the screen. Tinougl already understood what was going to happen next and said, "It looks like we will have to hire some security."

"I can't afford security," Morgan responded.

"I'll take care of the security." Tinougl responded, then he immediately dialed his Limo driver friend Bustamante and said, "I need you to come pick me up."

"You got all those new vehicles, why do you need the ride?"

"I'll explain it on the way."

CHAPTER TWENTY-FIVE

ARISTAPARA AND ORGANIZED CRIME TO THE RESCUE

Tinougl had some rather good intuition and figured it was late in the day and the crowds would not show up until in the morning. Hopefully he would get his run completed before he had to deal with the crowd.

"Where are you going?" Mòlìhuā asked with a frightful look on her face.

"I must go into the city to hire some security. I'll be back probably in a couple hours."

"I should probably go with you."

"No, stay with your parents, it's best you are not seen in the city with me."

"It's happening now, isn't it?"

"You remember what it was like at the transportation hub. That comes with fame."

Tinougl waited a couple more minutes watching some of the

news report then walked out of the house and predictably the Limo pulled in the driveway a few moments later.

Mòlīhuā stood by her man and had a worried look.

"All right, see you in a bit."

"Please be safe. You mean a lot to me."

"I will. And you mean a lot to me as well."

Tinougl was dressed in street clothes nothing to indicate he was anyone special. His communicator in silence mode was tucked into a special harness on the side of one of his legs, and some very capable spy weapons on his other leg in case his personal safety had issues.

"Where do you want to go?" Bustamante asked

"I assume you know the city well." Tinougl responded.

"Yes, I do."

"Good. I need to hire some security people. Take me to a security firm you know has some bad asses that can fuck some one up really bad if necessary."

"I know just the place. I've given a few of those goons rides a time or two.

They stiffed me but I'd rather be alive then argue with them."

"My kind of place."

In about ten minutes the Limo pulled in front of a storefront.

"This is it," Bustamante said.

Tinougl replied, "Wait here for me, I need you to drive me home."

Several of the bruisers inside had been drinking and taking drugs and were getting really cocky when the man wearing clothes that covered up most of his muscles walked into the storefront.

Instead of treating him like a potential client like they should have, one of the wise guys started mouthing off to Tinougl who ignored his pathetic outbirsts. A few of the other salty crew members knew when this guy wanted to kick some ass and started smiling because they knew a fight was going to break out any minute.

"What do you want."

"Some security."

"Yea you look like you need some security alright. In fact, I'm going to kick your ass to prove it."

"I really do not have time for this can I please talk to your boss."

The big guy was in the next room watching all this unfold. He was just about to stand up and go out and tell Ruckus to shut his *fucking* mouth and hear what the man had to say, but like a dumb shit, Ruckus lunged at Tinougl knowing he would beat the living crap out of the chump.

Ruckus had never dealt with a top galactic spy before. The other men didn't quite know what happened, it all moved so quickly, then Ruckus was on the floor unconscious, and at that time two others charged Tinougl who knocked their dumb asses out as well. The other three goons hanging out just stood there observing the three thugs unconscious on the floor were lying out the odds what would happen to them and on the better side of valor stood there.

The big guy (aka Aristapara), was utterly amazed and walked out with a cigar in his mourth and asked, "What do you want."

"Same thing I told these guys before they attacked me. I want to purchase some security."

"Looks like you don't need any security, you handled yourself quite well."

"I need security and I know you guys are not cheap, I will pay you well. Can we go some place where I can discuss with you, my situation?"

"Sure, come into my office." Aristapara said and added looking at the other three Amigos, "Clean up the mess and when our customer leaves, we are going to do a little sensitivity training."

Inside the office, the big guy said, "Have a seat."

"Thank you."

"Okay what's the deal, I just saw you fuck up three of the toughest bastards in the city in mere seconds and you think you need security?"

"My bride to be is a celebrity. Somehow someone tipped off the news we are here, and I now tomorrow morning there will be big crowds showing up wanting to see the Diva so I need some protection for their home and some mean bastards that can kick a few asses if the crowd gets out of control and tries to trespass on the property."

"About how many guys do you think you need?"

"I would like four guys from sunup to sundown or until the crowd dispurses."

"Alright I think we can handle it and it's not going to be cheap."

"I know that."

"How will you pay me?"

"Cash via credit transfers."

"Alright this is what it's going to cost." Aristapara threw out a number he jacked up a little about 25% more than he would charge customers to supply four hired guns.

"That works."

"Would you like to make a down payment, say one third?"

"Give me your phone number and I'll transfer the funds within the hour."

"How long do you think you will need my guys?"

"Until the idiots decide to leave us alone."

"That may take a while."

"I understand."

"I'm happy to help."

"I'm sure you are also good with investigations."

"That's correct. I have several private dicks that are the best in the business."

"I have another job for you to do that's unrelated to the security."

"Alright."

"I do not want anyone except the private dicks to know about this second job."

"That's understandable."

"I want you to find out who tipped off the news media, then I want you to put the fear of god in them and make them wish they never want to see us or hear about us again the rest of their lives."

"Wouldn't it be easier just to kill them?"

"When you put the fear of god into someone, it acts as a deterrent to others that might want to get cocky and cross me."

"As tough as you are, I know because you just beat up the toughest guys in the city, why do you not simply do it yourself."

"I'm sure you can appreciate this. My future wife and her family would not condone me doing such a thing. By not doing it and hiring you, I have plausible deniability."

"You are quite an interesting person. I've never dealt with someone like you before. Because you are such a good client, I'll put my best private dick on the case."

"I appreciate that."

"Where will my men be used?"

"When I call you shortly with the money, I'll give you the address. I'll be at their gate in the morning to greet your security guys. They will have shade and we'll supply them food, drink, and a toilet if necessary."

"I'll have a porta potty delivered there, it's best the men stay close to the perimeter. I know how these things work out."

"That's great. Thank you."

"My pleasure."

Aristapara stood up and held out his hand and puffed on his cigar and smiled and said, "I'll walk you out to your car."

"Thanks. What's your name by the way?"

"Aristapara."

"Aristapara, I'm Tinougl. Please do not advertise my name."

"Understand Tinougl. We take care of our clients privacy."

"Thank you."

"You're most welcome."

The three losers were coming to as the three amigos were getting them back on their feet and tidying up the place. Tinougl and Aristapara walked out to the limo which Aristapara knew well along with the driver, Bustamante.

The goons inside the business were mildly shocked. Aristapara never walked clients to their vehicles.

As the Limo pulled away to take Tinougl home, Aristapara walked back into his shop and said, "Okay dickheads, it's time for a little sensitivity training before you clowns wreck my business model."

When the Limo pulled into the driveway it was about dinner time and to Tinougl's satisfaction the crowd had not appeared, but he suspected tomorrow it would begin.

Tinougl went into the farmhouse and when greeted by Mòlìhuā and her parents, he said, "We will have security here in the morning. There will be four security specialists. Also, their company will deliver a portapotty that will be placed near the gate in case the men need to use a toilet.

This cemented the deal for Morgan. He now knew for a fact Tinougl was a man of the world and the galaxy and he had some fears as to what his daughter got herself into. If he knew the real story of Tinougl was a time traveller, it would crush him, so in a way he was lucky of the coceilment of Tinougl's mission and all that had transpired since Tinougl time traveled back 500 years.

The dinner was kind of quiet. Nobody was talking. It seemed like dread. Tinougl broke the ice and said, "I think we got enough of the fence done for now that we should hall all that hay out of the field so we can plow the field and get it ready for the next crop."

"Why the rush?" Karenna asked.

"Well, I was kind of wanting to try out that new tractor and have Morgan teach me how to use it."

"I would be most happy to give you all the pointers son."

"Thanks."

Tinougl then decided it was time to bring up a sensitive subject.

"I know that you know Mòlìhuā, and I are lovers. We've done a lot of unprotected sex and she could be pregnant by now. I would like to make our unification fully legal and registered as soon as possible."

Mòlìhuā lit up like a christmas tree, this was the final proof of Tinougl's intentions.

"It takes time to plan a wedding," Karenna stated.

"May I make a suggestion?" Tinougl said.

"Sure," Karenna responded.

"Tomorrow, we'll have security so we will be able to leave the farm and go into the city. We can go to the City Hall, do the official legal process, then schedule a wedding and celebration later, giving you the time, you need to prepare for it. Meahwhile Mòlìhuā can be legal partners and begin our marriage tomorrow."

Karenna was shocked, but she also knew what Tinougl said made sense especially with all the press coverage, her daughter would not look like a tramp if she were married to the man she was sleeping with and getting pregnant.

Mòlìhuā then spoke, "I would like to do what Tinougl has suggested, but instead of a Wedding, I would just like a reception here. We can invite all our special friends and not be swamped with strangers we have not had much dealing with, in our lives, just because they live in the valley near us."

Morgan then chimed in and said, "I want to go along with what Mòlìhuā said because after all, this is for her and Tinougl. it's what they want that counts."

"I'm very happy to just have a reception since we will be at the City Hall when they sign the unification," Karenna said, and actually felt relieved to not have to go through a very pompass ordeal that her daughter really didn't want. Besides that, the news media stated that over seven billion people bought subscriptions to her two videos, so they have already seen her dressed up the very best possible.

After dinner, they watched some more of the holographic news channel 100. Tinougl received a text massage on his communicator from Aristapara that said: "Thank you for the down payment. The men will be there at sunrise in the morning. The portapotty will not be delivered until a couple hours later. My private dick has made great progress on your second job. We will have a report for you in a couple days."

Tinougl replied, "Thank you for your support."

It was kind of a restless night for all, but since this was a special night knowing what was going to happen tomorrow, Karenna informed Morgan, "We need to go to bed early tonight, I want to get a good nights' sleep and take care of myself in the morning, so I look presentable."

"Alright dear."

Mòlìhuā knew her mother was giving her a gift as she knew what Tinougl the ultimate act did today was. His sincerity was proven by his actions. His intentions were real, and he turned out to be exactly like he seemed. Her mother knew Tinougl was going to receive some special loving tonight and needed to be left alone so her daughter could work her magic.

The two lovebirds were soon dancing the horizontal tango and tonight Mòlìhuā was the conductor of the band, fully in charge and saying things that not only shocked Tinougl but turned him on so much he had much stronger gratification. In a while just when he thought they were done and about to fall asleep, Mòlìhuā who was well read and had access to all those romance novels her room mate had back at Santorini de Shénshèng, crawled under the sheets and began performing fellatio on Tinougl that quickly reversed any prior drowsiness. Then when she knew she had him pumped up near the point of launch she crawled on top of him and performed a tremendous action that in short order caused the short countdown and the rockets were launched unexpectedly with great thrust. They were then in orbit together traveling through the cosmos in an ethereal domain that only true love can give.

The night ended too soon. Tinougl's eyes opened just about at sunup. He got up and put on his exercise clothes and exited the farmhouse. He walked out to the gate and as expected several vehicles came and Tinougl opened the gate for them so they could drive in the large yard.

The cars pulled over on the side of the driveway onto the grass to not block access. Five men exited the cars including Aristapara.

Aristapara stepped forward and held out his hand and quickly noticed Tinougl and his incredible build. Aristapara having been an INTEL specialist and worked for organized crime until he opened his own agency knew men didn't have builds like Tinougl unless they were into some very heavy-duty activity.

Thanks to his time in the INTEL community, he could spot a spook a mile away. He knew exactly what Tinougl was. He just didn't know who he worked for.

"Let's walk over here so we can have a little talk."

"Sure."

When they were far enough away where the goons could not overhear their conversation, Aristapara said, "My private dick tracked the person down who did all this to you."

"Yea who was it?"

"One of the guys at the vehicle dealership."

"The man who sold us the cars?"

"No, it's a guy with the nickname King Shark."

"What's next?"

"Private Dick is going to give him his nightmare tonight. The private dick says it would be best just as easy to kill the dude."

"No, I don't want him killed, that's not necessary. Just send the massage."

"Not a problem he'll know if he crosses you again, he'll lose his pecker."

"That's the way I want it."

"My men are here now. Another vehicle will be coming in a few minutes with some chairs and some shade fixtures that we'll have before your gate to check anyone that shows up that wants to go to the farmhouse."

"We'll be gone most of the day, so there will not be anyone here for visitors. After we leave turn away anyone that wants to drive in here and inform them, we are not home."

"That's perfect. That's what they will do."

"Alright Aristapara, I'm going for my morning run. Thanks for coming here with the updates."

"You are quite welcome."

The security force watched Tinougl take off. They knew he was flat out running at a very good clip. Aristapara knew only the very top-level echelon spies worked out this hard. Tinougl was a man of mystery, that was for sure. *He also knew how to make arrangements and where to go which says a lot.*

Two of the men got their asses beat by Tinougl yesterday, and after they received their sensitivity training, they knew to stay the hell away from this guy if they knew what was good for them. Aristapara knew how things are. This would not be the only time Tinougl would use them. In the future he expected other tasks, because handyman types were used for a lot of purposes. There would be future need and big payments because Tinougl probably already knew they were the really only firm in the city capable of doing what they did. Nobody else came close. They were expensive of course, but you must pay for talent, and you get what you pay for. Tinougl was one of the smart ones who knew what the price was and how it was important in order to handle important situations. In ten minutes, Tinougl was out of site so Aristapara got in his vehicle and drove back to the office, where he would enjoy looking at is bank account again.

Twenty minutes after he left the security force observed Tinougl come back to the farm moving along real fast and totally drenched in swet. They too saw the muscles and now understood, he was a man not to *mess* with.

CHAPTER

TWENTY-SIX

A VISIT TO CITY HALL

Karenna had already used the bathroom and showered and was working on making them something to eat.

Mòlìhuā was still in bed getting ready to get up and start getting ready for the big day. Her body was still recovering from the night before where she put every ounce of her being into pleasing Tinougl. She was happy because her efforts also helped him to please her. In love you get back what you put into it. When two lovers put forth the maximum effort, they reach these pateaus that most people miss out on.

Tinougl took a shower and put on his street clothes. Mòlìhuā soon followed him and took a shower and dressed and put on a pretty dress that Tinougl would be proud of.

After a quick breakfast that most of them did not want, they were scrubbed and ready to head for city hall.

"Which car are we going to take?" Morgan asked.

"I think we should just take a Limo; I'll call my friend. That way we can be delivered on the steps of city hall and not worry about parking."

"Great idea."

Tinougl called the Taxi-Limo driver Bustamante and in 15 minutes the Limo pulled up to the checkpoint. The security guys asked, "What are you doing here?"

"Tinougl called me and asked I pick him up. It looks like they are coming out of the house now."

The security guy looked and saw them coming so he knew it was legitimate and said, "Okay we must check everyone. Enjoy your day."

"Thank you."

The Limo pulled into the yard and made a U-turn and pulled up to where the four people were standing. They got in and the Limo left the farmhouse and headed for the city.

In less than ten minutes they were pulling up to the front of the city hall and the group got out and made their way into the building and saw the directions to the unification office, where they went.

It was lucky they arrived early, there were no customers.

"Can I help you?"

"Yes, Wánměi de Mòlihuā and I wish to register for a unification."

"Identification please?"

Tinougl and Mòlihuā knew what they needed to have with them and were ready. The form and the process were quite simple. The clerk scanned their identification, printed out the form and said, "Sign where indicated on the document."

Both signed and the clerk looked at the two individualsl with them and knew they were probably family members but had to ask the dumb question according to the law: "Do you have two witnesses to sign the unification?

"Yes."

"May I see their identification?"

"Morgan and Karenna were old school and always had their identification with them when they left the farm and went somewhere. They showed their identification, the clerk scanned them for the records, then stamped the document with the city seal and gave the couple the document which the city didn't need since the legal copy was in the city's computer archives and routed to several city departments that had interests in anyone possibly unifying, including law enforcement and the tax collectors."

The clerk then said, "That will be fifty credits for the fee."

Tinougl pulled out his communicator and wired the money to the city transactions department as required and was soon handed a receipt and informed. Congratulations, in the eyes of the public, you are officially and legally unified."

The couple faced each other and Mòlìhuā threw her arms around Tinougl, and they kissed as if there were no tomorrow. The clerk got slightly teary eyed looking at the magnificent demonstration of *Requited Love*. Morgan and Karenna threw their arms around the couple, and they all had a group hug in front of the clerk who didn't mind it since they were the only customers in the office.

Tinougl quickly came up with a great idea and said, "Let me call the Limo back and have him come pick us up and drive around the countryside for a bit, then when it gets around lunch time we can stop at a nice restaurant. Tinougl also said to Bustamante when he picked them up, take me to a reputable jewelry store so I can buy her a nice ring.

"I know just the place."

"I figured you did."

Soon they pulled up to a series of buildings and Tinougl said, 'You' guys all wait here, I have something I need to do."

The jewelry store wasn't well marked and unless you were specifically looking for it you wouldn't know it was there. Most of their salse were by referrels and that's the way the owner liked it.

Tinougl walked into the premises not looking special. He could easily pass for the average middle class based on his wardrobe he was wearing. He walked up to the store clerk who was behind a glass bullet proof window with speakers.

"How may I help you sir?"

"I was just unified with my bride, and I want to buy her a ring."

"People usually get a ring before the unification."

"We wanted to beat the crowd; we are doing it in reverse order."

"That's probably a smart move. How much are looking to spend?"

"The price isn't important; I want something that looks good."

"Take a look and let me know if you see something you like."

One tray of very expensive rings had Santorini de Shénshèng circular cut diamonds that only the wealthy could afford. Tinougl looked at that tray and said, "I want one of those."

"Those are very expensive sir."

"I can easily afford them."

"How do you intend on paying for the ring?"

"Cash Credits directly from my bank account."

"The minimum price for any of those are 50,000 credits."

"Not a problem, I can send you the money as soon as you write up the bill of sell and text me the balance which I can fill."

"Do you know what size you need?"

"Do you have a ring fitter?"

"Yes."

Give me a ring fitter you think will fit my little pinky. Tinougl held up his hand and the clerk put the plastic ring fitter in the tray below the glass window. Tinougl put it on and said, that's it. Do you have one this size?"

"Yes." The clerk pulled one up and showed Tinougl.

"I'll take that one but, in the contract, I want free fitting in case I need to bring her back and get it resized."

"No problem, sir, all our rings are sold that way because we know we do not always get the ultimate size usually until after the purchase and the person wants it adjusted to fit more comfortable."

"Great, lets do it."

"Sir what's your communicator number so I can send you the billing?"

Tinougl gave the clerk the number and immediately received the bill for 75,000 credits which he immediately paid out of one of his slush accounts. The billing had all the contractual information such as the free future fitting.

The clerk put the ring in a ring box and placed it down into the tray where

Tinougl picked it up and put it into his pocket. The clerk knew his name because it was on the billing information and said in the very nicest manner, "Thank you Tinougl for buying the ring today. That is one of our finest rings and it is rarely sold because most people cannot afford it."

"My bride is well worth it."

"What's her name?"

Tinougl knew this information was likely to be leaked out soon once the clerk discovered her, but the damage was already done at the vehicle dealership, so he informed the clerk. "Her maiden's name was Wánmĕi de Mòlìhuā."

"Lovely."

"Thank you."

Tinougl left the store, walked about thirty feet to the Limo where everyone inside was wondering where he was and what he was doing.

Tinougl went to the driver's window which was open and said, "We want you to drive us around and give us a mini tour until lunch time, then take us to a nice restaurant.

"Sure thing."

The driver, Bustamante enjoyed dealing with Tinougl who was such a pleasant person, yet full of surprises like this morning.

Soon they were on their way and before Tinougl's bride Mòlìhuā could quiz him on what he was doing, Tinougl said, "Mòlìhuā, I love you, but when you left the house this morning, you were not properly dressed."

"I wasn't?" Mòlìhuā suddenly had a frown on her face.

"No, you were missing something?" Tinougl said with an evil grin.

"What was I missing?" Mòlìhuā asked in a way that showed confusion.

"Yes, not to worry I picked one up for you so you will be properly dressed for the rest of the day." Then Tinougl pulled out the ring box and pulled out that exotic ring out of the box and placed it very efficiently on box Mòlìhuā's finger.

Karenna was virtually stunned. She knew that was a special ring that most likely cost a fortune. Her estimates were not too far off the mark since it had a Santorini de Shénshèng circular cut diamond that were only produced one place in the entire galaxy.

Tears were flowing down Mòlìhuā's eyes. Her emotional spike was quite severe. Happiness can be just as stressful as sadness because of the intensity at times. It was a good thing they were driving around sight seeing because it took Mòlìhuā a while to get a grip on herself.

Karenna was no less effected. Tinougl had stormed into their lives and turned their world upside down in such a short period of time.

Karenna also knew what she had to do. The couple needed some private and special time together. After lunch she said, "We are going to drop you off at a hotel and the Limo can take us home. We'll come and pick you guys up when you are ready to come home."

Mòlìhuā threw her arms around her mother and said. "Thank you so much for what you have done for me."

Once the Limo driver was given the game plan, he dropped Tinougl and Mòlìhuā off at the Grand Xenis Hotel, where only the wealthiest of Konhagar could afford to stay.

Tinougl and Mòlìhuā walked up to the receptionist.

"May I help you sir?"

"We want to check in."

"Do you have reservations?"

"No."

"I'm not sure we can help you."

"Behind Tinougl was a holographic screen for hotel guests in the lobby and they were playing reruns of Mòlìhuā's singing."

With an evil grin Tinougl asked, "Excuse me miss, but do you not find a striking resemblance to the woman singing on the holograph to this young lady?"

The condescending receptionist looked at the holograph, looked at Mòlìhuā a few times and said, "Is that really you?"

"When you check us in, I'll check in under my name so you will know who I am. I'm sure your facial recognition will soon be alerting you."

Facial recognition is really good because the computer starts working as soon as someone approaches the entrance. The hotel manager who overhears the audio from the front desk so he can tweak receptionists, if necessary, came flying through the door into the receptionist area of the lobby and said, "I'm very sorry Mòlìhuā, our receptionist didn't know who you are."

On the receptionist data terminal screen was big letters flashing "VIP" requiring her to inform the manager who was required to inform the management team of exceptional VIP visitors. In walked off the street was the current most famous DIVA in the Empire and the receptionist just insulted her!

If looks could kill, the receptionist suddenly realized she was going to have a very bad day.

"We would prefer you do not disclose we are staying in this hotel."

"We do not give out customer information."

Tinougl said, "Our parents dropped us off because they wanted to kick us out of the house for the night, so we came prepared with nothing, I assume you have fashion designers here that can properly dress us for evening dinner and entertainment?"

"Yes, sir we have everything. Would you like to check in now?"

"I want the reservation to me in my name," Mòlìhuā stipulated.

"Not a problem madam, do we have permission to charge your bank account?"

Artificial Intelligence in concert with Mòlìhuā's bank had immediately set up a link so the money transfer could happen seamlessly and as soon as Mòlìhuā responded in the affirmative, the account was linked so that all future charges would go to it and not create any hassles while they were guests.

"Sir I take it you are a confident of Mòlìhuā's?"

"He's, my husband. We were unified a few hours ago, his name is Tinougl."

The manager was utterly stunned. Standing before him just a few feet away was the biggest story in the empire these days, and she just got married!

Artificial Intelligence also immediately logged Tinougl and found his links and now the two were tied together in the reservation even though Mòlìhuā was paying for it. Since her recording just sold another billion subscriptions over the night, her wealth was now beyond anyone currently staying in the hotel.

The manager now knew he had to make some points because of this very embarrassing situation and said, "Mòlìhuā I'm very sorry if we disturbed you during the check-in process. One behalf of the Grand Xenis Hotel I'm putting you in a staffed penthouse at no additional cost."

"Thank you."

"Your penthouse is ready; may I please escort you to you're the penthouse?"

"Yes, that would be very nice, thank you."

The receptionist was worried when the manager came back down, he would probably fire her. She was crying a little already.

Tinougl knew the poor woman was only doing like they trained her so in the elevator he said to the manager, "The woman didn't know who we are. We are not dressed up like rich people, so she was only doing what her training directed her to do. Please promise me you will not do any adverse action against her in any way. She's probably going through a lot of stress right now because of all of this. I'm going to ask you to do me a personal favor."

"Yes sir, what is it."

"You have a nice flower shop here in the hotel, I'm sure."

"Yes sir, we do."

"I want you to go to the flower shop before you talk to the receptionist again and give her a dozen beautiful red roses and charge it to us and on the card, say, Casandra (on her name tag), we were pleased to meet you and on one of the most important days of our lives we send you our best wishes. Signed Tinougl and Mòlìhuā.

"Sir, I must say you are one of the kindest gentlemen I've ever met. Few people have your intuition and empathy like you just displayed. It will be my distinct honor do carry out that task for you. I'm also sure Casandra will appreciate you even more when I give her the flowers."

"Thank you, sir, I appreciate your help in this matter."

"My pleasure." The manager said and then thought, it's going to get wild in the hotel tonight.

The maid and the butler do not hang out in empty Penthouses. When the reservation is confirmed, they are on standby in the lounge or helping another employee when they are vectored to the Penthouse. The minute the manager confirmed the booking the butler and maid were well on their way to the Penthouse. Both were skilled in martial arts and as part of the hotel security apparatus had conceiled weapons and were obligated to protect the guests.

CHAPTER
TWENTY-SEVEN

THE PENTHOUSE AND
THE HONEYMOON

The Butler and the Maid arrived at the Penthouse about two minutes before the manager and the two guests arrived.

Thanks to artificial intelligence, the double penthouse door automatically opened and inside was the butler and the maid ready to take care of business. They went inside and the doors closed to give them privacy.

The manager said, "Mòlìhuā and Tinougl, let me introduce you to your butler Frimbro and the maid Contessa Riza."

Tinougl bowed out of respect and so did Mòlìhuā a second later.

"It's a pleasure to meet you." Frimbro said.

Contessa Riza quickly followed, "You look so lovely Mòlìhuā."

The butler Frimbro and the maid Contessa Riza received *their scramble briefing* on the way to the Penthouse. The only thing they needed to see was SVIP. The S meant "Special" which means the hotel had to go all out to please them.

Under circumstances like this when the hotel almost got caught with their pants down by a faulty reception, it was imperative *they didn't screw up again.* Furthermore, the manager now had to give the butler and the maid a special briefing which dealt with aspects of security and privacy and a lot of other things. There was no point in elaborating, so he cut to the chase.

"Mòlìhuā is now considered the top recording star in the Empire. In the past week the media announced she sold 8 billion subscriptions to a couple songs in a single day which means, we must not let up on our vigilance and allow other hotel guests to spoil their stay."

"I will do my upmost," Frimbro responded.

"And so shall I," Contessa Riza added.

"Thank you. They will want fashion consultants up here soon to prepare them for dinner. Due to a unique situation, they arrived without any luggage so we will be providing them anything they need tonight. One last thing before I leave and allow you to make them feel comfortable, is they are man and wife and that is a closely guarded secret. I do not want that to leak out of the hotel unless they make a public announcement in their own way on their own schedule."

"Sir, their secret is safe with us, and we will safeguard any and all information as we know how vital it is to their happiness."

"Thank you Frimbro, I knew you would understand, and I count on you, and you have never let me down before."

"Nor will I ever sir."

The manager now turned directly at Tinougl and looked him in the eyes with a glassy look and said, "I understand that security and safety are a primary concern of you and your bride. Frimbro and Contessa Riza are not only working in their roles as butler and maid, but they are also part of our security aparatus to help protect you. They are masters in martial arts and well armed to protect you should somehow our security boundaries get breached unexpectedly. I promise you can count on them."

"Thank you, sir, and thank you for spending the time with us giving us the special details that come with the Penthouse."

"It is my distinct pleasure and now with your permission I wish to go to the flower shop and take care of that matter you requested."

"Thank you for doing that."

"My pleasure. Please enjoy yourselves."

"Thank you."

The manager that had a nametag of "Randolph" turned and walked towards the double doors which quickly opened for him and shut after he departed.

"Would you two like a drink or is there anything I can do for you."

"Yes, I would like a drink and I'm sure Mòlìhuā would like a drink."

"This way please," Frimbro said as he led them into their Penthouse living room that was decorated with the quintessential best art money could buy.

"Would you like to make yourselves comfortable?"

Tinougl sat down on the sofa and Mòlìhuā sat beside him smiling very affectionately as her prince had come to her and lived up to everything he promised or indicated. It took her a while to accept the fact that he was being sincire about moving to this planet, especially when becoming part of Green Acres was on the menu.

"Madam, what would you like to drink?"

"I think I need a Lǐzǐ Guavastrian Elixir to calm my nerves, it's been quite a day."

"Hopefully we can make you feel comfortable so that you can fully relax."

"Thank you."

"And sir, what would you like?"

"I think I would like a Chamboree del Pàrà Mĕilì."

"I'll be back with your drinks momentarily."

Contessa Riza walked into the room and said, "Mòlìhuā, I just talked to the hotel's fashion designer, and she has a significant workload tonight and would like to know if she could bring her group up now to help prepare you for the evening?"

"Yes, that would be perfect."

"I will let her know immediately."

"Thank you."

A short time later, Frimbro came into the room carrying a silver tray with two drinks on it and sat the first one down on top of a decorative golden drink coaster sitting on top of a beautiful linen in front of Mòlìhuā and then a second glass in the golden coaster in front of Tinougl.

Frimbro then said, "I will be back in my room in case you need me. All you need to do is say Frimbro in a soft voice and artificial intelligence will notify me my presence is required to take care of any of your needs. Would you like me to initiate some music before I depart?"

"Sure, how about some soft classical music with a piano."

"Yes, sir I have the most splendid music I will play for you."

The music was delightful. The newlyweds were thinking it's too bad the fashion designer was on the way; they would have to delay the horizontal tango. The good news is they did such an excellent tango last night, they could wait a while to do it again.

~~~
~~~

The Limo drove down the two lane country road near Mòlīhuā's parents farmhouse and there were cars parked all over the place. News vans and pure chaos abounded. It took thirty minutes just to drive the last mile as the police were clearing out vehicles blocking traffic.

When the Limo signaled to turn into the farm, a police officer stopped the

Limo driver and asked, "Sir why are you trying to turn in there."

The driver said, "These people live there, you can check with the security guys. The police officer looked over to Aristapara's men and asked, "Is this Limo, okay?"

One of the security guys recognized the driver and said, "Yes, let him in."

The Limo drove into the yard and did a quick youturn and pulled up to the sidewalk leading into the house. The door automatically opened, and Morgan asked, "How much do we owe you?"

"It's all taken care of sir."

"Okay, thanks."

Morgan and Karenna walked up to the steps of the home and looked at the chaos on the nearby country road and Morgan said, "Tinougl is a smart guy, he knew this was going to happen."

"It's a good thing we dropped them off at the Hotel so they can have some privacy tonight."

"I kind of wish Tinougl was home, I feel safer when he's here, especially with all that."

News crews and individuals were out on the two-lane paved country Hiway with zoom lenses taking numerous pictures. And they were mildly perturbed they were not able to catch the Diva. Where was she?"

~~~

Tinougl and Mòlìhuā were half done with their drinks when the fashion designer and her complete makeover group arrived at the Penthouse.

"I'm sorry but we are terribly busy tonight, so we are going to have to prepare you both at the same time."

"Alright."

"Tinougl, you follow Mārcia to one bathroom and Mòlìhuā you follow Méisprīng to the other bathroom where we can start on you at the same time."

The main purpose of the bath was to prepare the hair for the hairdresser. Special chemicals and additives would make the hair turn into fairy dust and exquisite deigns.

Mārcia was shampooing Tinougl saw his tool and remarked, "I'm jealous of Mòlìhuā because I know what she gets tonight."

Tinougl saw her staring at it and said, "It's not the size that maters, it's the expertise on how you use it."

"I'm willing to learn."

"I've traveled far to find a woman like Mòlìhuā, she owns my heart."

"Awe that's so sweet. I like you."

"Thank you."

Tinougl's hair was prepped, and he was helped out of the tub dried and given a bath robe to put on then led into the spare bedroom that had the entrance to the bathroom, now a barber chair was already set up waiting for him.
~~~

The barber asked, "Would you like a *Cosmic Wave* hair cut?"

"No, one of my ex-girlfriends might find me."

The two laughed as the barber thought it was a joke. Soon the barber was crafting a hair stayle that more than made Tinougl look elegant.

While Mòlìhuā was getting her shampoo and special hair treatment,

Méisprīng saw the diamond ring and commented. "That's such a beautiful ring."

"Tinougl gave it to me today."

"That looks expensive, I've rarely seen one like it."

"Nor have I."

Mòlìhuā was soon dried off and put into a bathrobe and led out of the other bathroom to the master bedroom which also had a hair designer chair and hair drier all set up.

The hair designer went to work and created an elegant hair style. Thanks to her hair below her shoulders, the wavy creation manifested a surreal image fitting for the top movie stars. The film producers and directors would pay big bucks to make their starlets hair look so dazzling.

Then the makeup artists went to town on both guests and transformed them into images the public would crave. Then it was time to put on their garments and see how it turned out.

For Mòlìhuā, the fashion designer selected a golden woven satin sleeveless off-the-shoulder gown with a sweep and brush train featuring a sheath and a column that poured on the sex appeal. The full-length exotic dress matched her hair color with incredible imagery. With the makeup, the hair, and the dress, the famous singer Wánměi de Mòlìhuā would utterly stun everyone in the restaurant tonight that included a live band performing very nice, sophisticated music, soft to the ear, and only loud enough to not obscure the many conversations that would go on during dinner.

The fashion designer and Mārcia were alone with Tinougl when they had him look at the full-length mirror to determine if he liked what he saw. His remarks were, you did a fantastic job, I'm very happy. Mārcia a tease said, "You look so good if you were not with that princess tonight, I would let you take me and have your way with me. The fashion designer jumped in and said, "Only after I got done with him." They all chuckled.

"Alright, lets go see what your princess looks like."

Tinougl was led into the Penthouse living room and was asked to wait here. A moment later, here came the princess. Tinougl was more than amazed.

"May I make a request?"

"What can we do for you?"

"Do you have photographic equipment with you?"

"We always do in case there is a dispute."

"Could you take a picture of her and then one with us as a couple. I want to send to her parents tonight so they will now how lovely their daughter looks."

"I would be most delighted," the fashion designer said knowing she would get a gem in the process. One of these days, she knew that picture would be extremely valuable in her personal portfolio.

The fashion designer was also an expert photographer because it was often required as she figured things out or needed to give future clients some ideas as to how they could look.

After the pictures, the fashion designer said, "Those pictures are loaded in your personal file in our hotel computer network. It can only be sent to your personal communicator, or destroyed if you request, no other types of file transfers are allowed.

"How do I get them sent to my communicator?"

"Just make that request in this room and our artificial intelligence will immediately send it to your communicator."

"Just like that?"

"Yes."

"Alright, artificial intelligence send the pictures just taken to my communicator."

A soft voice in the background suddenly said, "Tinougl those pictures have been sent to your communicator."

"Thank you."

Tinougl pulled out his communicator and saw the pictures and immediately sent them to Mòlìhuā's parents. In the span of a few minutes, they directed the pictures from their communicator to their holographic projector and were in awe at the beauty of their daughter.

The fashion designer then piped in, "Tinougl, we have been alerted it's expected to be crowded in the restaurant tonight, I suggest you go there now.

Frimbro and Contessa Riza will assist us in restoring the ambience of your

Penthouse while you are gone."

"Thank you."

Tinougl looked at his beautiful bride and said, "Shall we go my dear?"

"Yes honey."

The couple made their way to the entrance of the Penthouse and there stood the butler Frimbro and maid Contessa Riza standing to one side and bowed as they passed by and Frimbro being the chief conductor of the operation said, "Please enjoy your evening. You both look stunning."

"Thank you."

Tinougl and Mòlìhuā left the Penthouse and walked to the elevator. As an SVIP they were tracked everywhere they went. Hotel security was watching them in the event they had to intervene due to nefarious activity.

In the elevator Tinougl asked the question, "Which direction to the hotel restaurant? The artificial intelligene answered, "Turn left when you exit the elevator."

Soon they were out of the elevator and heading to the restaurant. There was heavy duty facial recognition, especially for a SVIP.

When they entered the restaurant, the very attractive and sweet Maitra d' saw on her data terminal readout on the flatscreen mounted on her podium, SVIP singer Wánmĕi de Mòlìhuā arriving with her companion Tinougl. *Priority seating immediately.*

The Maitra d' recalled seeing this Diva on worldwide holographic news and well-well-well, there she was in incredible costume in front of her approaching with that incredibly handsome man she also saw during some of the video as it appeared she was singing to him. She also knew it was customary to use her personal name Mòlìhuā without the rest and as they got close to the podium, the Maitra d' said, "Hello Mòlìhuā and Tinougl. Your table is being prepared.

"Thank you."

"Give me one minute please."

The Maitra d' went into the restaurant and noticed a waitress putting a reserved sign on a table. The Maitra d' had the authority to place an SVIP in any reserved table and was grateful it instantly appeared, and went back to her podium and said, "Will you two please follow me."

Soon Mòlìhuā and Tinougl were seated, and the waitress immediately charged over to the SVIP table and got their drink orders.

The band was playing, and the female singer had a beautiful voice singing a song Mòlìhuā did not recognize.

When the waitress came back with their drinks, Tinougl said, "We will probably wait a while to order and enjoy a couple drinks."

"That's fine sir, I will check back with you from time to time, if you need me just look at me and jesture and I will know to come right away."

"Thank you."

Tinougl looked around the restaurant and didn't spot anyone he had seen before. Even though the restaurant was now only half full, there were substantial amount of people present and the night was still early

When they arrived and went to their table, surveillance on the restaurant wasn't yet conducted by Tinougl but he would soon be scoping out the clientele. He was happy he was dressed as nicely as anyone present. But he knew one thing, none of the women came close to matching Mòlìhuā's ellegence and preparation for the evening. Her makeup and attire were remarkably incredible. Tinougl wasn't the only person who thought that.

Chapter

Twenty-Eight

The Rose the Note and the Song

Reladondo bon Scrafatorious knew the couple was coming to Konhagar and after a few days basking in the sun at one of those planets that catered to the jet setters, Reladondo bon Scrafatorious decided to travel to Konhagar to try to recruit the starlet for some of his projects.

Thanks to the vehicle dealership leak he knew where to go find her and was merely waiting for the crowds to die down before he approached them. And in almost a sheer coincidence, here she was right now right in front of him in a semi open and available area of a very lavish restaurant where he could soon swoop in and beging the process.

Reladondo bon Scrafatorious recruited talent period. It didn't matter if it was male or female. He simiply wanted the best. And there the man was that she sang that song too while at Grand Plexis de Chiveltros who could easily make half the women here tonight instantly horny if he were available. His makeup job and fashion statement were the best of the very best. He would not stop at Mòlihuā. He would attempt recruiting the man who had those extreme features that drove women utterly nuts. He didn't want to spook the couple so he would wait until they finished eating, had a few more drinks and were socially prepared for him approaching them.

Suddenly, a new event took place that peaked Reladondo's interest real fast. A waitress walked up to Tinougl and handed him a vase with a rose in it that had a note attached. She sat the rose right in front of Tinougl and he opened the note to see what that was all about. The note said:

Hello Tinougl. I thought I was going to get fired today because I scewed up your welcome. Chalk it up to inexperience. When the manager came back from your Penthouse, I feared I was going to get fired on the spot. I was extremely weak and sad and wanted to cry. Then suddenly, the manager appeared with a dozen roses and instead of threatening me, praised me saying all kinds of nice things I think you had a lot to do with it. So instead of crying myself to sleep tonight, I'm very happy and I owe it all to you.

From the bottom of my heart. Thank you for being such a kind and decent gentleman to look out for me.

Casandra

Tinougl's eyes watered up a bit. Reladondo being a social engineer as well as one of the most successful agents to recruit talent, didn't miss a beat. He observed it all including the sadness Tinougl exhibited.

Tinougl felt that he was in an awkward situation and didn't have anything to hide so he handed the note to Mòlĭhuā who also read it. Amazingly her eyes watered up as well. She reached out and grabbed Tinougl's hand and squeezed it to send a private massage to him that she understood it all and was very proud of her prince charming for being such caring and decent person. The note was sat down on the table under the rose and vase. It would remain there until the couple left.

Mòlĭhuā felt the silent ringer buzzer on her communicator and pulled it out of the secret pocket in her outfit and looked. It was from her mother:

"There are huge crowds hanging out here waiting to see you and Tinougl keeping the police and the security men very busy. I recommend you do not come home tomorrow. Stay at the hotel a while until all this commotion dies down. Also, I loved those pictures. You look so beautiful and Tinougl looks so handsome. When we have the reception, I want you to dress up pretty like that again for me. Love Mother."

Mòlìhuā gave a happy smile which Reladondo did not miss.

The band took a break. The singer thought she recognized the beautiful woman sitting in the audience and during the break approached the table.

"Hello how are you doing tonight?"

"We are enjoying ourselves. I like your singing," Mòlìhuā said.

"You look so beautiful tonight, I love your hair and your dress," the singer said.

"You do not look too bad yourself dear."

"Listen I don't want to be nosey, but as a singer I have a curiousity. Are you that singer that's in the news visiting Konhagar?"

"Dear, if I answer that question do you promise not to tell anyone?"

"Absolutely."

"Yes, I'm Wánměi de Mòlìhuā."

"Oh, it's so wonderful meeting you, I feel privileged."

Mòlìhuā new how rough it is for a singer standing on their feet all night long asked, "What's your name dear?"

"My name is Kristina Ashmus."

"Kristina, would you like to join us for a drink?"

"I would love to."

There were four chairs at the table and Mòlìhuā gestured to the chair on her right between she and Tinougl. Kristina sat there and had a smile and was lit up. Tinougl turned towards their waitress and nodded his head, and the waitress approached immediately.

"Yes sir?"

"Would you please get Kristina a drink."

"Yes sir, I would be delighted."

In a couple more minutes Kristina had a big gulp of her drink which hit the spot. Here throat was slightly dry like happens to a lot of singers, so the drink quickly lubricated her throat which would help her feel far more pleasant when she started singing again.

They talked about trivial matters and had a pleasant conversation.

Reladondo liked the way the couple intereacted with the singer which went a long way to show how friendly and decent and caring they were.

A few moments before Kristina had to go back on stage she said, "Our band plays one of the songs you sang that was recorded."

"The the long one or the shorter one?"

"The longer one, though we would love to sing the shorter one, but just have not had time to learn it."

"Will you sing it this set?"

"Yes, and I have a wonderful idea. Why don't you come up and sing it with me?"

"What do you think Tinougl?"

"You know I love hearing you sing. But I must warn you that you might make me cry."

"You poor baby." Mòlìhuā tapped his hand.

Tinougl then said something that just about floured Mòlìhuā, "Since this is a very special day for us, it would actually mean a lot to me if you did sing it."

"Only if you promise to love me tonight."

"You can bet on it."

Mòlìhuā turned to Kristina and said, "Please let your band know and sing a couple other songs first."

"I will, thank you."

Kristina stood up and walked over and gave Mòlìhuā a big affectionate hug, then went back up on the stage and huddled with the band. The magic show was just about to start.

Reladondo couldn't quite make out what they were all saying but observing all the activity created a lot of sudden interest.

The next two songs it seemed like the band was supercharged. Even the audience noted the vast improvement of their delivery, especially the young singer in how she articulated the lyrics. She was a totally different person than before the break.

After two songs, the singer said, "Ladies and Gentlemen we have a special guest tonight that will be singing the next song with us. I'll let you figure out who she is."

When Mòlìhuā walked up to the stage people in the audience were somewhat mystified and some knew they had seen this woman before and were trying to recollect just where. Then as they looked at her and the table where she came and saw the very attractive man, they knew for sure they had recently seen them both.

Kristina knew how to sing exceptionally well. She also knew how to be a good backup singer. This was going to be all Mòlìhuā, but she would help her to her best ability.

With Mòlìhuā standing there in that glamorous golden dress and an exquisite hair style, she appeared movie star quality. Now with her full body exposed, her nice figure, her incredible makeup created that mystique that captured the imagination of the entire audience, men, and women alike. Then the music started.

Tonight, was a very special night for Mòlìhuā. Tinougl had made her dream come true and filled her heart full of love. She was feeling the love and broadcasting the love which modulated her essence with the spatial aperature of cosmic delight. She put her heart into that performance like never before in her life. She was making love to Tinougl on the stage. Every word and every sound were deliberate, and the interpretation and delivery were the essence of succuss.

Reladondo sat there utterly stunned. He also was a good observer of the audience; he also knew they were astonished. This gifted woman had reached into every one of their hearts. Half the women had tears in their eyes. They knew what Unrequited Love was, and this was not it, this was the real deal as she sent shivers down their spines and moved them like they had not been moved in a very long time. Even if they were in a seemingly dead relationship with a crapy husband, they somehow were feeling the love too. The eight-minute song was a perfect length for what it was doing to the audience. Finally, Mòlìhuā was done and Tinougl's eyes were watered up. He felt like a weak little boy who could not defend himself. Reladondo also had watery eyes. It hit him hard too.

The crowd went wild!

What a way to put the exclamation on a wedding day!

After a dozen thank you's and bows, Mòlìhuā gave Kristina a hug and returned to the table with Tounogl.

"Very nice."

"You're not afraid I blew our cover?"

"It's already blown, we will have to learn to live with it."

"Are you getting hungry now?"

"I suppose it's that time."

Tinougl turned to the waitress and gave a slight signal and she immediately proceeded to their table. She had on an ear bud and artificial intelligence backing her up would let her know when a table required service to expedite the service. She was usually ahead of the artificial intelligence by a few seconds which she enjoyed beating.

"How may I help you sir?"

"Could you do me a favor and ask the chef what he recommends tonight?"

"I will be delighted."

The waitress walked away and Tinougl a smart spy could see she was talking into her sleeve. She had a microphone there and received her orders via the ear bud.

A couple minutes later the waitress approached the table and said, "The Chef is going to send you out a surprise, it will be his recommendation."

"Thank you."

Within a couple minutes two waiters came with a cart that had food prepared on plates, which qickly ended up on the table settings and the aroma was rather pleasant. The meal was served and had several entrees of smaller servings so they could sample more. It took them a while to eat this way, but they always had a waiter beside them helping and refilling their drinks when necessary.

After the dinner the table was cleaned off and tablecloth changed, and the only thing put on the new tablecloth was the rose and the note that went with it.

Reladondo was curious as to what the note said.

In a few more minutes the band had another break and Kristina approached the table. Mòlìhuā said, "Kristina, please sit down with us and have a drink."

"Oh, thank you. My legs are just slightly sore, I need to rest up a little. I asked the band to take a slightly longer break this time."

"I wish we could do your other song tonight."

"Me too."

Tinougl chimed in, "I want to hear that one too. The name of the song is 'Dǎkāi Wánměi de Liánhuā,' do you think you can remember that?"

"Sure, I already know the name."

"This is my proposal, ask your band permission and Mòlìhuā can play the piano and sing it and you can back her up."

"That sounds ingenious. I like that idea. Let me go talk to our band leader for a minute."

Kristina walked up to the band leader and gave Tinougl's suggestion. The band leader had never heard such applause before, and the restaurant was still filling up with guests.

"Sure, bring her up after I get my drink because I want to enjoy her singing while I have a drink."

Kristina went back to the table and said, "The band leader wants to wait until he gets his drink in a couple minutes so he can enjoy your singing while he enjoys his drink."

Mòlìhuā chuckled and said, "That's perfect."

Kristina kept an eye on the band leader saw he was sitting down with drink in hand and nodded to her. It was time to get the crowd going again.

Kristina walked up to the stage and grabbed a microphone and said,

"Ladies and Gentlemen," our special guest will now perform another song which

I think you will really like."

When the crowd saw the lady with the incredible gold dress get up to sing again the applause elevated the closer, she got to the stage.

It's very seldom a singer gets a standing applause BEFORE the performance. Reladondo noted to himself.

Next huge surprise, Mòlìhuā sad down at the piano and Kristina stood next to her. The piano had it's own microphone setup.

Just before Mòlìhuā started playing as she wanted to wait until the applause died down, Kristina, said, "This song goes out to someone very special in the audience. The name of the song is *Dǎkāi Wánměi de Liánhuā*, written by the lovely Wánměi de Mòlìhuā.

Reladondo bon Scrafatorious, the greatest talent scout of all time sat there in high expectations and was waiting to get another jolt of emotional appeal.

The piano started and soon Mòlìhuā began singing.

Kristina had studied this song as soon as it became public and put a lot of effort into it because she knew her band cold shine if they nailed it.

Kristina was once again in a very helpful role as a backup singer which resonated Mòlìhuā's voice and created quintessential harmonics that multiplied the effect piercing the heart of every male listener in the restaurant. The women were captivated as well as the two women sang together as if they sung this song together over a long period of time. It was a much shorter piece a little more than six minutes long. Once again, Tinougl's eyes had watered, and he was looking right at Mòlìhuā and she was looking directly had him singing the entire time.

The magic between them was unmistakable. Reladondo had thought he had seen everything. Tonight, all his theories and ideas were blown out of the cosmos. This incredible couple had set a new bar and as he expected, when the song ended, the crowd was rowdy like he had never seen before. *And these wealthy people are supposed to be the calm and reserve crowd!*

Soon after some small talk between Kristina, Tinougl and Mòlìhuā, the couple stood up and walked out of the restaurant.

Reladondo saw they left the rose and vase behind as well as the note. He stood up and walked over to the table picked up the rose and smelled it and cleverly grabbed the note and had it in his hand without anyone catching the theft. The waitress walked up and saw the distinguished Reladondo smelling the flower. She knew he was an entertainment business powerhouse second to none so she politely said, "The couple left the rose behind but if you would like it, you may keep it."

"I don't mind if I do. Please give me another drink I want to enjoy another drink smelling this delightful rose."

"Certainly."

Reladondo went back to his table and sat down waiting for the drink. After the waitress served his drink and walked away, he took a nice long sip and opened the note and read it. This note clearly exposed the essence of the couple to take the time to help a poor girl who got in trouble with her boss by screwing up the way she did. Tinougl saved her in a major way. He was beginning to like Tinougl even more. He was different then most men, almost a rennassance man.

The couple arrived in their Penthouse. Contessa Riza and Frimbro were there to greet them at the door because they were duly warned by artificial intelligence the hotel guests were on their way.

"Welcome back, may we get you anything?"

"No, we are going to bed now, will you get us some sleeping apparel."

"Yes, give me a couple minutes and I will have that sitting out on your bed."

"Thank you."

Moments later Contessa Riza came out of the bedroom and said, "Your sleeping apparel is on your bed waiting for you to change. We'll take care of your clothes in the morning.

"Thank you."

"Do you guys know how long you will stay?"

"My mother told us to stay away from their home for a few more days.

We'll probably have to add on a couple days past that to make them miss us."

"Alright, we will be poised to assist you in any manner you need."

"Thank you."

Mòlìhuā walked towards the master bedroom and Tinougl followed her. Once inside Tinougl shut and locked the door as he didn't want to have someone accidentally walk in on them.

Mòlìhuā picked the sleeping attire off the bed and set it on the dressor and said, "I do not think we'll be needing this tonight."

The two then undressed and turned out the lights and began their transcendence into celestrial feasts and this was their honeymoon concerto on a theme from Paganini that exposed their hunger for that sweet combination that evoked the gratification of such a memorable day.

After a rigorous workout Tinougl said, "I don't want to lay in swet, us take a quick shower."

"Good idea."

"In the shower they held and caressed and after they dried off, they were slightly chilled, so they ended up wearing the sleeping attire afterall.

Chapter

Twenty-Nine

The Introduction to Reladondo bon Scrafatorious

Tinougl had a morning clock. As soon as his eyes were open, he got up and wondered where his street clothes were that he wore here. He thought of the other resorts he stayed in and thought maybe they did the same things and walked over to the closet and discovered his street clothes had been dry cleaned and his shoes and socks were there and he dressed, and went into the living room carefully shutting the door behind him and went into the living room and decided to check the artificial intelligence and in a calm low voice said, Frimbro can I see you please."

One minute later Frimbro appeared fully dressed and alert.

"What can I do for you Tinougl?"

"I want to go for a swim later can you obtain swimming clothes for Mòlìhuā and myself?"

"Absolutely. How soon do you need it?"

"I'm going for a walk then come back, hopefully Mòlìhuā will be awake by then and we can go to the pool together."

"I will make all the arrangements."

"Thank you."

"You are most welcome."

"One more thing, let Mòlihuā know I went for a walk I'll be back in a while unless she needs me, then I'll come back promptly."

"I will let her know when she is awake and comes into the living room."

"Thank you."

"You are welcome."

Frimbro followed Tinougl to the entrance and bowed as he left.

After the elevator ride, Tinougl was walking towards the front entrance through the lobby and there was Casandra. He walked up to her.

"Thank you for the rose and the note."

"Thank you Tinougl, you were very helpful to me, I don't know how to ever pay you back."

"There is one thing you can do for me."

"Sure, what is that?"

"Smile and be happy today."

"I will and you helped put this smile on my face."

"I'm glad."

Tinougl then walked out of the hotel and went for a walk. The hotel was located in a nice part of the city where care and concern were given to landscape and general cleanliness. There was no apparent dirt and grime. He couldn't run five miles, but he could certainly walk it and he did.

Instead of running 15 miles per hour he was walking briskly at almost four miles per hour and not working up much of a swet but was back at the hotel in about one and half hours. He walked past the receptionist Casandra who gave him a lovely smile and then took the elevator up to the Penthouse.

When he arrived, he discovered Mòlìhuā in the living room in her street clothes sitting next to a pile of objects that appeared to be swimming apparel for both of them.

Frimbro said you wanted to go swimming later.

"Yes, since we have a pool available, I would like to swim some laps."

"I suppose I could do a little swimming too, but I doubt I could keep up with you."

"That's alright, do as much as you like."

"Are we going to breakfast this morning?"

"Let me ask Frimbro a question."

Artificial Intelligence analyzed the conversation and notified Frimbro:

"Tinougl wants to speak with you."

Within a minute Frimbro asked, "What can I do for you Tinougl?"

"Do they serve breakfast and snacks down at the pool?"

"Yes, they do but the menu is not quite as robust as the restaurant."

"Alright, we will find out."

"You want to get changed now?"

"Sure. We can find out what they have on the menu and as a backup, we can always go to the restaurant."

Mòlìhuā then said the obvious, "Tinougl, I have a problem, I do not have enough clothes here."

"I'm sure the fashion designers can help you out."

"But what about street clothes?"

"We'll call them earlier today and tell them about that problem and have them bring us some street clothes as well."

"All right, that works."

It was a nice warm morning and there were already a dozen people at the pool with their same idea, breakfast pool side. Chief among them was no other than Reladondo bon Scrafatorious. Reladondo was at a table and chairs that gave him a great viewing area.

Reladondo spotted Tinougl leading Mòlìhuā out to the pool area and they too sat down at table and chairs with an umbrella on top. His first thought was *oh my god she is beautiful.*

Mòlìhuā's natural beauty was impressive. Makeup was probably not necessary. Her skin was so nice. She had stayed out of the sun most of her life and had no signs of wringles or premature aging.

They had their swim robes on so there wasn't a lot of body showing. Tinougl wasn't quite hungry and wanted to get the laps in and said, "Why don't you go ahead and order if you want. I'm going to swim first."

"Okay honey."

Tinougl took off his bathrobe and turned 180 degrees and sat his swim robe down on the chair. Reladondo got a full look then and said to himself, *you got to be shitting me.* Tinougl's body was not only impressive, but it was also spectacular!

Now Reladondo knew he had the dynamic couple. If he could get them into a movie together, he could blow the doors off the box office receipts! *Can a man really have those kinds of muscles?* It seemed rather impossible.

Tinougl then walked over to the pool and climbed in and started swimming. He pushed himself hard and did the 30 laps in no time at all.

Reladondo watched all this and took in every minute. But the best was about to come. After 30 hard laps Tinougl was exhausted, and his muscles were as tense as ever. He hoped he didn't get a cramp. Like all other good Hotels, they had a pool side SPA. Most of the people who went into the SPA's did so for other reasons. Nobody ever went in there with such tight of muscles full of lactic acid from the exercise. He didn't dare sit down or he knew he might cramp up and Mòlìhuā knew what he was going to do next, get a massage.

"I already know what you are going to do. Go get your massage. I'm going to order a snack and we'll talk about what we want to do when you get back."

"Alright honey."

Tinougl with his photographic memory saw the man he spotted last night in the restaurant, and here he was at the pool. For some reason he looked familiar.

Tinougl went into the SPA and discovered he got there at the right time. They were just opening and starting. He was their first customer.

"Hello, what can we do for you?"

"I did some power swims, and my muscles are tight, I need a massage."

"You came to the right place."

One of the massage technician ladies was next to the receptionist and said, "I'm available, us go."

She took Tinougl to her room. This beautiful blond lady had beautiful blue eyes and a nice body, but she didn't have very large breasts. But she was very pretty.

It was almost a universal policy from hotel to hotel, if you had been swimming, you were going to get a bath to get all the chemicals off your hair and body because the massage technicians could not stand the smell. Plus, the opioids and cannabinoids helped in a major way to soften up the muscles and prevent a Charlie Horse or a bad cramp.

It seemed like the massage technicians liked to get naked with their clients and as Tinougl found out some of them wanted to have sex. What he didn't know was it was only because of his body. Otherwise, they would never do it.

Once again Tinougl was treated to the naked splendor of a beautiful massage technician who adored his body. She was more ready and openly admitted she was ready for it if Tinougl wanted it.

"I'm a newlywed. I'm all sexed out. My bride has drained me, I'll pass."

Nevertheless, the woman worked on him with pleasure and 45 minutes later his muscle tightness was all gone. By the time he got back to the pool, Mòlìhuā had a good breakfast snack and was satisfied.

Tinougl sat down and that's when the illustrious Reladondo bon Scrafatorious decided to make his move.

Reladondo approached the couple and said, "Sir I do not know if you remember me, but we met at the transportation hub several days ago, and I gave you my business card. My name is Reladondo bon Scrafatorious."

Tinougl suddenly recalled the gentleman and said, "I remember you now, would you like to join us?"

"I certainly would."

Sitting close to Tinougl allowed Reladondo to see those incredible muscles, though they were not as prounounced as when got out of the water and went and got a massage.

"You knocked those laps out in the pool nice and quick."

"I pushed myself pretty hard, that's why I went and got the massage."

"Feel better now?"

"Oh yes I feel great."

"I was in the restaurant last night and heard Mòlihuā's performance. I must say Mòlihuā really motivated the crowd."

"It was our wedding day, so she probably sang a little more forceful."

Reladondo looked at Mòlihuā and smiled and said congratulations."

"Thank you."

Reladondo, never noticed it until now but there was that nice diamond ring on Mòlihuā's finger. He was very aware of jewelry because he had to do makeovers on movie stars and besides the hairdo, dresses, diets, and makeup, nothing came quite compelling as a woman wearing a lot of diamonds.

Reladondo knew those circular cut diamonds were excessively expensive since most of them originated on Santorini de Shénshèng where the finest and largest diamonds were sold due to one of the most prosperous diamond mines on the planet that had sunk a shaft down two miles below the surface of the planet and had to run powerful air-conditioning units around the clock to make it possible for the diamond miners to work.

No other source of extravagant diamonds could provide even a small supply of large diamonds that allowed craftsmen to create the exquisitee, shaped circular faced diamonds that gave the appearance of 1000 surfaces because of all the reflections created by the numerous angles of flat surfaces.

Reladondo bon Scrafatorious quickly analyzed Tinougl's voice was pleasant and attractive. As an expert in psychoacoustics, Reladondo knew they could filter and manipulate the voice if they had something good to work with in the beginning. It was crystal clear all the starlets in the Empire would crawl all over Tinougl if given the chance. One look at Tinougl's body and any of the starlets would accept a major role in a production to act and perform with him. The screen writers would taylor the stories to manifest scenes with the shirt off or a naked shot from behind.

Now all Reladondo needed to do was get the appropriate carrot.

"What are you guys going to do today?"

"Mòlìhuā's parents dropped us off here yesterday with only our street clothes on. We are going to call a fashion designer in to provide us with a few days of clothes to change in."

"Why don't you simply go home and pick up a few more items?"

"There are huge crowds camping outside her parents' farm, if we went there, we would be swarmed. We are staying away until the crowds die down."

"I have an idea, perhaps I can fly you there in my personal helicopter and get you right up to their home to avoid the crowds."

"You would really do that for us?"

"Yes, I like you for several reasons and want to do business with you in the future. I figure investing my time with you now is nothing more than a down payment on some of your time later."

"That makes sense."

"Especially after I make you a few offers you can't refuse."

"Such as?"

"Besides finding talented actors and singers, I also buy songs from obscure people who will never have a chance to become a star because of their drug addictions or obesity, or some other reason. I pay them good money and own the composition. I have four songs now I would like Mòlìhuā to record."

"I would have to leave that decision up to her."

Mòlìhuā the consummate musician and singer knew exactly what that implied. Those four songs could be as big as the two that already made her famous and decided to speak up. "I would like to hear the songs, perhaps I might be interested."

"Alright, I have a really good idea. There is a great studio merely blocks away from this hotel, we could practically just walk there. I propose you allow me to fly you to your parents' home, get some additional clothes, then come back here, get dressed up by the hotel's fashion designer. We could then go to the studio. I'll have some musicians and a singer there to perform the songs for you so you know how they sound, then do a dry run and if you want, then we could record them. I will give you 40% royalties."

"That's a lot of money."

"Some things in life are so important you have to pay for them, or you will never obtain them."

"True."

"Shall we, do it?"

"How about we go get cleaned up first, have the fashion designer make us look special, then we can fly to the farm, perhaps have a meal there, then come back and try out one of those four songs?"

"That sounds perfect."

"We'll contact you as soon as we are ready to go."

"I'll be ready."

"See you in a while."

Tinougl and Mòlìhuā went up to the Penthouse and was getting ready to call the fashion designer when Mòlìhuā said, "I want to take care of some other business before we call them."

The love tango only lasted a few brief moments. The two triggered each other's orgasms just a moment after stating that celestial coitus. After a quick shower they dried off and put on their street clothes that were dry cleaned while they were at the pool.

They walked out to the living room and Tinougl simply said, "Please send us the hotel's fashion designer."

The artificial intelligence asked softly in the background, "Tinougl, do you wish the hotel's fashion designer would come now to the Penthouse?"

"Yes, please."

"The fashion designer has been notified. I will let you know the Expected Time of Arrival as soon as they are ready to come to your Penthouse."

"Thank you."

A few minutes later, Frimbro walked into the living room and said, "Master Tinougl, the fashion designer and her crew are in the elevator on the way up to your Penthouse."

"Thank you, show them in when they arrive."

"I will be delighted sir."

As expected, two minutes later, Frimbro led the fashion team into the living room.

"Same as yesterday we will work on you two in parallel. What are you preparing for?"

"We are first going to fly with Reladondo bon Scrafatorious in my parents' home to pick up some more clothes and maybe have lunch, then we are coming back here and going over to a nearby recording studio for a possible recording if we can get it done."

Most music recordings had video as part of them and the fashion designer knew she had to really work on Mòlìhuā today because that image would be very important and responded, "We will make you look beautiful."

Also, we want you to provide us a couple of changes of street clothes since we didn't arrive with any luggage. We want you to select them and fit us with them before you put on our clothes we will wear for our outing."

"I will be most delighted and I'm very happy you are going to allow me to fit you with some casual clothes because we can select items that will make you look really good while wearing casual clothes in a less formal environment."

"Good, us get started."

"Give me a minute, I'm going to contact one of my assistants to bring up some additional clothing to try on."

"Sure."

In a moment the fashion designer was giving the assistant their marching orders.

"Now that we have that matter in hand, lets have you two take baths so we can shampoo your hair and get it ready."

They were soon shampood, dried off and in barber chairs getting their hair done and then came the makeup. What followed next was three changes of street clothes that were very sylish and attractive. They would be noticed walking around in those attires because they did look amazingly nice as they showed the brilliance of the designer.

Finally, they were ready to try on the more formal attire, a dress for the lady and a suit for the gentleman.

After they were dressed in these designer clothes and shoes, when they looked into the mirror, they felt exquisitee.

"This is very nice, I appreciate what you have done," Tinougl stated.

"You help us quite a bit because of your attention to your body and staying in good shape allows us to concentrate on the artwork instead of mitigating serious body issues."

"I think we are ready to leave now," Tinougl said as he really was glad, he made love to Mòlǐhuā, otherwise looking at her now, he would most likely send the fashion designers away and make love to her now and screw up her hair and makeup!

"You can go ahead and leave now; we'll clean up and Frimbro will escort us out."

"Alright, thanks."

Chapter Thirty

Helicopter Ride

Tinougl then said, "Please contact Reladondo bon Scrafatorious and inform him we are on our way to the lobby."

In the background with a soft voice the Artificial Intelligence reported, "Master Tinougl, Mister Reladondo bon Scrafatorious has been notified you are on your way to the lobby. He responded he will be there momentarily."

"Thank you."

The couple then departed the Penthouse and made their way to the lobby. Two minutes later while Casandra was smiling at the beautiful couple, Reladondo bon Scrafatorious arrived and said, "We need to go back into the elevator to get up to the roof top helicopter pad."

"Sure," Tinougl responded.

After the three were in the elevator, Reladondo said, "Take us up to the roof top, we have a helicopter waiting for us."

"What is your name sir?"

"I'm Reladondo bon Scrafatorious."

A moment later the elevator voice said, "Reladondo bon Scrafatorious, you are cleared for roof-top-flight operations access. Your pilot is in the helicopter waiting for you. Is Tinongle and Mòlīhuā your guests?"

"Yes, they are."

"Thank you for the confirmation."

The elevator arrived at the roof top a moment later. They exited the elevator that was in a compact room with a few chairs acting as a waiting room for helicopter arrivals. As they approached the door, it opened automatically using compressed air, and they promptly walked to the helicopter feeling the wind blowing across the top of the building.

The helicopter door was open and Mòlìhuā was invited in first followed by Tinougl and then Reladondo bon Scrafatorious. As to not damage the hair styles, the helicopter did not start up the rotor until everyone was aboard and door shut. Further to protect Mòlìhuā's hair design she was offered ear plugs instead of headphones. Tinougl was also given ear plugs for the very same reason.

The designer dress that Mòlìhuā illustraited two major points about her body that Reladondo quickly surmised, *her breasts and her posterior were second to none.* This woman physically was definitely star quality and since the latest report is her recordings had sold nineteen billion subscriptions, she actually was a superstar now in the eyes of the public.

Mòlìhuā's stratospheric rise to stardom was seldom experienced in the entertainment business. That part alone made her journey quite an extraordinary feat. Thanks to constant holographic news coverage, the address to the farmhouse was easily obtainable. A simple search on a computer or a data terminal immediately popped up the actual address. Once laid into the helicopter's fly by wire system and satellite navigation, they had a straight shot to the farmhouse since they were not flying near any airport or space port that would force them into a landing and takeoff pattern.

The journey by Limo was approximately fifteen minutes. By this helicopter going in a straight line, it was only five minutes.

The navigation system tagged the address, and the artificial intelligence determined a landing zone on the grass next to the driveway would be the perfect location to land.

The pilot had been instructed as soon as he landed to shut down the rotors as to not mess up their hair.

When they arrived, Tinougl looked out at the four security guys who looked stressed. The crowd was still large, and the police were constantly arguing with people that were parking their cars nearby possibly creating safety concerns.

Morgan saw the helicopter come down and feared it might be bad people who wanted an easy way in. As soon as he saw Tinougl and Mòlīhuā exit the craft, he suddenly felt a little better, then saw the other man with them.

Karenna was looking out the window at the helicopter and noted none had ever landed here before. That was another milestone that her daughter manifested no doubt.

Then she saw the two newlyweds leaving the helicopter all dressed up. People with telephoto lenses on their camera's were clicking away photographing this new sensation.

Karenna who was dressed nicely and looked wholesome came to the door to welcome them. Some of the news reporters quickly identified the famous Reladondo bon Scrafatorious who rarely traveled to a backwards planet like Konhagar, was also a sensational story for even being here. Not to say his ultra modern looking vertical take off and landing craft also deserved some mention. Seeing these three together immediately spurned on wild speculation. The thousand observers were making a lot of noise now including whistles, cat calls, and screams of begging for romance.

When the three approached the house, Morgan was standing besides Karenna and Mòlīhuā made the introduction, "Mother and Father, let me introduce you to Reladondo bon Scrafatorious, a notable entertainment recruiter from Santorini de Shénshèng.

"Pleased to meet you," Would you like to come in?" Karenna asked.

"Absolutely," Reladondo replied feeling uplifted seeing these wonderfuly normal people who no doubt raised their daughter well to create such a socially acceptable person. And now that he had seen Tinougl's body, he knew his daughter selected the best of the best to be with, meaning she had very fine taste and would not settle for next to none other.

The group migrated to the living room where, Karenna asked, "Can I get you guys something to drink?"

Tinougl remembering how nice Morgan's ferments were suggested, "I think we would like some of Morgan's ferments."

Morgan smiled and said, "I've been waiting for a special day to open up my last bottle of ferments I created during the very best harvest I ever had." "Sounds good to me," Reladondo remarked in a very friendly tone.

A few minutes later while Tinougl was enjoying this fantastic concoction, Reladondo commented, "This is one of the best ferment's I've ever tasted. If you can bottle a few more like this, I'll send one of my administrative aids out to pick it up."

"Sure, I can bottle you a few and have them ready in a couple days."

"I need an excuse to fly Mòlǐhuā out here again, what better a reason?"

Morgan chucked on that witty comment."

"Give me a couple days and it will be ready."

"Thank you."

Mòlǐhuā then shocked her mother by saying, "Mother, the reason why we came is Tinougl and I want to pick up a few more changes of clothes because we are going to stay at the Hotel a few more days until the crowds start dying down.”

“That's a great idea, I think you should.”

“Mother the other reason why we came is Tinougl and I were really missing you cooking.”

“Well, I can certainly fix you something to eat.”

“Mother let me help you.”

“Of course, dear if that's what you want.”

Tinougl being somewhat a sensitive person said, “Reladondo, I think you should invite your pilot in so he can get something to eat.”

“Tinougl, I'm sure he would love the offer, but he needs to stay with the helicopter in case the crowd breaks through the police barricade to take off right away to avoid them from possibly damaging the craft.”

“Alright, then I'm sure we can put together him a box lunch he can eat after he drops us off at the Hotel.”

“Good, I'm sure he would like that.”

In the kitchen Karenna handed Mòlìhuā an apron and said, “Put this on, I don't want you to get any spots on your beautiful dress.”

“Thanks mother, I appreciate that.”

The full-length dress with the high heels and tiny straps to hold up the top of the dress truly looked movie start quality with a woman madeup as well as Mòlìhuā. She now had several thousand pictures of her leaving the helicopter with Tinougl and Reladondo bon Scrafatorious being viewed all over the planet as well as several nearby planets by people interested in this new singing sensation.

Being filmed getting out of Reladondo bon Scrafatorious private helicopter immediately created vast speculation and had she not been with the sexy dude, many would have concluded she was Reladondo's new mistress, a fact he wouldn't mind in the least bit.

The men were talking, and Morgan assumed this famous talent scout was solely interested in his daughter and soon had quite a revelation.

"Are you going to have Mòlìhuā record some songs?"

"Yes Morgan, in fact after we leave here, we are going to a recording studio to work on a new song."

"It's good that you came all the way here to see my daughter."

"Actually, I came also to meet with Tinougl."

"He's a musician too?" Morgan asked in utter fascination.

"I've not yet pitched him the deal yet, but I'm producing a new holographic movie in a short time, and I want him to act in it."

"Really?"

"We've not talked about it yet, but we will after we get your daughter's song recordings on their way."

"Tinougl is that what you want to do?" Morgan asked.

"As long as it doesn't get in the way of my farm chores here working with you, I might consider."

"Tinougl, if you sign the movie contract, I personally will provide your father-in-law all the farm hands he needs for any jobs necessary."

Morgan sat there stunned.

"Reladondo, before I agree to such a venture, I would have to get Mòlìhuā's approval," Tinougl said.

"There are some love making scenes in the movie, the actors

are covered up and their nudity is not exposed, I could make sure Mòlìhuā plays the role of the woman so that she will not feel stress about you being under the covers with another woman."

"I'm sure she would appreciate that."

"It's just a small part of the movie so she would not have to be on the movie set too long."

"All right we'll talk about this at a later date. Us enjoy today now because in a while it sounds like Mòlìhuā will be working this afternoon."

"I'm confident after she hears these four songs, she will want to record them."

"If they are as nice as the two, she already recorded, I would love to hear it."

"Yes, those are great songs, but these four are as well."

"Why didn't you use the song writers?"

"Real simple, some can't really sing, and others are not photogenic."

"I understand that."

The men started smelling a nice aroma and before they could think about it, Karenna came into the room and said, "If you men would like, please come into the dining room, the food is ready."

Morgan stood up and Tinougl and Reladondo followed Karenna into the dining room where all the plates had been prepared with the meal. They sat down and were soon enjoying the essence of fresh food. Reladondo had payed big bucks for meals that didn't come close to the taste this good.

The ferments that Morgan produced were outstanding. Morgan now had a genuinely good customer who appreciated such mastership of brewing and fermenting and would pay handsomely for such exquisitee products.

There was a lot of small talk and nothing serious said during dinner and everyone had such a good time. The windows were open as there was a nice gentle breeze coming through. After everyone finished their meal, Tinougl said, "Reladondo why don't you go into the living room with Morgan and watch some holographic video while Mòlìhuā and I pack a few things."

"Sure, I would enjoy that," Reladondo replied.

The men watched some shows that were boring for Reladondo, but he was very polite and didn't really care because he would be leaving soon and heading to the recording studio where he planned on expanding the fame of his new find. And he also was given great thought to how the sex appeal of Tinougl would be when he had his shirt off exposing those incredible muscles. It was nothing more that picking the right script and narrative and he too would be a super star.

It did not take long to pack a couple days worth of street clothes, but the one item Tinougl appreciated the most was his running shoes and workout clothes so he could get back to five miles in the morning, then do some swimming to help cool him off. *Hopefully, the massage technicians would stop sexually harassing him.*

Based on Mòlìhuā's instruction, she had a bag of nicely wrapped up food for the helicopter pilot to eat when he landed at the end of his trip. As a country girl with a lot of common sense, she had a couple partially empty water bottles heated up in the microwave to almost boiling temperature to place in the thermos bags to keep the food nice and warm so the pilot would enjoy the taste better. She instructed Mòlìhuā to inform the pilot those water bottles were just to help keep the food warm and it worked like a champ.

Just before they left, Morgan had a selfish twinge and said, "Mòlìhuā, before you go, would it be possible for you to play that song, "Dǎkāi Wánměi de Liánhuā?"

Just before she was going to use Reladondo and his pilot as an excuse to leave, Reladondo interjected, "I would like to hear it as well."

"All right daddy, just for you."

At this time, it was apparent to Reladondo there was excessive noise coming from the country road with people yelling, screaming, and just the apparent noise manifested by 1000 beings out there in a party like mood. He almost asked if they could close the windows, but Mòlìhuā got to the keyboard and started playing the piano and singing the lyrics. The piano and the singing were loud enough to easily obscure the noise coming from the nearby road.

It was evident to Reladondo that Mòlìhuā had mastered this song. He also knew that with an orchestra in a studio they could easily improve the quality of the recordings to where nobody would want to hear the original recordings after hearing the refined product. To Reladondo, the song was way to short even though he knew it lasted over six minutes. Finally, the song was done and there was sheer quiet. Not a sound from the street!

That's interesting, Reladondo thought.

After the song, Mòlìhuā stood up and announced, "We'll be back in a few days, hopefully the crowd is gone by then."

They all filed out of the home and down the steps onto the sidewalk. It was impossible even for people out on the street 100 yards away to not be able to spot Mòlìhuā since she had on the designer dress and heels and a hair style that exemplified a super star. As soon as the crowd saw her, the applause was enormous. They had heard the song and the house acted as bellows and amplified it in a way where most of the people standing on the street could hear the essence of the song, especially the lyrics sung by such an outstanding singer.

This applause did not escape Reladondo who would start having his operatives do a public relations extravaganza and pay off certain journalists to manufacture the narrative of the super star.

Better yet, she was with the sexiest man on the planet by far, without stretching it one bit.

Tinougl carried the suitcase and Mòlihuā carried the pilot's lunch. They promptly got on the helicopter which then started up it's rotors and was soon airbornee. As the crowd saw her leave on the helicopter, they quickly assumed she was gone for good and would not be back at the farmhouse any time soon because they took a suitcase with them. The next day the crowd was mostly gone, but Tinougl wanted to continue the security for a while, which made the crime boss Aristapara happy because Tinougl was paying him handsomely. And then he smiled even more when he received a text from Tinougl saying he had another project, and they would soon meet to discuss the details.

The helicopter landed on the landing pad on the top of the hotel and the pilot shut down the rotors which stopped in a brief period. After the passengers were all out of the helicopter and inside the waiting room waiting for the elevator, the pilot took off and immediately headed for an auxiliary airfield a few miles away landed. The pilot smelled the food and was happy. After securing the helicopter, he walked 50 feet to a fence gate and then another 30 feet to his rental vehicle and got in and drove himself a few blocks away to his hotel, where he took that nice lunch up with him to check it out. He pulled the water bottles that were still nice and warm out of the thermal bag, then the covered plate and sat it next to him on the table and proceeded to try it out. He was suddenly delighted with the farm fresh food which exceeded his expectations by a wide margin.

Inside the elevator just before the door closed, Tinougl said, "I want to stop at our penthouse so we can freshen up. We'll meet you in the lobby say in fifteen or twenty minutes?"

"Sure, that works for me," Reladondo replied.

Chapter Thirty-One

Mòlìhuā's Recording Studio Adventure

After a brief time using the toilet and freshing up the couple were heading back to the elevator and soon down to the lobby.

Reladondo was there before them and noticed Casandra wasn't paying much attention to him. But when Tinougl came through the lobby she lit up like a Christmas tree and smiled like a woman who wanted something. But he also knew what her note said and why she would look fondly at Tinougl.

When you discover the truth about someone like this observing from a distance who doesn't know they are being observed, it becomes a meaningful indicator of the nature of their temperament. Reladondo now had a growing assessment of Tounogl and what he really was like.

As soon as they left the Hotel lobby, a Limo pulled up in the driveway and Reladondo walked directly towards it and it's door automatically opened.

"I thought we were going to walk."

"We are riding for enhanced security. You will understand in a few more days you have to be more careful."

The two blocks didn't take long to travel and when they pulled into the driveway of the studio circular driveway up to the front entrance, there were several men standing there who *were probably security by the looks of them,* Tinougl thought.

They were soon escorted into the studio and was taken into the recording room that had acoustic dampeners all around the room on the walls and ceiling and lead impregnated tiles on the floor. If nobody was talking, you could hear a pin drop.

Tinougl was taken into the control booth that had a very large glass multipane window for sound dampening as to not put any noise into the recording room.

A makeup artist and fashion designer were there and informed Reladondo bon Scrafatorious, "Mòlìhuā's attire is more than adaquate for any filming. All we need to do is touch up her makeup and slightly tweak her hair that has been blown out of position for the style she is wearing."

"How long will that take?"

"Fifteen minutes will be more than plenty of time."

"That's not bad. In the meantime, lets have the pianist play the song, and the singer perform it immediately afterwards so she can hear the timing of the lyrics. Then on the third cut, we will include the orchestra."

"Alright Mister Scrafatorious," the recording manager said.

The makeup artist said, "Mòlìhuā will you please have a seat here where we can work on you."

"Sure."

The manager directed the pianist, "Start playing 'Bǎochí Wéixiào Even if the Sun Isn't Shining'."

The piano portion of the composition was quite compelling. In the control booth with large instrument panel and numerous control and holographic displays along an entire wall next to the control panel desktop, the pure audio could be heard. Tinougl knew this was a purchased song. Reladondo owned it, but that didn't matter, it still was elegent. One day if he ever got the chance he would communicate to the originator, how talented that person is.

'Bǎochí wéixiǎo Even if the Sun Isn't Shining' is a seven and half minute long song, long for industry standards that try to keep songs down less than five minutes to avoid running the risk of boring the listener. If they liked it, they could play it multiple times.

"It truly was an "oh WOW" moment for Tinougl as well as Mòlìhuā who loved the melody. After the song was finished the control booth said, take five and we'll do the next cut with the singer Clara bon Xìngyùn."

Clara came into the room a moment later and walked to the acoustic microphone next to the piano. She had practiced this song often to get it down to the expectations of the original composer. Clara's problem is she was about 70 pounds overweight, and the excess weight distorted her face and would never enthrall the audiences. Clara was being treated by a medical staff to help her reduce weight so that one day she could perform, unfortunately it was always two steps forward and one step backwards and when she got depressed, three steps backwards, so her progress was painfully slow. Whether Clara would ever make it was questionable.

Mòlìhuā was handed a lyrics sheet to follow along. While she practiced the song later, Mòlìhuā would have the full sheet music with lyrics and the music score.

The piano started and Clara began singing. She had the song wrote to memory and could not help but stare at Mòlìhua with a hint of disdain. It erked her that she would be promoting this, for the Diva. But she had to go through with it or Reladondo would dump her, and she would then be blackballed in the recording industry. His medical staff was helping her with her weight problem, but she wanted instant gratification and let her emotions drive her sometimes when she should just chill out and get with the program, then she would arrive at stardom before she turned into an old hag. Otherwise, she ran the risk of never achieving it.

Hearing the singer and reading the words at the same time had a synergistic effect. Her voice was beautiful, and the composition was utterly outstanding. *If she could just cut back on a few sandwiches, her life could be turned upside down*, Mòlìhuā thought.

The piano with the singer did motivate the orchestra slightly. It truly was a beautiful creation. Soon the song ended, and the control booth said, "Take five and we'll have the orchestra perform with the piano and singer next.

In a few minutes the orchestra conductor walked over to the slightly raised area in front of the orchestra where he had direct eyesight with each musician. As soon as the control booth said, "Begin," the conductor raised his wand and started conducting the music. They all had automatic digital displays that were synchronized by artificial intelligence and the music slowly floated up the screen placing the active section in the middle of the display. It was totally hands off and made no sound.

The combination piano, orchestra and singer created a wonderful sound that enthralled Mòlìhuā as well as Tinougl. This was the sound quality that Reladondo knew would propel Mòlìhuā along her career and weight loss wasn't necessary for this princess.

As a pianist, Mòlìhuā could read sheet music very quickly. Some musicians could read 300 notes per minute. Mòlìhuā had been measured during several of her job interviews as having the ability to read 540 notes a minute. After hearing this song three times and reading the lyrics she was more than ready as she was asked to replace Clara bon Xìngyùn who then sat down, truly believing this new woman after just hearing the song three times could not compete with her operettic fundamentals.

Then reality struck. The conductor started the orchstra and the pianist added to the cocophony of tumultuous allegros and cosmic harmonics. And just when Clara assumed Mòlìhuā would strike out and must practice it 100 times just like she did, the angelic voice spontaneously sent shivers up Clara's spine. Mòlìhuā's singing was pitch perfect. Mòlìhuā's "aimed" projection and structure were far superior to Clara and Clara wasn't aware, Reladondo already knew all this, and she was almost ready to start crying over the realization she didn't hold a fiddle to this woman.

For good reason, every performance is recorded by the control booth so the conductor, director, and producer could critique the performance and measure where improvement needed to be made.

At the end of the performance after the conductor stopped the orchestra's last note, the control booth added another thirty seconds then secured the recording.

Reladondo had a Cheshire Cat smile because he knew the impossible just happened. The Diva Wánměi de Mòlìhuā hit a homerun in her first attempt. After giving instructions to the director and production managers, all the performers were directed to take a 15-minute break.

The conductor, director, production manager, and Reladondo went into the critique room that had a large table where people could take notes and argue about issues involved in a recording. At the table were special headphones for each person in the critique to hear cuts of the music which was digitally recorded.

After the four men were in the critique room setting next to each other at one end of the long table and Reladondo sitting in what amounts to the captain's chair at the very end, began the discussion.

Reladondo running the critique started the conversation.

"Well, what did you think."

The conductor who had a major voice in all this replied first:

"I was utterly amazed. Clara has sung this song probably 500 times. And she didn't come close a single time to match Mòlìhuā superior delivery."

"Any mistakes by the singer or the musicians?"

"Not a single one. I've never seen a one-shot deal like this in my entire career."

Reladondo looked over at the director and asked what do you think?"

"As you know we purposely put the cameras at angles and positions to hide the fact she was reading the music score. I was looking at all camera angles simultaneously on the holograph and listening to the music at the same time. Im not as good as the Maestro as far as analyzing the music, my expertise is the video. I thought the music was extremely good, and I can tell you unquestioningly, the video we have will go nicely with the recording. We really have now what we need for a production."

Reladondo looked at the man in the room with the most clout and asked the production manager, "What did you think."

"I have no idea how the hell we pulled this off in one attempt, which is probably a record we broke today, but I say it's a go. Us publish the video and the performance. I truly believe we got a winner and when the marketing guys get their hands on this, they WILL BE MOTIVATED."

Reladondo being a very wise person to avoid the pitfalls of a screwed-up production had a lot of common sense and said, "I agree with all of you, but we owe it to ourselves to listen to it one more time and watch the video in here and make sure it doesn't change our minds."

They all acknowledged, and Reladondo directed the control booth:

"Control booth, send the audio track and video of the last cut over to the holographic projector in the critique room."

The four men all put on their noise canceling headphones and the simultaneous time synchronized video and audio began. Seven and half minutes later when it all ended, Reladondo asked, "Did any of you change your minds?"

The conductor said, "hearing it again only reassured me that my original assessment was absolutely correct."

The director said, "That video is going to inspire a lot of people. She is such a gorgeous creature and we hit her at the best possible angles with what she is wearing."

The producer said, "I think we go live with this tonight and also if we had a venu to perform it to help get out the word, the marketing people would appreciate us in the morning."

Reladondo said, "I know just the place, let me have some privacy for a few minutes then I'll let you know what I have in mind."

The other men left the room and Reladondo who had the Hotel manager's phone number programmed into his communicator said, "Place a call to the manager at the Grand Xenis Hotel."

Soon Reladondo heard the customary "Hello how may I help you."

"Hi, this is Reladondo bon Scrafatorious I need to talk to you about a very hot topic."

"Is your stay in our hotel alright?"

"Yes, your hotel is wonderful. I need to discuss something else."

"What do you wish to discuss?"

"Remember last night you had that surprise singer the Diva Wánměi de Mòlìhuā perform a couple songs in your restaurant."

"Yes, I'm quite aware the phone has been ringing off the hook all day with people from the upper crust of society calling us congratulating us. It was a rather fantastic performance; one I will never forget."

"How would you like a better one tonight?"

"If that were truly possible, you know I would."

"Okay, I'm at the recording studio now. We have just recorded a block buster video and new song with Mòlìhuā singing that will be hitting the charts like crazy tomorrow. I'm willing to bring the Orchestra over there tonight to perform this new song with Mòlìhuā and our top pianist as you know has won many awards, if you agree."

"How could I not agree."

"That's kind of what I figured. Tell the regular band they are going to do their normal performance but around 9:00 we'll do that performance. Then they can start performing and at 10:00 after Mòlìhuā puts on a new dress, she can perform the song she played the piano last night with our orchestra. Then at 11:00 after she changes her dress again, her other song with my orchestra. They are ready to go. And one other thing. I want your fashion designer standing by with three new dresses. One she'll change into when she gets ready to perform each song."

"This is absolutely wonderful; would you like me to contact some of our exclusive guests and contacts in the community to give them heads up?"

"Yes, but I also want you to reserve a table about 10 feet away from the stage where, Mòlìhuā, Tinougl, my orchestra conductor, the director and the producer will be sitting with me."

"Absolutely."

"One other thing."

"Sure Reladondo, for what you are doing for me you can count on me."

"Your receptionist, Casandra is nearing the end of her shift, right?"

"Yes."

"I want you to put her in a Penthouse tonight at my expense, have the fashion designers fix her up and I want her sitting between me and my producer. I will be sitting next to Tinougal and Mòlìhuā to my right, and my conductor next to Mòlìhuā."

"What if Casandra doesn't wish to go?"

Tell her Tinougl specifically requested her, and she will receive a substantial bonus worth more than three months of salary if she agrees to hear the music. She's not required to do anything but listen to the music and tell me what she thought about it afterwards."

"I will relay the message to her, but I can't force her to go."

"Something tells me if you inform her Tinougl requested her, she would be delighted to attend."

"Is there something you know that I don't know?"

"It's a trade secret. I'm sorry I can't tell you. But I'm certain she will be delighted."

"Alright I'm a good messenger."

"We'll be back at the Hotel in a while I need to talk to the staff here now and give them their marching orders because I believe this will be a big event."

"With Mòlìhuā singing, I already know it will be."

"See you soon."

"Bye."

All Reladondo had to say was, "send the conductor, director, and producer back in the room please." Artificial Intelligence took care of the rest.

After the men were sitting with smiles of expectation on their faces,

Reladondo said, "It's a go. We are taking the orchestra over to the Grand Xenis Hotel tonight and I know for a fact some VIPs are being invited to attend."

"Their workday is almost finished," the conductor responded.

"Inform the orchestra, for this one-night performance which I know is a burdon to them, they will receive a month's pay as a bonus. Hopefully that will cheer them up."

"They will be on cloud nine."

Okay we are going live with this recording tonight. Director, get your video boys hot. I'd like to see this go live before we perform if possible."

"We have really good video, that's easy."

"You guys get the wheels rolling. Send Tinougl and Mòlìhuā here, I need to talk to them."

"Sure," the producer responded.

In a few minutes, Tinougl and Mòlìhuā walked into the room with smiles because the rumors were already floating, they did the impossible, a home run at the first swing at the plate.

"Listen I want to thank both of you for being so flexible and accommodative. Tonight, very well chart your future in a major way. You did such an excellent job singing Mòlìhuā, that we got a good audio and video recording on the first attempt. That is extremely rare in the entertainment business and rarely happens if ever."

The couple looked on with a significant curiousity as this all unfolded.

"Mòlìhuā, since we are going live with that recording tonight and your bank account will grow handsomely tomorrow, it's best we perform it tonight at a major venue."

"Sounds wonderful, but where could we go on such short notice?"

Mòlìhuā replied.

"The Grand Xenis Hotel manager has agreed to allow us to bring in the studio orchestra and you will perform three songs. At 9:00 you will perform this new song 'Bǎochí Wéixiǎo Even if the Sun Isn't Shining', At 10:00 you will perform Dǎkāi Wánměi de Liánhuā, and at 11:00 you will perform your other song. The orchestra has practiced those songs in expectation you would record it here. Would you like to sing those two other songs to hear the orchestra and how their music effects you?"

"Sure, but I have a request."

"What is your request."

"The singer in the band that's performing tonight, I want her singing back up with me in the other two songs."

"Sure, she did great last night."

"Thank you."

One other thing, you will be putting on three new dresses tonight. That's why the delay between performances. I want you to also wow the audience with your beauty."

Mòlìhuā looked on with an almost twinkle in her eye as she realized ALL her dreams were coming true, one right after the other.

"We all agree?"

"Sure, why not, I'm excited about this new song," Tinougl said and Mòlìhuā acknowled by moving her head up and down synchronized to Tinougl's comment.

"Alright us go into the recording rooms before the conductor cuts loose the orchestra on a long break."

They arrived just in time as the orchestra was just about to leave, get snacks and take a break. Artificial Intelligence had already informed them to stand by for another performance. A few of them had sour looks on their faces because they were thirsty and hungry.

"Alright everyone, please take your seats. We are now going to perform

Dǎkāi Wánměi de Liánhuā."

The orchestra wasn't greatly motivated but they liked the song and when the conductor started moving his wand, it was like he put a magic spell on them as they quickly responded to the movement of his wand.

The award-winning pianist had worked hard on this piece because the melody was so thought evoking and he was ready for prime time. When he kicked it into high gear, it seemed to have a synergistic effect on the orchestra. And then Mòlìhuā started singing. Perhaps it was because they were practicing with Clara, they didn't full appreciate the delivey that Mòlìhuā soon manifested. It was night and day difference. With a Diva singing the motivation was quite explicit.

Within thirty seconds of the seven and half minute performance, the orchestra was running on nitro glycerin with explosive results. Even though Reladondo knew he had three other new songs to produce in the next few days, he knew instantly, the quantification the orchestra had to the song. He also knew as amazingly as it seemed, he would be going LIVE with another song tonight. In his wildest ideas, he never ever expected to go LIVE with two Diva songs in one day. There could be no greater satisfaction. He almost felt like wheeping listening to all of it. He looked over at Tinougl and saw his eyes all water up. He knew there was some special attachment to that song. He would never pry; but he was glad it existed.

The six and half minutes went by too quickly, the band the conductor, the director, and everyone else in the recording studio had a severe letdown when the song endeed. They wished it could go on a lot longer.

Reladondo knowing he was up against some time constraints picked up the control booth microphone and said, "Okay relax for five minutes then we are going to perform that final song."

The orchestra was ready to go. Their insulin rush was now strong upon them, and their endorphins were resonating in their brains now. The conductor knew this five-minute break would help them prevent fatigue since they had a lot more to do later tonight.

The music started again and Mòlìhuā sang her heart out to her lover boy she looked directly at sitting there in the control booth. He took that very focused look and knew what she was telegraphing to him in her own way. It was the magic of love, and he took those ensembles of music intertwined with love directly into his heart. At that moment he forgot he was ever a spy. Now he was just human full of emotion evoked by the intensity of Mòlìhuā's love beams she cast upon him.

Then it all came to an end. They had finished.

It was crisis management time. Reladondo was running out of time and needed to make an off the hip shot and since the director and producer was in the control booth and he already suspected the conductor would give it a thumbs up, it was a no brainer.

"Okay guys we don't have time to go into the critique room. We have a lot of things to get done right away and get the orchestra over to the hotel in time to perform. Do we go live on these two songs tonight?"

The orchestra conductor said, "The music sounded great, I say yes."

The film director said, "The video is awesome, definitely a yes."

Reladondo looked at the producer who instantly knew he was on the hook who said, "Most definitely"

Reladondo then grabbed the microphone and said, "Conductor, give me a thumbs up if you think we should go live on those last two songs." The conductor put both thumbs up.

"Okay gentleman, we are making recording history tonight, going live in one night with three Diva songs. Do what you must make it happen."

"Call in all the Limo's you need to get the orchestra and their instruments over there with folding chairs and music stands and their music prompters. The manager is very flexible, you can setup even while the regular band is peroforming, we'll play these three songs during their three breaks."

The music conductor asked, "How soon will we play?"

"We must be ready for prime time exactly at 9:00 P.M."

As the chaos ruled everyone stepped up to the plate not only because they were extremely happy about the added income. They also knew they were doing something special in the recording industry that most likely would never be surpassed by going live on three new recordings in a single day on top of performing their new song at the opening devue at a prestigious venue.

Reladondo then hustled Tinougl and Mòlìhuā back to the hotel so they could be pampered and change clothes. When they walked into their penthouse, the fashion designer and her staff were there waiting. There was excitement in the air. Though they were quite utterly shocked what they were to do to Casandra tonight who was now up in a Penthouse taking it all in and having indecent thoughts about what she would like to do to Tinougl.

Chapter Thirty-Two

A Time for Love and a Time to Sing

With the special reserved table, they didn't have to hustle but by 8:30 they were walking down to the Grand Xenis Hotel Restaurant that was utterly amazing when they arrived. Chairs, tables, and all kinds of other things got moved around. It seemed more cramped but there was the orchestra sitting in their seats enjoying the band perform.

Tinougl and Mòlìhuā were the last to arrive and there was Casandra at the table with a makeover that was utterly shocking. She might have been attractive as a receptionist, and here she was smoking hot sitting next to Reladondo already having finished a drink that had significant calming effect to the point she was lovely and docile, just like Reladondo wanted.

When they approached the table all the men stood up. And bowed. There was an element of noise in the restaurant as people were eating, talking, and listening to the regular band perform. But the minute the couple came in and sat down, there was a mild ruckus as the gossiping was ablaze!

As soon as they were seated the Waitress was already handing them their regular drinks and treating like a king and queen. The music the band was performing was exceptionally good tonight as they were excited to get all the publicity. The singer in the band also had a make over and she was smoking hot as well and appreciative they could make her look so good as she wanted to make a couple guys in the band jealous of each other vying for her attention.

It was good they had thirty minutes to enjoy their drinks because it's exactly what Mòlìhuā needed to get the butterflies out of her tummy. Then at 9:00 the band leader walked off the stage carrying a microphone and handed it to Reladondo who walked over to the stage and started the announcement, "Ladies and Gentlemen, I'm Reladondo bon Scrafatorious the CEO of Scrafatorious Productions. Many of you have heard many of my talented performers in the past and some of the award-winning holographic videos and movies I've produced over the years.

Tonight, is a special night for me because I've done something I never was able to achieve before in my entire lifetime by going live on three major performances of our lovely singer Wánměi de Mòlìhuā who some of you know sang a couple of those songs here last night.

Tonight, will devue a new song 'Bǎochí wéixiǎo Even if the Sun Isn't Shining' Mòlìhuā recorded today and went live one hour ago, and I've been told has already been screened by over one billion viewers here and nearby planets." "May I now present to you the lovely Wánměi de Mòlìhuā"

Suddenly there was complete silence in the restaurant. All the waiters knew they were to stand down and not do anything during the performance.

Mòlìhuā walked up to the stage and Reladondo handed her the microphone and she saw the bands singer and gestured her to join her on the stage.

"As soon as the two women were together, Mòlìhuā nodded to the conductor who raised his wand and began the song."

The guests in the restaurant had never heard this song before. It was brand new. Thirty seconds into the performance they already realized the significance of the composition. The song fully captivated the audience who listend and watched the two lovely ladies sing, but they clearly heard Mòlìhuā doing the bulk of the singing, hitting all the high notes with great precision and the back up singer harmonizing her at different points along the way.

The song truly mesmerized the audience and just like the night before when the song ended there was a standing ovation and cheers that were very uncommon. The crowd went wild with applause.

The two women bowed twenty times saying thank you repeatedly.

Reladondo came to the stage and took the microphone from Mòlìhuā and said, "Wasn't she great!"

The applause roared back to life for another minute then Reladondo answered the calls for an encore by saying, "Ladies and gentlemen, Mòlìhuā is not done, she will be coming back after a break and sing you another song."

Reladondo knew to change the order of the next two songs. He wanted that heart crusher song Dǎkāi Wánměi de Liánhuā to be sang last because he knew exactly the impact it was going to have, especially for people sitting at his table including the illustrious Casandra.

Reladondo and Mòlìhuā sat down at the table and within seconds the chef and four assistants were there personally serving the VIP's which some of the restauranters too great interest in. They had to be very special to receive this level of SVIP treatment.

The manager who came into the restaurant to watch the performance went back to his office and answered a few inquiries by a few SVIP's and executives of the corporation that owned the hotel. His feed back was already indicating promotions were in store for his very innovative techniques that was driving the Hotel into a lot of fame. Reservations were now flooding in. These were exciting times.

The table was then served an entrée with the heads up that

Mòlìhuā needed to get something to eat, then get backup to the Penthouse and get into her new outfit.

Like on que twenty minutes later after Mòlìhuā had finished about one third of her serving, one of the fashion designers staff members dressed for the occasion came to the table and said, Mòlìhuā please come with me to the Penthouse so we can help you change into your next outfit.

Mòlìhuā then stood up and walked to the elevator with her and went up into the Penthouse and was fitted with another stunning creation that showed part of one of her beautiful legs.

There were some extra security men in the restaurant, the hallway by the Penthouse, in the elevator while Mòlìhuā was in it and from the elevator back to the restaurant she was surrounded by five security men who took her back to the table with about five minutes to spare. The big difference this time was:

Reladondo had a lot of diamonds he used for props on his starlets worth millions of credits were now on Mòlìhuā's arms, her neck and even on one of her ankles showing part of her thigh.

The glitter was utterly breathtaking and all this of coure was being filmed and would be broadcasted.

At 10:00 right on the dot the regular band stopped playing and exited the stage, Reladondo went back to the stage with the microphone. The conductor nodded indicating he and the orchestra, and the pianist were ready.

"Ladies and gentlemen, please welcome back to the stage our beautifully and radiant Wánměi de Mòlìhuā."

Mòlìhuā walked to the stage and signaled for the other singer to come join her. When the singer saw all those diamonds, she felt queezy. The sight was astonishing, and she knew she was singing with a person that was now super star quality. What she didn't know was the subscriptions to the three simultaneously released songs today were getting the media all around the Empire interested. They had not seen this subscription rate ever.

The audience that was here the night before heard this song with the local band that was nice, but nothing compared to a professional orchestra. Since more than half the people in the restaurant had not heard this song, they were fascinated. It was good this song was over eight minutes long because the audience did not want it to end. Every man in the place was in love with Mòlìhuā and those diamonds made her sparkle and gave them sexual inducements. Some of their wives would get some happy time tonight when they went to bed as the emotions rubbed off onto them.

Reladondo and the conductor were extremely proud of the orchestra tonight. Every member of the orchestra felt a part of this magical moment and they too played their hearts out articulating those notes with utter accuracy and interpretaion of it better than anyone before.

Finally, the song came to an end. The crowd was alive. The manager of the hotel stood in the back just shaking his head. And there he was looking at Casandra. One thing the manager knew vividly. Tinougl had touched three women's lives. He had Casandra sitting next to the top man in show business who would no doubt visit her later in her penthouse for the night with an indecent proposal if it were not a setup for Tinougl, which was another possibility. The manager instinctively knew that Tinougl probably had a lot to do with promoting Mòlìhuā to get her to the point of this stardom. And now he could see the change in the singer in the band. She was also destined for greatness because she didn't know it yet, but she escould receive royalties for tonights performance that would soon be broadcast around the empire. By morning she would be a millionaire.

The applause was as strong as before. The guests were having a tremendous night. Because of the lack of seating, the music was also played out at the pool that often-had guests there until mandatory closure around midnight drinking and listening to music. Tonight, those guests too were having a lot of fun and the music played out there with a great sound system, captivated them as well. They would certainly get their reservations in early tomorrow. When the manager walked out to the pool bar to talk with some of his staff and he inquired, "How's it going?"

"We've never seen anything like it."

The manager could see with his own eyes they had a full house. They have NEVER had a full house at 10:00 P.M. at the pool bar and the waitresses were all smiles because they were getting mountains of generous tips.

The table received another entrée by the chef and four of his staff. This helped immensely with their alcohol and elixir intake.

The recording studio staff, and the orchestra were extremely happy tonight. Everyone was smiling and poor Casandra was melting because she was thinking Tinougl would meet her in the Penthouse tonight and she would let him do to her whatever he wanted. She didn't know it yet, that wasn't in the cards.

Reladondo would console her later when prince charming didn't show up and secretly offer to take her to a planet, they were going to film a blockbuster film with the top 3 actors and actresses in the film industry with Tinougl in a leading role.

The Diva Mòlìhuā would be busy elsewhere guaranteeing her she would have exclusive access to Tinougl. But it would require her to give up some quid pro quo. Reladondo arranged through the manager the next day to give Casandra the day off so she could be at the pool in the morning when he would have arranged a swim call with Tinougl. He knew once she saw his body, she would give anything to taste it just one time.

That's how the entertainment industry was. Nothing was sacred.

After the entrée the fashion designer and bodyguards were there again.

The audience was starting to feel the surreal nature of this lady changing dresses, but the next dress would be the most provocative. Not that it showed more of her body, but simply by the color and the design.

The next dress Mòlìhuā was fitted with had diamon straps holding up the dress barely covering her perfect sized breasts. It was a purple full-length dress with a slit that showed off the right leg. The high heels accentuated that aspect. Her diamond neclaces and her diamonds on the sides of the rest and her high heels laced with diamonds created an imagery that was profoundly seductive. Since she was wearing two million in credits worth of diamonds, she had plenty of bodyguards. Mòlìhuā was no less than stunning. Her white pearl teeth and beautiful lips exposed a enticing smile. Her eyebrows and eye lashes were of perfect geometry. She had on a new hair style where where blond hair came down from her left shoulder and created the image that Tinougl would never forget.

Mòlìhuā arrived at 10:55 and not a soul had left the restaurant. There was a long line outside, but they had audio and vido pumped out to them, so they didn't miss a thing.

Reladondo bon Scrafatorious made his announcement exactly at 11:00. The orchestra was happy because they were fifteen minutes away from going home, so it seemed.

Mòlìhuā walked on stage and had sent word to the other singer she would do this solo because of special circumstances but was invited to sit next to Tinougl so she could evaluate the song and it's impact on him.

Reladondo made his announcement followed by Mòlìhuā who took the microphone from him and then said, "Ladies and gentlemen," thank you for allowing me to sing tonight. I dedicate this song to the man I love sitting on that table in front of me." The audio-visual technicians now put the spotlight on Tinougl. The audience was aghast looking at this incredible example of handsomeness. Even her boyfriend was movie start quality! They were not expecting this and Reladondo suspected she would dedicate the song to Tinougl, so he gave instructions to the recording studio video crew that was controlling the temporary lighting and all the augmentation of creativity that night.

Tinougl saw the brightness of the light and the audio-visual technicians had a split screen that was part of the imagery that was recorded as well as pumped out to the pool bar where sexy well-dressed women felt swooned by this incredible looking man who had the best film maker in the worlds top makeup artist beautifully enhancing every aspect of him.

The song began and the piano was pronounced as it led the incredible acoustic influence on everyone watching.

The extra light on Tinougl's face was slightly annoying but it did not screw up his ability to clearly see Mòlìhuā. There was a special passage in the song at the three-minute mark where the lyrics said, "I love you darling." When Mòlìhuā hit that part, Tinougl knew it would hit him like it usually did. There was a psychological trimmer and the tears started flowing. The women in the Piano Bar who could talk because they were not in the temporary concert hall soon had exlamations!

By the time the song ended, and the fanfare rose to a minor earthquake almost, the streams of tears were clearly flowing down Tinougl's face as if the dam had broken.

Mòlìhuā handed the microphone to the backup singer after saying thank you just one time. She then walked off the stage and walked over to Tinougl and sat down on his lap and threw her arms around him and began the most affectual embrace ever caught on film.

Reladondo observed all this up close and Mòlìhuā's scent which was fortified by priceless COFA DE COMA perfume quickly convinced him that the new Diva Wánměi de Mòlìhuā was his most successful exploitation of beauty in his lifetime. He also was sad that she already had a lover because otherwise he would pursue her to the ends of the Earth.

Out at the pool one of those extragantly and beautifully dressed honeys that was stuck out there because she didn't realize how fast the restaurant would fill up, said, "Poor baby. You can come to momma any time you want."

This sex goddess had the richest men on the planet and some from other Empire worlds always seeking her. And she was quite explicity in her comments and her friend knew she meant every word and would ride that man like he's never been ridden before. Tinougl had star image quality.

Everything that happened in this last song dovetailed nicely in the famed recording legend maker Reladondo bon Scrafatorious' plans. He had an inner glow because he knew by morning the publicists and PR people would be informing him the public's reaction to the Diva's lover.

Mòlìhuā whispered into Tinougl's ear, "I'm tired, us go up to the Penthouse."

Tinougl who was already agitated over the bright lights screwin up his precious moment responded, "Yes good idea."

Mòlìhuā stood up so Tinougl could stand up and Tinougl turned to Reladondo and said, "We are going up to the Penthouse, Mòlìhuā is tired and needs a break."

"Sure, I would like to escort you there because I have a proposal to make."

"Alright."

The three left the restaurant now a temporary concert hall and made their way up to the Penthouse with no less than six bodyguards and the jewelry escorts.

Once they got inside the Penthouse the jewelry escort took

possession of all the exclusive diamonds Reladondo had Mòlìhuā fitted with. The security guards and the jewelry escort then left the penthouse room, however two security men remained outside the Penthouse door for the rest of the night.

"What do you want to discuss?" Tinougl asked as he led Reladondo and Mòlìhuā into the Penthouse living room.

Nobody sat down as Tinougl expected this to be a short conversation.

"I would like to continue the recording of the next three songs tomorrow. This time we are not going to rush it. I promise you we will not work Mòlìhuā as hard as we did today. The reason why I had to do this blitz today was to send tremors through the public and give them shock and awe laced with sizzle to get the public relations effect we need for the publicists and the public relations group. Now that's all done, we can get the three recordings done at a more leisurely pace. My instruction to the studio is to do one recording a day, but not to go live until all three are ready to be published."

"That sounds reasonable."

"I have some thing for you Tinougl."

"What's that?"

"We are filming a new action thriller holograph movie and I'm going to give you the leading role if you want it."

"I suppose I could try."

"Good. While Mòlìhuā starts recording those three next songs tomorrow, I'm going to take you to Espranza de Topaxh to our main movie studio for three days to film a trailer and some of the initial scenes that do not require the entire cast and artwork. By the time we finish and release the video trailer, Mòlìhuā will have finished the recordings and I will set up another concert in the restaurant like we did tonight and put on a show right after we go live with those three new music videos."

"I'n willing to do it but I want to go for a run in the morning and do a little swim before we leave."

"Not a problem. I will see you in the morning. Call me when you are ready to leave. After you finish your swim the fashion designer will be here to dress you up for the trip."

"Alright."

The pompass and very successful Reladondo bon Scrafatorious then left the Penthouse knowing the two love birds needed to have a lot of sex to store some up for the three-day absence.

Mòlìhuā said, "I'm glad you will have something to do for three days while I'm working on those recordings."

"He's making us a lot of money, it's the least I could do for him."

"I kind of like the idea that I am married to a movie star."

"I was thinking it couldn't hurt your image if they do a good job producing the holographic drama."

With that meeting done and privacy back, the two were soon doing the horizontal tango with Tinougl releasing cauldrons of love to the purveyor of his joy.

Early in the morning Tinougl stirred and rose and after urinating, went to the closet and retrieved his running shoes and pulled his exercise clothes out of the chester drawers and put them on and left without disturbing Mòlìhuā currently in the most peaceful slumber.

He set up his communicator to alert him when he reached 2.5 miles and headed out. Casandra wasn't at the receptionist desk this morning, but a different lady and the manager were. The manager was beaming and spotted Tinougl and said, "Good morning, sir, going out for some exercise?"

"Yes, I'm going to do some running."

"Have a great time and we'll see you when you get back."

"Thank you."

The manager could see the incredible build on Tinougl and now knew most vividly whay a Diva like Mòlìhuā would pick him.

Tinougl got out and started running down the street in the direction where he knew afluent people lived and was deemed safer. After he reached the two point five miles, his communicator sounded the alarm. Tinougl then called. Aristapara the organized crime boss.

"Hello Tinougl," Aristapara said after seeing the caller I.D.

"Got time to talk?"

"For you anytime."

"Good, I'm out for a run and I'll send you my location from my communicator, swing by here and we'll discuss what I want in the next project."

"I'll be right there."

Tinougl was drenched in sweat, and it caused his workout clothes to cling to him further exposing his six pack abs and his bicepts and some of the muscles in his legs.

Five minutes after Tinougl zapped the location to Aristapara, a Limo pulled up and the window came down.

"What do you need to talk about?"

"I need some information." He then explained it thinking Aristapara could best get the information and he in no way would be linked to it.

After the transaction was completed, Aristapara said, "I like the way you operate."

"How so?"

"Cash in Advance."

"Thanks."

"One last thing."

"Sure."

"When my guys had King Shark in a good positon, they only cut his dick a little bit when they put the fear of god in him."

"Thanks, I appreciate your help in that matter."

"By the way, I subscribed to Mòlìhuā's videos. I'm very impressed. You have an incredible woman."

"Not bad for a farmers daughter."

"Not bad at all."

Soon the Limo was gone and Tinougl turned on the coals as he ran back to the Hotel.

Reladondo bon Scrafatorious spooks filmed him coming and going and soon Reladondo observed the video and saw him coming back to the hotel in the last mile as he curved around into view as the road curved to a straight section near the hotel.

Tinougl went up to the Penthouse, took a fast shower to clean off the swet and obtained swim apparel from Frimbro and made his way to the pool.

Tinougl didn't know the reality of it, but he had hidden cameras on him now. Reladondo bon Scrafatorious was surreptitiously filming him to see his body when it reached it's ultimate shape after the swim. He would utilize that in the video trailer they would soon be making. Tinougl didn't know realize the filming had already begun. Video from the restaurant, his running, and his swimming was concatenated into one of the most impressive video trailers ever produced for a super star at the beginning of his career.

Reladondo and a couple security men were there to meet Tinougl.

"I'm not going to try to keep up with you, but I'm going to swim with you," Reladondo said.

"That's fine, everyone has their own routine."

"Indeed, we do."

Reladondo had convinced Casandra to perform the horizontal tango with him last night and had informed her he would be back in about three days after he attended to some urgent business and requested, "Would you be so kind as to be available for dinner when I return?"

"Of course."

Casandra was extremely happy she had just had a fling with the movie mougle and knew the Hotel staff would be gossiping about her. Men who didn't give her notice in the past would soon be looking at her differently, especially if they saw the concert last night when she was all dressed for success.

When Reladondo left later that day, he informed the manager, "Have that Penthouse available for Casandra and she could remain while I'm gone for another three days. Also have the fashion designers dress her for work in the mornings and if she choses to remain in the Penthouse and have dinner in the restaurant, have the fashion designers dress her for dinner."

"Alright." The manager went on to say, "That concert last night was phenomenal. Even our pool bar was packed to maximum capacity so the people could watch the video and hear Mòlìhuā's singing."

"Thank you. I've already instructed the fashion designer to prepare Mòlìhuā each morning for her studio shoots and if she wants to perform in the restaurant with her new singer friend, to put her in something different each time."

"Absolutely."

"In three more days, she will have recorded another three songs. I would like to set up another concert at the restaurant."

"We are more than happy to showcase the lovely Mòlìhuā."

By the time Tinougl finished his swim and turned down a request from the attractive massage technician who wanted to copulate, he was feeling great and went back to the Penthouse and found Mòlìhuā was dressed and about to leave for the studio.

"You look beautiful."

"Thank you."

"I'll see you in three days. I hope I'm not a flop."

"I'm sure you will do great things. You are always great with me."

"I'll try my best."

They hugged and Mòlìhuā was out the door and the fashion designer then said, "We need to get you ready for your trip."

"Sure."

Chapter

Thirty-Three

Espranza de Topaxh Adventures

Tinougl was bathed and his bathwater was filled with special additives to create a mental transcendence to a more pleasurable plateau. Since Mòlīhuā was gone and they had complete privacy the young lady shampooing Tinougl's hair stripped down and hopped in the large tub with him and positioned herself where her womanhood could rub up against his tool. She would not insert it but since it was rubbing against her clitoris, she naturally got physically orgasmic in a while and Tinougl thbugh it felt rather pleasant the way she was shampooing him. Right after her orgasms died down, she rinsed his hair and was soon helping him out of the tub and drying him off and put him into a bath robe and she then put all her clothes back on and they departed the bathroom as if nothing special happened.

When the hairdresser asked Tinougl if he would like the *Cosmic Wave* hair design, he realized his cover was already blown and people would soon know all about him, so he said, "Why not."

With the *Cosmic Wave* hair design and the extremely sexy outfit on, Tinougl was ready for his day traveling to destiny.

Tinougl was in for his next surprise. Reladondo bon Scrafatorious had his own space transport that had the range to go to nearby solar systems.

Unfortunately, it's range wasn't good enough to get them to the Tartarnite Empire Capital City Santorini de Shénshèng, if they ever went there, they would be forced to take the high-speed public transport.

The trip to Espranza de Topaxh Movie Studio would only take a few hours to get there since that Espranza solar system wasn't very far away. The trip to Espranza de Topaxh didn't take as long as Tinougl expected and the studio was located on the side of the planet that was just now experiencing morning, so the film crew had a full day to work ahead of them.

Tinougl was led into the studio and today all his work would be teleprompted by a device next to the cameras so it would appear he was looking directly at the camera as he read off the script.

Reladondo bon Scrafatorious knew Tinougl had a great voice, and his mental intellect was superior, and he could handle the acting chores just fine with great articulation, form, structure, and projection.

By the end of the day, the film director knew he had a winner.

Just like at the recording studio at Konhagar, this film studio had it's own critique room which had artificial intelligence that assisted in splicing and moving sections of recordings around. While Tinougl was being taken to a nearby hotel and put into a Penthouse and offered a sedative and a snack so he could take a peaceful nap and would be awakend in a few hours and prepped for some public appearances, the critique began.

"What did you think?" Reladondo asked the director looking directly into his eyes. He liked this director in particular, because he never misrepresented the truth to him and called as he saw it never embellishing making sure Reladondo did not miscalculate important decisions.

"Reladondo, I don't know how the hell you keep finding these super stars, but you seem to have a nackt at spotting talent."

"Do you think we can have that video trailer done in three days?"

With the video you already supplied and what we filmed today, I know absolutely we will be ready to go live with the trailer in three days or less."

A couple consultants who were very keen to reviewer's most likely impressions and reports were then asked probing questions about what their impressions were.

"This guy is definitely a super star and when the women see the swimming pool and his running, their panties will melt away in utter lust."

"How the hell did he get a body like that?"

"I have my suspicions, but we are not going to go there. All the PR guys are simply to write the narrative he has one hell of a workout regiment."

After a few more round table discussions, it was time for everyone to take a break because they already had a fantastically productive day, and the big boss was happy.

The Grand Espranza de Topaxh Hotel had a night club Galant Simulacrum where a lot of movie stars hung out and flaunted their bodies. The richest men in the Empire were often seen here including the three Barracuda's husbands.

Tinougl was awakened in the evening and Reladondo bon Scrafatorious had a reserved table he had already sat down at and saved a seat specifically for Tinougl. Sitting at the table were a few of his starlets, some of which would be filming with Tinougl.

These starlets had all seen Mòlìhuā's concerts after they were informed who they would be working with. A starlet often rejects actors if they did not look suitable, because a bad looking actor could drag down their ratings as well. Just before these actresses were brought to the Galant Simulacrum for dinner and entertainment, they were individually given private showings of the portion of the video trailer completed. When they saw Tinougl's body the first notion they had was how the hell they could get into his bed before some of those other Bimbo's beat her to Tinougl.

With the *Cosmic Wave* hair design hair style and some of the sexiest men's attire available for movie stars, Tinougl was again prepared for prime time. He had no idea how many women he would make their panties wet tonight as they speculated on his application of his talents, they were sure he offered.

Most of the dinner guests in the Grand Espranza de Topaxh's quite famous Galant Simulacrum, had seen the blissful performance of the previous evening and this gorgeous man succumb to tumultuous allegros of emotions Mòlìhuā triggered. The fact the leading Diva had such an attraction to this man had quite an effect on other women who wanted to speculate on how good a lover he was. If he asked for voluneers right now, the line would stretch out of the restaurant and halfway down the block.

Needless to say, when Tinougl was escorted into the Galant Simulacrum there was a wave action as women watching other women turned to see what they were looking at and the whispers abounded.

The concoctions that Tinougl had that day prepared him psychologically for this grand moment. He was being filmed this very moment and all that would be dissected and spliced into the video traler.

Reladondo bon Scrafatorious was a genius and never missed a public relations trick. He currently had the two top starlets in the film industry sitting on each side of the chair that Tinougl would soon sit at. He also had a couple more honey's sitting across the circular table in direct view of Tinougl so he could enjoy the splendor of their bodies against the backdrop of the very fancy group performing in black tie behind them. A female singer every as beautiful as Mòlìhuā was there performing exquisite songs. Tinougl was in for a big surprise. The three songs that Mòlìhuā sang the previous night and one she would be recording while he was gone was in the works for the evening to help make him feel at home.

As soon as Tinougl arrived at the table, Reladondo bon Scrafatorious stood up and addressed the starlets waiting in great anticipation, "Ladies, here is your top course for the evening, may I please present your future colleague, Tinougl."

Tinougl bowed to the ladies and held his hand out to the first and most glamorous lady at the table sitting next to his chair. She held her hand out in response and Tinougl grasped it and kissed it and left her a subtle tounge lick that sent shivers down the woman's spine resulting in her own tulultuous Andante de la desires. He then copied his actions to the other woman sitting next to him and to say the table wasn't the least animated was a bit of an understatement. Then Tinougl sat down with all those smiles focused on him while the music played on.

In the film business rumors circulate like wildfire. With vivid speculation and expectations, tonight was the grand opening for Tinougl, who only had a single name that wasn't fitting for show business, so once again Reladondo and his public relations consultants had already come up with a solution added to his name and created the new star: Tinougl bon Brandenboynk. And soon enough all the top starlets wanted to be boynked by Tinougl.

The women were getting a little sassy because of lack of food and too many elixirs. Reladondo knew that and instructed the waiter to have Tinougl's drink and the food lelivered as soon as he sat down. The singer was told to start singing "Dǎkāi Wánměi de Liánhuā" as soon as the table started eating.

As to not screw up the timing, the performers took a short break while the chef and four assistants in their dress uniforms served the VIP's and explained to them what all the dishes were.

As soon as the table started eating and the Chef and his helper who were also directed to stand in a respectful pose during the song, the singer climbed up onto the stage and grabbed a microphone and said, "Ladies and Gentlemen, the next song I will sing is for our illustrious new film star Tinougl bon Brandenboynk who is with us here tonight."

Tinougl looked over at Reladondo who in turn, winked at him.

The food tasted great and Tinougl knew to play along with the programme. This is how things happened in the entertainment business. There were always reasons for everything. That's why some people who did this work were put on pedistals and enjoyed life, while others were crushed and destroyed as the victims of a system that took no prisoners.

The singer looked terrific had a full makeover making her look far better than she normally would while performing in this dinner night club. The song hit Tinougl like a ton of bricks and at the three-minute mark had that supernatural singularity that created those tendrils of tears slowly floating down his face captivating not only the women at the table, but also the singer herself who reciprocated with an even more powerful and romantic fashion. She had her eyes focused on Tinougl who was now bathed in colored lighting to create a surreal effect as it slowly transitioned between a colorful blue to purple and back in resonance of the singing.

Reladondo knew what he was doing most implicitly as he secretly recorded and studied the comments these women privately said to their screaners as they were shown the video trailer earlier in the day. He was watching the appearance of these women betray their earlier remarks. Tinougl had moved every single one of them. Reladondo took solace in what he observed and knew just like Mòlìhuā, Tinougl bon Brandenboynk was a growing super star and the tantalizing aspect of them being lovers would create vast interest in the media. Noting beats free advertising.

Reladondo didn't know why but the singer received a standing ovation. He somehow attributed it to the interactions between the singer and Tinougl which the crowd easily focused in because of the lighting effects.

During the next break the woman was taken to her change room and put on a new wardrobe and had corrective actions to her makeup while receiving some wonderful snacks of food similar to what the table in front of her was enjoying. Because of the longer time to fix up the singer, the band played a couple intrumentals until the singer returned and began her magic.

Just before her next beak she sang the eight-minute song to utter perfection and it made Tinougl quite happy because it brought back fond memories of Mòlìhuā. As soon as the song finished, and the great applause died down the singer went back to her change room and was put into a very classy low cut red dress with very small strings holding the top up and decorated with lavish diamonds not discimilar to what Mòlìhuā wore the previous evening.

Right near the end of the present set, the fantastic band and singer performed, 'Bǎochí Wéixiǎo Even if the Sun Isn't Shining'."

Now filled with fabulous food and exquisite drinks laced with the best pleasurizers in the Empire, Tinougl enjoyed this song like never before. It boosed his happiness and transfixed his observation on the singer who had been indoctrinated by Reladondo to focus those three songs on a single person in the audience, which she did. Psychologically, Tinougl took it as if she was singing it for him, and she really was and she knew in her heart if he wanted to make love to her tonight, she would let him. But she also knew those two venomous superstars sitting next to him already were vying for first shot. She would wait until the perfect time and place and instead of her waiting for him to ask, she knew how to turn the tide the other way.

After that song, Tinougl said, "Reladondo, I'm going back to my room to get some rest so that I can get up in the morning and do some running and swimming."

"Sure thing, Tinougl, I'll see you in the morning."

"Thanks for the entertainment."

"My pleasure Tinougl."

Chapter Thirty-Four

Margot bon Srofendorn and the Fabric of Time

Shortly after Tinougl returned to his Penthouse, the butler announced,

"Margot bon Srofendorn has requested permission to visit you."

This was the movie starlet on his left at dinner. "Sure, invite her in."

Margot came in and standing in the high heels gave a much better view of her splendid figure. She came in and Tinougl wasn't terribly sleepy yet figured he could entertain one of the top movie stars in the Empire for a while.

"Would you like something to drink?"

Margot was already feeling good but figured another might just help her get up the nerve to offer her body to Tinougl. Sure, I would like a Ràng wǒ Jiǎozhì Elixir. In a few moments as expected the butler brought in two drinks that were identical since Tinougl didn't request one, he simply assumed he would not mind trying this particular one that might open the flood gates of passion to the starlet.

Margot did not waste time downing that elixir and soon said, "I'm terribly sorry, but may I use your bathroom?"

"Sure, it's inside that room," Tinougl said as he pointed to the master bedroom and was feeling slightly invigorated by that fancy drink which no commoner could ever afford.

After a couple minutes Margot reappeared wearing a bath robe and said, "Tinougl could you please come in here for a moment there is something I wish to show you."

Tinougl feeling the buzz stood up and sheepishly went into the bedroom to see what she wanted and was slightly surprised she would have on a bath robe.

After he got into the master bedroom, Tinougl asked, "What did you want to show me?"

"This." Margot dropped the bathrobe to the floor revealing a movie stars body. It was indeed impressive. Margot walked over and shut and locked the door then walked up to Tinougl and softly kissed him on his lips and began to undress him.

At first, Tinougl was feeling a little shy and discomforted but as Margot worked his clothes off, she saw the little wet spot on his under garment and thus pulled it down and grabbed his erection and started performing fellatio on him. Tinougl didn't know what to do, he was feeling ecstasy. He didn't realize he had been drugged with a special narcotic *Damiana* that made men extremely exhilarated and psychologically elevated to the point he was throwing caution to the wind.

Tinougl would soon be acting with Margot not only tonight but in the studio tomorrow where her physical attraction to him created spontaneous energy towards him which Reladondo recognized as an award-winning performance. This movie trailer was quickly surpassing even the director's ambition by a large margin. Once in a great while does a stranger come into a studio and set it afire the way Tinougl was doing. If the studio knew he was a time travel spy, they would then really have one hell of a movie.

Tinougl then performed and soon gave Margot a symphony of allegros as her orgasms seemed endless.

Tinougl passed out and was in a deep sleep enjoying his neurological resplendence created by this wonderful creature.

The Butler and Maid were a combination security and public relations team that worked exclusively for Reladondo bon Scrafatorious. The Maid had the security code to unlock the door after observing the hidden video knew it was time to remove Margot to make sure there was no public scandal.

She went in and carefully awakened Margot who was sawing logs with her snoring and then placed her finger over her mouth to signify stay quiet please and helped her out of the bed and gathered up all her clothes and took her out of the room and helped her dress and fix her hair to make it appear it was just a social visit and no hanky panky went on.

Margot knew how the game was played and was grateful for the exit strategy and soon left the Penthouse with a big smile because her memory of her lingering orgasm didn't fade any time soon.

In another fifteen minutes she was in her own Penthouse lying down in her own bed falling to sleep fast after the Maid gave her those wonderful sleep inducers and was out until she was awakened in the morning.

Margot passed Tinougl who was getting into the elevator all sweaty from his five-mile run. She didn't quite remember all his muscles from the previous night, but she could see his splendid build with the swetty clothes clinging to his body. The image was truly better than any wet tee shirt contest.

"I see you are out exercising already?"

"I have to stay in shape."

"I'm glad you stay in shape," Margot said with an evil grin."

Tinougl had some remorse about screwing around behind his wife's back, but he realized he had been drugged the night before and all this was sanctioned by the puppet master who staged events to create an image and a reputation for a star that would increase public interest. As a spy he had been trained to spot ingredients in drinks in order to quickly get the antidotes to overcome potential hazardous situations. As he reflected on the previous night, he now knew his drink had a peculiar taste like a drink that had been spiked with a *Damiana* substance. He also knew rich men often drugged women with *Damiana* to have their way with them as it effected men and women in the same way creating chemical reactions in the pleasure center of the brain and stimulated sexual promiscuity.

Tinougl took a quick shower to clean off the swet, then put on his swimming attire and made his way down to the pool. There was Margot sitting with Reladondo snacking on her morning breakfast.

Tinougl gave his polite salutations to Reladondo and Margot, then excused himself and got into the large swimming pool and started his thirty laps. Even though he had just run five miles he swam with conviction. *Was it the regret he now felt that pushed him so hard* he wondered?

He made up his mind he would not fall into Margot's traps again during these three days. He realized how venomous she could be. The last thing in the world he needed now was a fatal attraction.

Margot watched with utter fascination as Tinougl worked out with extreme endurance. Finally, after his thirtieth lap he was drained of any strength left. Reladondo knew precisely what Tinougl would do next. He would be going in for a massage" so he would be able to function today.

While Tinougl was gone, getting his massage, Reladondo who

knew Margot quite well because he had sex with her a few times himself asked, "Did you fuck him last night?"

"If I did it's none of your business. You have a dirty mind Reladondo."

"Tinougl is my business. We can't afford any scandals with him right now."

Margot knew Reladondo quite well and knew she didn't want to end up like a few other starlets that simply vanished when they crossed Reladondo.

"Don't worry about me. I'm discrete and I do not broadcast my lovelife."

"Do me a favor and do not crawl in bed with him again tonight."

"What if he asks?"

"Something tells me he's not going to ask."

"Fine then, don't worry about it."

"I never worry."

Those word frightened Margot who would never get close to Tinougl again because she knew vividly the massage, she just received was her final warning.

But in her private thoughts she was overwhelmed with Tinougl's body, and she wanted him more now than before. But she also was a smart girl and wasn't going to piss off her meal ticket, Reladondo bon Scrafatorious who could also make her disappear.

The next few days were very similar to this day, except the two security men stationed at Tinougl's Penthouse door directed the half dozen starlets who came to visit and get laid that Tinougl wasn't available. When asked where he was, they responded, "Are you writing a book or something?"

Finally, they were done with the video trailer and Margot who acted the scenes with Tinougl felt herself was turning into a bitch in heat every time she got near Tinougl, and her body language flashed that lust and desire nicely into the film recordings they made. The soundtrack produced had superior psychoacoustics quality that helped bundle the trailer into a masterpiece.

CHAPTER THIRTY-FIVE
A NEW SONG

While Tinougl was traveling back to Konhagar the video trailer was being released and it too was soon engulfed in a chaotic almost calamity of affectuous desires of vast numbers of women, and four days later when it reached Tartarnite Empire Capital City Santorini de Shénshèng, the three Barracuda saw it advertised with blockbuster creations. They were stunned and Spicey along with Schemer were crying in their beers so to speak.

Spicey wondered if she should take a trip to Konhagar and try to make contact with Tinougl, but she also knew her husband was a vindictive prick and if she went chasing after Tinougl, he might do something like hire organized crime to hurt him. What saved Tinougl's life was the fact Spicey cared for him enough that she didn't want harm to come to him, so she stayed away.

That night the glorious couple were center of attraction in the Grand Xenis Hotel Restaurant as the manager was all smiles again and Casandra had greatly put a lot of smiles on guests faces as they passed her working as the Hotel Receptionist. The manager was uttely astonished to have such an incredibly beautiful receptionist there. His boses were also greatly impressed by the way the esthetics of the hotel were evolving. They appreciated this manager who was now making them lots of profit.

The couple sat down like before with the main production executives and Reladondo.

Tonight, was a special night because Mòlìhuā would soon swoon Tinougl with her three new recordings and actually had some quality practice time with the female singer that was with the band performing. They worked their act out together at the studio so when they appeared on stage for the first song, they were more than ready for prime time.

After Reladondo introduced Mòlìhuā, the beautiful singer made the announcement, "Tonight I have a new song that I will sing to someone special to me."

The place was packed, and the band had practiced this first song with the studio orchestra, so instead of taking a break they simply augmented the orchestra including providing the pianist who performed incredibly well.

Mòlìhuā announced the song title "How to fix a broken wing."

As Tinougl listened to the song, he wondered, *did I break her wing with my conduct at the Grand Espranza de Topaxh Hotel night club Galant Simulacrum?*

The band and the orchestra resonated the room with their combined sound. Tinougl was soon transfixed on every word Mòlìhuā sang:

What to write such a beautiful woman who humbles us mere mortals with her exquisitee features?

Something tells me she has a broken wing,

I wish I knew the magic to heal her heart and if I could only sing.

She is like a goddess, that transcends my thoughts to ethereal plateaus, where nobody knows, and only the luckiest goes.

Out in the galaxy is some creatures I know could fix her wing, but only I can heal her heart,

I have no magic potions,

I only have what is deep inside of me.

Some people might be confused between the essence of creativity and celestial art.

But for her, I do love her but do not really know her.

How can that be?

As the tendrils of essence passes through the cosmos and we detect those faint voices that only a few can hear,

You awaken and realize her beauty is so near,

Yet so far away.

You can't touch her physically, yet you can still love her.

So, what do you give her?

There is nothing you can give her but a piece of your heart and hope she cherishes it,

For you have traveled far and your own heart has had many ruptures,

That's life.

But if you can mend her broken wing,

She will soon learn; she has nothing to fear.

She loves you dear.

This song hit Tinougl like a ton of bricks. He now was remorseful and full of regret. He wished the hell he had never done it with Margo. Should he confess to her? Would she forgive him? It was a bridge to far for him to cross. His shame would soon mold his future as he knew he was a good spy and should never have allowed himself to be defeated by such a flimsy trick that is often applied by members of the opposite sex in honey pot schemes for clandestine activity.

He was also unaware that Reladondo had saved him but soon regretted it because he too wanted to taste the essence of this beautiful creature, Mòlìhuā. But since Tinougl delivered Casandra to him, as a gentleman he would defer to Tinougl to recapitulate his love for this beautiful singer.

The magical evening continued and finally after performing the third new recording, Mòlìhuā whispered in Tinougl's ear, "I want you to take me back up to the Penthouse and turn me into a naughty girl."

Mòlìhuā was ready and their separation for a few days greatly increased her desires for the man she knew only he could turn her on like he had witchcraft or magic ability.

CHAPTER THIRTY-SIX

AS TIME FADES AWAY

The movies and the singing performances continued for the couple who lived quite a successful life. After a few years, after Mòlìhuā gave birth to their two children, Tinougl decided he would play Mr. Mom and Mòlìhuā could continue with her singing career. The farmhouse was getting a little too small for the six of them so they hired contractors too add on more rooms and since money was no longer an issue, a large pool was put in so that Tinougl could swim in the mornings because he was slowing down and could not run as hard as he did as a younger man. His hair was starting to gray, and his two children eventually were reaching the age where they were going off to school and charting their own lives.

Tinougl was lucky he lived with Mòlìhuā's parents otherwise he wouldn't have survived. While he was swimming, Morgan and Karenna were at the pool's edge getting ready to get in and swim for a couple minutes right in front of them Tinougl stopped face down and didn't move. In a panic they used all their strength and were able to haul him out of the water before he drowned. In a short time, a helicopter ambulance arrived and took him to a nearby hospital. He had a three-dimensional scan of his body, and the doctor discovered the bad news.

Tinougl had a brain tumor, and it was well progressed.

After the medical consulations the doctor informed Mòlìhuā that Tinougl probably had one to two months left and the tumor was inoperable.

Mòlìhuā was devastated. She took Tinougl home in a Limo and would spend every day with him until he passed and cut off all her singing engagements.

Mòlìhuā decided to leave the kids at school at remote planets as to not disrupt their lives. She would inform them when they returned at the end of the school year what happened, and they would have a memorial.

The expanded farmhouse was larger, and their bedroom was was at the far end so Tinougl knew he could have a private discussion with Mòlìhuā where her parents could not hear them with the door closed.

He seemed happy and Mòlìhuā was trying her best to not break down. Then he decided to inform her the truth and an idea he had.

"What I'm going to tell you may seem rather strange, but you know me, we have been together all these years and everything I said came to be right?

"Yes, that's right."

"I have not revealed myself to you of who I really am and where I came from."

Tinougl then gave her the details of how he is a *time travel spy* and had actually accomplished his mission because his friend, organized crime boss Aristapara discovered the information for him he was sent to obtain.

"I'm sure the time machine is still there. I would like to go there get in it and go back to the future where I know they can cure me. I'll then try to come back to about this time."

At first Mòlìhuā thought Tinougl might be hallucinating which the doctor warned of. But after lengthy discussions and vivid detail about the future and several other things, Mòlìhuā who was so desperate for a cure that wasn't going to happen thought, *if he wants to spend his final days on this hallucination, I'll just play along since it will make him happy.*

After telling Mòlìhuā'sd parents a sweet lie she was taking Tinougl on a vacation to see his world and a few other places before he passed, they were on that high-speed transport making their way to Tartarnite Empire Capital City Santorini de Shénshèng. Tinougl wanted to stay where they met in the Cuìlǜ Resort Hotel. Since they were VIP's they had no problem getting room 1414 even though they were offered a Penthouse just for being there.

Tinougl was hoping that Guāiqiǎo and Tondron would still be there but assumed they would have been replaced a long time ago when new technology was implemented.

To his utter amazement, Tondron welcomed them back!

Somethings never change.

Tinougl only brought his backpack from many years ago. He had a few items with him to show his masters if the time machine still worked and he made it back alive. After saying their final goodbye Tinougl arranged for a Limo to take Mòlìhuā and himself up to where he hid the time machine years ago. His satellite fix on the location allowed him to lead Mòlìhuā directly to the spot while the Limo Driver waited for them. Tinougl gave the Limo driver instructions, "I'm going to a spot in the forest. I'm probably going to spend the night there making some bird observations. Mòlìhuā will come back to the Limo in a bit, take her back to the Hotel. She will come back and pick me up when I'm ready."

"Sure, thing mister."

It did not take much effort to get to the spot and the forest cover had put another few layers of debris on top the time machine, but Tinougl had no problem removing all the debris. He hoped it still worked because it meant the difference between life and death and now, he could finally complete his mission, though he would prefer to have remained healthy and stayed.

He did the proper sequence of actions and the time machine turned on and the access hatch opened.

With a heavy heart and hope for the future he hugged Mòlīhuā one more time and kissed her as they both had tears flowing down.

Stand back about twenty feet because this thing will emit a lot of energy when it takes me back to the future.

Then he said, "I love you and I will do whatever it takes to get me back here. Do not underestimate me."

"I've never underestimated you nor shall I ever."

"Good. Just think of this as a trip I'm going on. Tell your family I'm in a care center where a doctor is working on me who thinks there is a possible way of treating me. I will be back."

"All right, honey."

"Now step back so I can go."

Mòlīhuā was fully animated and somewhat in shock. This was the most bizarre thing in her lifetime. Nothing compares. She stood back twenty some steps and turned back towards Tinougl and the time machine. He waved to her, stepped into the time machine, and sat down and closed the hatch. Soon there was an eerie and funny sound unlike anything she ever heard in her lifetime. The time machine started emmiting strange patterns of light and soon the light waves resonated with the sound and the entire thing vanished. Tinougl was now gone to the future.

Mòlīhuā stood there and waited. She didn't know if he would ever come back, but she knew she would not bet against him.

Chapter

Thirty-Seven

Time Travel Spy's Next Mission

Cocilglu, the psychological mapper and psychoanalyst had recorded the conversation that took place over several days interspursed with trips to the medical lab where they detected a very small tumor, nothing like what he departed in the time machine with. Small tumors turn into big tumors, so Tinougl was operated on and with proton imaging they easily destroyed the tumor prevening future growth. Tinougl was healed. With his debriefing done and his vital intelligence that was actionable delivered he was soon offered another mission.

The briefing officer explained, this is one of the most critical time missions we have ever performed, and it is probably the most dangerous. You will have to volunteer to go. Nobody will be coerced into going.

"Where's the destination?" Tinougl asked.

"It's in the Azure-Tiānkōng of Konhagar," the director responded knowing some of Tinougl's recent time travel mission concerned finding out information about the radicals and troublemakers living in Azure-Tiānkōng.

"I'll go under one condition."

"And what's that?"

"After the mission is completed, you have to agree to send me back 480 years so that I can be with Mòlíhuā and spend the rest of my life with her."

"That's an extraordinary request."

"I'm sure you will not get any volunteers to go on your mission, especially when they find out all the details of how seriously dangerous Azure-Tiānkōng area is. If you want me to go that's my price."

"I'll have to take that up with the management."

"I'm going home for the rest of the day. Don't contact me again if you do not agree. Consider this my resignation if you do not agree to my terms."

"We've invested so much into your training and preparation; you can't just walk out on us like this."

"Just like you said, this mission has a 50/50 chance of surviving, it's extremely dangerous and I could get killed in the process. I'm not willing to take those odds especially in a place like Azure-Tiānkōng where they kill outsiders immediately upon detection, unless you are willing to send me back to the past like I requested."

"Go on home. I'll talk to my boss about it and see what he has to say."

Tinougl left the office foreboding, but happy he was now cured so that if he went back to the past, he could be with Mòlíhuā the rest of their lives.

It kind of felt weird looking into the mirror having aged twenty years then back as he was when it all started.

Everything was untouched as if he never left, but he knew otherwise.

The biggest mission of Tinougl's life was coming. That's what it would take to get back to Mòlìhuā. He was in a desperate situation that could only be resolved in the face of significant risk. He had the advantage over the enemy. If he died in the mission, it wouldn't matter because at least he would be spared the pain of being separated from his true love for the rest of his life, even though she lived 500 years ago.

Tinougl had plenty of time to kill so he decided to go to a research library and see if he could find any information of life and times 500 years ago.

Even though there was massive destruction of the planet in the past mega war, there were pockets of information saved, depending on which planet the information came from as there were planets that came out of the intergalactic strife with little or no damage.

The libraries data terminals were connected to vast resiovores of information. The problem was for security reasons there were no outside connectivity. All printed materials were scarce and were not permitted outside the library so if you wanted to read it, you needed to do it in the library under the care and concern of the caretakers who were available to answer questions, assist in research but most importantly, keep an eye on activity to prevent the materials from disappearing.

Tinougl who was twenty years more experienced than he was just a few days ago, was a patient and deliberate man. He had experienced true love and the extravagance of movie starlets and other interesting people he could now go research and attempt discovery.

Unfortunately, information concerning the planet most furthest from the Empire was the scarcest. It stood to reason because of it't remoteness.

On the otherhand, the entertainment capitol of the Empire, Espranza de Topaxh, was and still is the hub of entertainment and was virtually untouched during the war because of it's strict neutrality. It also was the chief location for the wealthy and the criminals to hide their wealth.

Espranza de Topaxh Banking Numbered accounts kept the government out of people's business. They didn't mind paying taxes; they just didn't like the criminal investigators using them as a boondoggle and a way to foster creeping investigations that often doubled in scope during the typical witch hunt and fishing expeditions.

There had been vast amounts of entertainment that came from Espranza de Topaxh because Reladondo bon Scrafatorious built up the entertainment business unlike anyone before or after.

Five hundred years ago was the perfect search because of all the major amounts of productions Reladondo performed.

Tinougl started searching about 450 years prior and started working his way backwards. Eventually he discovered Clara bon Xìngyùn who was so enthralled watching Wánměi de Mòlìhuā she virtually had her mouth wired shut and starved herself until the pounds came off and after the help of a little cosmetic surgery to trim off all the excess sking that resulted, she slowly turned into a Diva. She actually turned into a beautiful princess. *I wonder if Reladondo bon Scrafatorious had a hand in all that?*

Tinougl was a little apprehensive now as he feared what might have happened to Mòlìhuā as she got on with her life after his departure. It was like spying on a lover in the past. *People did it, but did it really matter?*

As Tinougl drilled down softly and peeled that onion by onion he looked for anything connected to Mòlìhuā, and he didn't find anything until he got close to his departure year. *I wonder what happened to her.*

Before he even found a single entry on Mòlìhuā he already seen numerous mentions of himself as he was a famous actor at the time he left. But he too suddenly disappeared. Although he knew why, he traveled back to the future.

Mòlìhuā disappeared about the same time he did in history. He hoped she didn't do something like go home and kill herself. Lovers have done that before when they lost the love of their life.

There was a lot of entries of Reladondo bon Scrafatorious, but that was expected. Soon he came across something that stunned him. They actually had some digital recordings that Mòlìhuā made, and he could download the music to his personal communicator.

It took about fifteen minutes to get all the files, then he closed his login to the library data terminal access and stood up and went home.

He sat back in his reclining chair and transferred the files to his home entertainment system and started playing all those songs that Mòlìhuā recorded. He cried himself to sleep. He missed that woman with all his heart. He felt so lucky to have spent the time with her. His profound love for her would never end.

Morning came and soon his communicator lit up.

It was no other than Kovloor, the time capsulee operator.

"Good morning."

"Sorry if I'm disturbing you Tinougl, but we are going to have a meeting about the new mission an an hour. The director wants you to attend and he wants to talk to you."

"Alright, I'll be there." Tinougl replied feeling reluctant but also knowing he had to get his life back on track and there was no need to be melancholic about a situation out of his control."

Tinougl did his morning routine and drank a vitamen and energy drink not knowing what the director would bestow upon him this morning.

When he arrived at work and into the conference room, Tinougl realized everyone was staring at him.

The director who was a pompass ass soon marched into the conference room and took his position at the end of the table and said, "Mission V35 is a go. Commence phase one immediately. Tinougl, I want you to meet me in my office in five minutes."

Tinougl was quite animated and was extremely curious how this would affect him. There were potentially four other time travel spies in the slot to make this mission, though it was strictly a volunteer mission. What Tinougl was not aware of is after receiving their briefings the other four spies opted out after saying they didn't believe it was possible to do what was being asked and they didn't want to risk their lives on an ill-conceived plan.

Tinougl found himself sitting across from the pompass director in a private meeting. The room was bug sniffed and certified for time discussions.

"I looked at your request and did a lot of classified evaluation with several of my analysts. After careful review it appears that you fulfilled your mission requirements to not affect the fabric of time during your last mission. In doing so you built in great trust with us."

"Thank you."

"If I permit you to take that one-way tip back 480 years ago, will you assure me you will not tamper with the fabric of time."

"When I go back 480 years so that I can be with Mòlìhuā, I plan on remaining on the family farm and enjoy my last years with her."

"You turned into a movie star back then, you could easily influence people."

"I made my last movie and retired and became Mr. Mom to be with my kids. Mòlìhuā continued to work which was okay by me because she was an artist and performance was in her veins.

"Alright I am willing to take the risk on that. But I want you to know this is a very dangerous assignment and you may get killed doing it and we wouldn't then be able take you back 480 years if you get killed in the mission."

"That's alright. I'm willing to take my chances."

"Okay this is your assignment once I give you the assignment, you know the rules of the game, the contract is in effect, and I can't cancel it."

"I understand all that."

"Alright. We will transport you back 250 years and provide you with an explosive device to assassinate Lord Ansator of the Konhagar Empire."

"Isn't that tampering with the fabric of time."

"The assassination is important."

"Why."

"We expect in a few weeks the Konhagar will successfully test the launch of their first-time machine and can then rearrange the past which means they can rearrange our future. If we wipe Lord Ansator out, it will kill their time travel program."

"You are right, the odds are barely 50/50."

"You agree to go?"

Under the condition I requested plus I want one other thing."

"What's that?"

"Alright I want you to invite Kovloor, Miltonzy, Cocilglu, and Remlesfy to come in the conference room with us and inform them my time travel ietnerary and give them permissions now to send me back 480 years the same time I came back from my last mission."

"Sure, if that's what you want."

"That's what I want."

In a few minutes, Kovloor, Miltonzy, Cocilglu, and Remlesfy were seated in the conference room with the director and Tinougl.

"Here's the holographic contract with Tinougl with my voice and facial signature. As soon as Tinougl completes mission V35 you are to immediately send him back 480 years to the exact time and place he returned from his last mission."

"Understood," Kovloor said speaking for the others present in the room.

After a few weeks of training and obtaining materials to be used in the mission Tinougl was ready. He had no fear because he would rather die than continue living without Mòlìhuā.

The day of destiny was upon them as Tinougl was escorted in the time machine and just like before prepped and in readiness condition. During his weeks of training, he worked out extremely hard. Instead of five miles and 30 laps it was 10 miles and 60 laps. The trainers recognized he was on a mission with passion and would give it his upmost to succeed. They had no idea how strong love can be and how people would rearrange their lives and go on hazardous missions just to pave the way to spend some more brief moments with the person they loved. The power of love was the strongest thing in the arsenal.

The countdown began and soon Tinougl was delivered to another desolate and remote location. He had his backpack and a few items that would seem innocuous if the were discovered. These ancient people that lived 250 years ago had no idea of the sweeping changes of chemistry that happened and what appeared to be a half bottle of hair wash, mouth wash bottle and a tube of toothpaste would create a deadly witches brew with amazing explosive power once mixed. All he had to do was be at the right time and right place to administer the kill.

This was a rough area where he was delivered with an ancient communicator that would work at the present time with stolen identity and accounts.

His facial recognition was altered slightly to match the black marketeer he portrayed. Thanks to his years as a movie star in another time and place, he was the perfect actor that his contemporaries had no idea he was capable of. Such acting skills would save his life and put him on a course of his ultimate destination if he didn't die in the process. Either way he was okay because as a dead person he would no longer spend hours regretting leaving Mòlìhuā behind. But he really didn't have much choice it was either go back to the future or die from that brain tumor he was now cured of.

The ruthless leader Lord Ansator of the Konhagar empire was identified and infiltrated only because Tinougl used organized crime boss Aristapara to find the roots to this fledgeling secret cell that was so discrete the Tartarnite Empire didn't know existed until it became apparent, they were were very close to building a successful time machine that would change everything. The disaster of the war four hundred years ago would be pale compared to what forestall in the future to the Empire.

Since they had no way of finding where this time machine research lab was secretly located in time to prevent it's launch, their only recourse was to change the fabric of time, a strict violation of their own rules. The governing council of the Time Travel Directorate decided they had no way out of this conundrum besides killing the man who would ultimately be the force behind it's development. They determined his assassination would push them back at least 100 years in development and give them enough time to work at dismantling the organization so they would not be a threat to the Empire. This time distance would not spare them. Another fact Tinougl would not learn in the process is he was being sent to kill his great great great grandson.

Tinougl had thus altered the fabric of time when he slept with Margo bon Srofendorn and created the illegitimate child she soon put in an orphanage where he grew up not knowing who his parents were and had a chip on his shoulder and joined the revolutionaries that Aristapara the organized crime boss helped identify including the sources of money to fuel the revolution. Bankers play both sides of a dispute such as Frederick bon Stoffengar. The impoverished revolutionaries would never be able to payback their debts. The bankers didn't count on it. They counted on bleeding the Empire to not only get their money back from the revolutionaries but also multiply the borrowing required by the regional administration to contain the threat.

The time machine had to arrive far from anyone. This desolate location existed where even the nomads didn't travel. There was nothing here to attract population or anything else for the matter. It was once part of the planet teaming with life that was bliterated in the great war almost one hundred and fifty years before.

The population of the planet was slowly coming back but it would be another 50 to 100 years before the population grew large enough to terraform this area using modern development techniques.

There was enough rubble and debris lying around to hide the time travel machine which was absolutely necessary for Tinougl to do before he left the area going due east to his target, a farm house that the future Lord Ansator of the Konhagar empire would soon visit with a dozen of his mercenaries to be with his wife before he went off into a pivitol battle that would once and for all wreak havoc on government forces to force their departure out of the great valley so the peoples could move on with self determination and not the burdensome control by government forces.

There would be too much firepower by these very capable mercenaries to take on directly. Tinougl would quietly kill a couple lookouts and place the weapon next to the house that would pulverize it with a massive explosion leaving no living persons inside.

Due to the extreme danger, Tinougl could only travel in the dead of night careful to keep an eye out for dangerous wild animals that would love to eat his flesh. His communicator had some secret circuitry built in that fed into the communicator that had sonic detectors and proximity sensors that fed his ear bud giving him heads up to external threats. The communicator was placed in a compartment in his clothes that protected it as well as prevented him losing it in the dark. All his cues were audio as to not deter him visual integration and sensory vigilance.

At the careful pace Tinougl took; his most significant need was water. The sensors in his communicator would find nearby water if it were there. He might have to dig down a few feet to get at that water that would be muddy at first, but he had measures to deal with that as well. Nothing would be better than a random thunderstorm that would fill a stream and he could refill his water bottles. At the velocity Tinougl was traveling, it would take three days to get to the target since he could only travel in the darkness of night, the anticipated time of the visit based on old records.

The revolutionaries assumed that this location was at such an extreme distance from society, it would be the ultimate safe house. They were absolutely correct until the innovation of time travel came about, and future generations read their biographies. Time travel was a curse to future generations that loved to bloviate about their past with an army of pompous phrases moving over the landscape in search of an idea.

Thanks to time travel, current generation of heros would be future demons. *But how far would they go?* Tinougl wondered.

If streams and valleys went eastword enough, Tinougl took them to avoid too much climbing and risk detection from the horizon. Staying down low was the best policy even if it took a little longer.

During the first night there were a half dozen wild animal scares, and they too hid out during the day and did most of their hunting at night.

The proximity detectors saved his life a couple times. Using sophisticated sound processing capabilities, the proximity detectors could warn Tinougl the speed and distance to a threat. His 18-inch-long thick knife was ready to slice. On the second night a group of six wild hogs approached and seeing a lone figure in the moonlight hastened their attack, thanks to the alerts and the skill of a deadly martial arts practitioner the knife went right down the middle of the skull of the first hog killing it rapidly and soon another three were dead and not moving before the trailing hogs procrastinated because their buddies were not moving. This was a blessing because Tinougl knew wild animals could smell blood for miles and in the daylight when all those other vicious creatures smelled the rotting carcuss in direct sunlight it would attract their attention and soon there would be an orgasmic like feast as many of these other animals came in for their fare share. Even their buddies took bites out of their shanks after watching some of the wild bird picking away at the carcass.

On the final night before the attack the communicator reported there was water dead ahead. This small Oasis out in the middle of nowhere was selected not only for it's distance from society but also it had natural springs and fresh running water near the shelter that was very nicely camoflauged.

Having that water meant he could make it back to the time machine and eventually get back to Mòlìhuā.

Many men would never go against twelve others especially knowing they were rugged fighters and had engaged the best armies of the Empire.

It was all about the element of surprise. All he had to do is swiftly kill a couple sentries, blow up the house and get the hell out of there.

He would make his attack in the middle of the night when vigilance decrement was at it's highest. His hope is one or both centuries would doze off. He had to look very carefully for trip wires. Hopefully his proximity detector would help. The last 100 yards would be on his hands and knees which he planned for and wore knee pads and nice thick cloves with super grip. That 18inch killer dagger would work handsomely killing the sentry like it did those hogs.

Mòlìhuā was worse than a narcotic in his mind now. It easily overcame any possible fear. His lifelong commitment to physical fitness now paid off as he was once again twenty years younger. He could easily sprint ten miles or swim 30 long laps around a large swimming pool and have sex four times a day.

He had another advantage, technology. He didn't want to run the batteries down on his night vision goggles that were far superior to any photonics these rugged fighters could possibly possess.

On his very slow creep to the two centuries, he eventually got his fixes on them. Now and then they would talk back and forth. Part of a good spy's training is to mimic a voice so that you could temporarily convince an enemy they were talking to a friendly in the cover of darkness.

Tinougl paid close attention to the sentry closest to him and soon mentally developed the dialect he would use to answer the enemy should there be any sudden chatter.

The last 30 yards took and hour of slow creeping along. The chatter happened about once ever twenty or thirty minutes, just two guys trying to stay awake through the night and their night watches. The last ten feet were the absolute slowest. Tinougl patiently waited dead in his tracks waiting for the expected chatter and eventually it happened.

One sentry asked, "Do you think we'll go into town this week for supplies?"

"It's possible we are getting low on supplies." The othe responded. That was it. Tinougl move swifly and did the silent deadly killing and carefully dragged the body behind some rocks where he would not be seen in case something went wrong with the explosives and they all came out looking they would not know which way to look.

Tinougl had to wait in this spot until the next chatter session and soon it happened.

"What are you going to do when we go to town."

"Don't know." Tinougl responded with a good copy of the dead man's voice.

Through the night vision he saw the other sentry on the side of the house turn around and appeared to be looking down a rough trail that probably headed towards the town. With his back turned towards Tinougl it made the silent kill much more efficient, which pleased him. Soon he was dead too and just laid down by the wood framed house. Tinougl went to the back of the house he guessed was by the sleeping quarters and he was very accurate in the assessment because of the window and put the final chemical in the explosive container with the three-minute timer and set it on the eave of a closed window with a fabric curtain blocking out any vision. From that position it would be a deadly kill as everyone inside would be incinerated in a flash. He had to walk silently away carefully looking for trip wires and observed a couple and worked past them and was soon 100 yeards away and then stepped behind a rock formation to wait and see the results. He had been counting for three minutes and knew it was about time the detonator went off. Sure, enough it did. The house was soon a gigantic fireball. Because of the revolutionairies stored amo and explosives right behind the wall he didn't know existed, the explosion was about ten times more than he expected and was glad he was behind that rock formation as the shrapnel and other fragments came whizzing by at great velocity. Had he been on the road he would have been cut down.

The explosion also had the effect of detonating all the trip wires and he heard a man cry out in agony as he was cut down by the trip wire. A chil went up his spine there was another sentry there he hadn't spotted who was probably sound asleep who got the crap scared out of him from the explosion he escaped barely by being on the other side of a large bolder. Unfortunately, he was so rattled he took off running like a scared deer and hit one of those trip wires and was soon bleeding to death.

As soon as the explosions died down, Tinougl started walking back to the time machine walking as abruptly as his body would let him. He knew he had to get as far away from that building as possible because government investigators would soon be on the scene since the huge explosion could see for miles was most likely detected by government forces who were looking for this group who had done the upmost damage in gorilla warfare fighting.

Tinougl knew time was at the essence and in the twilight when visibility was much better, he followed his locator beacon that gave a pitch if he were heading in the right direction and changed if he turned away accidentally. He wanted to finish this mission so badly during twilight hours before sunrise he was running at fifteen miles per hour just like he had on his gym clothes and spooked a group of wild animals that were chewing on the carcass he had left behind when he killed four of the wild hogs.

Every time he got a mile closer to the time machine his communicater gave him a new distance report. A little after sunrise he was within striking range of the time machine and looking back in the distance coul see the remaining smoke coming from the fire of the remains of the burning house over the horizon.

He knew if he kept going, he could leave this time today. He would be extra vigilant looking for objects and any possible signs of investigators.

Lucky for Tinougl there were plenty of investigators, but they were combing over the remains of the blown-up house where the occupants were discentigrated into a million pieces with the huge plasma of the bomb Tinougl set which cooked off all the ammo. Pieces of shell casings littered the area. They didn't know how but it seemed the rebel's ammo dump had blown up leaving a twelve-foot hole in the ground. Not much of the house remained. The only reason why they knew a house stood here is they were going to send in a squad to check it out, who would have probably been killed by the rebels had they attempted to attack them with all the firepower they had at their disposal.

Tinougl used every ounce of energy left in his body to keep going. He was no longer running on fumes; they were long gone. It was pure will and the nagging question: *How bad do you want it?*

By noon he was a short distance away from the time machine and with great super effort eventually got there and started clearing the debris off it then he heard the noise coming in fast from the distance. It was definitely a helicopter sound hugging the terrain to avoid handheld missiles that would easily kill them if they were up in the air.

It was now or never and Tinougl didn't care. He would rather be dead than stuck in this time zone. He released the top of the time machine and started it up and shut the top. The helicopter popped up and saw the time machine and was about to shoot a missile when the pilot saw the strange colorization and the phenomenal light waves going out in pulsating patterns like he never seen before and just before he pulled the trigger the light went away, and the object was gone!

All caught on gun camera video. Intel would be going over ths for a long- long time. Did this thing have something to do with the house blowing up?

When Tinougl hit the blue button to take him home to the present time, his vital indications showed he was near death as any living person had ever been before.

Then suddenly the time machine top opened and there was Kovloor looking down at him all smiles.

CHAPTER

THIRTY-EIGHT

THE FINAL DEBRIEFING AND THE FINAL TIME TRAVEL

Tinougl was soon in the office with Cocilglu sipping on a glass of Fonnegar elixir in his preliminary debriefing. This time it was happiness and not the misery he displayed when he returned the first time.

"You are all chipper this time. I suppose that means you didn't meet another woman and fall in love."

"That's right I got the job done and now I can go home for the final time."

"Any problems during the mission?"

"No. The planning was perfect. INTEL finally got it right the first time."

"This was a critical mission; it had a huge impact on society for the future."

"Yea I can imagine a madman with a time machine weapon could be very destructive."

The Psychiatrist decided for Tinougl's better mental health he would not let him know he killed his great great great grandson he didn't know existed.

After Tinougl finished the drink feeling great because the time machine restored him back to his original body before he went on the mission.

Tinougl was then ushered into the director's office, and they had their final meeting.

"You fulfilled your end of the bargain. So, I'm going to prove to you I am also good on my word. I wanted to personally thank you for saving us from the destructive power of a mad man with a time machine."

"I appreciate that it means a lot to me."

"When you arrived and we took you through the process and had you remove all your clothes and get deloused and changed into official Time Force uniform, we obtained what you wore when you arrived. it's sitting there on the table. We are going to send you back to the exact time and location you returned from four hundred and eighty years ago. I assume you want to be dressed the same way you left."

"Yes, that would be kind of handy."

"Go ahead and change your clothes and I'll escort you to a time machine that is now ready to launch you back to the past."

With the biggest smile on his face, Tinougl quickly changed and put those clothes back on. The only difference would be he would return looking younger which he didn't mind. At least that's what he thought.

"Alright, I'm ready to go."

The director walked Tinougl all the way to the time machine and after Tinougl climbed inside, the director said, "If you do not plan on using the time machine, would you mind sending it back to us right away."

"Sure, I do not mind at all."

They shook hands and in another ten minutes those toroids were cycling in cosmic frequencies and the time machine took Tinougl back to the forest."

Mòlìhuā now crying as if it were the saddest day of her life turned around to see what all the noise was about and suddenly there was Tinougl standing there by a time machine and he said, "Where do you think you are going?"

Mòlìhuā ran back to Tinougl and threw her arms around him sobbing like a little girl and held on for dear life. After she regained her composure, she asked the obvious question: "Did they fix you?"

"Yes, the tumor was removed, and all my brain functions are back to normal."

"Did they die your hair you look younger."

"We need to talk about that, but for now, I need to hide this thing, can't let it be found."

Between the two of them, the time machine was covered up nicely with debris from the forest where it would accumulate a lot more.

They walked out to the road and the Limo driver was still there thinking the woman would not be back for a while from the sound of it but it's okay because he was being paid well and his payments were coming in real time as each minute was billed to central banking and as soon as the trip was completed, the balance due of zero would be posted since the tirp and the tip were already paid.

They went back to the Cuìlǜ Resort Hotel and made up for lost time.

To give a plausible cover story, the couple concocted a story where they tried an ancient healer to gave Tinougl herbs which killed his tumor and his body slowly drained it away. They actually went by such a healer and took some of his tea to make Mòlìhuā look younger. It was a very old man. Tinougl who had a photographic memory now realized, this was one of the old men who was sitting at the park bench years ago.

"Excuse me sir but did you used to go to Santorini de Shénshèng Central Park with two other gentlemen next to the lake and sit together on a park bench?"

"Why yes I did."

"Are those two men still alive?"

"No, they are gone now."

"I'm sorry."

They stayed at the Cuìlǜ Resort Hotel for two weeks and on the last night, they were in the Dining Hall listening to a lackluster band. Tinougl wanted to hear Mòlìhuā sing so he summoned he waiter who approached and asked:

"What may I do for you Tinougl?"

"I would like to talk to the manager please."

"Sure, I will go get him, we'll be back in a few minutes."

Shortly the manager who Tinougl didn't know asked, "How can I help you sir?"

"Sir, you may not recognize me, but my screen name is Tinougl bon Brandenboynk and I'm a Espranza de Topaxh Academy Award winner."

"Now that you mention it yes, I recognize you and I watched all your movie holographs."

"This is my wife the singer Wánměi de Mòlìhuā."

"Oh yes I remember her too, fantastic voice, incredible success and you are still performing from what I understand."

"That is correct."

"What would you like me to do for you Tinougl?"

"Would it be possible for my wife to sing a song. She can play the piano while she sings in case the band doesn't know the song."

"I would love to hear her sing, let me as the band leader to take a short break as soon as this song is over, and I'll bring him over to your table and you can ask him if they know her songs."

"Thank you. I appreciate it."

"My pleasure. it's not every day we get to hear a famous singer in here."

The band finished the song a moment later and the manager walked up to the band leader and asked him to come to their table and he introduced them.

"Liángshuǎng, this is Tinougl and the lovely recording star Wánměi de Mòlìhuā. She has agreed to sing a song for us tonight and she can play the piano, if necessary, does your band know any of her songs?"

"Yes, we do. One of her songs is a classic and we get asked to perform it now and then and I think we are good at it."

"Which song is that?"

"Dǎkāi Wánměi de Liánhuā."

Tinougl jumped in and said, "That would be perfect."

"Would you like to sing it now?"

"I would love to."

Let me go get my band prepared and let them know what we are going to do then I will introduce you."

"Thank you Liángshuǎng."

True to his word, Liángshuǎng got the band ready and then he made the announcement. "Ladies and Gentlemen, we have a real honor tonight of having a recording star here to sing for us. Please let me introduce the lovely Wánměi de Mòlìhuā.

Since this was their last night before heading home and visiting the rigors of life, the two had fashion designers give them a makeover. Tinougl was his young self very strong and athletic but Mòlìhuā looked great with the makeover and designer dress and high heels. It was as if she stepped back in time twenty years.

Many people in the venue knew who she was and had heard her performances many times before and she was the last person they would expect here tonight. This resort hotel had seen better times.

Just before the music started playing Tinougl said to the manager, "Please have a seat and listen to this with me."

The manager said, "Thank you," and took a chair next to Tinougl so he too could look directly at Mòlìhuā.

The music started playing and Mòlìhuā started singing just as nicely as she did twenty years before. Right around the three-minute mark Tinougl's eyes watered up that song hit him hard every time. There was some psychological attraction to it he didn't recognize.

Had Tinougl discussed this situation with Cocilglu psychological mapper and psychoanalyst, the good doctor would have probably informed him that three-minute mark in the music is when you fell in love with her. That moment is indelibly etched into you mind or so it seemed.

Mòlìhuā suspected Tinougl would do this and to celebrate his recovery she poured her heart out in the singing. She had no idea he almost got himself killed just to do a mission to be with her again. His road back to her led through hell and back. And he was more than happy to make that journey because it gave him a second chance in life with the woman he loved.

The manager gazed back and forth a few times checking out Tinougl's reaction and saw the tears streaming down. It affected him as well.

The crowd was electrified and as soon as Mòlìhuā ended the song, the crowd came to their feet in thunderous applause. The manager was so grateful because he knew this one performance alone would bring back some clientele. He then started scheming in his mind to try to come up with some inducements to get them to stay over a few more days.

Mòlìhuā came back to the table after saying thank you a dozen times and multiple bows. It was if that one performance gave her back five years. Or was it the herbal tea?

"Why do you have to leave tomorrow?"

"We've been here two weeks."

"Any pressing things back home?"

"No, I stopped doing movies to play Mr. Mom raising our kids and she canceled her performance engagements so I could come here for some medical treatments."

"I hope everything worked out for you."

"Yes, I'm cured."

"We do have the best doctors here."

"I think the doctors where we came from mis-diagnosed it. We went to an ancient medicine doctor, and he gave me some herbal teas and I'm fine now."

"I'm glad that worked out for you."

"Thank you."

"Listen this is what I would like, and it may help her get back into the swing of things of performances again."

"What do you have in mind?"

"I'll move you up to a penthouse right now. Room service will move all your belongings and you get the Penthouse for free, just come here in the evening and sing a song or two."

Before Tinougl had a chance to intervene, Mòlìhuā said, "I have one condition."

"And what is that Madam?"

"I want the band to come in here a few hours before the Dining Hall opens for the dinner crowd and practice my songs with me so I can get them groomed up to sing at least a half dozen of my songs and be very professional about it."

"Sure, we'll do that."

"I also want the band members in black tie and the female singer in a designer dress. I want her given the same makeover as I get. And as part of that I want three dress changes for she and I during the night. Afterall if I'm going to perform, I want her to be smoking hot and we'll fill up your dining room."

"Madam you are true to my heart, I would love to do exactly everything you requested because I know it will be a smashing success."

"Thank you for believing in me. I will not disappoint you."

"I already know that."

"Say during the break ask the band leader if they can do another one of my songs, I'm ready to sing tonight if they are ready."

"Mòlìhuā, it will be my greatest pleasure."

During the next break the band leader Liángshuǎng came to the table and said, Mòlìhuā I think we can do 'Bǎochí wéixiǎo Even if the Sun Isn't Shining'."

"Good, I'll be ready to sing it with your band in your next set. And I want your singer to sing it with me. She has a good voice and will resonate my sound nicely. I know it will be slightly cumbersome for her, but I'm sure we'll get it done."

"I'll let her know."

The manager decided he would stick around because it sounded like another song was coming right up.

"What would you guys like to drink?"

"Lǐzǐ Guavastrian Elixir," Mòlìhuā said.

"Give me what she's having," Tinougl added.

"I'll be back with your drinks momentarily," the manager walked over to the band leader and said, "Play a couple of your songs to give me and the guests time to have a drink. I'll come up and introduce Mòlìhuā just before she sings."

"Understand, we'll play two songs and pause."

The manager went over to the bartender and said, "Give me three Lǐzǐ

Guavastrian Elixirs for our guests and myself."

"Coming right up."

"In the span of one minute the three drinks were made to utter perfection and poured into three glasses and the bartender put them on a tray for the manager who took over to the table and personally served the two guests."

The waitress beat feet to the table and the manager handed her the tray and said, "Thank you."

The band started playing and the manager and his guests continued their conversation not talking to loud to offend the crowd or the band. The band knew these were VIP's so if they wanted to talk, that was ok."

"You know Mòlìhuā got her start up on that stage in this hotel."

"She did?"

"Yes. We left here together and started our life living with her parents, and still do. We added to the farmhouse because it was too small for her parents and our kids. We are still there even though I made movies and she recorded songs."

"How's life on the farm?"

"It's wonderful, I call it Green Acres. I helped her father rebuild it after many years of neglect because of terrible debt."

"You help out with all the farm work?"

"Definitely, I stopped making movies so it wouldn't distract me."

"Isn't making movies more lucrative?"

"It's not as fun as driving a tractor."

The conversation continued and gave the manager quite satisfaction because these superstars were not condescending pompous people. The were down to Earth and very reasonable. More than that, they could demand huge fees for such a single appearance, and they are doing it just for fun. Incredible!

The manager looked at the drinks and they were almost gone so he gave the waitress a signal which meant send over another round of drinks.

The drinks arrived a minute before they were done with the

second song and Mòlìhuā looked satisfied for the moment, so the manager asked, "Are you ready to sing now Mòlìhuā?"

"I'm more than ready."

"Alright give me a minute to set it up."

The manager walked up to the stage and grabbed the microphone from the band leader and said, "Ladies and gentlemen, I'm the manager of the Cuìlǜ Resort Hotel and I'm very happy that we have an award-winning movie star and a recording artist staying in the resort. Tonight, our wonderful guest Wánměi de Mòlìhuā got her start right here on this stage. Some of her early recordings were released from this very stage back then. Please welcome the beautiful Mòlìhuā."

The crowd was into it and people were calling friends in the resort to give them heads up to come down to the restaurant that now seemed like it was quickly filling up like the manager had not seen in a long time.

Mòlìhuā who was dressed very beautifully, and such a wonderful soul walked up to the stage and took the microphone from the manager who then walked back to his seat, and looked at the other singer and smiled then grabbed her hand and turned around to the growing crowd and said, "Ladies and gentleman, I want to point out that handsome man sitting next to the manager.

"I began my life journey with him. Since then, he has filmed movies and supported my singing career by retiring from a lucrative film career to play Mr. Mom and raise our kids so that I could continue my career. He's such a fantastic person. I'm going to ask you all a question now. Do you think he should go back to making more films?"

The crowd went wild with "YES YES YES."

"Alright I'm going to dedicate this next song to the love of my life sitting in front of all of you tonight."

The other singer was almost terrified and Mòlìhuā would calm her nerves by holding her hand like her best friend. It was a shock to stand next to and sing with a recording star Diva dressed so beautiful.

As the music started and Mòlìhuā started singing right next to the band's singer, she heard the beauty in Mòlìhuā's voice, and her hand calmed her, and she started to add to the luster as a good back up singer resonating her voice and harmonizing very nicely.

This was a beautiful song and it sold 27 billion subscriptions and made Mòlìhuā extremely wealthy so she could send her two children to the finest schools in the Empire so they could rub elbows with the people who were the power brokers and the intergalactic banker's children.

The manager was a brilliant thinker and he saw the restaurant fill up. About the time Mòlìhuā finished the song, almost every seat in the Dining Hall was taken. The manager was eternally grateful. And to add to his pleasure, his assistant approached him and whispered in his ear, "their belongings have been moved up to the Penthouse."

When Mòlìhuā returned to her seat after the rowsing applause, the manager who already had the waitress replace their drinks with fresh chilled ones said, "I've already had your belongings moved up to a Penthouse. When you leave here the elevator will direct you where to go."

"Thank you," Tinougl said though he already missed his robot friends.

In a while the band took another break and as the singer was stepping down from the stage, Mòlìhuā walked over to her and said, "I loved the way you sang that tune and helped me by making it far more beautiful. You have a wonderful voice; would you please come to the table and join me and my husband for a drink?"

The young lady was enthralled and said, "I would love to."

The two ladies sat down and Tinougl was extremely happy. Going from a war zone where he almost got killed to here in a few hours would humble most people.

"What is your name dear?" Mòlìhuā asked.

"My name is Lili Pàoténg.

Mòlìhuā knew that Lili's dialect meant Pàoténg was her last name and thus knew to call her Lili in their conversations.

"Lili, as you can imagine I personally know the great talent scout Reladondo bon Scrafatorious, if you promise to work hard with me over the next few days, when I go home, I will contact him and ask him to give you a review. I think your voice is so nice, he has songs ready for you to record."

"Of course, I would work hard with you because you inspire me, and I have learned a lot singing your songs."

"All right dear, I expect in the next few months you will be given the opportunity to perform numerous hits that will exemplify the essence of your expertise."

"I'll try my best."

"That's all I can ask of you. Do you know any of my other songs?"

"Yes, we have performed one of your latest songs, "Ài de Xiāngliào, in the morning."

"Would you like to sing that with me after your break?"

"I would love too."

The two lady's chit chatted about trivial things for another ten minutes, then Lili Pàoténg said, "Just walk up to the stage with me. The band leader likes this song and if you are singing it, he'll be very happy."

"My pleasure dear."

The manager and Tinougl sat there taking it all in. Tonight, was one of the happiest evenings the manager had in a very long time as he looked around and saw the restaurant had filled up to almost maximum capacity as various parties had called upon their friends to come see this Diva sing.

When the two ladies reached the stage, Lili Pàoténg walked up to Liángshuǎng and said, "Mòlìhuā's going to sing with us again. She wants to perform 'Ài de Xiāngliào in the Morning.'

"That's wonderful, that's one of our best songs."

"It just got better."

"All right, lets get started."

Liángshuǎng sat down at the piano and the other group members had their instruments including the percussionist who would add greatly to this song as the drums and chimes were ingeniously applied throughout.

The music started and the instruments played for the first thirty seconds with the piano giving a tremendous lead in for the two talented singers.

There would be no harmonizing this time as Lili Pàoténg resonated Mòlìhuā's voice throughout. The crowd was energized as it was quite apparent this was the best performance of the night since the band was very proficient with this particular song as it was one of their showcase tunes often, they closed out the night with and got the crowd the most enthused. When you walk off the stage with good applause is always uplifting to the band. This would not be the last song for them tonight, but it would be the most memorable.

Once again Mòlìhuā's voice enthralled the audience as she looked directly at Tinougl knowing what the poor man had just gone through. One day she would pester him to tell her what he did while he was gone those few seconds he disappeared. He finally decided to let her know in their final years together since she had earned the right to know his most inner thoughts. When she discovered what he had to do to get back to her, it touched her heart deeply because it conveyed to her the quantity of love, he had for her to be willing to die for her, if necessary, just to get back to be with her. Few women know their husbands' deep feelings like this, and many make assumptions that are off the mark.

Mòlìhuā and Lili Pàoténg put forth an incredible performance. Everyone in the room knew this legendary singer and the young lady were delivering one of the greatest performances that most of them would ever see in their lifetimes.

When the song ended, they might as well have closed the curtain, because the crowd was rejuvenated in the most spectacular fashion. The standing ovation was loud and thunderous. The band was entranced by the response. Looking out on the full house that started out as another dull evening that morphed into all this had quite a huge psychological impact on every band member. They now had complete fondness towards their benefactor who just put them on the map.

The manager was mesmerized by all this and said to himself, "The hell with it, I'm going to have another drink!"

It took a full ten minutes for the crowd to die down. Mòlìhuā dressed nicely in a designer dress sat down next to Tinougl who did something he rarely did, showing this type of reaction in public. He reached out to Mòlìhuā and pulled her closer and gave her an inspiring kiss. That too caused a standing ovation. The manager sat there just floating in his happiness that was augmented by the elixir he had downed in the most profound fashion and was even more animated when he started thinking about tomorrow and the big galla they would put on. He would certainly contact his short list of preferred clients and see if they wanted reserved tables as he expected another blowout performance.

After they finished their drink Tinougl sitting next to the

manager said, "We are going to leave now. I want to get up in the morning and do some running and swimming."

Reladondo bon Scrafatorious had been traveling to Tartarnite Empire Capital City Santorini de Shénshèng because he knew the news about Tinougl's health and knew Mòlìhuā would take it hard and using his vast spy networkd discovered they were staying at the Cuìlù Resort Hotel which he felt bad about since he knew the hotel had seen it's better day.

Tinougl and Mòlìhuā were up in their Penthouse getting to know the butler and the maid when Reladondo pulled into the hotel and checked in. Since he was a VIP, the manager who was now back in his office was notified the VIP was arriving, so the manager popped out to greet him. The bellhop had his small amount of luggage because he was traveling light and would simply buy changes of clothes directly from the fashion designer, he knew was available in this resort hotel.

Chapter

Thirty-Nine

They Meet Again

"Good evening Mr. Scrafatorious, thank you for choosing our hotel resort."

"You are quite welcome. Is your restaurant still open?" Reladondo asked starting to feel a little hungry.

"Yes sir, it will be open for another few hours, would you like to go there now?"

"If you wouldn't mind I would."

"Fine, the bellhop will take your luggage up to your Penthouse and I'll escort you into the restaurant."

"I appreciate that."

The table where Tinougl and Mòlǐhuā had been sitting, was still open because they had not yet taken the reserve sign down and the waitress was waiting for instructions. The table was cleaned off and beautiful linen tablecloth changed and was virtually ready for resort guests."

The manager was now very pleased with the screwup so he could seat the famed film maker Reladondo bon Scrafatorious in direct view of the performers that were now super animated by the audience reactions to their music.

"What would you like to eat so I can give your order directly to the chef?"

"Tell the chef to surprise me with something good."

"I certainly will. Would you like something to drink?"

"Yes, thanks to my friend Tinougl, I've grown fond of Chamboree del Pàrà Mĕilì."

"Are you referring to the man that is with Wánmĕi de Mòlìhuā?"

"Yes, absolutely, how's he doing?"

"He was in very good spirits tonight, but I must say when Wánmĕi de Mòlìhuā started singing one of her songs, he started crying."

"I think I know the song. It hits me too."

"I believe it effected me as well sir."

"How did the crowd like it?"

"When they first showed up tonight, this place was half empty and I assumed it would be another dead night. Now look around, this was the only empty table available, only because they just left." "I'm sorry I missed them."

"Don't worry you can see them tomorrow."

"I thought they were leaving tomorrow."

"Luckily they are staying."

"Why the change in plans?"

"This was a very auspicious night for us because Wánmĕi de Mòlìhuā sang several songs with the band and created all this excitement and I pitched them to stay a few more days. Wánmĕi de Mòlìhuā agreed to stay because she wants to work with that singer. She thinks she has a future and informed her if she worked really hard over the next few days, she would introduce you to her."

"I'm looking forward to the introduction."

"Let me go place your order and get your drink."

"One thing sir, I do not like eating alone, would you mind joining me?"

"I would be delighted."

The manager then left and got their orders in and immediately returned with two glasses of Chamboree del Pàrà Měilì. Then he thought, *what a night!*

Reladondo got instant gratification with the combination of the Chamboree del Pàrà Měilì and the girl's voice. She really was good, and he knew that if Mòlìhuā worked with her for a few days, he might just have a new song or two he purchased to have her record. He was also happy he happened to be in the Tartarnite Empire Capital City Santorini de Shénshèng that now had one of the best recording studios in the entire Empire.

Within ten minutes the Chef and a couple of his assistants came out pushing a cart warmer with sampler entrees for the two men. Impressing the VIP and the manager at the same time gave the Chef ample satisfaction along with the fact they had far more food orders than normal and out in the Dining Hall, he could see why. The place was buzzing tonight and wasn't the dull place it had slowly shrank into.

The food was fantastic as the Chef selected what he knew was the best of the best that only the wealthier clients would order. The manager was quite animated though feeling slightly inebriated by engaging in consumption of drinks with the VIPs, but it was all worth it as tonight turned things around for him. His boss would be happy when the reports started flowing in.

Lili Pàoténg was the real deal as far as Reladondo was concerned.

He knew that once Mòlìhuā groomed her, she would be ready for prime time. The manager asked, "Would you like to meet the singer?"

"No, if you don't mind, I want to wait until Mòlìhuā introduces us tomorrow."

"As you wish sir."

"Thank you."

After eating the meal and a second Chamboree del Pàrà Měilì, Reladondo knew it was time to get up to the Penthouse. There was a chance he might see Tinougl in the morning swimming. He'd then find out what his prognosis is.

What a terrible shame such a good handsome screen actor develops an ilness like this.

"I'm going to call it a night. I want to get a good night sleep and deal with some things tomorrow."

"Thank you, Mister Scrafatorious, for staying with us tonight."

My pleasure, and please call me Reladondo."

"Sure, thing Reladondo."

"See you tomorrow."

<center>~~~</center>

Tinougl woke at his normal time in the morning, however he felt slightly lethargic with the recent multiple time travels which was far worse than jet lag. He knew how to deal with it and got up and put on the running clothes he had requested and without disturbing Mòlìhuā left and was soon out running like he knew he could when he was a younger man. Those five miles came easy. And he was soon showering and putting on his swim attire.

Mòlîhuā was awake and dressed and wasn't interested in swimming today and said she was waiting for the fashion designers to arrive to prepare her for her looks today. She knew she had been spotted and the public knew she was here, so she had to dress up like a recording star to be seen in the public.

Tinougl went to the pool and didn't pay attention to who was there because quite frankly he didn't care. He got in the water and started swimming the 30 laps. There was someone there who did care. It was no other than Reladondo bon Scrafatorious having breakfast and hoping to see Tinougl.

And there he was. It was almost shocking. He looked exactly like he did twenty years ago when he made those few movies. *He hadn't changed a bit! And there he was, a sick man about to die knocking off 30 laps! What the heck is going on?*

There were three old hags sitting there also watching and they knew this man. They were equally shocked. They hadn't seen him in twenty years and here he is looking the same. They too were entranced.

Tinougl didn't know who the old hags were, nor did he care. He certainly didn't recognize them.

At the end of his thirty laps, Tinougl got out of the pool and his muscles were inflated by the exercise and he did feel the inflammation and worried about sustaining a cramp and saw the SPA was open. He dried off and put on his swim robe and sandals and was heading to the SPA when suddenly blocking his path was no other than Reladondo bon Scrafatorious!

"Wow you look great Tinougl, what the hell have you been eating?"

"All that farm fresh food I've been growing on my Green Acres."

"Well, I probably need to start coming over there for dinner. it's worked well for you."

"Having a sexy beautiful woman in your life helps out as well."

"How's Mòlìhuā doing?"

"A lot better since I got cured."

"Your tumor?"

"Yes actually."

"What happened, I thought it was inoperable?"

"We came here and visited the best doctors in the Empire who wrote me off and said, there was nothing they could do."

"One day later when I was feeling a little nausea, I went into an old timer's medical herbs and spices place and he prescribed a certain tea for me, said it was known to shrink tumors."

"It worked?"

"Yes. In a month's time I was feeling energetic and went for a run and a swim which surprised Mòlìhuā who insisted I go back to the doctors and get checked. By the time they checked the tumor was down to the size smaller than a pea, which they could easily kill off with their proton zapping technique. That along with the tea has eliminated the tumor. I'm good to go."

"You look fantastic for a man your age. In fact, you look quite a bit younger than the last time I saw you. Perhaps I need some of that tea."

"Funny that you mention it, Mòlìhuā was thinking the exact same thing so we went back to the store and discovered the elderly gentleman had passed away and they were closing the store down and had sold off all their merchandise. The elderly gentleman never shared his secrets with anyone, so those old medical remedies are irrevocably gone forever.

"That's a terrible shame. Society is missing out on what is perhaps one of the greatest secrets of all time."

"I'm lucky I met him before it was too late."

"What are you doing now?"

"I'm going over to get a massage."

"Maybe I'll go with you and get one too."

"All right us go."

The receptionist was happy to see the men because lately there was so few clients, they were now down to just two massage technicians.

"Can I help you gentlemen."

"We both want massages."

"Alright this is Ami and Năizuĭ

"Can you massage us in the same room so we can talk?"

"Sure, but you will have separate baths due to new management policy." "That works."

The two men were soon enjoying the hot bath and shampoo as well as all the preliminary massages.

They were soon lying on tables parallel to each other getting a good massage from the two women.

"Tinougl, now that your cured and your kids are off to school, have you thought about getting back into movies?"

"Since the farm is getting kind of lonely since Mòlihuā's parents are kind of quiet unless she's around, I suppose I could try it again."

"You were a natural actor, just give me the word and I'll put you into a full feature movie."

One of the massage technicians was getting captivated by the way these men were talking and asked, "Who are you guys?"

Reladondo smiled and said, "This is the famous actor Tinougl bon Brandenboynk."

"You are?"

"Yes, and the other gentleman is the movie and recording star producer Reladondo bon Scrafatorious," Tinougl responded.

"I want to be your sex slave while you are staying in the Resort!" the young lady exclaimed."

"I'm sorry my wife takes good care of that tasking, but Reladondo could probably use some soft off's."

"What's a soft off?"

"It's a condition of older men when they get to hold a beautiful woman like you in his arms."

"I would certainly be willing to provide soft offs," The beautiful young lady advertised with a big smile.

"I'll keep you in mind," Reladondo replied.

"What do you have planned for today?" Reladondo asked.

"Mòlìhuā is going to meet with the band performing in the Dining Hall and practice some of her songs with them so she can perform them tonight."

"I certainly want to see that."

"There is a young singer in the band she thinks has a good future after she grooms her a little bit."

"If anyone can inspire a young singer, it's Mòlìhuā."

"You got that right."

"Last night the band sucked until Mòlìhuā lit a fire in them."

"Say, I have an idea to help the young lady. How about when

we get done here, I'll contact the recording studio I use here in Santorini de Shénshèng and have them bring over an orchestra like we did for your wife's recordings to improve the sound quality a bit."

"Are they ready to perform her songs?"

"I'll have their conductor practice them today to get their proficiency up."

"All right, I'll let Mòlìhuā know the plan."

"Good, I'll talk to the manager who I know after we leave to get his permission."

Reladondo then turned to Nǎizuǐ, the prettier and better built of the two massage technicians and asked, "What time do you get off from work today?"

"They have cut my hours down because of the lack of customers, I'll be leaving at two this afternoon."

"When you finish, I'll give you one of my business cards. I want you to come up to my Penthouse as soon as you finish work today so I can have you dressed up in a nice evening designer dress to be my date tonight at dinner and watch the performance."

"I would love that!"

The other massage technician had a sour look on her face being passed over for the other girl.

~~~

Mòlìhuā met the band in the Dining Hall after it closed and they started practicing six songs. It was hard work, but they were energized knowing it would be a special night.

After a few hours it was time to take a break and let the staff
~~~

prepare for the evening when the manager came in and had some news.

"Okay guys and gals, you need to stay for about thirty more minutes, we have an orchestra coming in that you will play with you tonight, it's going to be a big show. They want to do the first song you plan on performing tonight before you leave."

The band leader Liángshuǎng asked, "Mòlìhuā which song do you wish to sing first?"

"That's easy one to pick. I want to sing the song that will make my husband weak at his knees and make him cry right off at the start, 'Dǎkāi Wánměi de Liánhuā.'"

"Great song choice, I like it," Liángshuǎng responded.

About that time, Reladondo bon Scrafatorious came whisking into the room followed by workers carrying chairs and music stands with the digital flatscreen music prompters.

"I should have figured it out that you were somehow involved."

"How are you doing Mòlìhuā?"

"Fine Reladondo, good to see you again."

"I met Tinougl this morning, we had a nice talk and he and I jointly came up with this idea."

"When you two guys get together interesting things seem to always happen."

"Including an announcement that will be made tonight."

"And what is that?"

"Tinougl has agreed to play the role of the major actor in a new

Holographic Movie I'm going to produce."

"Is there a sex scene in the movie?"

"You know there is."

"All right, the only way I'm going to allow him to do that film with you is to put me in as the actress he goes to bed with."

"If you want to play the role, I'm sure the two of you could act the bedroom scene really well."

"Reladondo, just between you and me, what happens under the covers stays under the covers. I plan on being fully nude and if he wants to really do it during the filming, I'll make sure he's not acting."

"You got me excited already. Good thing I have a date with a young lady that is going to give me a soft off tonight."

"What the hell is a soft off?"

"Tinougl will let you know tonight."

Shortly after the conversation decayed into nonsense, the orchestra was already set up and the Conductor approached Reladondo and said, "We are ready to perform. We have thirty minutes; we can probably get two or three practice songs in."

"Alright go ahead, I'm going to sit down and listen with the manager." The good news was all the chairs and equipment were set up in what would be considered wasted space as there wan't the need to have extra tables set up due to the recent low turnout that typically happened these days.

Mòlìhuā and the band had already practiced 'Dǎkāi Wánměi de Liánhuā' and were proficient in their interpretation of the music producing vey high quality sound. When the conductor started and the band musicians quickly synchronized, the sound quality improved about ten notches and the staff setting up for evening meals were temporarily transfixed as it all unfolded.

Reladondo bon Scrafatorious was the happiest person in the room because he knew standing in front of him singing their hearts out were two Diva's. And on top of it he had a film star currently up in his Penthouse getting made out exquisiteely for tonights event.

Because the band and the orchestra were well synchronized, in the 30 minutes they had left to practice they were able to jam in four songs. The conductor approached Reladondo and said, "I believe they are ready."

"I know they are ready," Reladondo said smiling and added, "I really appreciate you pulling this together as quickly as you did."

"It's real simple Mr. Scrafatorious, you have helped us out a lot in the past and the least we could do was return the favor."

"You have done it in a major way. When I produce this recording, I'm not going to take any proceeds. My fee will go to all the musicians performing tonight."

"They will definitely like that sir."

"Especially if I get a few billion subscribers."

Those words almost made the conductor dizzy as he knew this amounted to a large paycheck. He also knew his musicians would never complain again all the hard work he made them do in the past when they looked at their bank accounts.

While Reladondo was dealing with the musicians, Nǎizuǐ was getting her make over. She was already extremely happy because she got tips from both men even though she was giving Tinougl a massage. Her tips amounted to almost three months pay. She too was lightheaded and the pleasurizers she received in the bath water as well as the drinks, was quickly turning her into a great 'soft offer' where she would perform with her athletic ability developed by the rigorous exercise of applying massage therapy.

By the time the practice session was over, Tinougl was dressed and when Mòlìhuā arrived with Lili Pàoténg to get her dressed up, she said, "Tinougl you need to go down to the Dining Hall because we need all the extra space for preparing two women."

"Not a problem, I'm kind of thirsty."

Tinougl was looking really good tonight. He even let the hairdresser give him a *Cosmic Wave* hair design. His black-tie suit fit perfect for his athletic build and the suntan he got during his last time travel running back to the time machine was still apparent adding to his luster. He didn't know this, but a lot of women's panties would get wet tonight while fantasizing about him.

Tinougl took the elevator down and headed for the all too familiar Dining Hall where his life changed considerably and gave him some unique experiences with the Barracuda's. He wondered what happened to them in twenty years.

The three Barracudas tried the best they could, but they were not able to over come gravity and old age. They knew their candle had gone out a long time ago, something they wretchedly accepted as a fact of life.

When Tinougl entered the Dining Hall, the Maitre d' saw on her podium tablet digital display this man Tinougl is a VIP and reserved table number two had his seat which was diagrammed on the tablet display.

"This way Tinougl, to your reserved seat," the Matre d' stated. Tinougl walked in front of the three Barracuda and didn't recognize them. Age had not treated them well. He sat down observing his name printed on the small, reserved marker panel. Tinougl got his favorite drink Chamboree del Pàrà Měilì. It was kind of boring sitting there alone, but when the orchestra musicians started showing up in black tie and seating themselves that at least made up for some for the monotony of sitting alone.

Thirty minutes after Tinougl sat down waiting to see how the two Diva's turned out was joined by Reladondo bon Scrafatorious and the massage technician Ami.

Tinougl was impressed with how the young massage technician Ami looked. *She's probably going to be a terrific 'soft off' coach.*

All the musicians and orchestra members were ready, all that was needed now what the two Diva's that were not far behind.

The manager came into the Dining Hall and saw the tables were quickly filling up with guests. Fourteen of the tables were reserved and only a third of them were seated. He knew that was going to be changing soon because those tables were reserved for reliable clientele.

People were already ordering drinks and a few dinners. The waitresses were already active, just the way he liked it.

The manager was soon in a state of shock. There was the illustrious massage technician Ami dressed up sitting next to Reladondo bon Scrafatorious with a smile that only the most talented *soft offers* could possibly display. Her exquisite designer clothes and hair style changed her completely. She was already good looking as a massage therapist and here she was with no other than Reladondo bon Scrafatorious that had a reputation of spoiling young ladies that pleased him. He seriously doubted she would be showing up for work in the morning as she undoubtedly would be working overtime tonight.

The old Barracuda that were getting more sassy as the years drug on were there lined up looking upon that table with disgusting evil. The manager knew what they wanted, fresh meat. They were far more than carivoires, they gave vultures a bad reputation as being too feeble.

The fashion designer explained to the two ladies, "Make them wait, let them all be anxious, it will add to your allure when they are wondering when the hell you are going to show up. Make them feel almost panic, then waltz in and give them the sexual thirst they have great desires for.

The women soon were on the elevator looking at each other.

One thing they both knew was they were each very attractive tonight. The fashion designer worked her magic not only in the designer full length dresses they wore, but also the hair styles and the exquisite makeup. Both women had appealing breasts and the thin straps that held up the front that barely covered their breasts showed enough cleavage to create that seductive allure for the men in the audience.

"It didn't matter how well we sing tonight; the men will want sex with us so badly, they could care less how well we perform," Mòlìhuā said with an evil grin.

"I feel a lot calmer knowing I will be singing with you and not by myself."

"I feel a lot calmer knowing you will be standing beside me and the men in the audience will be clamoring for your body, they will quickly forget how well I sing and miss any mistakes I make."

Just like the fashion designer said, as they waltzed into the main Dining Hall towards the band and the orchestra, they could see there was panic on the faces of a lot of people. Their arrival was timed perfectly for the moment and the greatest impact.

As the women approached the stage, Reladondo bon Scrafatorious stood up and walked up to the stage with them, he already had a microphone in his hand waiting for this moment.

"Ladies and Gentlemen, it is my great honor to introduce to you the recording star legend Wánměi de Mòlìhuā and her new singing contemporary, the lovely Lili Pàoténg."

Even without singing a note there was a standing applause greater in volume than the band had ever received AFTER a performance.

This was a special song and a special time for Mòlìhuā. Her husband sitting directly in front of her next to Reladondo bon Scrafatorious had gone through a lot to be able to be here with her today. She didn't quite know the hell the time travel spy had gone through to be able to stay alive and get back to her in the past few days. She would reward him because she suspected he went through a lot. She would sing her heart out and give him the significance of the emotions she now held for him.

Mòlíhuā knew at about the three-minute mark in the song he would display those emotional tendrils she evoked by creating that memory from a long time ago, when he stole her heart.

Reladondo bon Scrafatorious the movie maker and recording exec knew this song well. He casually observed Tinougl at a slight angle and as expected at that three-minute mark when something triggered the emotion from long forgotten memories, his yes watered and the droplets were undeniably a symbol of acquiessence to a very strong and dangerous spy that nobody in the room knew existed except for his sweet lover.

He couldn't help remembering, shutting the cover of his time machine as the helicopter popped over the horizon getting ready to pickle some very nasty and deadly missiles which would kill him and prevent him from ever seeing his lover againg.

The slight hesitation of the pilot seeing the strange color patterns coming off the time machine is the only thing that saved his life. Life and death were mere seconds away.

Just as the helicopter pilot was pressing the fire button on the control stick, the object disappeared. The missile flew through open air and detonated when it crashed into large boulders a few feet beyond. Whatever it was had disappeared.

The performers had planned to sing this song with the orchestra and then do their next song by themselves and alternate like that performing every other song with the orchestra. As soon as the song was over, there was a rambunctious standing ovation. Mòlíhuā bowed and said thank you a few times and then walked directly over to Tinougl and sat down on his lap and kissed him.

All the noise around them was shielded as they entered their special time and place and the love flowed between them. Nobody knew that just a week ago Tinougl was dying from a brain tumor. However, his travel back to the future helped take care of that, but to get back to the present time, he had to sign his soul to the devil and go on that extremely dangerous mission that had at best a fifty percent chance of survival. Because of the likelihood whoever went on the mission would be killed, stopped any volunteer and only Tinougl stepped forward with an extraordinary demand. Had it not been how important this mission was the director never would have agreed to sending him back in time afterwards so he could continue his life living five hundred years before.

Soon, Mòlìhuā was singing another song and the crowd was animated like they had not been for many years while this resort slowly decayed. The singing duet quickly turned things around and every seat was filled with satisfied resort guests.

After the second song, the two Diva's went back to the Penthouse and put on their second evening designer clothes that elicited pure lust in most of the men in the audience when they returned.

And finally for the last two songs they changed dresses again and this time the designer had a big surprise for them. Since Reladondo bon Scrafatorious used a recording studio nearby for his movies and entertainment recordings, he always had a stash of diamond jewelry. When the women came back for the final series of songs, they were escorted by six security men with conceiled weapons to safeguard all those fabulous diamonds they were wearing that put the final sizzle on the Divas.

Few people present had ever seen two sexy Diva's like these two. The rapture they evoked not only helped the men in the audience, but because they made those men so tremendously horny, their women would soon be enjoying the results of their motivation.

Reladondo bon Scrafatorious knew he had a winning act and shortly after the women finished singing and went back to the Penthouse, he too left and took the massage technican Ami he met that morning and dressed her up for the occasion, back to his penthouse, where he could teach her the exquisitee details of how to give an older guy, a soft off.

511

CHAPTER FORTY

TIME TRAVEL SPY BACK TO THE FUTURE

Time passed and the two grew older. Mòlìhuā's parents slowly faded away and the children became adults with their own families.

Since Mòlìhuā was practically twenty years older than Tinougl, she passed away at an age when many people do. Tinougl was devastated and took Mòlìhuā's passing very hard. Without her, life didn't feel like living.

Tinougl was very lonely and unhappy being by himself. His children lived on other planets and had lives of their own. He was viewed as an old timer and the children took him for granted as they had their own issues to contend with.

One day, Tinougl made that fateful decision. There was no longer any point remaining, so he knew what to do. He wasn't going to waste twenty years here sitting around watching the plants grow. He kind of missed being a spy. The thrill of success and the agony of defeat was the life of a spy.

After putting together his final letters to his children including copies of his will and power of attorney giving it to his older son, he knew they would not receive probably for a couple weeks, he booked a high-speed transport flight to Tartarnite Empire Capital City Santorini de Shénshèng and checked into the

Cuìlù Resort Hotel that had been renovated thanks to him and Mòlìhuā's efforts.

In room 1414 he once again was pleased to see Guāiqiǎo and Tondron.

The next morning, he took a Limo out to where he had hidden the time machine so many years before. He paid the Limo driver and said, "I'm going bird watching and will call you when I need a ride back."

The Limo turned around and went back to the city.

Tinougl easily found the time machine and cleared off all the forest debris and opened it up. He got inside and hit the blue button and moments later he was back to the future one minute after he had left.

People had taken bets on whether he would return. The director bet he would return. When asked why he took that bet the director said, "It's actually simple. First and foremost, he's a spy. In due time he will miss the spy business and be back."

"Does he have another mission already?"

"Yes, in fact I have something in mind for him and we are going to get approval to do the mission. I think as soon as we complete the debrief, he'll be ready to start the training and we'll deploy him a few weeks later."

Paul D. Escudero

保罗·道格拉斯·埃斯库德罗

March 29, 2022

AUTHOR'S NOTE:

This is a work of fiction. There are no living persons in this book. Infact none of the story takes place on Earth.

This is a story about a time traveller spy. If you have read this far, then you know that throughout the story, the time traveller's controllers did extensive training and preparation to instill in the Character Tinougl to not do things that would possibly change the fabric of time and history.

The first mission the time traveller spy goes on is to get information only. They didn't know exactly how long it would take but assumed since he was only seeking information, he could get it and travel back to the future in a relatively short period of time.

The way this time travel worked; it would appear he was only gone for one minute. However, in a different time and dimension his existence could be quite different, especially if he deviated from his prime directives and did time travel violations and changed the fabric of time. In some cases, time travel spies did not come back, either their missions failed, or they chose not to come back. The time travel directorate had no ability to discover either case unless the time traveller left behind significant evidence that would survive harsh conditions and the passage of time.

The time travel spy Tinougl carried out heroing espionage in the past that gave his superiors the notion he was a team player and would carry out his assignment with professionalism and a great deal of fidelity.

Traveling back five hundred years didn't seem such an extraordinary event just to acquire actionable data.

When the time travel spy Tinougl assessed the situation where he set up shop in a resort hotel, he quickly found no clues to track down for the information he sought. Eventually after several instances of quintessential

delight with a few wealthy women who lived in Penthouses at the resort, he meets a singer Wánměi de Mòlìhuā. About the time he meets Mòlìhuā her social name, he is getting clues of radicals on the planet Konhagar that may be linked to the information he was seeking.

As a trained spy Tinougl knew it would be extremely risky to travel to

Konhagar by himself with the possibility of creating visibility with the current Empire government. On the otherhand if he went there with his girlfriend to meet her parents that would create an excellent cover story and not raise any suspecians.

So as the time travel spy goes about seducing the young lady, he is quite successful at it. As he anticipated she would eventually bring up the subject of meeting her parents. After their quantification of the romance has succeeded it was only natural for him to respond he wanted to meet her family. This lovely singer at this phase of the relationship gets lucky and is becoming a successful Diva with fantastic income.

As they put together the plan to visit her parents the money is rolling in and by the time, she reaches her parents home she has became quite wealthy. When she confronts her father as to why he is driving the hovercraft instead of the family vehicles, the truth comes out. He's a financial wreck and the bank is playing hardball trying to sieze his farm She quickly intervenes and eliminates his debt and the time travel spy who has substantial credits with him to bribe people as necessary is also able to help out and between the two of them, they slowly rebuild his farm back to it's former glory.

During a trip to a vehicle dealership to buy vehicles the farmer had been forced to sell to pay all his farm hands, one of the sales force personnel discovers this woman is the Diva everyone is looking for and for a price he sells the information to a media outlet.

Now that their cover is blown and the time travel spy knew the crowds would show up the next day, he visits an organized crime boss to purchase protection and security men for the next day, he also hires the boss to find out who blew their cover. Evenntually the salesman was identified and had the fear of God put in him. Later the time travel spy who had no legitimate leads to the source of the information hires this same organized crime boss to go find it for him.

The two lovers remained living with her parents and eventually establish a family. The time travel spy realizes he had failed as a spy and fell in love with the woman that he did not want to leave. Their journey through life continued for many years where they lived a life based on mutual love and respect. One day unexpectedly the time travel spy passes out as he was going for a swim in the family swimming pool that had been recently built. Luckily his wife's parents were able to pull him out of the pool before he drowned.

The doctors soon assessed the time travel spy had an inoperable brain tumor and gave him approximately thirty days to love.

At this moment in private conversations with the woman he

loved he disclosed who he really was and what he was doing on the planet but assured her after he fell in love with her, he ended his career as a spy. At first, she thought he might be hallucinating, but he assured her if she went with him to the city he originally arrived and hid the time machine in a nearby forest so he could return back to the future with the INTEL he was sent to gather. They traveled there and discovered the time machine was still there and intact. He said to her he would go get healed with future technology then come back, but he might have to go on another mission first to bargain for a trip back to this time and place.

Indeed, when he came back to the future, he arrived one minute after he left.

During the debriefing he informed the psychiatrist everything that happened while he was gone.

The next mission was so dangerous it was a volunteer only type of mission with the forecast of a 50 percent chance of survival. There were no volunteers and based on agency policy none of the time travel spies could be coerced or forced to go on a mission with such poor odds. The time travel spy said he would volunteer under the condition that after he completed the mission, he be sent back 500 years to be with his true love. During his time travel back, the tumor had shrunk and his youth was returned and doctors were able to detect the tumor and remove it before it became dangerous, hence he would no longer be ill when he returned.

The time travel spy is then sent back in time to deal with a group of rebels that would one day build their own time machine and in the present time they only had a few weeks before the rebels could deploy their time machine and reek destruction upon the Empire. The time travel spy was deployed to a remote area where he had to travel at night to avoid being captured and get into position to deal with the insurgency. This was a heroing eventure with some real danger and close calls. Upon completion of the mission at the exact time he was getting into the time machine to return a helicopter pops above the horizaon and was coming right at him and launches missiles. The outcome of that missile strike narrowly missed destroying the time machine at the critical moment.

Now with the mission complete and having earned his trip back in time to his lover, he's sent on his way where he has new adventures. At this time the people in the time travel agency took bets as whether he would come back or not. The director bet he would come back, everyone else had the opposite bet. If you read the book, then you know what happened.

Is there really the possibility of time travel or travel to other dimensions? How would we know? Our scientific community on a galactic scale are merely cosmic cockroaches with very little knowledge of the Universe. To underscore how the scientific community lacks so much information you might as well call them cosmic cockroaches, they don't even know whats going on at Jupiter, Saturn, and other planets. Since they do not know about our own planets in this solar system that tells me they really do not know about the universe or whether time travel and other unique situations can occur.

In the study of electronics scientists know about singularities and how that is involved in transfer functions. Is time travel merely another transfer function our cosmic cockroaches have not discovered?

If you had time travel ability is there any time you wish to go back to change? And why would you?

Throughout this book I have names and places that are manifestations of the Chinese language. I've published three Chinese Language Novels that are sold by Amazon and one of them, Radiant Destiny is sold by many book sellers.

My name is signed in Chinese as well. I have some hot steamy love and sex with Chinese woman in my book Pluto II. I've studied Chinese History, translated several books to Chinese and read them in Chinese. I'm currently getting rusty in Chinese because

I've been publishing books in Japanese,

German, Russian, French, and Spanish. I even have a book starting in Portugese.

All the countries that use the languages listed in the previous paragraph have interesting histories and cultures. Russian in particular has a significant impact on classical music. If you read my triple language book Tauceti Incident in English/Russian/German or the latest version in English/Russian/French, I give great tribute to Russia and how in the past they contributed very positively to America's future. In the past century we've of course had turbulent times with Russia because of the policies of the Communist Party that is diabolically opposed to the United States and worked many years to undermine us. One Russian informed me Russians hate Americans for one reason, they want what we have but are too lazy to work for it.

Well not all Russians are lazy some are very industrious and very intelligent. One of the Russians I think we need to pay attention to is a very well educated astro physicist: Khabibullo Abdusamatov. I would dedicate this book to Khabibullo Abdusamatov if I had his permission. If anyone knows him ask him for me and in later editions I will.

What is so specciall about Khabibullo Abdusamatov? In the height of the global warming hoax, he warned about the pending mini-ice age and has evidence to back it up. You know just a couple of days ago in late March, the Great Lakes still had 30% ice cover and of course Hudson Bay is still iced over.

Great Lakes Surfaace Environment Analysis (GLSEA) puts out daily ice charts. On March 28, the Great Lakes still had 15.6% ice cover. [glsea_cur.png (1024×800) (noaa.gov)] On April 6, 2022, Great Lakes ice cover was still about 12%. Does that sound like warm to you?

I would like to see relations with Russia to improve. It takes two to tango, but it also takes two to be friends. To Russia with love as James Bond said.

This book depicts space and travel and many other things that might seem far fetched. But just think, many things Isaac Asimov wrote in the 1940's in now coming true. Eventually we'll get down space travel and figure it out. In the meantime, with the Navy's release of UFO video and other disclosures, I think it's time people skeptical about Aliens realize the world is not flat, nor is the

Universe. Ask your self, "Why would Aliens want to come visit Cosmic Cockroaches?"

God help us if Aliens bring a big can of RAID. Now start thinking about the sound of some of those RAID commercials on TV.

This science fiction thriller has a lot of romance and sex in it. They teach sex education in schools now. Anyone 16 or over already knows about the birds and the bees, and many of them have already experienced sex even if you wish to not believe it. When did you first experience it? Now look at your kids and extrapolate they started the same time you did, and you are not such a great parent afterall because they did it behind your back and really do not care what you think about it.

There are a lot of stories about singers and music in this book and a time travel spy who is built so excessively well, the women melt in his arms. Why pay such a high tribute to singers? How often have you listened to music in the past? When you are driving somewhere, do you listening to music on the radio? I know I am all the time. Everything from classical music to pop and rock. I'm listening to music right now in fact one of my favorites: <u>Kurt Atterberg (1887-1974) :</u>

<u>Piano Concerto in B flat minor (1927-36) **MUST HEAR** - YouTube.</u>

That is one of the greatest compositions I've ever heard. it's very uplifting.

I'm mentioned on Wikipedia because of the illustrious composer Hanns Wolf: Etract from Wikipedia:

Literature[edit]

Hanns Wolf was recognized in Peter Hollfelder's *Lexikon Klaviermusik* in 2005.[28]

Wolf's piano concerto was mentioned in Paul D. Escudero's *Pluto II: Voyage to the end of the Universe* when Greg listened to it to achieve a "Hemi-Sync Reality" during meditation.[29]

By the way did you know CIA used Hemi-Sync?

In 1983, The CIA Wrote A Bizarre Report About Transcending Spacetime With Your Mind | IFLScience

I have a paperback coming out in April 2022: Arizona Alien Adventure. It also gets deep into hemi-sync and meditation. In that book I provide links where you can go to get meditation music. If you really want to master meditation, go to a Zen Buddhist organization and they can effectively teach you if you are a willing student.

In conclusion: In the future will we have time travel spies?

The axiom of time travel: If you have time travel spies in the future that means you have them now.

GLOSSARY

Ài de Xiāngliào in the Morning - [Spice of love in the morning] Love song. [Chinese: 爱的香料 'Ài de Xiāngliào (Spice of Love)]

Ami and Nǎizuǐ: two massage technicians in later years at the Cuìlǜ Resort Hotel

Argecibo: Time Traveller Spy Tinougl's home world [Part of his cover story.]

Aristapara: organized crime bossAzure-Tiānkōng: Rebel area located just about

8,000 miles West of the family farm on planet Konhagar

Bǎochí Wéixiǎo Even if the Sun Isn't Shining - Love Song. [Bǎochí Wéixiǎo - PINYIN for keep smiling; Chinese: 保持微笑]

Bustamante: Limo driver at Konhagar

Chamboree del Pàrà Měilì: Drink/elixir

Cocilglu: psychological mapper and psychoanalyst

COFA DE COMA: perfume

Cosmic Wave: hair style

Cuìlǜ Resort Hotel 翠绿 Emerald Green Resort Hotel

Dǎkāi Wánměi de Liánhuā: Love Song 打开完美的莲花 [Chinese: Opening the perfect Lotus]

Espranza de Topaxh: planet and location for Reladondo bon Scrafatorious main movie studio

Madam Estele bon Stoffengar (aka Spicey). Husband is

Intergalactic Banker: Frederick

Gradvolchin Hog Farm [Gradvolchin is a type of Alien hog with sharp front teeth for tearing into flesh]

Galant Simulacrum: Grand Espranza de Topaxh Hotel Night Club

Grand Xenis Hotel on the planet Konhagar

Guāiqiǎo: Cuìlǜ Resort Hotel room robot's name 乖巧 [Chinese meaning: clever]

Konhagar: Planet where Wánměi de Mòlìhuā parents live, also planet that has Azure-Tiānkōng rebel area.

Kovloor: time capsulee operator

Liángshuǎng: band leader at Cuìlǜ Resort Hotel in the final chapters

Lili Pàoténg: Singer at Cuìlǜ Resort Hotel in the final chapters

Lǐzǐ Guavastrian Elixir: exotic drink

Lord Ansator Rebel leader of the Konhagar empire and also Tinougl's great grea great grandson

Madalyn bon Donkers: Cuìlǜ Resort Hotel Dining Hall waitress

Mǎshāwáwá 玛莎娃娃 Mǎshāwáwá Female Cuìlǜ Resort Hotel Hotel room robot [Chinese meaning: Martha Doll, in honor of the great pianist Martha Argerich]

Milton: Artificial Intelligence at Grand Plexis de Chiveltros

Miltonzy scientist controlling the toroidal electromagnets

Plexis de Chiveltros: Planet Tartar moon

Ràng wǒ jiǎozhì elixir 让我角质 [get me horny elixir]

Reladondo bon Scrafatorious: film and music recording mogol

Remlesfy: Time Travel Staff member.

Vicky Bon Adenauer (aka Sparky), Husband: Sandstrum

Santorini de Shénshèng: Tartarnite Empire Capital City

Sěphámy bon Cǎoméi (aka Schemer) - Intergalactic Banker Vangrelle's lonely wife

Stephany bon Srofendorn: Film actress and mother of Tinougl's great great great grandson.

Táozi: 桃子 [Chinese meaning: peach] Narrator for Tartarnite Empire Capital

City Santorini de Shénshèng Central Park video

Tartarnites the name of people of the Empire

Timestronauts: Time Travel Spies

Tinougl: Time Traveller Spy; later known as Tinougl bon Brandenboynk (film actor stage name for brief career)

Tondron: Cuìlǜ Resort Hotel Room Holograph personality

Trombocante del Sporbosa: Elixir at the Cuìlǜ Resort Hotel very strong drink

Wánměi de Mòlìhuā: singer and one of the main characters often referred to as Mòlìhuā

Xiǎomāo: 小猫 Waitress at Grand Plexis de Chiveltros Dining Hall Yuánběn: Robot at Grand Plexis de Chiveltros Milton AI

圣托里尼的岛神生: Shèngtuōlǐní de Dǎoshénshēng [Chinese construction of city named Santorini de Shénshèng]

保罗·道格拉斯·埃斯库德罗: [Chinese for Paul Douglas Escudero]

www.ingramcontent.com/pod-product-compliance
Lightning Source LLC
Chambersburg PA
CBHW071956190726
48293CB00001B/53